D0031115

Almost, Maine

Almost, Maine

John Cariani

Feiwel and Friends
New York

A Feiwel and Friends Book
An imprint of Macmillan Publishing Group, LLC
120 Broadway, New York, NY 10271

Our books may be purchased in bulk for promotional, educational, or business
use. Please contact your local bookseller or the Macmillan Corporate and Premium
Sales Department at (800) 221-7945 ext. 5442 or by email at
MacmillanSpecialMarkets@macmillan.com.

Library of Congress Cataloging-in-Publication Data is available.

ISBN 978-1-250-10291-1 (hardcover) / ISBN 978-1-250-10290-4 (ebook)

Book design by Mike Burroughs
Feiwel and Friends logo designed by Filomena Tuosto

First edition, March 2020

10 9 8 7 6 5 4 3 2 1

For northern Maine and the people who live there

Prologue

There is a place in northern Maine that is so far north, it's almost not in the United States.

It's almost in Canada.

But not quite.

Not many people live there.

Not much seems to happen there.

And the things that do happen there seem pretty ordinary. Especially to the people who live there.

But some extraordinary things did happen there once—on a Friday night in the middle of winter, not too long ago.

Or maybe it was a long time ago.

No one quite remembers.

Actually, no one is even sure that the extraordinary things even happened.

And no one is even sure that the place actually exists.

But it's somewhere we've all been.

It's a place called Almost.

Welcome.

1

Ginette and Pete had always been close.

As friends, first.

They had grown up together. And learned to do just about everything together, like swim and fish and shoot and play chess and skate and cross-country ski and ride snowmobiles and ATVs across northern Maine's wide-open spaces and impenetrable forests.

But the summer before the winter when all the extraordinary things did or didn't happen, they became more than friends.

Pete's mom and dad took them to the Northern Maine Fair in Presque Isle, the largest city in Aroostook County, which is the largest county—and one of the least densely populated counties—east of the Rocky Mountains.

Going to Presque Isle was always exciting. It was an hour east of—and a world apart from—Almost. (It had a four-story building and once had over ten thousand people.).

Going to the Northern Maine Fair was doubly exciting, because of all the rides and all the food and all the games. And all the people.

Ginette and Pete rode a carnival ride that zipped and flipped and spun them almost sick. And Pete grabbed Ginette's hand the first time the ride zipped and flipped and spun her and Pete—and held on to it the whole ride.

And Ginette felt a strange lightness fill up her insides while Pete held on to her hand. It made her feel like the lights from the carnival rides were glowing inside her. And like she was somehow weightless as the ride zipped and flipped and spun them.

And Pete felt the same strange lightness while he held on to Ginette's hand.

After the ride, they recovered from being almost sick.

And then they recovered from the strange lightness they had felt when Pete was holding on to Ginette's hand.

And then they felt well enough to get some fried dough smothered in confectioner's sugar. And they walked around the midway while they ate it.

And then they played some carnival games.

Ginette won herself a giant stuffed frog at the milk-jug toss.

And Pete won nothing. And may have felt bad about winning nothing. So Ginette slid her hand inside his and held it to make him feel better.

And they walked around the midway holding hands. And felt that strange lightness fill up their insides again.

But they stopped holding hands when it was time to go home. Because they had met up with Pete's parents again, and they weren't quite ready to hold hands in front of them.

And then they didn't hold hands the rest of the summer.

And they didn't hold hands when they started school at the unified high school up in Fort Kent.

Maybe because they weren't quite ready to let everyone know—including themselves—that they were ready to be more than friends.

But one fall day when Ginette got home from school, she found out that her black Lab, Dill, had died—for no reason other than that he had finished up living his long life.

And Ginette called Pete and told him what happened.

And he stopped by. And they went for a walk in the woods. And Ginette took Pete's hand and held on to it while they walked. And when they were deep enough in the woods, she started crying and told Pete that she didn't know what she was going to do without Dill. And Pete hugged her to comfort her. And when he did, Ginette felt that strange lightness fill up her insides again. And it made her feel like everything was going to be okay. Even though she was so sad about Dill.

After that hug in the woods, Ginette felt like she was ready to be more than friends with Pete. And in school the next day, she slid her hand into his on their way to science class.

And on their way to geometry, Pete slid his hand inside Ginette's hand.

And they walked around holding hands a lot after that, happy that they had tacitly decided that they were more than friends.

And that was enough for them for a while.

That is—until the Friday when all the extraordinary things did or didn't happen. That day had started out in an unusual way. School had been canceled. Because of snow. And snow days were rare in Almost. Because people from Almost, Maine, are snow-removal experts. But so much snow had fallen during the early-morning hours on that Friday that the experts couldn't clear the roads fast enough with their plows to make them passable for school buses. So school had been canceled.

Ginette's mom heard the news on the country radio station out of Presque Isle and sneaked into her daughter's room to shut off her alarm so she could sleep in.

It was almost eleven when Ginette woke up. And she panicked a little when she saw the time and hopped out of bed and stumbled into the hall trying to figure out why she had slept so late.

"Mom?" she called.

"Oh! I was just about to wake you, sweetie!"

"What's—"

"Snow day!" Ginette's mom raised her arms in the air, fists clenched, as if she had won something.

Ginette looked out the window and saw all the snow and smiled. Snow days are unexpected gifts of free time and fun. A snow day on a Friday is even better, because it makes for a three-day weekend.

"I'm gonna go check in on Mémé," continued Ginette's mom. Mémé was Ginette's grandmother. "And then I'll probably head in to work, if the roads are good." Ginette's mom was a server up at the Snowmobile Club, which would have plenty of business on a snow day. And she went on to tell Ginette not to eat crap and lay around all day, and Ginette rolled her eyes a little and said she wouldn't. And then her mom said she wanted her to shovel the roof and the driveway and a path to the propane tank—and to ask Pete if maybe he could help her. And Ginette said she would even though she didn't want to shovel, because that would eat into the free time the snow day had given her. And it wouldn't exactly be fun.

"And then you and Pete can go over to Mémé's and help her shovel out," suggested Ginette's mom. And she grabbed her coat and her bag and headed out.

And Ginette made herself some Life cereal for breakfast. With chocolate milk. Which her mom would definitely think was crap. And then she watched a little bit of a game show and some of a soap opera, because that's what she did when she was home sick or when it was a snow day.

And then she called Pete and asked him if he'd come over and help with all the shoveling she had to do.

About an hour later, Ginette and Pete were shoveling off the flat roof of Ginette's mobile home.

And then they shoveled her driveway and a path to the propane tank so Mr. Pelletier could deliver more gas so Ginette and her mom could stay warm.

And then they went over to Mémé's and shoveled her driveway and cleared a path to her garage. And they brought in five bags of wood pellets from the garage so Mémé would have enough fuel for the week to keep her house warm.

And then Mémé fed Ginette and Pete a late lunch of grilled cheese and tomato soup. And they all wondered if a late lunch should be called dunch or linner. And decided that linner was more accurate, since a late breakfast was called brunch—but also decided that dunch was much funnier.

After dunch—or linner—they went over to Pete's and shoveled out the mailbox at the end of his driveway. And shoveled a path to the oil fill so Mr. Pelletier could deliver his heating oil, too.

And then they went tubing on the hill behind Pete's house.

And then they made pizza with Pete's mom and dad. And ate it for dinner.

And then they played chess.

And Ginette won. And Pete sulked a little.

And then Pete's mom asked them what they were going to do their science projects on, which were due on Monday.

Pete had chosen to do his on map projections. And no one quite knew what map projections were, so he explained, "The Earth is a globe, right?"

And everyone said, "Yeah."

"Yeah, and when you try to represent its three-dimensional surface in two dimensions, it creates distortions. Like, if you draw a map on an orange, say, with a marker, and then peel it and flatten it out, the images at the 'poles' get distorted—they get bigger. Which is why Canada and Russia and Greenland look so giant on maps. So I'm gonna talk about that."

Pete's dad fake-yawned and groaned, "Snoozefest," and he grabbed his son and gave him a noogie to let him know he was kidding and everyone laughed and Pete's mom said, "Guess somebody's gotta think about . . . maps." And then she asked Ginette what she was going to do her presentation on, and Ginette said, "The northern lights." And Ginette's mom said, "Ooh!" And Ginette explained that the northern lights appear when massive storms on the sun shoot streams of tiny charged particles into space. Those particles hurtle toward the Earth and collide with atoms in the atmosphere, exciting them and disrupting their natural state. The excited atoms want to return to their normal states, and when they do, the energy they give off is manifested in colorful little bursts of light, called photons. When enough photons are present, the northern lights appear.

Pete's dad was impressed with Ginette's presentation, because he had seen the northern lights his whole life and had never known what caused them. "Now that," he proclaimed, "is a whole lot more interesting than maps!" And everybody laughed, and as they did, Pete took Ginette's hand, because he was proud that she had impressed his dad.

And Ginette felt that strange lightness again. This time it felt like the northern lights were inside her. And she felt like Pete was one of those charged particles from the sun and he was disrupting her natural state and creating bursts of light inside her.

And she wondered what it meant.

And then she wondered what it meant that she and Pete were holding hands in front of his parents. Did it mean that they were more than more than just friends? Did it mean that they were boyfriend and girlfriend? And that they were dating?

She wanted to know. She wanted to name whatever it was that they were.

But naming what they were would mean assigning words to whatever it was that was happening between them. Which might minimize whatever it was that was happening between them. Because words can make things that seem huge in your heart seem small and insignificant.

But Ginette was willing to take the risk. Because the lightness inside her made her feel like something really wonderful was about to happen to her and Pete.

And it wasn't going to happen while they were hanging out with Pete's parents.

So Ginette got up and told Pete, "Come on," and headed toward the door to put her coat and boots on.

Pete followed Ginette and asked, "Where are we going?"

And Ginette said that talking about the northern lights made her want to go outside and see if they could see them. Because it was the perfect night for them. It was clear, and there was no moon. And she had read that solar storms were currently raging on the sun. So chances were better than they usually were that the northern lights would appear.

And if they didn't see them, Ginette added, they could just do some stargazing.

Pete didn't really care if they saw the northern lights or not. He wasn't interested in outer space like Ginette was. He was more interested in the Earth.

But he was more interested in Ginette than he was in the Earth. So he was going to go with her to see if they could see the northern lights. Or just stargaze.

So Pete put his coat and boots on and they grabbed their backpacks and their flashlights and headed out to a place that was specifically designated for looking at the night sky—a tiny parcel of land called Skyview Park on the eastern edge of Almost.

The little park had been created by some folks who Pete's dad called a buncha hippies. They wanted to make Almost, Maine, a dark-sky destination—a place for astro-tourists to visit and look at the stars. Because northern Maine was the largest light-pollution–free swath of land in the eastern United States.

And so the buncha hippies built an observatory—a small wooden platform on a little hill on the edge of Norsworthy's Potato Farm. And they put a red wooden bench on the platform so people would have a place to sit when they wanted to stargaze.

Once the observatory was built, the hippies got in touch with experts from the International Dark-Sky Association and invited them to come check out the observatory and determine whether Almost qualified as a dark-sky destination.

The experts hadn't shown up yet, but the hippies were hopeful.

The only way to get to Skyview Park from Pete's house was on Almost's main road—which had two names depending on which way you were going. If you were going east toward the big towns in eastern Aroostook County, you were on the Road to Somewhere.

If you were going west toward the wooded wilderness of northwestern Maine, you were on the Road to Nowhere.

Skyview Park was west of where Pete lived, so he and Ginette headed west on the Road to Nowhere.

As they walked, Pete slid his hand into Ginette's. It was a warm night for midwinter in Almost, Maine—nineteen degrees. And there was no wind. So they didn't need gloves. Ginette felt that strange lightness fill up her insides again while they held hands. And she wondered what she and Pete were. And couldn't wait to find out.

In about ten minutes they reached the path that led up the little hill to Skyview Park. The path had been plowed already—probably by the buncha hippies so they'd be ready if any experts showed up to deem Almost a dark-sky destination.

It was a little before 7:30 when they reached the observatory platform and its red wooden bench, both of which the hippies had also cleared of the snow that had fallen earlier in the day.

Ginette and Pete clicked off their flashlights and slid them into their backpacks and sat down on the bench—Ginette on the west side of it; Pete on the east side. They tucked their backpacks underneath them and then sat up and looked out across the snow-covered potato fields that stretched endlessly to the north in front of them.

And then they looked up.

"Wow," said Pete.

"Yeah."

An uncountable number of stars twinkled above and in front of and behind and all around them. They felt like they were close enough to touch and far, far away—all at once.

The Milky Way's thick band of stars arced overhead. It made the universe feel infinite. And it made the stargazers feel infinitesimal.

And humble.

The northern night sky will do that—make you feel humble. Because when you can see as many stars as Ginette and Pete could see, you can't help but realize that there has to be more—much, much more—than just . . . you.

As Pete gazed skyward and took in the spectacular northern night sky, he wondered why he hadn't ever gone to the observatory before.

It was probably because he felt like there was so much he needed to learn about the Earth that he didn't have time to pay attention to the heavens.

But still—he should have been aware of the majesty above him. And he turned to Ginette and confessed, "You know . . . I don't think I've ever done this."

"Done what?"

"Just . . . sat outside. Looked at the stars."

"I think a lotta people here don't."

Ginette's dad used to tell her that people from northern Maine didn't realize how lucky they were to be able to see the stars. He was from a place where people couldn't see very many of them but everyone was reaching for them. But in northern Maine, people could see just about all of them, it seemed. But not many people reached for them. He told Ginette before he left to make sure she'd never stop reaching for them. And Ginette promised she wouldn't.

"You've been missin' out," chided Ginette.

"Yeah," said Pete, marveling at the stars. "So . . . what am I lookin' at?"

"Well—"

"I know the North Star, 'cause of scouts," said Pete, looking directly above them.

"Kay."

"And I know a couple constellations, like the Big Dipper and the Little Dipper."

"Well, those aren't constellations. They're asterisms."

"Huh?"

"Just—star patterns we all recognize. They're inside constellations, which are bigger. Like . . . both of the Dippers are inside the Ursa Major constellation."

"What's Ursa Major?"

"The bear."

"I don't see a bear."

"No one does. Just like no one sees Cassiopeia—but everyone sees the W." Ginette swiveled southward and pointed out a W-shaped asterism that is the identifiable part of the constellation Cassiopeia. Pete swiveled southward, too, and saw the W, and nodded, because he had seen that W before.

Then Ginette pointed out the Pleiades, or the Seven Sisters, a small, bright cluster asterism that is part of the constellation Taurus, the bull, which Orion, the hunter, was fighting. Ginette helped Pete see Orion's shield and his weapon—a club, which he was going to use to subjugate Taurus.

"Wow," said Pete.

"What?"

"I guess I just didn't know you knew all that," said Pete, nodding skyward.

"It's just stuff my dad taught me." Ginette shrugged. "He used to take me here."

"My dad thinks this place is hippie-dippie," said Pete.

"That's too bad. Everybody should come here. Or at least look up once in a while. To help them remember that things are possible. Everybody needs help with that from time to time."

Pete wondered if Ginette needed to be reminded that things were possible. She seemed like the kind of person who thought anything was possible.

But Ginette's mom wasn't great at seeing what was possible. She was a great person and a great mom, but she was very practical and too often dwelled on what was *im*possible. And that had been wearing on Ginette lately.

"It helps me remember to dream, coming here." Ginette missed her dad again, because he was a dreamer. But not a doer. Which was why Ginette's mom had to ask him to leave. "You know," continued Ginette, "I want to go up there someday. Space."

"Really?" asked Pete.

"Yeah." Ginette felt like she belonged up there, among the stars and planets. More than she belonged on Earth, sometimes.

"Wow."

"You've gotta be really smart to go, though," said Ginette, wondering how a girl like her would ever get to space—and then wondering if she should have shared her secret dream with Pete.

"You're really smart," said Pete. "You could totally go," he added, looking up at the stars.

And Ginette looked at Pete and watched him as he stargazed. And she couldn't have been happier that she had shared her secret dream with him. And that strange lightness surged through her body again. This time, it felt like it was giving her the courage to come right out and ask him if they were going out or dating or if they were boyfriend and girlfriend or what.

And she almost asked right then and there. "Pete?" she started.

"Yeah?"

But then she chickened out. And said something that wasn't the question that she wanted to ask Pete. It was a statement—something she wanted him to know.

"I just . . . had a lot of fun today."

"Me, too."

"I always have fun with you."

"Yeah." Pete smiled. "Me, too. I mean—I always have fun with you, too. Not with me."

"I know what you mean," laughed Ginette. She was happy to hear that Pete always had fun with her, too. And it made her feel that strange lightness again. And the lightness gave her the courage to try—again—to ask him if they were dating or going out or if they were boyfriend and girlfriend or what.

"Pete?" she asked.

"Yeah?"

The lightness she was feeling grew inside her and seemed to take control of her body and she felt like it was hijacking her head and her heart and it suddenly pushed three small, immense words out of her mouth.

"I love you."

Whoa. That was not quite what Ginette had intended to say. She had intended to ask Pete something like, "Are we dating?" or "Are we boyfriend and girlfriend?" or "Do you like me the way I like you?"

But she didn't ask any of those questions.

Or any question at all.

She went straight to another statement: "I love you."

And she felt like some sort of cosmic shutdown was happening. Like all motion in the universe was ceasing. She could have sworn it made a sound—like the *vvvrrrmmm* of a giant machine losing its power.

And she just stared at Pete.

And Pete just stared at her.

And neither of them breathed.

And then Ginette suddenly gasped for air as if someone had just revived her with CPR, and she laughed a loud laugh.

And couldn't believe what she had just said.

And her laughter decrescendoed into a hopeful smile.

And she looked at Pete and waited for him to say something.

But he didn't say anything.

And then Ginette's smile turned into a look of concern.

And then it turned into a pained frown.

Because Pete still wasn't saying anything.

He was still just staring at her. Like a deer frozen in headlights.

He stared at her for so long like that, that Ginette felt like she had broken time.

And then Pete suddenly gasped and sucked in some air as if he, too, had just been revived by CPR.

And he turned away from Ginette. And looked out at the horizon, his eyes still wide.

And then Ginette turned away from him. And looked out at the horizon. Her eyes were wide, too.

And Ginette and Pete sat in the silence. And the stillness. For a while. And the stillness felt like it was full of motion. And the silence felt like it was full of sound.

Ginette had stopped breathing again, so she suddenly had to suck down some more air so she wouldn't pass out. She turned to Pete, who was still staring out at the horizon, and grunted a throaty, frenetic laugh again, hoping to coax some kind of a response from her best friend. Or former best friend. Or future boyfriend. Or whatever Pete was. And her laughter seemed to echo around in the still, quiet night. Even though there was nothing for the sound to bounce off, so there couldn't have been an echo.

And Pete didn't respond to Ginette's weird laugh.

So she looked back out at the horizon. And felt her mouth dry up, as if all of her saliva was racing up into her eyeballs and becoming tears. No, no, no. No tears, Ginette pleaded with herself. No tears.

But it was too late. Tears were falling.

They were hot.

And her neck and her head were, too.

And she could hear her heartbeat loud in her ears. And she could hear the sound of her blood whooshing through her veins and arteries. And she felt prickly all over. And like she might start sweating. Even though she was cold.

She wished Pete would say something. Anything.

But he didn't.

And Ginette's heart suddenly got so heavy.

And it sank.

And sank.

And sank.

And she decided that she just needed to get out of there—and fast. But when she tried to get up to go, she couldn't—because her body wouldn't move. Because that strange lightness she had been feeling had been replaced by a strange heaviness. It made her feel like she had a black hole inside her—and it was going to suck her body inside of itself.

Oh, what had she *done*?

She wished she could unsay what she had said. But once something is said, it can't be unsaid. And Pete had heard it. She knew he had heard it. And anything that's heard can never be unheard. That's one of the greatest tragedies of being human. Once something is heard, it lives inside the hearer's head and heart and can do good or do damage for the rest of their life.

WHY ISN'T HE SAYING ANYTHING?!? screamed Ginette to herself.

Pete would have been able to answer that question had he been able to hear it.

And his answer would have been that he was simply shocked by Ginette's confession. It was nowhere near anything even remotely close to what he was expecting her to say. So it was taking him a long time to process what she had said.

But after maybe a minute—the longest minute of Ginette's life—Pete had finally processed what Ginette had said.

And had figured out how he felt about what she had said.

And that strange lightness he had been feeling filled up his insides and seemed to course through his body and made his heart swell and seemed to force four words—urgently and breathlessly—out of his mouth: "I love you, too."

And everything stopped even more than it was already stopped.

And Ginette and Pete felt like they were suspended in time and space—not breathing, not thinking, not moving.

And then . . . Ginette felt like some sort of cosmic upshifting was setting the universe in motion again.

And Ginette and Pete were breathing and thinking and moving again.

And both of them were feeling that strange lightness fill up their insides again. And this time it was reconfiguring their chemical compositions and molecular structures. Which may have explained why they were both feeling tingly all over. And why they were feeling weak and powerful all at the same time. And more alive than they'd ever felt.

Ginette suddenly shivered. Not from the cold. But because her natural state had been disrupted and she had too much energy and nowhere to put it. Like when a charged particle from the sun collides with an atom in the Earth's atmosphere and disrupts its natural state. The energy it creates has to be manifested in some way. In the case of an atom, as light. In the case of Ginette, as a shiver.

"You okay?" asked Pete.

"Yeah." Ginette shivered again. She felt depleted—but exhilarated. And like she had just been revived from a deep sleep.

"Are you cold? Do you wanna go?"

"No, no, I just wanna sit. Here. Like this. Close." She realized that she wasn't actually sitting close to Pete at all. So she slid closer to him.

And they sat in the stillness and the silence. And the silence no longer seemed like it was full of sound. And the stillness no longer seemed like it was full of motion.

And neither of them knew what to say. Maybe because so much had just been said.

And for a while neither of them knew what to do.

Until Ginette decided that she wanted to be closer to Pete. So she slid a little closer to him and said, "I feel so close to you tonight."

"I'm glad," laughed Pete. He felt close to her, too.

"It's nice to be close," continued Ginette. "Like we are."

"Yeah," agreed Pete.

Ginette slid closer to Pete. And they both chuckled as she did.

And then she slid closer to him again. And Pete chuckled with her as she did.

And then she slid closer to him again. Until she was sitting right next to him.

And then Pete lifted his arm and put it around Ginette and pulled her in even closer to him.

And Ginette tucked herself into Pete's long torso and leaned her head on his shoulder, chuckling some more as she did so.

"What?" asked Pete.

"This is just . . . really nice."

"Yeah. It is."

Ginette laughed a funny little laugh. And her heart raced.

And Pete laughed a funny little laugh back. And his heart raced.

And then their hearts stopped racing and they felt a calm like no calm they had ever experienced.

And Ginette took Pete's hand in both of hers. And held it.

And they sat in silence and took in the night sky.

And enjoyed the serenity.

And Ginette wondered if maybe this was the great thing that she felt like she was about to experience. Because it sure was great.

After a few of the best moments either of them had ever experienced, Ginette said, "You know, right now, I think I'm about as close to you as I could possibly be."

And she laughed a little, wondering why she had said such a thing, and looked up and out at the night sky.

And Pete thought about what Ginette had just said—that she was as close to him as she could possibly be.

And then said something that could only be described as unexpected: "Well, not really."

Pete's words were like the sound of a needle getting scratched across a record on a turntable—a jarring interruption of some of the most beautiful music Ginette had ever heard. She turned to Pete. And wondered if she had heard him correctly. "Huh?" she asked, puzzled, but smiling to cover the hint of concern she felt.

"Not really," Pete repeated.

"Not really what?" Ginette asked.

"You're not really close to me. At all."

Ginette pulled her head away from Pete and looked up at him, searching his eyes for an explanation.

"If you think about it a different way," Pete explained, "you're really actually about as far away from me as you can possibly be."

More confused, Ginette recoiled a little from Pete.

"I mean," continued Pete, "if you think about it technically—if you're assuming the world is round, like a ball . . ." Pete gathered some snow, and the heat from his hands melted it enough for him to make a decent-size snowball. His hands felt like they had an ice-cream headache. He reached into his bag and pulled out his flashlight and clicked it on and tucked it under his arm to illuminate his makeshift globe. "See," he continued, "if you're assuming the world is round, like a snowball, then the farthest away you can be from somebody is if you're sitting right next to them."

Ginette wasn't following.

"See, if I'm here . . ."

Pete pointed out a spot on the snowball facing them that represented him.

"And you're here . . ."

Pete pointed out a spot on the snowball that represented her, just to the left of him.

". . . then . . ."

Pete traced a path with his finger all the way around his miniature globe to demonstrate the immense space between them.

And when his finger returned to the point on the snowball that represented him, he said, "That's *far*."

And he looked at Ginette, in awe of what he felt like was an important discovery.

Ginette looked up at Pete, puzzled. "Huh?" she queried, her face all screwed up.

Pete demonstrated again, this time with more props. He reached into his backpack and grabbed his bag of gorp and took a peanut and a green M&M out of the bag and tucked his flashlight under his arm again and continued. "See, if this is me . . ." He held up the peanut. "And I'm here . . ." He shoved the peanut into the snowball, facing them, to represent himself. "And this is you . . ." He held up the green M&M. ". . . and you're here . . ." He placed the green M&M directly to the left of the peanut, but then moved the M&M in the opposite direction of the peanut—all the way around the snowball—until it was close to the peanut again—but on the other side of it. And then he shoved the M&M into the snowball next to the peanut and said, "That's far."

And then Pete looked at Ginette, in awe of his discovery.

"Yeah," Ginette muttered, wondering why Pete was telling her this. She looked to him, hoping for more of an explanation.

But none was forthcoming. Pete was just smiling goofily, excited about his new definition of what it means to be close to someone. To him it was a happy revelation: He and Ginette had just confessed their love for each other. And they were going to have to get to know one another in a brand-new way. He suddenly felt like the space between them was enormous, because their world had changed— they were in unknown territory and had so much to learn about each other. And he couldn't wait to learn all about Ginette and fill that space. And get close to her again—a new kind of close.

But Ginette didn't know that this was what Pete was thinking. Because she felt like he was saying—in a cruel, cryptic way—that he felt like he was far away from her. Or didn't want to be close to her. Or something.

So she moved away from him. Because she didn't want to be close to him if he didn't want to be close to her.

Pete clocked Ginette's move away from him. And explained brightly, "But now . . . you're closer!" And this was true, according to his newly formed theory on what it means to be close.

Ginette turned to Pete. He was still smiling goofily. Which irritated her. "Pete . . ." she said, hurt and confused. And then said nothing more. And exhaled—a little exasperatedly.

Pete kept smiling and earnestly asked, "What?"

"Nothin'," Ginette said, sliding farther away from the guy she had just professed her love to.

Pete responded to Ginette's second move away from him by triumphantly repeating, "And closer!"

Ginette looked back at Pete and wanted to ask him what the heck he was saying. So she could understand what he was saying. But she was so irked by him that she didn't want to understand what he was saying and decided that she just needed to leave.

She leaned over and grabbed her backpack, unzipped it, pulled out her flashlight, and clicked it on. And then zipped up her backpack and stood up to go—but stopped. And felt a deep sense of loss—like she had just missed out on experiencing the greatest joy she would ever know. It made her feel hollow. And heavy. Both at the same time.

But then she shook the hollow heaviness off, slung her backpack over her shoulders, and started to leave.

She didn't really know where she was going. Wherever it was, it was going to be somewhere Pete wasn't.

Home, probably.

When she had taken barely one step, Pete called out hopefully, "And closer!" Because, to a conventional thinker, Ginette was getting farther and farther away from him. But to an unconventional thinker, she was getting closer to him with every step away from him she took.

Ginette stopped and turned to Pete and shone her light on him.

"Right?" Pete asked, shielding his eyes from the light but still smiling and expecting Ginette to be wowed by his radical new theory on what it means to be close.

Ginette looked at Pete like he was crazy and shook her head and turned and started to go again. And had barely taken one more step when Pete said almost triumphantly, "And closer!"

Ginette stopped. And turned to Pete, who still had a goofy grin on his face.

And she tried to understand what he was saying. But couldn't.

Part puzzled, part hurt, and mostly annoyed, she started to leave again.

But when she had taken just one more step away from him, Pete called out, "And closer."

Ginette stopped. And turned to Pete again.

And shook her head and shrugged again, completely at a loss.

And then continued on her way on the path out of Skyview Park, which was taking her west alongside the Road to Nowhere.

And with every step she took, Pete called to her, eagerly explaining that she was getting "closer and closer and closer and closer . . ." to him. Which made Ginette walk faster and faster and faster and faster, because she really didn't want to hear that anymore, especially when the fact was, she was getting farther and farther and farther and farther away from him.

It wasn't long before all Pete could see of Ginette was her silhouette against the pool of light from her flashlight. It was getting smaller and smaller and smaller and smaller the farther away she got. And it started dropping out of sight as she descended the little hill that the observatory was on.

And then it disappeared.

And Pete was alone.

And his goofy smile faded.

And he started to panic a little. Because this was not quite how he had planned for the evening to go. He didn't know exactly how he had planned for it to go—but this was definitely not it.

He suddenly didn't like his theory very much. Because—while it was true that Ginette was getting closer and closer and closer to him with every step she took, it was also true that she was getting farther and farther and farther away from him.

Oh, no.

What had he done?

He had just experienced one of the greatest things he would ever experience. And now . . . well, it seemed he had ruined it.

He wanted to get up and go after the girl he loved.

But he couldn't move. Because that strange lightness he had been feeling had been replaced by darkness—and a painful heaviness. It made him feel like he had a brick of osmium, the densest naturally occurring element, in his gut.

And he was scared and confused.

And embarrassed.

So he just sat. On the bench. Alone. Trying to figure out what to do.

And Ginette walked.

2

Ginette made her way west along the path from the observatory at Skyview Park, which ran parallel to the Road to Nowhere, until the path and the road merged.

As she walked, she wondered why she was leaving Pete behind.

A few minutes ago, she had told Pete she loved him.

And—it took him a while—but Pete eventually told her that he loved her, too.

And now Ginette was hurt and sad and confused—and leaving Pete behind.

And she shouldn't have been leaving Pete.

She should have been staying with him and sitting on the bench with him, basking in some sort of afterglow or something.

But she wasn't staying and sitting and basking in any sort of glow.

She was leaving. Because when she poured her heart out to Pete and told him that she thought she was about as close to him as she could possibly be, he said, "Not really."

He could have said, "Yeah."

Or, "Cool."

Or nothing.

But he said, "Not really." And then went on to say that Ginette wasn't really close to him at all. That she was actually about as far away from him as she could possibly be.

What did he *mean*?

And why had he said that—*when* he had said it?

Soon the path merged with the Road to Nowhere, and Ginette crossed the road for safety, so she would be walking against traffic, so she could see the headlights of oncoming vehicles before they saw her.

She stayed close to the snowbanks—which were almost as tall as she was. And continued west.

And, at 7:50, she came to the Gallaghers' potato farm, where Ginette's mom had picked potatoes when she was a teenager, back when the farm was still operational. Schools in northern Maine closed for three weeks every fall so high schoolers could help farmers get their crop out of the ground. Not many farmers employed hand pickers anymore, so Ginette hadn't been able to find work over the last few harvests. But she'd be sixteen in the summer—old enough to work on one of the Norsworthys' mechanical harvesters in the coming fall. And she hoped Mrs. Norsworthy would hire her.

As Ginette walked, she wondered what she was going to do with the rest of her evening.

She'd be home—alone. Because her mom was working.

And she wasn't sure she wanted to be alone.

But that's what she was.

And then she started wallowing in her loneliness—and wondered if she was going to be alone for the rest of her life. Like the Gallaghers' son, East—who was about to experience one of the extraordinary things that did or didn't happen on that Friday night.

But East Gallagher didn't feel like he was about to experience anything extraordinary when Ginette walked by his house.

It had been a pretty ordinary day.

He had plowed some driveways.

And shoveled some walkways and paths to oil fills and propane tanks.

And now he was eating his dinner: noodles with hamburger and butter and some peas and potatoes.

When he was done, he let Hound lick off his plate, and then he put it in the white enamel-coated cast-iron basin in his kitchen.

He looked at the Wildflowers of Maine clock over the sink and it told him it was 8:20. Time for bed. East still woke up at 4:30 a.m. like he did when he was a farmer. So he still went to bed at 8:30.

He headed over to the staircase landing and flicked off the downstairs lights and flicked on the upstairs hall light. "Come on, Hound." Hound obeyed and started up the stairs a little more slowly than he used to, and East followed, a little more slowly than he used to. And the two large creatures lumbered up the stairs. When they reached the second-floor landing, canine and human shuffled into the room East had slept in his whole life. It was a large room with a big picture window that afforded a view of the backyard and, beyond it, the first potato field his parents ever planted.

Hound hauled himself up onto the bed with some help from his owner. East pulled the covers back and his old pup thunked down on his side of the bed and curled up into a dog doughnut. East kissed Hound on the head and pulled the covers over him and wished he could fall asleep as fast as his best friend did. Then he turned his bedside lamp on and went to the bathroom and brushed his teeth and then flicked the hall light off and went back into his room.

He was about to get out of his Carhartts and Scotch-plaid flannel and turn off his bedside lamp and slide into his side of the bed—when he found himself drawn to his bedroom window. He stared out the glass pane and had the strangest, strongest feeling that someone was out there. Someone he wanted to know. Or needed to know.

But he couldn't see anyone—or much of anything, save for his reflection in the glass. So he went over to his bedside lamp and switched it off and went back to the window.

His eyes eventually adjusted to the darkness, and he could make out the silhouettes of the old barn and the Dr. Seuss–like spruce trees in his backyard, and beyond it, the expanse of the old potato field.

And he couldn't shake the feeling that someone was out there.

But he couldn't see anyone. Which wasn't too surprising. Because it was dark out there.

And then he shook off the feeling, because why would anyone be out there in the middle of the night in the middle of winter?

So he peeled off his Carhartts and his flannel and went to bed. And lay there for a while. And was cold. Bedrooms in Maine are always cold in winter.

But soon his body heat warmed the bed covers enough that he started to drift off to sleep—but only started. Before he completely fell asleep, he was roused by a strange lightness that seemed to be filling his insides. The lightness made him feel like he had the glow of a welding torch burning inside him. And like he was floating in an inner tube on Echo Lake in the summertime.

It also seemed like it was what made him get out of bed and go to the window and look outside again.

East cupped his hands around his eyes and pressed his hands against the glass and stared out into the darkness, certain that someone was out there—someone he had to meet.

And then he slid his Carhartts on over his boxers and pulled his flannel over his gray T-shirt and hurried downstairs, where he put on a coat, pulled on some boots, grabbed his Maglite, and went outside to see who he might find out there in the darkness.

Motion-sensor lights flicked on when he went outside. They illuminated a portion of his backyard—and peeved him a little, because the light they threw allowed him to see only what was in his immediate vicinity and not what was out there in the darkness. And what he was looking for was out there in the darkness.

So he trudged through the deep snow, passed through the pool of light, and made his way into the darkness. Shortly after he did so, the motion-sensor lights flickered off. And he couldn't see a thing. So he stopped and let his eyes adjust to the lack of light. As they did, he thought about how strange darkness is. It's not there. But you can't see through it. Not without a light, anyway. So he clicked on his Maglite and continued on his way to see if anyone was actually out there in the old potato field.

The going was difficult because the snow was thigh-deep in places. But he persevered. And after about a five-minute traipse, he stopped. Because he felt like he wasn't alone.

Someone was definitely out there, he felt.

"Hello!" called East—loudly enough to be heard but gently enough not to frighten anyone.

"Hello!" called a woman's voice cheerily. East shone his Maglite in the voice's direction. And it revealed a woman looking intently up at the sky.

She looked like she was modeling winter clothing for a catalog that sold expensive and stylish winter clothes to people who live in warm places so they have something nice to wear when they visit winter on the occasional weekend. Her jacket was white and had a brightly colored flower pattern exploding all over it. And she had a cerulean blue hat on—with matching scarf and gloves.

And she looked cold.

And it wasn't cold.

It was nineteen degrees.

The woman looked like she definitely wasn't from northern Maine.

Or from anywhere in Maine.

Or from anywhere where winter actually happened.

East wondered why she was standing in the middle of his yard—in the middle of winter—in the middle of the night—staring up at the sky.

"I thought I saw someone out here," he said, hoping the woman would explain what she was doing in his yard. But she didn't say anything. So East said, "I was about to go to bed and I thought I saw you from my window."

The woman didn't respond and just kept looking up at the sky.

East followed her gaze upward to see what she was looking at.

It was just the same old northern night sky that he had been looking up at his whole life.

And then he looked back at the woman and asked, "Is there something I can do for you?" He hoped he sounded like he was there to help.

The woman turned to East and said, "Oh, no—thank you, though. I'm just here to see the northern lights."

And then she smiled and resumed looking skyward.

"Okay," said East, and he wondered if maybe she was one of those astro-tourists he had been hearing about. "Okay," repeated East. "It's just that—it's kinda late." It was about 8:45, which was late for East but not for the woman. "And you're in my yard."

"What?—Oh, no!" cried the woman, genuinely concerned. "I am?"

"Yeah."

"Oh, I'm sorry!" The woman was definitely from away, East decided, because she said she was "saw-ree" the way people from away did. (Northern Mainers say they're "sore-ee" like Canadians do.) "I didn't know I was in anybody's yard!" continued the woman, sounding flustered.

"Well, you are, but it's okay—"

"I thought I was just in a random field," interrupted the woman.

"Well, it used to be a potato field. But now it's just . . . my yard."

"Oh," said the woman as she looked out over the snowy landscape.

"Well, I hope you don't mind that I'm here. I'll see them tonight— the northern lights—and then I'll be gone. I hope you don't mind!"

"Is that your tent?" asked East, having espied a dome-shaped silhouette a few yards away from the woman.

The woman looked to where East was shining his Maglite. "Um . . . yeah, yes!" The woman was nodding and smiling.

"You've pitched a tent," said East blankly.

"Yeah—"

"In my yard."

"Yeah, so I have a place to sleep after I see them. I hope you don't mind!"

"Well," began East. He didn't really mind or not mind that this stranger had pitched a tent in his yard, but the woman was getting the feeling that he did, in fact, mind that she was there, and she didn't want to inconvenience him, because she didn't like to inconvenience people. "Oh, no!" she cried, "You mind, don't you?"

"Um—"

"Yeah! You do! Oh, no! I'm sorry!" she cried, pronouncing sorry in her from-away way. "I didn't think you would!" She pulled her cerulean gloves off with her teeth and took a glossy, folded-up wad of paper out of her jacket pocket. "See, I read that . . . um . . ." The woman shoved her gloves in her pocket and unfolded the wad of paper, reading from it as she continued. "I read that you wouldn't mind. See, it says in your brochure that people from Maine live life 'the way life should be,' and that, in the tradition of their brethren in rural northern climes like Scandinavia, they'll let people who are complete strangers like cross-country skiers and hikers and bikers just camp out in their yards if they need to. They'll just let you."

East wondered who had written this brochure—and why she thought it was his.

"Is it true?" continued the woman. "That they'll just let you? Camp out?" The woman stuffed the brochure back in her pocket and retrieved her gloves and put them back on. "I'm a hiker," she clarified. "Is it true? That they'll just let you stay in their yards if you need to?"

Before East could answer, the woman was providing information that was more cryptic than illuminating.

"'Cause I need to. Camp out. 'Cause I'm where I need to be. And I came a long way to be here—I'm from a part of the country that's a little closer to things. I've never been this far north before. Or east." The woman took in the sky and the wide-open, empty space of the northeasternmost corner of the United States. She felt like she was in a forgotten place. Unthought of, even. Which is one step below forgotten, because forgotten places were once at least thought of.

"Anyway," she continued, still marveling at the wide-open space, "it feels like the end of the world. And here I am at the end of the world, and I have nowhere to go, unless it's *not* true, I mean, *is* it true?" asked the woman, turning to East. "Would you let a hiker who was where she needed to be camp out in your yard for free? I mean, if a person really needed to?"

"Well—"

"Really, really needed to?"

The woman fell silent and waited for East's answer. Which wasn't forthcoming, because East was a little overwhelmed by all of the woman's questions. There were so many of them. And they seemed more like demands than questions. Which, East had come to learn, was how people from away often asked their questions.

But East didn't seem to mind all of the woman's questions/demands. Because he just wanted to help her out in any way he could. "Well," he began, "if a person really needed to stay here and camp out . . . well, I wouldn't want to get in the way of that, but—"

"Oh!" cried the woman, interrupting him and rushing him. "Thank you!" she exclaimed. And the next thing East knew, she was hugging him, and her face was embedded in his torso.

He smelled like woodsmoke and gasoline, and the woman felt like she wanted to smell that smell for the rest of her life.

And she felt a strange lightness start to fill up her insides. It made her feel like she had the glow of the Milky Way inside her. And like gravity might lose its hold on her.

East was also feeling that strange lightness—again. This time, it made him feel like part of him was levitating—as if his one self had become two, and his levitating self was looking down at the earthbound one that was being embraced by the woman. But then the woman suddenly pulled away from him, and East felt his floating self crash back down into his earthbound one. And he felt like a magical spell had been broken.

"I'm so sorry I did that," said the woman, stunned by all the feelings she was feeling.

"It's okay," said East. He hadn't minded at all that the woman had hugged him.

"I don't know why I did that. I guess I just really appreciate you letting me stay here—so I can do what I need to do. You have no idea how much it means to me. Thank you."

"Sure," said East.

And the woman smiled and focused her attention skyward again.

And East watched the woman watch the sky. And felt like he could have watched her forever.

And then the woman suddenly gasped and said, "Oh, no!" And she started pressing her hands to her chest as if she was having trouble breathing.

"What's wrong?" asked East. "Are you okay?"

The woman had gotten her flashlight out of her backpack and flicked it on and started searching frantically for something around her campsite.

"What's wrong?" repeated East.

The woman shone her flashlight on East and suddenly gasped again and cried, "Oh!" She had found what she was looking for.

"What?"

"I need that!" The woman was pointing at something East was holding.

East looked down to where the woman was pointing.

And was surprised to find a small brown paper sack in the crook of his arm.

He had no idea he had been holding it.

Or how long he had been holding it.

Or how he had gotten it.

Or that the woman had been holding it the whole time they had been talking.

He simply hadn't seen it.

When the woman had hugged him a few moments ago, it

had gotten lodged between their bodies and a seamless transfer occurred—so seamless that neither East nor the woman realized that the bag had exchanged owners.

East held the small brown paper sack out to the woman, and the woman snatched it from him. "Thanks," she said, holding the bag close, relieved to have it back.

"Sure," said East.

And then the woman clicked off her flashlight and put it back in her backpack and resumed looking at the sky. And hoped that East would go back inside his house and let her do what she needed to do.

But that wasn't going to happen. Because East was too intrigued by this woman.

And he wanted to know why she was there.

So he said, "So . . . I don't mean to bother you, but did you say—when I came out here and asked you if there was somethin' I could do for you—did you say that you were here to see the northern lights?"

"Yeah," said the woman, happy that East wasn't asking her about the brown paper sack that she had just recovered. "I'll only be here tonight. I'll see them tonight. And then I'll be gone."

"Um, well . . . you never really know if you're gonna see 'em, you know. They're not on a schedule or anything. So you might not see 'em *tonight*."

"Oh, no! I'll see them!" insisted the woman. "Your latitude is good."

This was true. Almost, Maine, is just far enough north that the northern lights appear there fairly frequently. And—good thing—because the woman had forgotten to renew her passport, so getting to Canada would have been tricky, and she didn't have the time—or money, really—to get to Alaska, so Almost was her best option for doing what she needed to do.

"And the time is right: there's no moon so moonlight won't obscure them," continued the woman, and she looked up at the sky, and East did, too, and together they tacitly confirmed that there was, indeed, no moon. "And—most important," the woman added, "solar activity is at an eleven-year peak right now, so everything's in order, and boy, you have good sky for it. It's so huge here," she gushed, "and dark." The woman shifted focus earthward and scanned the horizon. "And, you know, it's flatter here than I thought it would be. I thought it'd be more mountainous."

"Nah. Mountains are way south and west. We just have some hills. And woods. And farms."

"Oh." They took in the landscape the woman had just described. And then the woman asked, "So what kinda farm is this?"

"Potato."

"Oh, yeah, you said."

"And broccoli," added East.

But then he remembered it wasn't a potato and broccoli farm anymore and was about to correct himself when the woman asked, "So you're a farmer?"

"No. Used to be. But not anymore."

"Oh."

"I sold off most of my land a few years back after my folks died," explained East. His mom and dad had hit a moose on their way home from a Maine Potato Board meeting in Presque Isle and only the moose survived. And East still wasn't quite over it. "And now," he added, "I'm a repairman."

"Oh."

"I fix things," he explained. And then immediately wished that he hadn't. Because it's pretty obvious what repairmen do.

And then the woman snorted. And seemed to be laughing.

"What?" asked East, hoping she wasn't laughing at him. "What's so funny?"

"Nothing. It's just—you're not a lobster man."

"Um . . . nope." East stifled a laugh, because the woman said *lobster man*—instead of *lobsterman*.

"And I guess I thought that everyone from Maine was a lobster man and talked in that funny way like they do in Maine. But . . . you're not a lobster man, and you don't talk that way."

"Nope." East was smiling a little, eager to debunk a common misconception. "You're not Downeast. You're up north. And we don't really have an accent up here."

"So I'm hearing."

"And, plus, the ocean's a couple hundred miles away, so . . . it'd be an awful long ride to work if I was a 'lobster man,'" continued East dryly, making sure to say *lobsterman* the way she did—like it was two words—because he wanted the woman to know he was having a little bit of fun at her expense.

"Yeah, I guess it would be," laughed the woman, rolling her eyes at herself, and then they laughed together at her misconceptions and at his dry wit until they realized they had nothing else to say.

And the strange lightness they had been feeling filled their insides again.

And that feeling confused the woman. And she suddenly remembered that she was on a mission and that she needed to get back to doing what she needed to do in order to accomplish it.

So she said, "I'm sorry—you know what? I really need to get back to . . ." And she pointed to the sky to let East know that she needed to get back to doing what she was there to do.

"Oh, sure," said East.

"And—I really appreciate you letting me stay here. And look for the northern lights. I just really need to do this, and . . . thanks for being so understanding and accommodating—"

The next thing either of them knew, East was hugging the woman.

And then, just as suddenly as he was hugging her—he wasn't.

Because he had pulled away from her.

And was now standing stock-still, facing her, a little stunned.

The woman was also a little stunned.

"Oh, gosh—I'm—I'm sorry," stammered East.

"It's okay," said the woman. Even though she wasn't sure it was.

"Are you okay?"

The woman wasn't sure she was.

"I'm real sorry I did that," East added, imagining what it must have been like for this small woman to have had a big lug of a man like him come at her and wrap her up in his arms. "It's just . . ." The strange lightness East had been feeling grew inside him—it felt like it was possessing him, even—and it seemed to take control of his body and push the rest of the sentence he had started out of his mouth and make him gutturally blurt out, "I think I love you."

And then he felt like everything stopped.

And he found himself unable to breathe. And unable to move.

And his face was the picture of contrite befuddlement.

The woman's eyes widened and bugged a little as she took in her host's unexpected confession. And then she recoiled a bit and may have even taken a step or two away from East as she skeptically uttered, "I'm sorry—what?"

And East started breathing again and conferred with himself for a moment. And decided that what he had just said was indeed true. "Yeah. I saw you from my window—no—wait: I didn't actually *see* you. I just . . . *felt* . . . like you were out here when I was looking out my window . . . and . . ." He thought some more to make sure what he was about to say was true. And when he was sure it was true, he continued, "And I loved you. Before I even saw you."

And then East shrugged helplessly.

And everything was silent and still.

And East stood facing the woman, still looking contritely befuddled, trying to process what he had just said.

And the woman stood facing East, trying to process what she had just heard. His profession of love was a little disconcerting—because it had come from a complete stranger. But it seemed sincere and, ultimately, harmless. So the woman was gentle as she quashed her lovelorn host's romantic overtures. "Well . . . that's really nice of you to say, but, um, there's something I think you should know: What you just told me? I'm not here for that."

"Oh, no!" East really didn't presume that the woman was there for him to love her. And he couldn't quite believe he had just professed his love to a complete stranger—even though there was no doubt that he loved her. "I didn't think you were!" he contended, defending himself.

"I'm here to pay my respects," continued the woman. "To my husband."

"Oh, no," groaned East. He had just told a married woman that he loved her.

"Yeah. My husband. Wes. I'm here to say goodbye to him. 'Cause he died recently."

"Oh, no." East had just told a grieving *widow* that he loved her.

"Yeah. On Tuesday, actually."

"Oh."

"Yeah." And that was all she wanted to say on the subject. Because she really didn't want to get into it.

But something about East made her want to get into it.

So she did.

"And the northern lights—did you know this?—the northern lights are actually the torches that the recently departed carry with them so they can find their way home to heaven, according to the people who first lived here." The woman knew this because she had been reading *The Big Book of Who, What, Where, When, and Why* with her story-time kids at the library. And one of the entries was about what the northern lights were—and where, when, why they appeared. "And, see," she continued, "it takes a soul three days to make its way home to heaven, and Wes died on Tuesday night—three days ago—and I flew in to Presque Isle on Wednesday—in the morning—and then I hiked Wednesday and Thursday and today, until I found a spot that was dark enough . . . and that felt right. And when I got here today, well, it just felt *right*, and it's so *dark* here, and—anyway—this is Friday! This is the third day, so, you see, I *will* see them—the northern lights—because they're gonna be him. He'll be carrying one of the torches." The woman looked up and started scanning the sky. "And, see, I need them to be him, because I didn't leave things well with him, so I was just hoping I could come here and say goodbye to him . . . but what you just *said*—just a second ago? That's going to get in the way of me saying goodbye to him, I think, and so I think I'm just going to go find another place to do what I need to do."

And the woman started making her way toward her tent so she could pack up and go, and, as she did, East protested. "No—wait! Please don't do that. I'm sorry!" The thought of the woman leaving made East's insides feel heavy and dark. And he realized that they had felt that way for a long time. And he didn't want them to feel that way anymore, which made him desperate for the woman to stay, and he begged, "Please don't go! I don't really know what happened."

"Well, *I* do. *I* know what happened," retorted the woman sardonically.

The woman collapsed her tent and started packing it up into a small pouch and converted the poles that gave it its structure into trekking poles. East marveled at the amazing design but was surprised to find that he was more interested in the woman than he was in the excellent design of her ultra-packable tent. Which she probably saw in the same catalog that she had found her expensive and stylish clothing in.

"Please wait!" East begged. "Like I said—I'm not the kind of person who does things like . . . what I just did."

The woman continued to break down her campsite.

"Please—don't go," pleaded East. "Just—do what you need to do, and . . . and I-I-I . . . I won't bother you."

The woman realized that all she wanted in the world right now was for this guy to stay and bother her, and she had no idea what to do with that feeling, so she ignored it and continued packing up her things so she could be on her way.

"Maybe just consider what I did . . . a-a-a-a . . . a very warm Maine welcome."

From any other guy, such a hokey appeal would have been creepy. But from East, it was earnest. And charming, somehow. And it took the woman by such sweet surprise that she stopped packing up her things.

And the lightness she had been feeling filled up her insides again. And seemed to make her acquiesce and say, "All right."

East was overjoyed that the woman was going to stay in his yard. And he immediately apologized again for hugging her: "I'm real sorry I did that."

"It's okay," the woman said, in a way that made East feel like it really wasn't and that she would like for him to stop apologizing and stop talking to her and let her do what she was there to do.

And East took the hint and said, "Well, good luck. And if you need anything—somethin' to eat or some heat . . . or the bathroom—just give a holler."

"Okay. Thank you."

East was a little embarrassed that he had just offered the woman his bathroom. But she'd need a bathroom sooner or later, he figured. So it wasn't an unreasonable thing to have offered.

And then he turned and was about to go—but, before he did, he realized that he didn't know the woman's name. And she didn't know his. So he said, "And, just so you know: I'm East."

"I'm sorry?" asked the woman, turning to East.

"My name's East."

"Oh." The woman considered the unusual name. And then asked, "Like the direction?"

"Yeah," East answered, and he went on to explain his unusual name, like he had done countless times in his life. "It's short for Easton." And he took a few eager steps toward her as he explained his name. "It's the name of a town—that way"—East pointed east—"where I was born." And then he offered more of an explanation so the woman wouldn't have to ask for one. "There was a mess-up on the birth certificate: a son, *Easton*, born in the town of *Matthew*, Maine. Instead of the other way around."

The woman seemed to pity East when she learned the origin of his unusual name. "Oh," she said with a wincing smile. "I'm sorry."

"Don't be. You didn't name me."

The woman smiled, conceding East's point.

"And—anyway—I like my name," continued East.

"Well, good."

And then the woman congratulated East on his recent birthday.

And East thanked the woman and appreciated her thoughtfulness.

And then the woman—who had completely forgotten why she was where she was—asked, "So . . . Easton, huh?"

"Yup."

"Yeah, I passed a sign for there on my way here, and, by the way, where is 'here'? I couldn't find it on my map." The woman pulled her cerulean gloves off with her teeth again and pulled a map out of her jacket pocket.

"Um . . . well—"

"Where *am* I?" asked the woman, unfolding her map.

"You're in unorganized territory. Township 13, Range 7."

East went on to explain that over half of Maine's land area—an area the size of the states of Vermont and New Hampshire—was unorganized territory. Back when the country was being put together, surveyors went out and started mapping the wild places. And those wild places were divided into townships that were about thirty-six square miles each. Almost was one of those townships.

The woman looked on her map for this "Almost" place, but East warned her, "It's not gonna be on your map, 'cause it's not an actual town, technically."

"What do you mean?"

"See, to be a town, you gotta get organized, and we never got around to getting organized. So we're just . . . Almost."

"Oh."

"Plus, we're *almost* in Canada."

"Okay." The woman nodded.

"And almost *not* in the United States."

"Okay."

"So . . . Almost."

"Okay." Appropriate name, supposed the woman.

And she wondered what in the world this "Almost" place was.

And then decided that she needed to get back on task and said, "Okay, well—I'm just gonna do what I need to do, here, if that's still okay?"

"Oh, yeah, sure," said East, and he reminded the woman again to let him know if she needed anything and the woman said, "Thanks," and East turned to go. And as he did, the woman added, "And my name's Glory, just so you know."

East turned back to the woman and felt that strange lightness fill up his insides again and said, "Hi, Glory."

And Glory said, "Hi." And felt the strange lightness fill up her insides again, too.

And Glory didn't quite know how to deal with the lightness she was feeling and suddenly directed her focus back up to the sky.

And East didn't know how to deal with the lightness he was feeling, either, so he turned and started to make his way back to his house.

And he felt a deep, strange sense of loss as he did.

And so did Glory.

And then Glory realized that she was feeling a sense of loss because she had actually lost something.

Or was missing something.

And then discovered that the small brown paper sack she had been carrying was no longer in her possession.

"Oh, no!" she gasped. East heard Glory and stopped and turned to her. "Oh, no!" uttered Glory again. And she dug her flashlight out of her backpack and started searching the area for what was missing.

But it was nowhere to be found.

"What's wrong?" asked East. He saw her flashlight beam dancing on the snow, and when he shone his Maglite on her, he saw her frantically searching the area around her campsite.

"Glory?" he called, rushing back to her. "Are you okay?"

Glory was emitting strange grunts and groans and gasps as she searched.

"What's wrong?" repeated East.

"My heart!" called Glory.

"Huh?"

"My heart!" Glory repeated, clutching at her chest, her breathing labored.

East wondered if she was having a heart attack—even though she seemed far too young to be having a heart attack. "Where is it?" gasped Glory, searching more frantically.

Glory shone her flashlight on East and was about to ask him to help her find what she was looking for when she gasped, "Oh! *You* have it!"

"Huh?"

Glory was pointing at something East was holding. "In that bag, it's in that bag!"

East looked to where Glory was pointing and saw that he was holding the brown paper sack in the crook of his arm—again. And wondered how on earth it had gotten there. He didn't know that when he hugged Glory, it had become lodged between their bodies again, and another imperceptible transfer had occurred.

"Please give it back. Please, I need it!" Glory demanded, struggling to breathe.

"Yeah, sure, here," said East, going to Glory and offering her the bag—which she grabbed and held close.

"Thank you," said she greatly relieved, her breathing starting to normalize.

"You're welcome," said East, completely bewildered.

Glory looked back up at the sky. And tried to make like nothing had happened.

And East stood and stared at Glory. And wondered if he had heard her correctly. Had she just said that her heart was in that bag?

Glory felt East's eyes on her and kept looking at the sky, hoping that East would go away so she wouldn't have to explain what she had just said was inside the brown paper bag she was clutching.

But East wasn't going away. He was staring at her. And trying to make sense of what had just happened. And—even though he knew it wasn't any of his business—he couldn't help but ask, "Um . . . I'm sorry, but, did you just say that your . . . heart . . . is in that bag? Is that what you just said, that your *heart* is in—"

"Yes," interrupted Glory. He had already asked the question once, and there was no need for him to repeat it.

East thought long and hard about Glory's answer. And then finally remarked, "It's heavy."

It was. But Glory chose not to let East know that she concurred, and said nothing. Because she was too busy trying—and failing—to find a way out of having to explain what she knew she was going to have to explain.

"Why is it in that bag?"

"It's how I carry it around," said Glory curtly.

"Why do you have to . . . carry it around?" asked East.

Glory almost told East that she really didn't want to get into it. Because she really didn't want to get into it. At all. But there didn't seem to be a way for her to *not* get into it.

And maybe a part of her felt like getting into it with him.

So she got into it.

"It's broken," she confessed—and she was surprised to feel that strange lightness fill up her insides again. This time, it felt like an unburdening. And it felt good.

"Oh," said East.

Glory expected East to have an opinion about her strange answer. But he didn't. Instead, he simply asked, "What happened?"

"Wes broke it."

"Your husband," said East, making sure he was remembering who Wes was.

"Yeah. He went away."

"Oh," said East, saddened by the revelation.

"With someone else."

"Oh, no," groaned East.

"Yeah. And when he did that . . . well, I felt like my heart was gonna break. And that's exactly what happened. It broke."

Glory paused and checked in with East to see if he believed her.

And he didn't seem to believe or disbelieve her. He seemed to be listening without judgment and without forming an opinion. Which was how he usually listened.

"And," she continued, "it hurt so bad, I had to go to the hospital, and when I got there, well—I didn't know this, because I was out cold—but . . . I guess it had broken."

This was actually true. Glory had developed takotsubo cardio-myopathy, a weakening of the heart's left ventricle that can occur as the result of severe emotional or physical stress—like when a husband leaves his wife for another woman. It's also called broken-heart syndrome, and most people recover from it quickly with no lasting damage.

But not Glory. Her case was extreme: when she arrived at the hospital, doctors discovered that her heart had actually broken in two.

Glory eyed East before she continued, gauging how crazy he seemed to think she was.

But he didn't seem to think she was crazy at all. He still just seemed to be listening.

"I almost died, I guess," she continued. "But they hooked me up to a machine that resuscitated me and called in an expert"— fortunately Glory lived in a place where there were lots of experts— "and the expert took the two broken halves of my heart out of my chest, and when he did that, he somehow managed to drop them on the operating room floor, and they broke into nineteen pieces."

Glory held up the brown paper bag she was holding.

"Slate," Glory explained, shaking the bag three times. The shards in the bag clanked together as Glory shook them, making a jangly, earthy sound as they did. "It turned to slate," added Glory.

After East took a moment to process what he had heard, he said the only thing he could think of to say to someone who had just told him that her heart had turned to slate: "Great for roofing."

Glory turned to East and wondered what in the world she was supposed to do with that information.

And East shrugged a little. Because he had no idea what she was supposed to do with that information.

And then Glory turned her focus back to the sky.

And East watched Glory watch the sky. And marveled at her and what she had been through. And then asked, "How do you breathe? If your heart is in that bag, how are you alive?"

Glory tapped her chest a couple of times. "Artificial."

"Really?" asked East, increasingly fascinated, and trying to figure out how an artificial heart might work.

"Yeah." Glory was touched by East's earnest interest. And seeming lack of judgment. "When my real one broke, we didn't have time to wait for a donor to give us a real one. And there aren't nearly enough real ones to go around."

"Oh," said East. And then he thought. And looked at the small brown paper sack Glory was holding close while he did. And then he pointed at it and said, "So . . . that's your heart."

"Yeah."

"The one that broke."

"Yeah."

"And the one in there"—East pointed to Glory's chest—"is artificial?"

"Yeah."

East thought. And then pointed to the heart that was in the bag Glory was holding. "So why do you carry this one around with you?"

"Well, because they gave it back to me when I left the hospital," answered Glory. "So I figured I must need it, that it must still be . . . important. I mean—it *is* my heart."

"Yeah. But it's broken," said East.

"Yeah—"

"'Cause your husband left you."

"Yeah, but—"

"For someone else."

"Yeah—"

"Well, why are you paying your respects to a guy who left you?"

"Well, because that's what you do when a person dies, you pay your respects."

"But . . . he *left* you."

"Yeah."

"And it seems to me that a man who leaves somebody doesn't deserve any respects," reasoned East, building a case.

Glory defended herself—and her husband. "Well, I just didn't

leave things well with him, and I'd like to apologize to him. That's all."
Glory focused on the sky again, hoping that East would be satisfied
with that explanation and let the rest go.

But East wasn't letting the rest go. "But he *left* you," he argued.

"Yeah, but—"

"*He*'s the one who should apologize, not you."

"Yeah, well—"

"Why should *you* have to apologize?"

"Just because."

"Because *why*?"

"Because I killed him!"

East froze. And tried not to look alarmed. And managed to say,
"Oh."

"Yeah. And I'd like to apologize."

East wondered whether or not he was in danger and took a couple of tentative steps away from Glory.

And then the strange lightness Glory had been feeling expanded
inside her and made her want to tell this kind, gentle man everything. He seemed to have believed everything she had told him thus
far. Maybe he'd believe the rest of the strange story that had become
her life over the past couple of years.

"See," she explained, "Wes had come to visit me at home, after
I had had my surgery—which had gone really well: my artificial heart
was in my chest, and it was pumping, and I was breathing and doing
most of the things I used to be able to do. And *then* . . ." Glory paused,
rolling her eyes at the implausibility of it all before continuing, "Wes
calls me up last Tuesday—I was eating my dinner—and says he wants
to stop by to see me. And I don't really want to see *him*, but I do want
him to see that I'm doing well—really well, actually—without him.
And so I tell him to come on by. And he does. And *then* . . ." Glory

snorted sardonically and then continued, "He's not even there for five minutes and he starts *crying*, and telling me that the woman he left *me* for . . . had left *him*! Do you believe that?"

East didn't answer. Because he didn't have enough information yet to know whether he believed or disbelieved. He was just listening.

Glory continued. "And *then* he tells me that he wants me back! I mean, can you believe *that*?"

East didn't answer again—again because he didn't have enough information yet to know whether he believed or disbelieved. He was just listening.

"And I said, as nicely as I could, 'Wes, I'm sorry. I have a new heart now. It doesn't want you back.' And I know that sounds harsh, but it was the truth, and I owed him the truth. And I should have left it at that . . ." Glory paused and fought off some sadness as she relived her last moments with Wes. But then shook the sadness off and continued, "But I didn't—leave it at that. And I told him that even if my old heart had been working, I didn't think *it* would want him back either. And *that* . . ." Glory sighed and tumbled into a deep sadness as she finished her story. "That just *killed* him."

East realized that he had been holding his breath since Glory revealed that she had killed her husband. Because he thought that she had *actually* killed her husband.

But now he realized that she hadn't *actually* killed her husband.

She may have contributed to his demise.

But she hadn't killed him.

And he exhaled for the first time since Glory had said that she had killed her husband. "Oh-oh-oh," he stammered, relieved to learn that Glory wasn't a killer. "So you didn't . . . actually *kill* him."

"Yes, I did! Because he got so sad that my new heart didn't want him back that he just tore outta my house . . . and ran outside . . .

and a bus was coming, and he didn't see it, and . . ." She struggled to say what happened next, because it upset her so deeply. "And it just took him right out."

"But . . . that wasn't your fault. That was just . . . fate. Or somethin'."

"No. It was my fault. At least—partly. Because I wished some pretty terrible things for him after he left me."

"Well, that seems understandable."

"It's not, really. You've got to be careful what you wish for." Glory looked at East, ashamed of what she may have wished for her ex-husband. "Anyway, I'm just here for some closure. I just want to say goodbye to him in my own way—not as his sad ex-wife at some big public service—but just . . . privately." Glory started to fall into another deep sadness.

And East tried to catch her fall by hugging her again.

And when he did, he felt that strange lightness fill up his insides again.

And Glory felt it, too, and she pulled away from East as soon as she did. Because it scared her, that lightness. Because it made her feel like it might make her do things she didn't normally do—like kiss a man she hardly knew.

Like East.

Which she suddenly did.

And then, as suddenly as she was kissing him, she wasn't.

And East had the brown paper bag in his possession again—and was suddenly kissing Glory back. And then pulling away from her.

"I'm sorry," he said.

Don't be, thought Glory. And she kissed him again.

And then pulled away again.

And then gasped, "I'm sorry."

And East said, "Don't be! I love you!"

"Well—don't do that!" Glory groaned, wincing, because East couldn't possibly love her; he had just met her.

"Well, I can't help it!" said the quiet stoic, who was suddenly getting loud and emotional.

"Well . . ." Glory saw that East had the brown paper bag again, and she grabbed it from him. "Help it!" she commanded.

"Why?" demanded East.

"Because! I won't be able to love you back! I have a heart that can pump my blood and that's all! The one that did the other stuff is broken! It doesn't work anymore!" This was an inaccurate series of statements, because Glory was clearly feeling all the things that hearts make people feel. So either her artificial heart was doing more than just pumping her blood, or the one she had been carrying around was doing all the "other stuff" it used to do. Whatever the case, one of her hearts had moved Glory to kiss East again.

And when Glory pulled away from East, East had her heart again.

And Glory grabbed it right back.

And then East kissed Glory again.

And pulled away again.

And East had her heart again.

And Glory grabbed it back again.

And East grabbed it right back and pleaded, "Let me have this!"

"No!" Glory lunged and tried to get her heart back again, but East kept it away from her, which wasn't very difficult, because he was tall, and she was not.

Glory lunged again—but failed to retrieve her heart.

East was impressed that someone with an artificial heart was so spry and strong. *Modern medicine is a wonder*, he thought.

And then Glory lunged again, without success.

And this went on for some time—Glory repeatedly lunging for her heart, East repeatedly keeping it just out of reach.

From a distance, they looked like a couple of kids playing keep-away.

Until one lunge landed Glory face-first in the snow.

"Oh! Are you okay?" asked East, rushing to Glory to help her up, because he felt terrible that he had just made her face-plant.

Glory flipped onto her back, sat up, and demanded, "East, give that back to me."

"No!"

"It's mine!"

"But it's broken! It's no good like this!"

"But it's my heart," pleaded Glory.

"Yeah. It is." East held Glory's heart above his head, out of her reach, and declared, "And right now, I have it."

East looked up at the brown paper bag and said, "And I can fix it."

And then he looked at Glory and said, "I'm a repairman. I repair things. It's what I do."

Glory took in what East had said. And wondered what his being a repairman had to do with anything.

And then realized it had everything to do with everything.

And she contemplated what East was proposing.

And what it implied.

And then she scowled and scoffed, because there was no way East could possibly do what he had just said he could do, whether he was a repairman or not.

But . . . then she couldn't help but wonder . . . what if he *could* do what he just said he could do?

What would happen?

East took off his coat and spread it out on the snow, lining up, in front of him. And then knelt down and placed the brown paper bag on it. He rubbed his hands to warm them. And then cupped them over his mouth and exhaled to warm them some more. And then took hold of the bag. The paper around the opening was so worn, it felt more like cloth than paper.

And then he checked in with Glory as he started to open it.

And paused. Because she didn't seem to want him to open it.

But she didn't seem to want him to *not* open it.

So East opened it.

And as he did, Glory inhaled sharply as if she was afraid that opening the bag was going to hurt her or something. And she held her breath.

And then stopped holding it.

Because she realized that the bag was open—and she was okay.

And she felt that strange lightness fill up her insides again. It felt like it was permanently replacing the darkness and heaviness that had been inside her since Wes had left her for someone else.

It also felt like it was making room for something else.

Something she thought she would never feel again in her life.

Something like what she had felt when she first met Wes. But—different.

East started to take the nineteen pieces of slate out of the bag. And he laid them on his coat.

Glory watched him do this.

And then she looked up—partly because she couldn't watch what East was about to do, partly because she couldn't believe he was about to do what he had said he was about to do, partly because no one wants to see their heart laid bare, but mostly because she was looking for answers to questions she didn't even know how to ask.

And then . . . she saw them.

The northern lights.

They were hovering and pulsing in the star-filled sky above, filling it with streaks of red and green and yellow and white and even blue and purple.

Glory was stupefied.

"Wow!" she whispered as she took in the otherworldly display. "Wowwwww!" she whispered more quietly, as not to disturb them. "They're so beautiful."

And they were—so beautiful that Glory forgot for a moment that they were why she was there. And that they were what—and who—she had come to see.

But she remembered soon enough what and who they were—and why she was there. And when she did, she called out and up into the night sky, "Oh! Wes!" The northern lights seemed to become stiller, as if they were waiting to hear what she had to say. "Wes!" Glory repeated. And then she waved to them, calling, "Goodbye!" And then she repeated the farewell—maybe because she wanted to make sure he had heard her: "Goodbye, Wes!"

And then she did what she had come to Almost to do. And she apologized.

"Wes! I'm—sorry! I'm so sorry!" she said to the sky.

And she was. So sorry.

Because she really did feel partly responsible for his demise.

And she really was sorry he was gone. And that they had parted on such strange terms.

And then she stood in silence as she took in the celestial phenomenon above.

And then she called out one more time, "Goodbye, Wes!"

Glory wondered if Wes had heard her.

And then the aurora seemed to pulsate, as if in appreciation.

And Glory felt sure that Wes had heard her.

And she felt like she had completed her mission.

And then she turned to the man who had said he could repair her heart. Because she felt like she needed to thank him. "East," she began—but stopped, because he wasn't there.

And his jacket and the pieces of her heart weren't there either.

Glory looked around for him.

And found him a few moments later when the motion-sensor lights on the farmstead's old barn came on and revealed East's silhouette moving against the white of the snow and the white of the old barn until it disappeared through the side door and into the building.

And then she saw the lights inside come on.

And then she followed East. Because she wanted to know if he was doing what he had said he could do.

She crossed into the pool of light that the motion-sensor lights were throwing.

And she got to the door that she had seen East disappear into.

And opened it.

And she entered the old barn.

And she saw East place the slate shards that were once her heart onto a workbench.

And she watched him examine the pieces of slate for a while. He seemed to be contemplating how he'd be able to make the nineteen pieces into something whole again.

Glory almost stopped him. Because she realized that maybe she didn't need him to make those nineteen pieces whole again. Because maybe her old heart didn't need repairing anymore. Because it—or maybe her artificial one—was loving him just fine.

But she didn't stop him.

Because she didn't want to interrupt him.

Because he seemed so peaceful.

And he was. Because he liked fixing things for people more than anything in the world.

So Glory stayed where she was.

And watched this man named East do what he said he could do.

3

Ginette passed the old Gallagher homestead and thought
about how sad her mom had gotten when East decided to stop growing potatoes on his farm.

And then she thought about how her mom had been talking a
lot lately about how so much of northern Maine was full of things
that were once something—but weren't anymore. And that the forest
was slowly taking them back.

Things like the ghost locomotives up at Eagle Lake.

And the general store in Dyer Brook.

And the abandoned trucks and farm equipment that can be
found all over the northern Maine woods.

And farms—like the Gallaghers'.

As she walked, Ginette wondered if she and Pete were one of the
things that had once been something—but now weren't.

And she realized that maybe they were.

Because, while they were sitting together on the bench in their
newly named love, Pete had said that he and Ginette weren't close to
each other at all—that they were actually about as far away from each
other as they could possibly have been.

And now Ginette was getting even farther away from Pete with every step she took.

And that made her feel a kind of loneliness she had never felt before.

It was 7:55 when Ginette reached St. Mary's, a small white Catholic church a quarter of a mile down the road from East's house. St. Mary's didn't have its own pastor, so Father Tom from Sacred Heart in Caribou went to Almost to say mass once a week—on Saturday evenings at six o'clock.

There was usually a supper or a social hour after mass at St. Mary's, and then Father Tom would look in on whoever needed looking in on.

And then he'd head back to Caribou so he would be available for Sunday morning services at Sacred Heart.

Father Tom had called Chad Buzza on the night when all the extraordinary things did or didn't happen, like he usually did. Chad worked part-time for St. Mary's. He maintained the building and the grounds and the small cemetery behind the church. Father Tom was calling to make sure Chad had plowed the parking lot and that the church was prepped for Clair Gudreau's funeral the next morning and for mass in the evening.

Chad told Father Tom he had everything under control.

And then Father Tom asked him why he wasn't out doing something fun on a Friday night, and Chad said he had gone out to dinner with a girl earlier, and Father Tom said, "Good for you," and then Chad realized he was going to have to go to confession, because he hadn't gone to dinner with a girl. He was *supposed* to have gone to dinner with a girl. But she had decided she didn't want to go to dinner with him at the last minute. So he didn't go to dinner with her. And, instead, went to the Moose Paddy and got a burger for himself and a turkey club sandwich and a corn chowder for his mom. His mom was surprised to see him home so soon. And Chad said that his date had to cancel at the last minute because there had been an emergency—nothing too serious—and his mom said she was sorry but that she was happy to have him around for dinner and happier about her turkey club and corn chowder.

After dinner, he drove his old Dodge Ram over to St. Mary's and plowed the driveway. And listened to some thrash metal while he did. Ginette heard a muted version of the loud, thrashy music as she passed by the church. And wondered why anyone would ever want to listen to music like that.

When Chad finished plowing, he shoveled the path to the front entrance of the church, poured some sand on the steps so people wouldn't slip, and then went inside and made sure the heat was working. And then he swept a little and made sure the bathroom was clean and made sure Father Tom had vestments and that there were candles and that everything was ready for Clair Gudreau's funeral the next morning.

When he was sure everything was ready, he closed up the church and headed outside to his truck and was about to get in and head home when a Ford F-250 pulled into the church's parking lot. The F-250 belonged to Chad's best friend, Randy Lowery, who got out of his truck and seemed agitated. Randy had a brown paper bag in one arm and a flashlight in his other hand.

"Hey," called Chad.

Randy didn't answer and turned and started heading toward the snowbank behind the church.

"You okay?"

Randy didn't answer again.

"Hey, where ya goin'?" Chad asked.

"I need a beer," called Randy. He had a six-pack of Natural Light beer in the bag he was carrying, and he didn't want to drink it in the church parking lot, because that just didn't seem right.

Chad grabbed his flashlight from his truck and followed Randy, who had climbed to the top of the snowbank and was climbing down the other side.

When Randy reached the base of the other side of the snowbank, he plunked himself down on a snow boulder, jammed the butt of his flashlight into the packed snow so it could serve as a torch, and looked out over the cemetery behind St. Mary's—which looked no different than the potato fields that surrounded it, because the snow was deeper than the headstones were high.

Eventually, Chad plunked down on the snow boulder next to the one Randy was sitting on, jammed his flashlight into the packed snow, and asked, "Are you okay?"

Randy scoffed and looked out across the cemetery and into the Norsworthys' potato fields.

"What's up?" asked Chad.

Randy made a *pshh* sound and shook his head. "Things with Yvonne went about as bad as they coulda gone."

"Oh. Sorry, pal." Chad watched his best friend take a swig of his beer. "If it makes you feel any better, my date with Sally didn't go so good, either."

"Naw," grunted Randy. "Don't even. There's no way it was anywhere near as bad as my night, so . . ."

"Mmm, I don't know—"

"It was bad, Chad. *Bad!*"

"I hear ya, but—"

"Yeah, but you're not *listenin'*!"

"No, *you're* not listenin', Randy, 'cause I'm tryin' to tell ya that I had a pretty bad time, *myself*!" exploded Chad, surprising himself, because he wasn't an explosive guy.

"Whoa, okay, relax," said Randy. And he felt bad that he had been so wrapped up in how awful his own date had gone that he hadn't bothered to check to see how his best friend's date had gone. And, while he was sure that there was no way that Chad's date had gone worse than his, Chad had just kind of lost it a little. So maybe it had gone worse. So Randy offered his buddy a Natty Light—and the proverbial floor—and said, "Let's hear it."

Chad cracked the beer open. And took a swig. And didn't say anything for about a minute. He was really hurting. And Randy was concerned. Because Chad looked sadder than Randy had ever seen him look—sadder than he looked when his rabbit died. And when his grandpa died. And when his last girlfriend broke up with him. In fact, Randy hadn't seen Chad hurt like he was hurting since he was eleven—when he burned half his house down when he was playing with sparklers indoors.

Randy felt his ears and his head and his neck get all hot, because he felt like Chad was going to cry, and he didn't like crying. And he had dealt with a lot of crying that night already.

So he looked away from Chad and tried to figure out if he was going to stay or go—and he almost got up and left. But something inside him told him he needed to stay. So he did. And he looked at Chad and said impatiently, "What's up, bud? What happened?"

Chad was about to answer when his breathing hitched. And a wave of sadness overcame him. But he quickly pulled himself together and began his sad story. "She said she didn't like the way I smelled."

Randy looked at Chad. And then furrowed his brow and screwed up his face and shrugged and asked, "What?!?"

"Sally told me she didn't like the way I smelled," repeated Chad. "Never has."

Sally Dunleavy was a great girl. She was the receptionist for Visiting Nurses of Aroostook up in Fort Kent. She and Chad had known each other for years, but when Chad called to inquire about having a nurse come in to take care of his mom as she started breast cancer treatment, they really hit it off.

But a couple of months later, when Sally called to let Chad know that a new nurse named Pam would be looking in on his mom, she asked him out. Apparently she wasn't seeing Randy's cousin Tim anymore. And so they went out on a date on the Friday night when all the extraordinary things did or didn't happen.

And it hadn't gone so well.

"Sally Dunleavy told you that she didn't like the way you *smelled*?" asked Randy, flabbergasted.

"Yeah."

"When?" Randy really wanted to know when you would tell someone you're out on a date with that you don't like the way they smell.

"Pretty much as soon as I met her."

Well, at least she didn't lead him on, thought Randy.

"I picked her up," continued Chad. "And she got in the truck. And we're backin' outta her driveway—and all of a sudden, she started breathin' hard and coverin' her mouth and nose with her scarf and asked me to stop. And she got outta the truck and said she was sorry and that I was a nice guy—but she couldn't go out with me because she didn't like the way I smelled, never had."

"What?!?" Randy winced.

"And she slammed the door and left me sittin' right there in her driveway."

Randy was stunned. "'Cause she didn't like the way you *smelled*?" he asked in disbelief.

"Yeah."

"Well what kinda . . . ?" Sally was a really nice person. But telling someone that you don't like the way they smell on a first date . . . is just not nice. And didn't sound like the Sally Dunleavy he knew. "Well, want me to talk to her?"

"No."

"I could talk to her."

"No!" Chad really didn't want Randy to talk to her because he'd probably just yell at her, because that's how he dealt with people who crossed his friends.

"Jeez." Randy sneered a little and got a little sad because he really liked Sally and thought she and Chad would make a great pair. Then he laughed a little and tried to make light of the situation. "I mean, I don't mind the way you smell."

"Thanks," snorted Chad.

"And, you know," continued Randy, "I don't think this is about you and the way you smell. This is about her. I don't think she's ready, yet. For dating. 'Cause I don't think she's over Tim. It's only been a couple months. And she's tryin' to get herself out there again, but she's just not ready, you know. That's all it is, pal."

Chad didn't say anything and just took a swig of his beer. And wondered if what Randy had just said was true. And decided that it definitely wasn't and that Randy was just trying to make him feel better. "Whatever," he shrugged.

Randy and Chad sat in the northern Maine silence and drank their beers.

And then Chad laughed a little and realized that he had actually come to enjoy telling Randy about his dating disasters. There had been several since they started dating again after their longtime girlfriends dumped them a couple years ago. Jenny Lovely broke up with Chad because she felt like she didn't make him happy. And that didn't make her happy.

And Kelly Clockadile broke up with Randy after they had a big blowout one night. She said she was tired of his temper.

So Chad and Randy found themselves single again. And they probably should have stayed single and done some work on themselves. But they weren't the kind of guys who did work on themselves. Maybe because they didn't like themselves very much.

So they started dating every chance they could. Because they thought they'd definitely like themselves better if they could find a couple of girls who liked them.

But none of them seemed to like them, for whatever reason—in Sally's case, because she didn't like the way Chad smelled.

"Anyway," said Chad, "I told you it was bad." He took another swig of his beer and belched impressively and then continued. "So, I'm guessin' I'm the big winner tonight, huh? So . . . I get to pick tomorrow." Randy and Chad went on most of their dates on Friday or Saturday nights. And they usually met up afterward to check in—and often to commiserate. And the one who had the worse date got to pick what they were going to do for fun the next day. And Chad was sure that his date had been worse that night, so he said, "And I pick bowlin'. We'll go bowlin' in Caribou, supper at the Snowmobile Club, coupla beers at the Moose Paddy, and just . . . hang out."

He offered up his can of beer for a toast. And waited for Randy to toast him back.

But Randy didn't.

So Chad toasted himself and chugged. And thought about how

maybe he shouldn't drink as much as he did. But it was the only thing that made him feel less sad. So he decided that he would think about maybe not drinking as much as he currently did another time. And he finished his beer and then tried—and failed—to crush his empty beer can on his head, because he had never quite learned how to execute that move. And then he got up and tossed his mostly crushed can into the brown paper bag that Randy had brought the beer in. And then he grabbed another beer and cracked it open and sat back down on his snow boulder. And he was about to ask Randy when he wanted to go bowling tomorrow when Randy calmly droned, "I didn't say you're the big winner."

"Huh?"

"Did I say you're the big winner?"

"No, but—"

"No," interrupted Randy, staring out across the cemetery and into the Norsworthys' potato fields and out at the horizon. "All that's pretty sad, Chad, and bad, but you didn't win."

"What do you mean?"

"You didn't win."

Chad knew there was no way that Randy could beat what had happened to him with Sally, so he challenged Randy. "You can beat bein' told you smell bad?"

"Yup," said Randy, still staring off into the distance.

Randy's calm confidence intrigued Chad. And he said, "Well, then," holding out his hand and offering Randy the floor.

Randy took a deep breath as if he was about to say something. But instead belched more impressively than Chad had. And then he sighed. And seemed really sad—sadder than Chad was, even. And Chad was shocked. Because he had never known Randy to be sad. He had known him to be angry. But never sad.

And Chad was about to ask him if he was okay when Randy grunted, "Mine's face broke."

Chad heard Randy. But didn't quite understand what he had just said.

"Huh?" asked Chad, screwing up his face.

"Her face broke," repeated Randy.

Chad let his head drop and tried to make sense of what Randy had just said. And then he turned back to Randy and repeated, "Huh?"

"You heard me. Finally friggin' get to go out with Yvonne LaFrance and her face breaks." Yvonne LaFrance lived in Portage and worked at the general store there, and whenever Randy saw her, he'd ask her out, and every time he did, she'd say she was seeing somebody. And she always was, because she was pretty and kind.

But a couple of weeks ago, Randy was ice fishing on Portage Lake and when he stopped by the store for a coffee, he said he still hoped he'd get a chance to take her out someday and she said, "How about someday soon?" And that someday soon turned out to be the Friday night when all the extraordinary things did or didn't happen.

Chad tried to figure out what Randy had meant when he said that Yvonne LaFrance's face had broken. "Her face . . . ?" He couldn't finish the question, because he was aghast.

"Broke, dude, it broke. How many times are you gonna make me say it?!" snapped Randy.

Chad wasn't trying to make Randy keep saying that Yvonne's face had broken. He was just trying to understand.

"Told you it was bad," chuckled Randy sardonically.

And Chad wasn't denying that it was bad. He was just trying to figure out how Yvonne's face had broken. He sure hoped Randy hadn't hit her. Randy had broken a lot of guys' faces. Because he had punched them. Because they had made him mad.

But Randy would never hit a girl. Chad was sure of it.

"Well . . . how did her face break?" Chad asked, hoping it wasn't as serious as it all sounded.

"When we were dancin'."

The word *dancin'* stuck to the air like a fly sticks to flypaper.

Chad and Randy did not dance.

Not even at their proms. Which is probably why their prom dates had dumped them on prom night.

"*Dancin'*?" Chad smirked.

"Yeah . . . ," Randy said, in a way that let Chad know he wasn't happy about having gone dancing.

Chad conjured up an image of his best bud dancing and couldn't help but laugh—hard. But not so hard that he couldn't ask the all-important question, "Why the heck were you dancin'?!?"

"'Cause that's what she wanted to do!" snapped Randy. "On our date! So I took her! Down to the Rec Center. They had a bean supper at five and then lessons at five thirty and then you dance all night. And they teach together dancing—how to dance . . . together. And we learned that thing where you throw the girl up and over your shoulder—"

"Whoa—what?"

"It's just this fancy move she wanted me to try with her." It wasn't just Yvonne who wanted Randy to try it. Lalaine Deshain, the country swing dance instructor from Presque Isle, thought that Yvonne and Randy were really good dancing together. And she was particularly impressed with Randy's ability, so she showed him how to do a complicated over-the-shoulder flip with Yvonne, because she thought he was strong enough and that they were both skilled enough to execute it. And then she supervised them when they tried it, and Yvonne faced Randy and put her left hand on his right shoulder and jumped up, and Randy guided her body with his right hand, and she glided over his back and over his head and she landed on her feet, facing him. And Lalaine gleefully shrieked, "Yes!" and told them to try it again, but to incorporate the fancy flips into the other moves they had learned. And then she went over to teach some less-skilled newbies some basics like the cuddle and the jitterbug step.

So Randy and Yvonne tried the over-the-shoulder flip again unsupervised, this time incorporating it into the other moves they had learned. But that second time they tried it, Yvonne asked Randy to throw her a little higher, for fun. "And I said sure," said Randy, continuing his story, "and, well . . . Yvonne's pretty small . . . and I'm pretty strong, and when I threw her up and over—a little higher—well . . . I guess I threw her a little *too* high or somethin'."

"Oh, no," groaned Chad.

"Yeah." Randy took a moment to relive the incident, and then added, "And she landed on her face."

Randy took another moment to relive the incident. And then added, "And it broke."

Chad took the same moment to imagine the incident. And didn't know what to say. This was truly one of the saddest things he had ever heard—and also one of the most absurd. And something about the absurdity of it made him want to snicker. But he didn't, because he could tell that the big guy was pretty broken up about what had happened. So he stifled his snicker.

And the fellas sat in silence for a long time.

And Randy relived his dancing debacle. Over and over.

And Chad relived his imagined version of the dancing debacle over and over. And wondered if Yvonne was okay. And took a swig of his beer. And hoped he never broke anybody's face.

And Randy hoped that Yvonne was okay, too. And took a swig of his beer. And vowed that he was done with breaking people's faces. On purpose or accidentally.

And then he crushed his can on his head and tossed it in the paper bag he had brought his six-pack of beer in. And Chad wished that he was as good at crushing a beer can on his head as Randy was.

And then Randy grabbed another beer and opened it and started drinking it. And then shared the kicker to his story: "I had to take her to the emergency room."

"Oof," groaned Chad.

And then he tried to imagine the drive to the emergency room.

And then wondered which emergency room Randy had taken Yvonne to. "Fort Kent?"

"Huh?"

"Fort Kent or Caribou?"

"Oh. Fort Kent."

Chad shook his head in pity. It was thirty-eight miles to Fort Kent. "That's a drive," he said flatly.

"Yup."

Randy relived the thirty-eight-mile drive to Fort Kent.

And Chad imagined the thirty-eight-mile drive to Fort Kent. And then asked, "What'd they say?"

"What do you mean, 'What'd they say?'"

"At the hospital?"

"What do you think they said? They said her face broke, dude."

"Yeah, where?"

"Orbit—somethin'." Randy indicated his eye and couldn't remember the term "orbital fracture," so he said, "Her eye bone and cheekbone broke."

"Oof." Chad took a swig of his beer. And then asked, "Blood?"

"Oh, yeah." Randy took a swig of his beer and then sneered, "And she *cried*!"

"Hate that," griped Chad.

"The whole way."

"Ugh."

"And then—when we get to the hospital—she asks me to call her old boyfriend—who *lives* up there—to come be with her!"

"Oh, no!" Chad half groaned and half exclaimed.

"Oh, yeah!" Randy took a swig of his beer. "And I call him. And when he gets there, he asks me to 'please leave.' As if she was *his*."

Chad hissed. And took a swig of his beer.

"He's as small as she is," added Randy wryly.

And Chad laughed. And the beer he had just drunk sprayed out of his mouth and up his nose.

And Randy laughed, too. At Yvonne's tiny boyfriend. And at the absurdity of it all. And at Chad's spit take.

And Chad coughed for a while and eventually recovered from the beer that had gone up his nose.

And then the guys sat in silence for a bit.

And Randy relived his drive to the hospital in Fort Kent.

And Chad imagined Randy's drive to the hospital in Fort Kent. With Yvonne. And all her blood. And all her tears.

And then he made a weird sound—a combination of a snort and a chortle and a scoff.

"What?" asked Randy.

"That's just pretty bad," said Chad in grand understatement.

"Yup," nodded Randy, almost triumphantly.

"And sad."

"Yup."

"So . . . I guess you win," Chad capitulated.

Randy raised his arms, fists clenched, assuming a championship pose. "Yes!" he bellowed.

Chad laughed and said, "That right there might make you the big winner of all time!"

"Yup!" Randy bellowed louder, fists still clenched, arms still raised.

"Baddest-date guy of all time!" announced Chad, egging Randy on.

"Yaaaaaaah!" cheered Randy, strutting like a rooster.

"Congratulations!" cheered Chad.

"Thank you!" grunted Randy and he assumed the championship pose again and opened his mouth wide and made a sound like there was an imaginary crowd cheering for him.

And Chad laughed.

And then Randy dropped the championship pose.

And it was quiet again.

And the guys fell into a deep sadness as they contemplated their worst dates ever.

And then Chad managed to pull himself out of his sadness and asked Randy, "So what do you pick tomorrow?"

Randy shrugged and said what the winner always said. "Bowlin'. Supper at the Snowmobile Club. Coupla beers at the Moose Paddy. Hang out."

Chad said, "Good."

And then he wondered if someday they'd pick something else as the prize.

And then he air-toasted Randy.

And Randy air-toasted back.

And then Chad finished his beer.

And Randy finished his.

And crushed his empty can on his head.

And Chad didn't quite crush his empty can on his head.

And then Randy made like his crushed beer can was a basketball and he pretended he was in the closing seconds of a championship game, and he counted down, "Three! . . . Two! . . . One!" and made a buzzer-beating shot into the paper bag that he had brought the Natty Light in. And then he made like an imaginary crowd was roaring for him in adoration. And then said, "And now, Chad Buzza for the win!" to let Chad know it was his turn to be the hero.

And Chad got up and fake-dribbled and pulled up.

And missed his buzzer-beating shot.

And his almost-crushed empty beer can clinked and clanked on the packed snow and finally settled behind the bag.

And Randy made the sounds of an imaginary crowd booing.

And the guys laughed.

And their laughter melted away and they slid into another sad silence. Which Chad tried to pull himself out of by laughing. And his laugh sounded like a dying animal.

Randy looked at Chad, wondering what the heck the sound he just made was. "You okay?"

"Yeah. I don't know. Just . . . sometimes I don't know why I bother goin' out. I don't like it, Randy. I hate it. I hate goin' out on these . . . *dates*." Chad's voice was getting high and phlegmy. "I mean, why do I wanna spend my Friday night with some girl I might *maybe* like, when I could be spendin' it hangin' out with someone I *know* I like, like you, you know?"

"Yeah," Randy laughed, and wondered why they put so much effort into the 'big maybe' that was dating.

"I mean . . . that was rough tonight," continued Chad, and he kicked at the snow and started pacing. "In the middle of Sally tellin' me how she didn't like the way I smelled . . . I got sad."

"Yeah, well, you're always sad."

"No. This was different. This was a new kind of sad."

Randy really didn't want to hear about Chad's new kind of sadness.

But Chad really wanted to tell Randy about it. So he did. "And all I could think about was how not much in this world makes me feel good or makes much sense anymore."

Randy stopped breathing for a second and hoped Chad wasn't going to tell him that he wanted to kill himself or something.

"And I got really scared," continued Chad, still pacing. "'Cause there's gotta be something that makes you feel good or at least makes sense in this world, or what's the point, right?"

"I guess . . ." Randy was trying to figure out what he was going to do if Chad said he wanted to kill himself.

"But then . . ." Chad stopped pacing and continued, "I kinda came out of bein' sad and actually felt okay, 'cause I realized that there *is* one thing in this world that makes me feel really good and that *does* make sense, and it's you."

The words flew out of Chad's mouth—before the thought they were trying to describe had even been fully formed.

So Chad wasn't quite sure what he meant by what he had just said.

And Randy wasn't quite sure what he had just heard Chad say. Or what Chad meant.

And the guys felt like everything had stopped—like some kind of cosmic shutdown had occurred.

And they sat in the midwinter northern Maine silence and stillness.

And Chad started to feel a strange lightness suddenly grow inside him. It made him feel warm and weightless—like the gentlest fireworks ever were going off inside him, and like helium was filling his body. And—like he had been released from a great sadness.

But then, just as suddenly as it had come on, the lightness was being replaced by a strange heaviness—and not the usual heaviness he felt inside. It was an even heavier heaviness. And it made him feel like it was going to pull him to the ground.

Chad fought the feeling that he was going to fall, and, as he did, Randy suddenly hopped up—so fast that it felt like he had single-handedly jumpstarted the cosmos and made everything start moving again, and the stillness gave way to motion and the silence gave way to sound as Randy got to his feet.

And Randy decided that he was going to ignore what Chad had just said—whatever it was that he had just said—and carry on as if it had never been said—if it had even been said at all.

"Well, I'm gonna head," Randy said gruffly, and he started bending down to grab his flashlight and his bag of beer when Chad realized that he could no longer fight the strange feeling that he was going to fall.

And then he fell.

His knees buckled.

And his legs crumpled.

And he couldn't get his hands out of his pants pockets in time to brace his fall.

And he face-planted onto the snow.

Suddenly and completely—and almost in slow motion.

Randy witnessed Chad's strange face-plant.

And tried to figure out what had just happened.

And wondered if Chad had had a seizure or something. His cousin from Frenchville had a miniature pony that had some sort of neurological disorder and would periodically collapse. Maybe Chad had a similar condition.

"What is wrong with you?" demanded Randy, implying that a lot was wrong with Chad. Because something was definitely wrong with Chad. Because of what he had just done. And because of what he had just said.

Chad didn't answer Randy's question. And slowly started getting up, brushing the snow off his beard and his face and his coat and his jeans as he did.

When he was on his feet again, he looked completely bewildered.

And so did Randy. "You all right or what?" he asked in a way that let Chad know that the only answer he would accept was yes.

"Yeah," answered Chad unconvincingly.

"All right. Well, I'm gonna head," he said again, and he grabbed his flashlight and his bag of beer.

"Yeah," said Chad. "Me, too."

"I gotta work in the mornin'," said Randy, and he started to make his way up the snowbank.

"Yeah, well, let me know when you're done, and I'll pick you up whenever you want."

Randy didn't really want to hang out with Chad tomorrow and felt like maybe he didn't want to hang out with him ever again, and said, "Oh, I don't know, Chad. I'm helpin' Lendall—he brought me on to work on Marvalyn and Eric's roof, and—"

"Well, whenever you're done, just let me know."

"Well, their roof collapsed, you know? So it's gonna be a big job."

"Well, just give me a call when you're done."

"I don't know when we'll be done—could take all day—so let's just bag it."

"Well, you can't bag it!" cried Chad, almost pleading.

Chad was deeply regretting saying what he had said—even though he hadn't planned to say it—and hadn't meant to say it. And he started to feel like he was losing his best friend because he had said it. And the heaviness that had made him crumple to the ground grew inside him again and made him feel like he could barely stand. "You're the big winner!" he reminded Randy as he tried to remain upright, "So I can be ready whenever you want me to come pick ya up."

"You know what—?"

"Just say when and I'll be there!"

"You know what, Chad—?"

"'Cause you can't bag it! We gotta—!"

"Chad! You know what?" Randy held his hand out in front of him—like he was stopping traffic—to let Chad know that the conversation was over and that he was getting a little ticked off. "I'll see ya later!" And he knew he was lying. Because he wouldn't be seeing Chad later—or ever again. If he could help it.

And he made his way back up the snowbank.

And Chad said, "Okay," and he watched Randy go. And he felt for sure that he wasn't going to see him later. Or ever again. And he didn't want that. So he tried not to sound desperate when he called, "Hey, Randy!"

Randy ignored Chad and continued climbing the snowbank.

And then heard the *oof* sound that a body makes when the wind gets knocked out of it from a sudden fall.

Randy turned and directed the beam from his flashlight onto Chad.

And it revealed Chad facedown in the snow.

Again.

Because Chad had suddenly and completely fallen down—almost in slow motion—again.

Randy was now convinced that Chad had the same thing wrong with him that his cousin from Frenchville's pony did.

"Hey!" called Randy. And he made his way down the snowbank to make sure Chad was okay. Because, even though Chad had said something that Randy didn't quite want to understand, he didn't want to leave Chad there if he had the same thing wrong with him that his cousin's pony did. "You all right?"

Chad pushed himself up out of the snow. "I don't know," he answered.

"What the—here . . ." Randy grabbed Chad by the arms and hauled his former best friend up onto his feet again.

"Thanks," said Chad, brushing snow off himself again and wondering what in the world had just happened.

"What was that? You okay?"

"Yeah. I just . . . fell."

"Yeah," scoffed Randy. "I kinda figured that out. Has this happened before?" he asked, shining his light in Chad's eyes to see if he could diagnose a neurological impairment.

"No—just . . ." Chad thought. Deeply. And for a while. And tried to sort out what had just happened. And what he was going to say. And he felt that strange lightness fill him up again. And it made his heart swell this time. And he gasped a little and pressed his hand on the part of his chest where his heart lived.

"What? What's wrong?" asked Randy, suddenly wondering if Chad had a heart condition, and not a neurological one.

Chad looked at Randy and answered his question honestly and truly: "I think I just fell in love with you there, Randy."

And Chad looked at Randy.

And then he suddenly and completely—and almost in slow motion—crumpled to the ground again, his knees hitting first and the rest of his body following until he had face-planted in the snow again.

Randy jumped away from Chad as he fell.

"Whoa," said Chad, laughing, and feeling a little delirious—but freer than he had ever felt. "Yup—that's what that was. Me falling in love with you."

Randy stared at Chad, wondering what the heck was happening. And started backing away from him slowly—like he was possessed. Or dangerous.

Chad started to get up again.

And when he was back on his feet, he looked at Randy and suddenly and completely and almost in slow motion crumpled onto the snow again.

And he laughed again—a confused, amused laugh.

But Randy was not amused. And he charged Chad. "What are you—drunk?" he demanded.

"I don't think so."

"Get up!" Randy bent over and pulled Chad into an upright position, and Chad protested, because he knew he was just going to fall down again. And he was right, because, no sooner was he upright than he was past upright and crumpling down onto the snow-covered ground again.

"WOULD YOU CUT THAT OUT?!?" Randy yelled apoplectically.

"WELL, I CAN'T HELP IT!!" Chad yelled back, sitting up. "IT JUST KINDA CAME OVER ME!! I'VE FALLEN IN LOVE WITH YA, HERE!!" Chad had never heard himself speak with such force or authority before. And neither had Randy. And it scared both of the young men.

Randy took in what Chad had just said. And didn't move. For a while.

He was so angry.

"Chad," said Randy. His voice was low, and his demeanor was eerily calm. "I'm your best buddy in the whole world," he began. "And I don't quite know what you're doin' or what you're goin' on about . . . but . . . what is your PROBLEM?!? What are you DOIN'?!? YOU'RE MY BEST FRIEND!"

"Yeah—" protested Chad weakly.

"OR YOU USED TO BE!" roared Randy. "AND WHEN YOU'RE FRIENDS—WELL, YOU DON'T MESS WITH THAT! AND *YOU* MESSED WITH IT!" He started back up the snowbank. But realized he wasn't done yet and wheeled around and charged Chad again. "'Cause, you know somethin'?" he said, his voice calm but intense. "You're about the only thing that feels really good and makes sense in this world to me, too, and now you've gone and fouled it up, by doin' this whatever-it-is-you're-doin'"—he indicated Chad, who was still sitting in the snow—"And tellin' me . . . what you told me." He couldn't bring himself to repeat exactly what Chad had told him, because it was the most disgusting thing he had ever been told. "And now," he added, "nothin' makes sense at all!" And then he roared again, "AND NOTHIN' FEELS GOOD!"

Randy turned and started to go back up the snowbank again, taking off his Red Sox cap and wiping his brow, because now he was sweating. And then he stopped again. And he slapped his cap back on his head and he suddenly turned toward Chad. He wanted to charge down the mound of snow and pummel him like he had done to the dozens of other guys that had crossed him in his lifetime.

But he couldn't bring himself to hurt Chad—because the poor

guy looked so helpless. And what if he actually had something wrong with him?

But he needed to let him know that he had done something unforgivable, and he yelled, "YOU KNOW, YOU'VE DONE A REAL NUMBER ON A GOOD THING, HERE, BUDDY!! 'CAUSE WE WERE FRIENDS!! AND THERE'S A LINE WHEN YOU'RE FRIENDS THAT YOU CAN'T CROSS! AND YOU . . . *CROSSED* IT!"

Randy was about to turn and finish the climb up the snowbank and head back down the other side to his truck when he suddenly and completely fell down—almost in slow motion: his legs crumpled, and his knees hit the packed snow of the snowbank, and he listed to one side and tumbled down the snowbank until he reached its base and skidded to a stop about a dozen feet from Chad.

His flashlight came skittering down behind him and disappeared somewhere in the fluffy snow at the bottom of the snowbank.

The guys felt like everything had stopped again. And another cosmic shutdown had occurred.

And everything was silent and still again.

And Randy started feeling a strange lightness suddenly grow inside him. It made him feel like he had a road flare burning somewhere deep in his guts. And like gravity had no hold on him, even though it had just pulled him to the ground.

He felt like that lightness had gently jump-started the cosmos and made everything start moving again, and the stillness gave way to motion and the silence gave way to sound as Randy blew some snow and some snowy snot out of his nose and rolled over onto his side and sat up and looked around to see if he could locate Chad.

And he found him—about twelve feet in front of him, sitting up and looking at him, totally dumbstruck. Because he had just witnessed Randy's crumple and tumble down the snowbank.

It seemed that what had happened to Chad had also just happened to Randy.

Chad felt the lightness start growing inside him again.

It was the same lightness that Randy had just started feeling.

And then Chad and Randy realized that all they wanted to do was get to one another.

Because they knew they needed to be with each other.

So they started to get themselves up off the snowy ground and back up onto their feet so they could make their way to one another.

They were a little dazed and a lot unsteady.

And they looked to one another.

And there was enough starlight that each could make out the whites of the other's eyes.

And they searched one another's eyes for an explanation of what was going on. Because they didn't know where else to look.

And then—suddenly and completely—and almost in slow motion—they collapsed again, knees first, with the rest of their bodies following.

And they found themselves facedown in the snow again—twelve feet apart.

And they did not want to be twelve feet apart.

So they got up on their feet again to see if they could get themselves closer to one another—without falling down.

But when they were upright, they looked at each other, and their knees buckled, and they crumpled to the ground again, face-planting in the snow.

Frustrated but not defeated, they slowly lifted their heads up out of the snow.

And they got up again.

And looked at one another again. But crumpled to the ground and splatted in the snow again, face-first, when their eyes met.

Randy and Chad tried several more times to get up onto their feet—but with no success. Until they were too tired—and maybe too discouraged—to try getting up anymore.

Because they were no closer to each other than they had been when they started falling.

And then they flipped over onto their backs, because it's not particularly comfortable to lie facedown in the snow.

And when they did, they saw the northern lights pulsing and dancing in the sky above them.

They had been hovering up there since the first time Chad had fallen.

But neither of them had seen them, because they were too busy falling.

In love.

But now they were seeing them.

And they were pretty spectacular.

But not as spectacular as what was happening to them.

And, after a while, they wondered if they'd ever be able to get up again. And if they'd ever be able to walk again—so they could get out of there. Because they didn't want anyone to find them there, lying in the snow behind the church, and wonder what was happening.

Because what would they tell people?

And then they got scared.

Really scared.

And then the northern lights faded.

But what Randy and Chad were feeling for one another didn't.

And they sat up and still wanted nothing more than to get to one another.

So Randy rolled onto his stomach again and started crawling on his belly toward Chad.

And Chad started crawling on his belly toward Randy.

And when they got to each other, they reached out to grab hands.

And had no idea what was going to happen next.

4

As Ginette passed St. Mary's, she thought about how glad she was that Pete didn't like thrash metal music—like whoever was plowing the parking lot did. And she thought about the music that he did like to listen to—old country songs that his dad would play for Ginette and Pete on his record player.

A lot of those songs were story songs that made Ginette feel like she had read a whole book in three minutes.

And, as she walked, she wondered if she'd ever get to listen to those songs again. Because she probably wouldn't be going over to Pete's anymore, now that they weren't together.

And she wondered how they had gone so quickly from being together to being so far apart.

And then she stopped wondering, because she knew why.

It was because of Pete—and his stupid theory on what it means to be close. Why the heck did he have to say that she wasn't really close to him—and that she was actually about as far away from him as she could possibly be—when she was leaning right up against him?

She was confounded.

And hurt.

And when people get confounded and hurt, their faces look like what Ginette's face looked like as she made her way home on the Road to Nowhere.

It was 8 p.m. when Ginette reached Ma Dudley's, an old farmhouse that was about a quarter of a mile down—and across—the road from St. Mary's. Ma and her husband of fifty-seven years, Sunny, had converted the farmhouse into a boardinghouse decades ago, and they rented seven rooms for daily, weekly, or monthly rates.

As Ginette walked past the boardinghouse, she saw Ma and Sunny dancing together in the living room through the big picture window. And she couldn't help but stop and watch them as they swayed back and forth in a warm yellow light to some music that seemed like it was bouncy—but gentle.

Marvalyn LaJoy was watching the old couple, too, from inside. She had just come downstairs from her room on the third floor and was on her way to the laundry room in the basement to switch her clothes from the washers to the dryers. And, as she passed the living room, she saw Ma and Sunny dancing to some gentle old-time big-band music.

And she stopped and watched the sweet sight.

And she wished that she and her boyfriend, Eric, danced together like Ma and Sunny.

But they didn't.

And when Ma and Sunny kissed, she tried to look away, because it's creepy to watch people kiss when they think they're alone.

But she couldn't look away. And she wondered if she and Eric would kiss like that when they were old.

They hadn't kissed like that in a while.

Maybe they would again someday—when their circumstances improved.

"Oh!" Sunny had caught sight of Marvalyn standing in the doorway and was surprised to learn that what he thought was a private moment wasn't actually private.

"Hi, Mr. Dudley!" Marvalyn smiled, embarrassed that she had been caught staring.

"Huh? Oh!" said Ma simultaneously, turning and seeing Marvalyn and pulling away from her husband.

"Sorry!" chirped Marvalyn. "Hi, Ma! Sorry!"

"Hi, Marvalyn," Ma mumbled coldly. She was not very happy that such a tender moment had been observed—and interrupted.

"Didn't see you there!" Sunny said, smiling sheepishly.

"Yeah—sorry—I was just—I've got some laundry in, and I've gotta check on it. You two look so good together, dancin'!"

"Naw," snorted Ma, mortified that someone had seen her and Sunny dancing. And kissing.

"Yeah!" countered Marvalyn.

"I like to think we've still got it," said Sunny, winking as he took the needle off the record, stopping the music.

"You do!" giggled Marvalyn.

"Pshh," said Ma. "Listen, you better get down there and finish up. It's after eight."

All laundry had to be completed by 10 p.m.—house rule.

"Oh, I just have to switch stuff over to the dryer," said Marvalyn.

"You got plenty of time, dear," assured Sunny.

"Yeah—sorry if I interrupted anything," said Marvalyn, and she started toward the door to the basement.

"You didn't interrupt nothin'," barked Ma. She knew this was a lie and was deeply disappointed that she and Sunny had been interrupted. But you sacrifice some privacy when you operate a boardinghouse.

"G'night, Marvalyn," said Sunny.

"'Night!" called Marvalyn, and she headed down the stairs to the basement.

When she reached the staircase landing, she hung a left and entered the laundry room, a public, utilitarian space that had two washing machines, two dryers, two clothes-folding tables, and a bench in the middle of the room—and lots of signage, reminding people not to overload the machines and to clean out the lint filters. One of the signs read, "Ma Dudley isn't your mother. So clean up after yourself."

The washing machines weren't quite finished with their cycles when Marvalyn arrived, so she turned on the radio that was on the shelf between some laundry detergent and some fabric softener and an old coffee can labeled "the pay-what-you-CAN." And she tuned the radio to the country station out of Presque Isle. A song about sunshine, summertime, and six-packs came on, and Marvalyn turned it up and danced and wished it was summer. And then went over to the bookshelf to see what there was to read while she killed the couple of minutes that were left on the spin cycle.

Someone had added a magazine called *YOU!* to the magazine collection—probably the new girl who had moved in on the second floor a few weeks ago. Her name was Vivian. Or Vicky. Or Veronica. Or some weird name that began with a *V*. She seemed like a really nice person.

Marvalyn felt herself get all tingly when she saw what the cover story of the *YOU!* magazine was: "*YOUR GUIDE TO A MARVELOUS LIFE: Be the Best YOU Ever!*"

Because it seemed that the current issue had been written especially for her.

Marvalyn had always hoped she'd have a marvelous life. Her mother hoped so, too. That was why she had given her daughter her unusual name: Marvalyn. It was a name to live up to.

But Marvalyn hadn't quite lived up to it yet.

But she still hoped that she'd be able to. And maybe the *YOU!* magazine article on how to have a marvelous life could get her back on track.

Marvalyn had just started reading when a buzzer cut through the country music on the radio and let her know her clothes were clean. She put her *YOU!* magazine on the dryer and unloaded her laundry from the washers and transferred the wet clothes to the dryers and threw a couple of fabric softener sheets into the machines, and then she closed the dryer doors and set the timers for thirty-five minutes and hit both start buttons. She put a dollar (for the use of the machines) and a couple of quarters (for the detergent and fabric softener she had used) into the pay-what-you-CAN, picked up the *YOU!* magazine, and started reading her article again, eager to see what she needed to do to make her life marvelous.

A song about what a girl needs to do when she has leaving on her mind came on the radio while she read.

And then a song about what a girl should do with a guy who's dead weight came on.

And then a song about what a woman needs to do to restart her heart came on.

And then some commercials came on.

By then, Marvalyn had finished the article on how to have a marvelous life. It was mostly about how important it is to exercise and eat better. And to limit your alcohol intake. And to stop smoking if you smoke. And to start following your bliss and pursuing your dreams.

Marvalyn thought that maybe it was time for her to start pursuing her dreams again. But she had no idea how to go about doing so.

So she thought maybe she'd try following her bliss first. But she didn't know what her bliss was. Which is sad for a young woman whose last name is LaJoy.

So she decided that, first, she was going to work on exercising and eating better.

Which she would do after she started limiting her alcohol intake.

Which she would do after she stopped smoking.

Which she would do after she had one more cigarette.

She had about twenty-five more minutes, she guessed, before her clothes would be dry, so she dragged the magazine off the dryer and shuffled over to the bookshelf and dumped it where she had gotten it. And went outside and sat on the front porch and smoked the last cigarette she would ever smoke and looked out over the potato fields of Norsworthy's Potato Farm. And took in the sky. And the stars. And wished upon a couple of them. And took a few more drags on her cigarette. And thought about how that cigarette really did need to be the last one she ever smoked. Because she needed to start taking better care of herself so she could be marvelous, like the *YOU!* magazine article said.

Then she thought about maybe going to Sandrine St. Pierre's bachelorette party at the Moose Paddy. It'd be going strong, she bet. And it'd be fun, she bet. And a lot of her friends would be there, she bet. And she hadn't seen her friends much lately.

But she didn't want to go to Sandrine St. Pierre's bachelorette party without telling Eric she was going. Because that would make him mad.

And she didn't want to wake him and ask him if he minded if she went, because that would make him mad, too.

So she decided to just stay home.

She could read the rest of the *YOU!* magazine once she finished her laundry. There was an article about getting the right pair of jeans and how they could make you look ten pounds lighter. Marvalyn wondered if there were jeans that could make her look twenty pounds lighter.

Or forty.

She finished her cigarette and wondered if she'd gain more weight if she stopped smoking.

And hoped she wouldn't.

And then she headed back inside and went back down to the laundry room. When she got there, the radio was playing a song about what happens when you break up with someone in a small town. And she danced a little and wondered what her life would be like if she broke up with Eric—but then realized that she wasn't quite ready to wonder about that, so she stopped wondering about it and sat on the bench and read the other articles in her *YOU!* magazine.

She read the one about the jeans.

And one about how makeup could save her life.

And one about gratitude.

And one about healthy versions of everyone's favorite desserts. They looked gross.

And the next thing she knew, the dryers' buzzers were cutting through a song about what love isn't, alerting her that her clothes were dry. And she got up and unloaded her clothes and dumped them on the clothes-folding table and then went back to the dryers and cleaned out the lint filters for the next user, because that was a house rule, and Marvalyn was a rule follower.

Then she grabbed the ironing board and unfolded it, because she had to iron Eric's work clothes. The old contraption resisted and screeched at Marvalyn as she did, and she made a mental note to WD-40 the thing the next time she used it.

Once the ironing board was set up, she got the iron off the shelf where the pay-what-you-CAN was. Then she went to the deep stainless-steel sink by the washing machines and filled the iron's water chamber and then plugged it in and set it on the ironing board and started folding her laundry while she waited for it to steam. She folded towels and T-shirts and underwear and sweatshirts and sweatpants and jeans, and then she paired the socks, and then placed what she had folded and paired in her laundry basket.

The iron had been sighing with steam for a while, letting Marvalyn know that it was ready to be employed, so she gathered up Eric's work clothes—khaki pants and navy and gold polo shirts with the Dollar Discount Plus! emblem on the left breast pocket—and prepared to iron them. They were wrinkle-free, but Marvalyn ironed them anyway. Because she wanted Eric to look good for work. Or as good as he could look. His work clothes were getting too small for him. She wondered when he had gotten fat. He was skinny when they had met.

After she ironed the five Dollar Discount Plus! shirts, she hung them on a rod above the clothes-folding table and concentrated on pressing a perfect crease into one of Eric's pant legs—as if that crease was going to get Eric promoted from assistant manager to full-fledged manager. Even though Eric said he didn't want a promotion—because his job at the Dollar Discount Plus! was temporary. He wanted to get a job at the paper mill. There was an opening on the machine that made butter wrappers.

But Marvalyn encouraged him to inquire about a management position at Dollar Discount Plus!, because if he could become a manager there, they would be set.

And then she suddenly stopped ironing. And just stared at those khaki pants. And then slammed the iron down on the ironing board. And crumpled the pants up into a ball and tried to make them as wrinkled as you could make a pair of wrinkle-free pants. And chucked them into her laundry basket.

She wouldn't have done this had she known that Steve Doody, another tenant at Ma Dudley's, had come down to switch his laundry from the washers to the dryers. He had started his wash when Marvalyn had gone out to smoke the last cigarette she would ever smoke. And then had gone back to his room.

Steve was surprised to see Marvalyn in the laundry room. It was a Friday night, and people weren't usually in the laundry room doing their laundry on Friday nights. Because Friday nights were when most people were out doing something fun. Like going to the Moose Paddy. Which is what Steve's brother, Rob, was doing on the night when all the extraordinary things did or didn't happen. He went there every Friday night to have dinner and drink beer and play darts and pool and foosball with his friends. And Steve stayed home and did the laundry—one of the few chores he was able to complete unsupervised.

Steve recognized Marvalyn as the woman who had moved into Ma Dudley's a couple of weeks ago. But he didn't know her name. Because he hadn't met her yet. And he hadn't met the man she moved in with yet, either.

He stopped and stared at her for a while, hoping she'd turn and see him.

And wanted to meet her. He liked meeting people.

But she seemed angry. She was pulling a bunch of polo shirts off their hangers and crumpling them up and chucking them into her laundry basket. So Steve decided to not bother her. And he sat down on the bench facing the washing machines and opened up a three-hundred-page black marble composition book he had brought with him that was labeled THINGS TO BE AFRAID OF and started studying it while he waited for his wash to finish.

Meanwhile, Marvalyn unplugged the iron and shook the water out of it into the sink. And then, while she was coiling its cord, her wrist touched the iron's hot surface. "Dammit!" she hissed, and she dropped the iron, and it bounced the way heavy metal-and-plastic items bounce. Marvalyn grimaced and shook her hand rapidly back and forth as if that would make the pain go away.

Steve wasn't quite sure what had happened, but then Marvalyn said, "Ow!"

And then Steve knew exactly what had happened: Marvalyn had hurt herself. He had learned a long time ago that *ow* is something people say when they hurt themselves.

He closed the composition book he had been studying and put it in a black backpack that he always had with him. And he pulled another black marble composition notebook out of it labeled THINGS THAT CAN HURT YOU and opened it to a page about two-thirds of the way through and took a stubby pencil out of his shirt pocket and added the word *irons* to it.

Then he looked at Marvalyn, who had made her way to the sink so she could soothe her burn with cold water and then picked the iron up off the floor, inspecting it. It seemed to be fine. It said it was heavy-duty. And then she licked her right index finger and touched it to the iron to see if it was still hot, and it wasn't. It was only a little warm. So she wrapped the cord around it and returned it to the shelf where it lived.

Then she scooped her laundry basket up and held it under one arm and tried to get the ironing board to collapse into its flat resting position. But it was arthritic and screeched again and wouldn't flatten, so Marvalyn had to drop her laundry basket and focus on getting it closed. And Eric's work shirts and pants spilled onto the floor in a messy clump. Marvalyn grabbed the spilled clothes and chucked them into the basket. They were wrinkle-free. They'd be fine.

And then she refocused her attention on closing the ironing board. It seemed that the only way to get it to collapse fully was to stand it up on its feet, press the lever under the ironing surface to release the legs, and then gently guide it—with gravity's help—into a flat, closed position on the floor. Which she had finally managed to do. Then she picked up the ironing board and slung it under her arm and turned around to put it back where it lived. As she did so, the flat face of the ironing board walloped something. She didn't know what. But whatever it was—she had hit it pretty hard. And she turned toward whatever it was she had hit. And saw nothing but a gangly kid—or maybe he was a young man—flopping onto the floor. And she gasped and realized that he was the thing she had hit. She had been so absorbed in her ironing and in her thoughts and in her country music that she was completely unaware that there had been anyone else in the laundry room.

"Oh, no!" she cried, dropping the ironing board and rushing to Steve. "I'm sorry! I'm sorry! Oh, honey, I didn't see you, are you okay?!?"

"Yeah," Steve replied. He hopped to his feet as if nothing had happened and looked for his book of THINGS THAT CAN HURT YOU, which had been sent flying.

"No, you're not! I smashed you with the ironing board, I wasn't even looking! Are you hurt?"

"No," said Steve, having located his THINGS THAT CAN HURT YOU book—which had skittered under one of the clothes-folding tables.

Meanwhile, Marvalyn frantically tried to make everything right. Like she always did. It was her best quality. And her worst. "Oh, you must be!" she insisted. "I just clocked you! Where did I get you?"

"In the head," said Steve.

"In the *head*!?!" cried Marvalyn, deeply concerned that she had injured this poor guy. "Oh, God!"

Steve was making his way back to the bench, having retrieved his THINGS THAT CAN HURT YOU book from under the clothes-folding table.

"Okay, listen," ordered Marvalyn, "I need you to sit down and stop moving."

Steve obeyed and sat down and stopped moving.

"Come here," ordered Marvalyn, going to Steve. Which confused him. Because when you tell someone to come here, they're supposed to go to you. And not the other way around. "Where in the head did I get you, exactly?" continued Marvalyn.

"Um, right here, I think." Steve pointed to the top of his head.

"Oh, no," Marvalyn groaned. "Are you okay?" she asked, sitting down and checking Steve's eyes, and then holding her index finger in front of them and moving it from side to side to see if he could follow it. "Are you okay?" she asked again, trying to think of what else she had learned about diagnosing head injuries in her one semester in the nursing program at Northern Maine Community College in Presque Isle.

"Well, is there any blood?" asked Steve.

"No," answered Marvalyn, perplexed by the question. She was wondering why he would have thought there might be blood. Sure, he had suffered a good hit to the head. But she was sure she had hit him with the flat surface of the ironing board. And a blow from the flat surface of an ironing board isn't going to break skin.

"Is there any discoloration?" asked Steve.

Marvalyn wondered why he would be asking if there was any discoloration when she had hit him on the top of his head. Hair would cover any bruising. And Steve had a lot of short, thick black hair. But she checked his scalp for blood and for bruising to be sure. And found neither.

"Any swelling?" asked Steve.

There was no swelling either. Not yet, anyway. "No," she answered.

"Then I'm okay." Steve gave Marvalyn a thumbs-up and smiled a smile that didn't look like a smile. It looked like a smile that someone who was trying to make the right emotional choice would make.

"Okay," said Marvalyn, not quite sure what to make of this kid—or this guy—who smiled strangely and asked peculiar questions. "Well—I'm really sorry, about that. I didn't even see you," she added.

"It's okay. Most people don't," stated Steve simply and not seeking sympathy.

But Marvalyn didn't hear him, because she was on her way out of the laundry room. "You stay right there; I'm gonna go get you some ice," she called.

"No, you don't have to do that."

She stopped and turned to Steve. "Yes, I do, and some aspirin. To keep the swelling down and for the pain."

"Well, I don't feel pain."

Marvalyn didn't know how to respond to such a bizarre statement. "What?"

"I can't feel pain."

Marvalyn didn't know what to make of what Steve had just said.

"Okay," she said, convinced that she had seriously injured this kid. "Listen, I need you to be still, okay? I was gonna be a nurse, so, I know: You're hurt. You just took a good shot right to the head, and it could be serious. You might have a concussion."

"No, it's not serious," countered Steve. "I don't think an ironing board could really hurt your head, 'cause, see, ironing boards aren't on my list of things that can hurt you." Steve offered Marvalyn his book of THINGS THAT CAN HURT YOU.

"What?" Marvalyn asked, and she tentatively took Steve's book and read—and pondered—its title.

"Ironing boards aren't on my list of things that can hurt you."

"What are you talking about?"

"Plus, there's no blood or discoloration or swelling from where I got hit," Steve continued, excited to be able to explain his situation to someone. "So, I'm okay."

"Well, that doesn't mean—" Marvalyn was going to finish her sentence with, "you're not hurt," but she couldn't, because Steve was still talking.

"And my list is pretty reliable, 'cause my brother Rob is helping me make it, and I can prove it to you!" Steve got up and picked up the ironing board as Marvalyn opened his THINGS THAT CAN HURT YOU book. "See," continued Steve, approaching Marvalyn from behind, "I bet if I took this ironing board, like this, and hit you with it, that it wouldn't hurt you," and, suddenly, Steve thwacked Marvalyn in the back of the head with the flat part of the ironing board and continued making his point as he did so. "See? That didn't hurt!" he proclaimed.

"Ow!" Marvalyn cried, and she jumped up off the bench and dropped the book of THINGS THAT CAN HURT YOU, rubbing her head with her hands. "Why did you do that?!?" she asked.

"Oh, no," said Steve, concerned and confused. Marvalyn was hurt. Steve knew this because she had just said, "Ow." And she seemed to be afraid, because her eyes were wide, and Steve had learned that, when people are afraid, their eyes get wide.

"God, why did you do that?!? What the hell was that?!" Marvalyn seemed more irritated than scared now, because she was realizing that she wasn't actually hurt. She had just been startled.

"I'm sorry," said Steve earnestly. "Did that hurt?"

"Yeah! Of course it did!"

"Oh, no! I didn't think it would."

"God," Marvalyn sighed, her irritation subsiding, because this young man seemed truly contrite—and quite harmless.

"I'm really sorry!" cried Steve, picking up his book of THINGS THAT CAN HURT YOU. "See, I didn't think it would," he continued, flipping through the book. "See, ironing boards are not on my list of things that can hurt you, but, gosh, maybe they should be on my list, because that ironing board hurt you. And you were afraid it hurt me just a couple minutes ago."

"What are you talking about?" Marvalyn asked.

"I have a list of things that can hurt you, my brother Rob is helping me make it, and ironing boards aren't on it."

"Well, that ironing board . . . hurt me," Marvalyn said impatiently—and almost hostilely. And then she realized that she didn't want to be hostile to this guy. Or boy. Or whatever he was. He seemed fifteen one moment, thirty the next.

"Yeah," agreed Steve, pondering.

"So . . . you should add it to your list," said Marvalyn snidely.

"Yeah!" agreed Steve enthusiastically. Marvalyn watched as the odd young man dutifully added *ironing boards* to his list of THINGS THAT CAN HURT YOU.

And she wondered if ironing boards actually belonged on that list and was about to tell him that they didn't—but before she was able to, Steve had closed the book he was writing in and asked Marvalyn, "Should I be *afraid* of ironing boards?"

"Well, no, but if someone swings one at your head and wallops you with it, then, yeah, maybe you should be."

"Well—" Steve pulled another black marble composition book out of his backpack, this one labeled THINGS TO BE AFRAID OF, and continued, "See, I have a list of things to be afraid of, too, but ironing boards aren't on this list either."

"Well, they shouldn't be, really," said Marvalyn, fascinated by the second composition book.

"No?"

"No, you shouldn't be *afraid* of ironing boards."

"But they can hurt you," argued Steve.

"Yeah, but—"

"So I should be afraid of them."

"Well, no—"

"So I *shouldn't* be afraid of them?"

"Right."

"But they can *hurt* me."

"Well, if they're used the way you just used that one," she said, pointing to the ironing board on the floor, "then, yeah, they could hurt you, but—"

"Oh, oh, oh!" Steve exclaimed. "So they're kind of like the opposite of God!"

It took Marvalyn a moment to process Steve's strange epiphany.

"What?!?" she finally asked, part dumbfounded and part amused, and completely interested in the explanation.

"Well, ironing boards can *hurt* me, but I shouldn't be *afraid* of them," Steve reasoned, "but *God*, my brother Rob says, God won't ever hurt me, but I should *fear* Him."

Marvalyn considered what Steve had just said for a moment. And then responded, "I guess." She found his reasoning to be sound. She had never quite thought about God in that way before. But it seemed to her like a perfectly good way to think about Him. Or Her. Or whatever It was, because she wasn't quite sure what God was. If everyone was made in His image, maybe He was a She half the time. Or maybe He was neither a He nor a She. Or maybe God was both He and She. Who knew.

Steve ultimately decided not to add ironing boards to his book of things to be afraid of, because they didn't fulfill the criteria. And grumbled, "Boy, this is getting really complicated."

"What is?"

"This business of learning what hurts, what doesn't hurt, what to be afraid of, what not to be afraid of."

"Okay—listen—are you sure you're okay?" chuckled Marvalyn nervously. "You're not makin' a whole lotta sense, here, pal."

"Yeah, I am. I have congenital analgesia."

"Huh?"

"I have congenital analgesia. Some people call it congenital insensitivity to pain. And some people call it hereditary sensory neuropathy type four, but it all just means I can't feel pain."

"Congenital ana-what?" Marvalyn hadn't quite caught what Steve had called his disorder.

"Analgesia. You can hit me if you want to, to see."

"What?—No!"

"Yeah!" Steve offered Marvalyn his book of THINGS THAT CAN HURT YOU. "With this!"

"No!" Marvalyn got up and moved away from Steve.

"Yeah! Go ahead! It won't hurt! See?" Steve whacked his head with his book of THINGS THAT CAN HURT YOU.

"Stop!" cried Marvalyn.

Steve whacked his head again.

"Don't!" begged Marvalyn.

Steve whacked his head again. "Now you try!" he said, offering Marvalyn his book again.

"NO!!" insisted Marvalyn, and she grabbed the book out of Steve's hands so she could put an end to his twisted game.

"Okay," said Steve. "You don't have to hit me. Most people don't. Hit me. When I ask them to. Most people just go away. You can go away, too, if you want to. That's what most people do when I tell them about myself. My brother Rob says I just shouldn't tell people about myself, because I scare them—that's why they go away, he says—so I've actually recently put 'myself' on my list of things to be afraid of, but—"

Before Steve could finish his sentence, Marvalyn's curiosity had gotten the better of her, and she crept up behind him and walloped him on the back of the head with his THINGS THAT CAN HURT YOU book.

"Oh, my gosh! I'm sorry! I can't believe I just did that!" Marvalyn was horrified by what she had just done.

But Steve was thrilled. "You hit me! Most people go away, but you didn't! You hit me!"

"Yeah! I had to *see* if it really wouldn't hurt—did it hurt? Are you okay?"

"Yeah, I don't feel pain!"

"Right, you don't feel pain, of course you're okay! But—are you sure?"

"Well, is there any blood?" asked Steve.

"No," answered Marvalyn, kindly, but a little condescendingly, because a smack on the back of the head with a composition book wouldn't cause someone to bleed.

"Any discoloration?"

"No," smiled Marvalyn. A smack on the back of the head with a composition book wouldn't cause someone to bruise.

"Or swelling?"

"No," smiled Marvalyn. A smack on the back of the head with a composition book wouldn't cause any swelling.

"Then I'm okay," said Steve, giving Marvalyn a thumbs-up.

"Well, you can be hurt and not even look like it," said Marvalyn.

This didn't match up well with Steve's worldview. And he started to protest. "But—"

"Trust me," interrupted Marvalyn. "There are things that hurt you that make you bruised and bloody and there are things that hurt you that don't make you bruised and bloody and . . . they all hurt."

Steve pondered this paradigm-shifting piece of information.

And Marvalyn felt like she had overshared.

And then decided that she needed to get back upstairs, because Eric might be wondering where she was. So she got up and said, "Here," and gave Steve back his THINGS THAT CAN HURT YOU book. And then she went to gather her laundry and head back up to her room. But then stopped. And turned to Steve, who was staring at her. And wondered how it was possible that she had never even seen him before and suddenly asked, "Do you live here?"

"Yeah." Steve nodded. "Through there." He pointed toward the hall beyond the entrance to the laundry room. It led to the basement apartment he and his brother shared.

"I haven't ever . . . seen you," said Marvalyn. "I mean—I'm new here—but I've never even . . . seen you."

"I don't go out much."

"Oh."

"It's not safe."

"Oh." Marvalyn imagined that there was a lot in the world that was unsafe for someone who couldn't feel pain. And then she pitied him for a moment. And then just wanted to know more about him. And wanted him to know more about her. Like her name, for starters. So she said, "I'm Marvalyn."

"Yeah, I know," said Steve. "Ma Dudley told me when I asked her who you were. We saw you and your husband move in."

"Oh—no—he's not my husband," corrected Marvalyn so quickly and defensively that she made Steve feel like he had done something wrong.

"Oh. Sorry," said Steve.

"No—it's okay. We probably seem like we're married. But he's just my boyfriend," clarified Marvalyn, smiling.

"Oh." Steve wondered why Marvalyn was smiling. She didn't seem happy. Which made Steve wonder if she had chosen the wrong facial expression to go with her emotional state.

"But maybe someday he'll be my husband, because I love him!" declared Marvalyn. And then she wondered if that was true—and then realized that she didn't want to be wondering such a thing in front of a stranger, so she stopped and went on: "Anyway, our roof collapsed from all the snow in December. We're just here until we can get our feet back on the ground."

"Oh, well that's good, 'cause that's what Ma Dudley says her boarding house is—a place where people can live till they get their feet back on the ground."

"Oh," said Marvalyn, smiling.

"Yeah, we've been trying to get our feet back on the ground our whole lives, my brother Rob says."

Marvalyn nodded, wondering how long it would take for her and Eric to get their feet back on the ground.

And then she pitied herself a little. And then pitied the odd manchild again—whose name she still didn't know. And suddenly asked, "So, what's your name?

"Steve."

"Steve what?"

"Doody."

"And you've lived here for . . . how long?" she asked.

"Couple years."

Marvalyn wondered how it was possible that she didn't know these brothers, Steve and Rob Doody, who had been living at Ma Dudley's in Almost, Maine, for the past couple of years.

She didn't know that the brothers were from Winterville and had moved to Ma Dudley's after their house had gotten foreclosed on. And she had never met them because Rob worked nights and Steve never went out.

And she suddenly felt like something wasn't right about Steve's situation. And like he needed help. And like she could help him. But before she could figure out how she might help him, Steve said, "You guys are loud."

And Marvalyn got flustered and stammered, "H-huh?"

"You and your boyfriend. You yell and bang."

"Oh. Sorry." Marvalyn and Eric were going through a rough patch. And there had been some yelling. And maybe some banging.

But she didn't think that Steve could possibly have heard them all the way down in the basement. So she asked, "Did you . . . hear us . . . from down here?" She was afraid to hear the answer.

"No. But the new lady who moved in on the second floor said that you guys yell and bang a lot and that she can hear you."

"Oh." The "new lady" Steve was talking about was Vivian—or Vicky—or Veronica—from the second floor. And Marvalyn realized she'd better apologize to her for the noise.

In the meantime, she apologized to Steve. "Sorry about that. We're goin' through a rough patch. Sorry."

"Didn't bother me. I didn't hear ya."

"Well—I'm glad! So, um, listen, it was nice to meet you, but—"

"Nice to meet you, too."

"Yeah, but I've gotta get back to my boyfriend, 'cause he's waiting for me, actually, I think. We had a fun little stay-at-home date night," she said, wanting Steve to know that she and Eric were happy—when they weren't yelling and banging. "So I'm gonna go back up and hang out with him, so maybe I'll see you around, okay?"

"Yeah."

Marvalyn gathered her laundry basket and started to go. The washing machine that had Steve's laundry in it buzzed to let him know his wash was done. Marvalyn was startled by the sound. And stopped. And, from the entrance to the laundry room, she watched Steve get up and remove the clean clothes from the washer and transfer them to the dryer.

She was fascinated by him.

"What's it like?" she suddenly asked. Marvalyn didn't feel like she was the one who had just asked that question. She felt like another version of herself somewhere deep down inside her had asked it for her.

Steve jumped a little at the question. He didn't know Marvalyn hadn't left. And he was happy she hadn't, for some reason. "Huh?" he asked.

"What's it like? To not feel pain."

"Oh. I don't know," Steve answered honestly. "I've never known what it's like to hurt, so . . . I don't know. I guess it just feels . . . normal, to me."

"You're kind of lucky, you know. In a way."

"Yeah. I know. My brother Rob says I'll never have to worry about getting addicted to painkillers. So that's lucky."

That wasn't quite what Marvalyn had meant when she said that Steve was kind of lucky to not feel pain, but she couldn't deny that it was true. "Yeah, I guess," she concurred. And then she wondered if Steve's condition was genetic or the result of some sort of trauma, so she asked, "So . . . were you born this way?"

"Yeah, congenital means 'present from birth,' so yeah."

Okay, so—how did they figure out you had it?"

"I never cried."

This was true.

Steve didn't cry when he was born.

He didn't cry when he had a diaper rash.

He didn't cry when he started growing teeth and bit his tongue until he bled.

He didn't cry when he burned his hand reaching into a campfire to retrieve a rogue toasting marshmallow.

He didn't cry when he reached for a spoon that had been dropped into boiling water.

He didn't cry when he stepped on a nail with his bare foot.

He didn't cry when he fell down the stairs and broke his ankle and walked around on it for hours before anyone noticed the swelling and the bruising.

But his mom cried a lot. She felt all the pain her son couldn't feel. And it was all too much for her.

And the way she took care of her pain took her away from her family.

So Steve and Rob's grandma raised her daughter's sons.

And when she died, Rob became Steve's legal guardian. Which was nothing new, because he had always been Steve's main caregiver anyway.

"So . . . can you . . . *feel* . . . things?" asked Marvalyn.

"Kinda."

Marvalyn suddenly poked Steve. "Did you feel that?"

"Yup," laughed Steve, surprised by Marvalyn's forwardness. "I can feel the pressure. But . . . that's it. 'Cause I don't have fully developed pain sensors. They're immature, my brother Rob says, and because they're immature—"

"How does he know that?" interrupted Marvalyn.

"Oh, he reads, and because they're immature, my development as a human being has been compromised, he says, but he teaches me what hurts, though."

"Why?"

"So I won't ruin myself. I have to know what hurts, so I know when to be afraid. See, my mind can't tell me when to be afraid, 'cause my body doesn't know what being hurt is, so I have to memorize what might hurt."

"Okay." This made sense to Marvalyn.

"And I have to memorize what to be afraid of." Steve opened his book of THINGS TO BE AFRAID OF to a random page, eager to show Marvalyn all the things that his grandma—and Rob—had helped him learn to be afraid of. Almost all of them corresponded to items in his THINGS THAT CAN HURT YOU book. "Things like"—Steve pointed to a random item on the page—"guns."

He turned to another page and pointed to a random item on it. "And bears."

He turned to another page and pointed to a random item on it. "And oven burners that are orange and red."

Then he turned to a page almost at the end of the book and pointed to a random item on it. "And—oh, this one's newer: fear, I should fear fear itself. I don't really know what that means, but the second President Roosevelt said it."

He turned the page and pointed to a random item and said, "And—this one's new, too—pretty girls."

And then he realized something.

And he looked at Marvalyn. And got extremely uncomfortable.

"Pretty girls?" asked Marvalyn.

"Yeah," said Steve, looking at Marvalyn. "Like you."

Marvalyn laughed. And then almost cried. Because it had been a long time since anyone had told her she was pretty. She knew she used to be pretty. But she didn't think she was anymore. She thought she was just fat. And old enough looking that she wasn't getting carded anymore.

"Like me?" she asked.

"Yeah." Steve was uncomfortable. And confused.

"Well, why should you be afraid of pretty girls?" asked Marvalyn, smiling.

"Well, because my brother Rob says they can hurt you 'cause they make you love them, and that's something I'm supposed to be afraid of, too—love—but my brother Rob says that I'm really lucky, 'cause I'll probably never have to deal with love, because I have a lot of deficiencies and not very many capacities as a result of the congenital analgesia."

"Whoa, whoa, whoa—wait—what do you mean you're never gonna have to deal with love? Why would he say that?"

"'Cause I'm never gonna know what it feels like, Rob says."

"Well, how does he know that?"

"'Cause it hurts."

"Well, it shouldn't."

"And, plus, I have a lot of deficiencies and not very many capacities, Rob says."

"You know what, a lot of people do."

Steve had never thought about what Marvalyn had just said—that maybe a lot of other people had a lot of deficiencies. And not very many capacities. It made him feel like maybe he wasn't as different from other people as he had always been told he was. And he hadn't felt like that in . . . well, he couldn't remember ever feeling like that.

He looked straight into Marvalyn's eyes—and he hardly ever looked straight into anyone's eyes. And Marvalyn felt a strange lightness fill up her insides. It made her feel like she had sunshine from a sunny spring day inside her. And like she had just let go of the rope swing at the quarry pond and was suspended in time and space.

And it made her feel like she had some promise in her.

And it made a strange combination of compassion and desire surge through her body.

And it made her lunge toward Steve and want to kiss him.

So she did.

Hard.

Steve made a sound that was part gasp and part groan upon receiving Marvalyn's kiss. And his instinct was to resist. But he gave in to the kiss before he resisted. And he felt still and calm as he did.

And he couldn't remember the last time he had felt still and calm.

And then he felt a strange lightness fill up his insides. It was as if a gentle fire from a fireplace was flickering inside him—and it made him feel like he was floating. The last time he remembered feeling that way was when he was little and had fallen asleep on the couch in front of the fireplace and his grandma would carry him to bed.

He felt safe in her arms. And protected—and wanted.

And he felt the same way while Marvalyn was kissing him.

Better, even.

And then he started kissing Marvalyn back. Which made the lightness Marvalyn was feeling grow. And it almost hurt—because it made her feel like her organs were shifting. It seemed to be reviving something in her that she didn't even know was dead. And that scared her. So she broke away from Steve, horrified by what she had just done.

"Oh my God!" she gasped. "I'm sorry—I'm so sorry. I don't know why I just did that. Are you all right? Are you okay?"

Steve was staring at Marvalyn, dopey and confused.

"Hey! Are you okay?" Marvalyn asked again, more urgently.

Steve touched his lips. "Well . . . is there any blood?" he asked, which was the question he had been trained to ask.

"No," answered Marvalyn, touched by the sweet response.

"Any discoloration?"

"No." Marvalyn smiled with a mix of pity and wonder. "And no swelling, either," she added to save some time.

"Well, then . . . I'm all right," said Steve unconvincingly.

Marvalyn and Steve sat in a stunned silence for a moment.

Neither of them knew what to do.

And then Marvalyn realized that she actually did know what to do: she needed to get out of there. And go back upstairs. To Eric.

"I'm . . . sorry," she said as she scrambled to her laundry basket. As she tried to pick it up, it slipped out of her hands and its contents flopped out all over the place. "Come on," she growled, and she started gathering the spilled laundry so she could go back upstairs to Eric.

She checked in on Steve as she did.

He was lost in thought, trying to figure out what had just happened to him.

"I'm so sorry I did that to you," said Marvalyn. "I shouldn't have done that."

"No. You shouldn't have," agreed Steve. "Because you have a boyfriend."

"Yes, I do," answered Marvalyn sheepishly. She had gathered all the spilled laundry and was starting to go—because she really needed to go.

"And you just kissed me."

"Yes, I did," said Marvalyn, stopping. And not knowing why she was stopping.

"And it's Friday night and you're doing your laundry."

Marvalyn wished that she had gone to Sandrine St. Pierre's bachelorette party at the Moose Paddy. Or that Eric hadn't fallen asleep in front of the hockey game. If either of those things had happened, she wouldn't have just kissed a kid who she hoped to God was eighteen. "Yes, I am," she acknowledged.

"And people who love each other, they don't kiss other people and do their laundry on Friday nights—I've learned that." Steve was working hard to solve the riddle of the girl who had a boyfriend but who had just kissed another boy. "And," he continued, "people who are in love with each other—they go to the Moose Paddy on Friday nights. And they kiss each other. They don't kiss other people."

Marvalyn heard the truth Steve was speaking. And it paralyzed her for a moment. "Yeah, well . . . ," she began—and didn't know how to finish the sentence.

"You know what?" Steve added, building a case. "I don't think that's love, what you and your boyfriend have."

"Yeah, well, you know what?" Marvalyn tried to put a stop to Steve's line of reasoning and then tried to refute his assertion—but couldn't. And just said, "I have to go. I've been down here longer than I should have been and he's gonna wonder where I am, and he doesn't like it when he doesn't know where I am."

"Who?"

"Eric."

"Your boyfriend."

"Yup."

"Who you love a lot."

"Yes."

"Even though you just kissed me."

"Um . . . yup." Marvalyn felt really bad that she had kissed Steve. But that kiss had felt so good. Because it was the kind of kiss that a girl who had a marvelous life would give to her marvelous boyfriend on a Friday night.

"Wow," said Steve, "I'm going to have to talk to my brother Rob about this—"

"No! Don't talk to your brother Rob about this!" There was a rule at Ma Dudley's about fraternizing among tenants. And what Marvalyn had done to Steve would definitely have qualified as fraternizing. And Marvalyn didn't need anyone to know that she had been fraternizing with Steve. So she started to go, but stopped—because the almost-nurse in her felt compelled to help her almost-patient. "And do me a favor: tell your brother to stop teaching you.

'Cause whatever he's teaching you . . . isn't something you wanna know."

"But I have to learn from him—"

"Look, I was gonna be a nurse, so I know: you need help. Your brother shouldn't be reading . . . whatever it is he reads. And he shouldn't be telling you that you have a lot of deficiencies and not very many capacities." Marvalyn had been told the same thing—but with different words—too often lately. And she didn't appreciate being told that. "And he shouldn't be—I don't know—deciding—for you—all the things he's deciding for you."

"Huh?"

"You know what, I gotta go."

"Right. You gotta go. You're leaving. I knew you would. That's what people do."

"I'm sorry, but I told you, Eric doesn't know where I am—"

"Your boyfriend?"

"Yes, my boyfriend. I've told you that ten times."

"No you haven't. You've only told me three times." This was true. Steve had counted.

"Okay, well, I've told you three times that Eric is my boyfriend, and I've told you I don't know how many times that he doesn't like it when he doesn't know where I am, and he doesn't know where I am, so I need to go." Marvalyn started to leave again but realized that she had forgotten to put the ironing board away—which Steve had used last when he clocked her in the head with it. And Ma Dudley had a rule about leaving the laundry room as you found it. And Marvalyn was a rule follower, so she dropped her laundry basket and picked up the ironing board. And it sprang open as she did so, because it hadn't been closed fully. And she struggled to close it again.

Meanwhile, Steve had taken a seat on the bench and was staring at the clock on the wall. It said it was just before nine o'clock now, so he figured his clothes would be dry by a little after nine thirty. Which was well before ten.

And then he went back to work, poring over his books, making sure he knew about all the things that could hurt him and all the things he needed to be afraid of.

Marvalyn finally got the ornery ironing board folded up again and latched into a closed position, and, as she turned to put it away, she somehow managed to wallop Steve in the head with it—in exactly the same way that she had not even twenty minutes ago. And Steve went flying off the bench again, in much the same way as he did earlier, and keened, "OW!"

Marvalyn jumped and cringed when she hit Steve this second time. "Oh, no!" she cried, dropping the ironing board and rushing to Steve. "I'm sorry! I'm sorry! Oh, honey, I can't believe I just did that to you again! Are you okay?!?"

"OW!" howled Steve.

"I'm so sorry. Are you okay?"

"OW!" moaned Steve. He was clearly in pain.

"I'm so sorry—where did I get y—" Marvalyn interrupted herself when she realized what Steve had just said. "Wait: What did you just say?"

"Ow," Steve replied. He looked bewildered and terrified.

And he was crying.

For the first time in his life, possibly.

Because he was in pain. For the first time in his life.

And he was afraid—for the first time in his life. Because he had no idea what was happening to him.

Marvalyn saw the tears rolling down Steve's face.

And she saw his pain.

And his fear.

And she wanted to rush to him and comfort him. And make sure he was okay.

But she didn't. Because she realized that—maybe for the first time in his life—he was okay. Or—he was going to be okay. Because he was going to have to learn how to work through pain. Just like she—and just about everybody else in the world—had to.

And besides—she wouldn't have been able to make him okay.

Because she couldn't make anyone else okay.

She could only make herself okay.

And she needed to get to work on making herself okay.

So she grabbed her laundry basket and told Steve that she was sorry—so sorry—but she had to go.

And she started to flee but stopped before she exited the laundry room. "I know it doesn't feel like it right now—but you're gonna be okay."

And then she exited the laundry room and ran down the hall and rushed up the stairs and into the living room and was about to go up to her room on the third floor—when she stopped again.

Because she didn't want to go upstairs. Because Eric was there. And she didn't want to see him. Ever again.

And she decided then and there that she was going to leave him.

She didn't have much money, and she didn't have a job, and she didn't have any family she could go to, and she had become distant from her friends because Eric liked it that way.

So it was going to be difficult for her to leave him.

But she had a car—an old Chevy Malibu.

So she could just go.

And when she realized that she could just go, that strange lightness filled up her insides. And it made her feel like maybe there was still a chance that she could be marvelous.

And she went upstairs to get her coat and her keys. So she could just go. And not come back.

She had no idea where she was going to go. But she was going to go.

If Eric was still asleep.

And even if he wasn't.

5

As Ginette made her way past Ma Dudley's, she wondered if she would have someone to dance with when she was as old as Ma and Sunny were.

Half an hour ago, she would have thought that that someone would be Pete. Because she and Pete had just told each other that they loved each other. And it seemed like they were together or that they were girlfriend and boyfriend or that they were dating—or something. And—whatever they were—it seemed like they were going to live happily ever after.

But they weren't living happily ever after.

They were living—sadly ever after.

At least, Ginette was. Because she and Pete weren't dating and they weren't girlfriend and boyfriend and they weren't together.

They were nothing—maybe not even friends anymore.

And that made Ginette's heart so, so heavy.

And she wallowed in a deep, deep sadness as she continued west on the Road to Nowhere.

* * *

It was 8:05 when Ginette found herself approaching the Moose Paddy, which was about a quarter of a mile down the road from Ma Dudley's.

She hated the name of Almost's local watering hole. It had been so dubbed by its proprietors, a couple of brothers from Bangor who wanted the place to sound Irish—yet local.

Instead it sounded like what a moose's bowel movement leaves behind.

A cackle from the Moose Paddy's parking lot interrupted Ginette's wallow in sadness. She looked across the Road to Nowhere, and a few exterior sodium lights allowed her to see the silhouette of a guy and a girl laughing and hugging and kissing and making their way toward the Moose Paddy entrance.

Jimmy Pelletier had pulled into the Moose Paddy's parking lot moments ago and had seen the same girl and guy laughing and hugging and kissing. And it made him miss having someone to laugh with and hug and kiss.

But then he remembered that that was why he was at the Moose Paddy on the Friday night when all the extraordinary things did or didn't happen—to see if he could find himself someone to laugh with and hug and kiss. And maybe even love.

And he could thank Mrs. Roy for giving him the confidence to see if he could find someone to laugh with and hug and kiss again (and maybe even love). Because Mrs. Roy's pellet stove—a furnace that burned compressed sawdust pellets—was on the fritz that night. And since Jimmy ran Pelletier's Heating and Cooling, he was the guy people called when their home's main source of heat was down. And he always made sure to answer people's emergency calls. Because—in the wintertime in northern Maine—it's a matter of life and death when a home has no heat. So when Mrs. Roy called with her pellet stove emergency, Jimmy went over and cleaned and recalibrated her stove and got it working again.

Mrs. Roy thanked Jimmy and paid him for his trouble with a five-dollar bill and a bag of chocolate chip cookies—which Jimmy graciously accepted. (He had a pay-what-you-can policy for senior citizens—and anyone—on fixed incomes.) And, as he was about to leave, she asked him what he was doing with his Friday night.

And Jimmy said not much.

And Mrs. Roy asked him if he going out on a date or anything.

And Jimmy said he wasn't.

And Mrs. Roy said that she didn't mean to be all up in his business, but he needed to get himself out there again and move on from Sandrine, his old girlfriend, and start dating again. Because he was a catch, she said. Because he ran his own business. And he was a good guy. And he still had some looks.

Jimmy thanked Mrs. Roy for the confidence boost.

And told her that he just might head on over to the Moose Paddy. And get himself out there again. And move on.

And so he did.

He sat in his Pelletier's Heating and Cooling van for a moment after he pulled into the establishment's parking lot.

And promptly lost his confidence. Because Sandrine had done a real number on him.

But then he reminded himself what Mrs. Roy had said—that he was a catch. Because he ran his own business. And he was a good guy. And he still had some looks.

So he got out of his van and made his way toward the Moose Paddy's entrance. And as he did, the lack of confidence he was feeling faded away. And he felt a strange lightness fill up his insides. It made him feel like he had the glow of a fired-up pellet stove inside him. And like he had the butterflies. And it made him feel like things were going to go his way. And that wasn't something that he felt very often. Most of the time he felt like things were not going to go his way. At all.

His confidence restored, Jimmy pulled the worn, chunky oak Moose Paddy door open and left the cold, quiet northern Maine night behind him. And he eased into the warm, piney, buzzy, and dimly lit Moose Paddy. The place smelled like old and new beer. And old and new fried food.

He passed the coatroom—an actual room for coats and snowmobile suits and paraphernalia for those who arrived by snowmobile— and looked around at the knotty-pine walls and up at the knotty-pine ceiling and down at the knotty-pine floors and remembered some of the crazy things he and his buddies had done inside those walls and under that ceiling and on those floors many years ago.

He approached the bar, which dominated the establishment and had seats all the way around it. A giant chalkboard above the bar listed the beers that were on tap. It also announced the night's special: "Drink free if you're sad. Just tell us you're sad, and you'll drink free. Honor code applies."

Jimmy wasn't sad, so he ordered—and paid for—a Bud Light.

While he waited for his beer, he saw a lot of girls he vaguely knew dressed in shiny clothes. They were cackling and drinking rounds of shots and wearing tiaras and boas and BRIDE SQUAD hats. Some bachelorette party or something.

He got his beer and left a big tip (because he could) and passed a couple of regulars who were sitting at the bar. It had been a while since Jimmy had been to the Moose Paddy and he was surprised by how old those guys had gotten. Some of them stopped him and asked how his parents liked retirement. He said it suited them just fine. And they told him to say hi to them for them. And he said he would.

Then he headed to the back of the establishment, where it was quieter, and he eventually found a table near the pool tables and the dartboards and the restrooms. The jukebox was playing an old song about a crazy little thing called love. And he bopped his head a little to the music. And he took off his Pelletier's Heating and Cooling jacket and draped it over the back of his chair, because it was warm, and then started scoping out the place.

And he soon lost his confidence. Because he realized that most of the women who were there were going to be young. And he was not young anymore. He was pushing thirty. And to be single at thirty in Almost, Maine, meant you'd most likely be single when you were forty. And when you were fifty. And when you were sixty.

And just when he was about to get up and grab his coat and go, something wonderful happened.

He saw Sandrine.

She was coming his way—from the ladies' room, he guessed. And she seemed to be gliding in slow motion right toward him. She looked beautiful—in her tight jeans and a shimmery purple shirt and boots that made her much taller than she actually was.

He hadn't seen her since she'd left.

And he felt that eerie lightness again. It made his whole body tingle.

Jimmy rose to greet Sandrine and held out his arms to embrace her. But then she walked right by his table and suddenly seemed to be moving at regular speed as she headed back toward the front of the Moose Paddy.

Jimmy watched her walk toward the front for a little too long.

And then realized he'd better act or she'd be out of earshot, and he called out—a little too loudly—"Sandrine!?!"

Sandrine stopped and started turning toward the guy who had called her name.

"Yeah?" she asked. She was in a giggly fog. Because she was happy. And she had done a shot of peach schnapps not too long ago.

But as soon as she saw Jimmy, she came out of her giggly fog and got still and sober.

Because Jimmy was the last person in the world she wanted to see right then. She almost recoiled and said, "Oh, God." But didn't, and instead forced a smile and gave her ex-boyfriend a warm greeting. "Jimmy! Hi!"

"Hey!" said Jimmy, smiling way too hard. Sandrine smiled back, a little horrified, and a little shocked. She couldn't believe that—on that night of all nights—she had run into the guy that she had managed to avoid for almost a year.

But Jimmy could believe it. Because he had just been feeling that things were going to go his way that night. And it looked like they were!

He took off his Pelletier's Heating and Cooling hat—which he had designed—and tried to straighten his hair and make himself look as good as he could. And hoped to God that Mrs. Roy was right—that he still had some looks. His work kept him in pretty good shape. He hadn't gotten as fat as all of his friends had. He just felt short. Because Sandrine was in boots that made her taller than him. And it never bothered him when Sandrine wore shoes or boots that made her taller than him when they were together. But now that they weren't together anymore, it bothered him for some reason.

"Hey!" Jimmy said again, still smiling way too hard and approaching Sandrine.

"Hey!" Sandrine replied, smiling back.

"Hey!" Jimmy said again, because he couldn't figure out what else to say.

"Hey!" Sandrine responded, because—well, what else could she say?

"Heyyyy!" said Jimmy again, and he moved in on her and bear-hugged her way too long and way too hard.

Sandrine didn't really accept the hug. And definitely didn't return it. And may have tried to squirm out of Jimmy's grasp. But Jimmy was so happy to see her—and hug her—that he didn't notice her attempt to escape, and when he finally released her, he asked, "So, how you doin'?"

"I'm doin' pretty good! How are you doin'?"

"I'm good, I'm good!" And he thought this was the truth. But then realized that it wasn't. Because he was lonely. Bone-crushingly lonely. And seeing Sandrine made him realize just how lonely he had been since she left.

But he didn't want Sandrine to think he was lonely. And that he wasn't doing well. So he smiled harder. Which made him look a little maniacal.

And Sandrine smiled harder, too. Which made her look a little maniacal, too.

And then Jimmy realized that he wasn't talking.

And that Sandrine wasn't talking.

And Sandrine realized that she wasn't talking.

And that Jimmy wasn't talking.

And it got terribly awkward. So Jimmy tried to save them from the awkwardness by restarting the conversation. And asked, "How are ya?!?" And immediately realized that he had just asked a slightly different version of that question.

Sandrine gamely answered the question again honestly. "I'm good, doin' good, great!"

"Good!" Jimmy searched for something else to say but could only manage to ask, "How are ya?" again.

"Great, great!" Sandrine nodded and smiled a lot to try to ignore all the awkwardness. Which was good of her.

Jimmy felt like he was drowning. This reunion couldn't have been more awkward. But he didn't let on that he felt like he was drowning and said, "Well . . . good!" way too enthusiastically. "That's great!" he cheered.

"Yeah!"

"That's great!" he said again.

"Yeah."

"That's great!" he said again, trying to come up with something else to say.

"Yeah!"

"That's great!" he said again, overly enthusiastically.

"Yeah!"

"You look great!" he said, happy to have finally come up with something else to say.

"Naw!" protested Sandrine.

"You look great!"

"Thanks."

"You do. You look so great!"

"Thanks, Jimmy," said Sandrine, a little put off by Jimmy's enthusiasm.

"So pretty. So pretty."

"Okay, thanks," she said, putting an end to the ridiculous exchange—because Jimmy was starting to creep her out with all his compliments.

Jimmy smiled at Sandrine and admired her loveliness for a moment and then said, "Here, have a seat," and he pulled the other chair at his table out and offered it to her.

Sandrine protested. "Oh, no, Jimmy, I can't—"

"Aw, come on," interrupted Jimmy, "I haven't seen you in . . . well, *months*."

"Yeah—"

"And *months*."

"Yeah." Sandrine was well aware that she hadn't seen Jimmy in months and knew that she owed him an explanation. But she really didn't want to have to give him one right then.

"And months and months and months and months and months and months and *months*."

Jimmy wanted to make sure Sandrine knew exactly how many months it had been since he had seen her: nine.

"Yeah," said Sandrine contritely.

"How does *that* happen—live in the same part of the world as someone and never see 'em?"

Sandrine shrugged and said, "I don't know," even though she knew full well how to live in the same little corner of the world as someone and never see them: duck and cover and run. Which she did any time she saw him anywhere.

And—she stopped going to the places he went. She started going to a different church—St. Thomas's in Fort Kent instead of St. Mary's. She went to a different grocery store—the Hannaford's in Caribou instead of Paradis's in Fort Kent.

Jimmy was aware that he was making Sandrine uncomfortable. But that was okay. He was owed an explanation. And he decided to make her more uncomfortable. And so he said with a smile, "I mean, I haven't seen you since that night before that morning when I woke up and you were just gone."

This was a cryptic way of saying that he hadn't seen her since she left.

It took Sandrine a second to decipher what Jimmy was saying. And when she did, she knew she needed to sit down and explain why she had slipped out on him after he had fallen asleep on that spring night a little less than a year ago.

Fortunately, the table Jimmy had chosen was tucked away in the corner—but still had a good view of the front, so she'd be able to see if anyone she knew was coming her way before they saw her. Because she really could not have anyone see her there with Jimmy.

As Sandrine sat down, a pained look came over her face. "Listen, Jimmy," she began. But before she could say anything else, a waitress breezed over to the table and interrupted her. "Look at you two, tucked away in the corner over here! Lucky I found ya! Are the man and his lovely lady ready for another round?"

Jimmy liked the idea of Sandrine being his lovely lady. "Sure!" he chirped.

But Sandrine emphatically set the record straight. "Oh, no! We're not together!"

It was awkward for a moment. And they all heard the jukebox playing an old rock song about how someone was just what the singer of the song needed. And Jimmy realized that Sandrine was just what he needed and started to explain that he and Sandrine used to be together and were hopefully going to be together again someday soon, but Sandrine interrupted him again and urgently reiterated, "We're not together."

Then Jimmy tried to explain their unusual situation. "Well, we used to be—"

But Sandrine interrupted and made sure the waitress understood her: "We're not together."

"Okay," said the waitress, puzzled. She looked at Jimmy. And then at Sandrine. And then back at Jimmy. And wondered if she should stay or go. And then decided to go, because it was pretty awkward. "Well, holler if you need anything," she said as she left.

"We will, thanks," called Sandrine.

The waitress stopped and turned to the unhappy couple, and said sternly, "No, really: You gotta holler. It's busy up front. There's a thing goin' on up there, and we're short-staffed, so—holler!"

"Okay, thanks," said Sandrine, and the waitress was gone.

Sandrine turned back to Jimmy. And he was smiling a goofy smile. Because he was convinced that Sandrine really was just what he needed. And he was hoping that what Mrs. Roy had said was true—that he was a catch. Because he was hoping to get caught—and kept, this time—by Sandrine. But before he could get caught, he needed to make sure she wasn't seeing anyone—so he could see if he should even bother trying to get caught. So he asked, "So, are you here with anybody, or . . . ?"

"Um . . ." Sandrine looked down and then nodded toward the front of the Moose Paddy and said, "Just the girls." She was telling the truth, but not really answering the question that she well knew Jimmy was asking. Because she just didn't feel like it was the right time to tell the whole truth. Because she needed to apologize to him and explain why she had left him so unceremoniously before she told him anything else.

"Oh!" said Jimmy. He felt like he had just won the lottery, because if Sandrine was there with a bunch of her girlfriends—on a Friday night—well, then, she probably wasn't dating anybody.

"Yeah. We're, um—just . . . girls' night out!" she chirped, feeling like she was lying even though she wasn't, really.

"Oh! All right, then!" exclaimed Jimmy a little too enthusiastically.

"Yeah. We're in the front," said Sandrine, and then she decided to abandon any attempt to apologize and/or explain why she had left him. Because she wasn't at the Moose Paddy to explain herself to Jimmy. She was there for a very different reason. So she got up and said, "And, you know, everyone's going to be wondering where I am, so I should get back to them." And she started to go, but Jimmy hopped up and almost aggressively blocked her path, preventing her from leaving. "Whoa, whoa, whoa!" he said. There was no way she was going anywhere. Not without an explanation or an apology.

Sandrine was taken aback by Jimmy's behavior—and Jimmy immediately sensed this, so he eased up and pleaded, "Come on! Please stay! I haven't even seen ya. Your girls'll survive without ya for a minute or two."

The last thing Sandrine wanted to do was stay with Jimmy. But he was winning her over with those hangdog eyes of his—the same ones that had won her over when she met him at the Spring Singles Service at St. Mary's last April. So she forgave him his quick eruption of aggression—as inappropriate as it was—and stayed.

"So . . . what's been—here—" Jimmy offered Sandrine her seat again. "So what's been goin' on, whatcha been up to?"

"Well . . ." Sandrine realized it was now or never. She needed to tell him everything so she could leave with a clear conscience and never have to deal with him again. "Um—"

But before she could say anything else, Jimmy interrupted her to make sure she knew that he was still a catch: "Did you know I took over my dad's business?"

"Yeah, I heard that," responded Sandrine. "That's great," she added, making no effort to sound enthusiastic. And then she tried to steer the conversation back to what she wanted to tell him, but couldn't, because Jimmy was already elaborating.

"Thanks, yeah. I run it now."

"I heard that."

"I'm runnin' it."

"Heard that."

"Runnin' the business." Jimmy really wanted Sandrine to be impressed with him and his new situation.

"Congratulations. Good for you," said Sandrine, genuinely happy that Jimmy was doing so well.

"Thanks, yeah, we still do heating and cooling."

"Yeah?"

"Yeah, and we've expanded, too. We sell and maintain and service pellet stoves now."

"Wow," said Sandrine, unsuccessfully feigning interest. She couldn't have been less interested in hearing any details about Jimmy's heating and cooling business. Because she just wanted to come clean with him and leave. But she had missed her chance. And now she'd have to listen to him yammer on about how well his business was doing before she'd be able to find another one.

"Yeah, so, like I said, business is super good. Been busy. Real busy."

"Good."

"I'm on call a lot. Weekends, holidays, you name it, 'cause, you know, your heat goes, people die, it's serious."

"Yeah."

"I was thinkin' about makin' that the motto, actually, of the company: 'If your heat goes, you could die.' But that's a little dark, I think, maybe."

"Mm. Maybe." The reasons why Sandrine couldn't be with this guy were all coming back to her. Even though they'd never really left her. Jimmy had great intentions. But, too often, they were misguided.

"Anyway, I do a lot of house calls. Like—I just was at Mrs. Roy's.

She had a problem with her pellet stove shuttin' off outta nowhere, so I went over and it just needed a cleaning, and I had to recalibrate it and adjust the augur, and she's good to go now."

"Well, that's really good of you, Jimmy."

"Yeah, well, I have the time, you know, to help people. 'Cause I'm not tied down to anyone, so I can, you know, give the guys who work for me their holidays off—like I work Thanksgivin', Christmas—so they can be with their families, since I'm all alone this year."

Jimmy worried that reminding Sandrine that he was all alone this year sounded like a ploy to get her to feel bad for him. And then he realized it was a ploy to make her feel bad for him. Because he wanted her to feel bad for him. Or at least realize how bad she had made him feel. Because she had hurt him. And he wanted her to know just how badly she had hurt him.

Sandrine wanted to offer Jimmy some solace—she knew she owed him that. But before she could, Jimmy made sure she understood just how alone he was and said, "Yeah, I don't have anybody anymore, really. I mean, my sister got canned, so she left town."

"Right . . ." Sandrine had heard this. The paper mill in Madawaska had restructured and Jimmy's sister had been laid off, but, fortunately, she had found work at a plant in Pennsylvania that made toilet paper out of recycled coffee cups.

"And Mom and Dad retired and headed south."

"Yeah, I heard that."

"Vermont."

"Oh."

"Yeah, winters there are a lot easier."

"Oh."

"Yeah, and then Spot went and died on me."

"Oh, Jimmy, I didn't know that." For the first time, Sandrine forgot how awful she felt about seeing Jimmy and became genuinely concerned for him. And genuinely sad for him. Because Spot was the fish Sandrine had gotten Jimmy at the pet store in Edmundston, New Brunswick, to celebrate their one-month anniversary. And Jimmy loved that fish.

"Yeah. He was old, it was his time." Jimmy was almost crying—partly for Spot, but mostly because he was so sad about losing Sandrine.

"I'm sorry, Jimmy." Sandrine was overwhelmed by how sad Jimmy was. Over a fish.

"He was a good fish, though," added Jimmy. And then a couple of tears started to make their way out of his eyes, and they rolled down his cheeks. And Jimmy brushed them away—but not before Sandrine saw that he was crying. And she got extremely uncomfortable, like most people do when men like Jimmy cry. "But—so," continued Jimmy, "like I said, I really don't have anybody anymore."

Sandrine said she was sorry again.

And Jimmy said thanks. And looked up at her. And Sandrine saw the sweet guy she almost fell in love with. And Jimmy saw her see that guy. And saw his chance to get her back—and took it. "So, listen," he said, "I was wonderin': Would you like to come over?"

"Huh?" Sandrine was stunned by the question, because that was the last thing in the world she wanted to do.

"It'd be fun!"

"Oh, no—"

"Yeah! We could catch up, hang out?"

"Jimmy—"

Sandrine was about to say no again when the waitress was suddenly at their table again. "So, I forgot to tell ya, don't forget! Friday night special at the Moose Paddy: Drink free if you're sad. So if you're sad, or if you two are ready for another coupla Buds or somethin', let me know, all right?"

Jimmy said, "All right!" at the same time that Sandrine said, "We're good, thanks!" And the waitress only heard Sandrine and hustled away, calling, "Okay!"

Sandrine watched the waitress leave. And Jimmy watched Sandrine watch the waitress leave. And when Sandrine turned back to Jimmy, she was met with Jimmy's hopeful mug and a question. "So . . . what do you say?"

"Huh?—Oh, um—"

"You wanna come over, for fun?"

"No, Jimmy. I can't. I can't. I really gotta get back with the girls."

"Naw—"

"Yeah, Jimmy, yeah," she said, standing. "I gotta. 'Cause, see . . ." She blew air out through her cheeks as if she was about to do something really difficult, like deadlift a lot of weight. "Oh, gosh." She laughed a little and then continued. "I've been meanin' to tell you this for a while . . ." And she looked her ex-boyfriend right in the eye and confessed, "There's a guy, Jimmy. I've got a guy."

Jimmy felt like he was going to throw up. Or pass out. Or both.

He had totally forgotten to consider the fact that Sandrine might have met someone else.

"Oh," he said, trying not to let on how completely devastated he was.

Sandrine nodded apologetically. And she had much more to say. But she couldn't say it. Because she didn't want to hurt Jimmy any more than she felt like she already had.

And Jimmy didn't want to let Sandrine know how hurt he was by this news. So he stepped up and forced himself to handle it like a champ.

"Well . . . good for you," he said, mustering a smile, and quoting Mrs. Roy. "Gettin' yourself out there again. Movin' on."

Sandrine said, "Yeah." And almost left it at that. But that wouldn't have been the whole truth. And she needed to tell him the whole truth.

So she did.

"Um—Jimmy," she began gently. And then she paused and braced herself for what his response would be to what she was about to tell him. "It's actually more than me just gettin' myself out there and movin' on. Um . . . this is my . . ." She looked toward the front of the Moose Paddy and then back to Jimmy, and then finally came out with it. "This is my bachelorette party." She smiled and shrugged. And gestured toward the front. And Jimmy didn't seem to be comprehending. So she added, "I'm gettin' married."

The words hit Jimmy like a slow-motion left hook to the face. And a right jab to the gut.

Sandrine smiled weakly and shrugged apologetically.

And then she showed Jimmy her engagement ring.

Seeing the ring hit Jimmy like a slow-motion *right* hook to the face. And a *left* jab to the gut.

And he felt like he was falling. Even though he was sitting.

And felt again like he was going to pass out.

Or throw up.

Or both.

And he looked so sad—like he was never going to feel any kind of happiness again. Ever.

And Sandrine couldn't bear to see him looking so sad. That's why she had left Jimmy by slipping away in the middle of the night. It's really hard to tell someone who loves you that you don't love them back. It's easier to just disappear. So you don't have to see their sadness. So that's what she did. It was her way.

And it was a bad way to be.

"Wow," said Jimmy, looking like he was going to cry again when he surprised himself—and Sandrine—and smiled and said, "Well, that's great! Congratulations."

"Thanks." Sandrine smiled with all her teeth. And Jimmy smiled back. And then his smile faded. And he just stared at Sandrine. And realized something. And said, "I thought you said you weren't gonna do that. Get married. Thought it wasn't for you, you told me."

Sandrine stopped smiling and looked at the floor. And then looked at Jimmy and smiled again apologetically. And then shrugged her shoulders. And stopped smiling again. And looked at the floor again.

Jimmy got the message. "Guess it just wasn't for you . . . with me."

And then Jimmy didn't say anything for a while.

And Sandrine didn't say anything for a while.

And then Jimmy almost spiraled into a deep despair.

And he almost really let Sandrine have it for having disappeared on him.

And he thought about going up to the front and ruining her bachelorette party.

And then he thought about just leaving.

But he didn't do any of those things. Instead he made like he was happy for Sandrine and all her good news and asked, "So who's the lucky guy?"

Sandrine was aware that Jimmy was taking the high road and appreciated his kindness. "Um . . . Martin LaFerriere." She smiled gleefully, because Martin made her so happy. "Do you know him? The, uh—"

"The game warden?"

"Yeah."

"From Ashland?"

"Yeah!" Sandrine's smile got bigger.

"Wow!"

"Yeah!"

"Well, that's . . . awesome!" cheered Jimmy, through slightly gritted teeth. "He's . . . *awesome!*"

And Martin *was* awesome. Jimmy had *some* looks. But Martin had all of them. He was tall. And his torso was shaped like a triangle. And his jaw was square. He actually looked like a superhero. Heck, he was a superhero. Because game wardens are superheroes. They do things like fight forest fires and save lives and stop drug trafficking into and out of Canada and make sure people treat the wilderness well. And come to the rescue when the wilderness doesn't treat people well.

Sandrine agreed with Jimmy. "Yeah. He is. He's pretty awesome," she said, beaming.

"I mean, he's a *legend*!" enthused Jimmy.

Martin LaFerriere *was* a legend. Last summer he made all the local papers—and even the national news—when he rescued a hiker who had gotten lost on Shepalojo Mountain. At night. During the forest fire.

"If you're lost on a mountain in Maine, he's the guy you want lookin' for ya." Jimmy was working way too hard to disguise his jealousy as he praised the guy that was going to be Sandrine's husband.

"Yeah . . ." Sandrine wondered if Jimmy was okay, because he was looking maniacal again—because he was smiling so hard—because he didn't want Sandrine to be able to tell how badly he was hurting.

Because he wanted to be the one who was about to be Sandrine's husband.

He got even more animated as he extolled Martin's virtues. "I mean, if you're lost out there in this big bad northern world, Martin LaFerriere's the guy you want to have go out there and find you."

"Yeah," said Sandrine uneasily.

"And he found . . . you." And Jimmy wasn't covering up his sadness anymore.

And Sandrine felt terrible. "Yeah," she said, looking down at the floor.

And then neither of them said anything.

A country version of an old song about life in a northern town was playing on the jukebox. Jimmy started thinking about how he had lived his whole life in a northern non-town. And then he thought about how he'd probably die there, too. And wondered if he was going to die there alone. He suddenly got so scared of being alone that he didn't hear Sandrine say that she was sorry that she had never told him about her and Martin.

"Jimmy?"

"Huh?"

"I said I'm sorry I never told you. About me and Martin."

Jimmy wanted to say it was okay and not to worry about it, but he couldn't, because it wasn't okay, and he wanted her to worry about it. So he didn't say anything. Which put the burden on her to figure out what to say next.

"I actually thought you would have known, I thought you woulda heard. About Martin and me."

"How would I have heard?" asked Jimmy.

"Well, you know, people talk."

"Not about things they know you don't wanna hear, they don't. And that's not somethin' I woulda wanted to hear."

Sandrine couldn't deny that.

And Jimmy and Sandrine didn't say anything for a while.

And then Jimmy realized that he had lost Sandrine. To Martin. And decided to be gracious in defeat. And took a deep breath. And held it for a moment. And finally said, "Well . . . congratulations."

"Thanks, Jimmy." The thanks were sincere, because the congratulations were sincere.

And then Jimmy and Sandrine didn't say anything for a while.

And then Sandrine decided that it was time for her to say goodbye and go back to her bachelorette party. And she was about to do so when Jimmy inhaled sharply—as if he had just been startled awake—and asked, "So when's the big event?" He genuinely seemed to want to celebrate his ex-girlfriend's good fortune.

"Um . . . tomorrow!" replied Sandrine, wincing apologetically.

The word *tomorrow* hit Jimmy like another punch—to the gut. And he couldn't breathe for a second. And when he could breathe again, he half stated and half asked, "Really."

"Yup." Sandrine smiled sheepishly.

"Wow."

"Yup." Sandrine shrugged.

"Wow," said Jimmy again, because he couldn't come up with anything else to say.

And he stared at his beer bottle for a moment.

And Sandrine watched Jimmy stare at his bottle. And felt bad for him. And realized how wrong she had done him.

And then Jimmy gathered up all his gumption and said, "Well, then . . ." And he downed his beer, and then stood up and hollered to the waitress, who had said she would be somewhere up front. "HEY!"

He raised his right arm and waved to get her attention. Which was going to be difficult, because the dance floor was filling up. Someone had just put on a rap song about big butts.

"Jimmy! Shh!" Sandrine tried to make herself disappear, because she didn't want anyone to see her with him. "What are you doing?" she whispered intensely, and she got up and stood in front of him to block him from view of the girls who were at her bachelorette party.

"Gettin' our waitress. She said holler if you need anything, so I'm hollerin'," explained Jimmy matter-of-factly, unaware—or maybe not caring—that he was making Sandrine uncomfortable.

"HEY!" he yelled again, and then asked Sandrine, "What's her name?"

"I don't know—Jimmy, what are you doing?"

"We gotta celebrate! You got *found*! By Martin La-friggin'-Ferriere! He's . . . quite a guy." Jimmy paused and looked Sandrine dead in the eye and said in all earnestness, "And so are you. I mean—you're quite a girl. Or—person. Just—you're awesome is all I'm tryin' to say."

Sandrine looked down and was about to say that she wasn't awesome, because an awesome person doesn't leave a guy the way she had left Jimmy, but, before she could, Jimmy was calling to the waitress again. "HEY!" he hollered, raising his right arm and waving to the waitress.

As he did so, his unbuttoned shirtsleeve slid down his arm enough to reveal some kind of marking on the inside of his forearm.

Sandrine was trying to shush Jimmy and had looked toward the front to make sure no one in her bachelorette party was seeing her with her ex.

When she turned back to tell Jimmy that she didn't want to celebrate with him, she noticed the marking on his arm. It looked like a tattoo.

"Hey, Jimmy—whoa! What's that?" Sandrine was pointing to—and almost touching—the marking on his arm.

"What?" Jimmy looked to where she was pointing and realized that the tattoo he had gotten after Sandrine disappeared on him had been revealed.

"*That!*"

"Oh . . ." Jimmy quickly dropped his arm, pulled the sleeve of his blue work shirt down to cover up what he didn't want Sandrine to see, and tried to button the cuff. "Nothin'. Just—a tattoo."

"What?!?" she cried, totally intrigued.

"A tattoo." Jimmy tried to get back on task and hollered to the waitress, waving with his other hand. "HEY!"

"No way!" said Sandrine. Jimmy wasn't the kind of guy who she ever imagined would get a tattoo. "When did you get that?!?"

"Um . . . after you left," said Jimmy, and he hollered to the waitress again to try to deflect attention from the skin art on the inside of his forearm. "HEY!" he hollered. But the Moose Paddy was busy and the song about the guy who likes big butts was playing, so the waitress probably couldn't hear him—and was nowhere to be found.

"Well—what's it of, what's it say?" asked Sandrine, trying to grab Jimmy's tattooed forearm.

"Nothin', nothin' . . ." Jimmy really didn't want to talk about his tattoo or let Sandrine see it, so he pressed his right arm close against his body, holding tight to the cuff of his sleeve, and he waved to the waitress with his left hand again. "HEY!" he hollered, but, as he did so, Sandrine grabbed hold of Jimmy's right arm and tried to pry it away from his body. Jimmy resisted. "No, don't—"

"Jimmy! Come on! I wanna see your tattoo!"

Jimmy realized there was no way out, so he gave in and let Sandrine take his arm, and Sandrine pushed his sleeve up and positioned it—

and herself—so she could see what the tattoo was. And she saw that it was an assemblage of letters. In Old English-style font:

𝔙𝔦𝔩𝔩𝔦𝔞𝔫

"Villian," read Sandrine.

"Villain," Jimmy quickly corrected. But Sandrine didn't really hear him. Because she was staring at the tattoo and reading it again to herself.

"Who's Villian?" asked Sandrine earnestly.

Jimmy shook his arm free of Sandrine's grasp and pulled his sleeve down, covering the tattoo, and testily corrected her: "Villain." And realized that he was going to have to explain his tattoo. And that was the last thing in the world he wanted to do.

"Huh?" asked Sandrine, looking for clarification.

"Villain. It's supposed to say 'Villain.'"

"Well, it doesn't say 'Villain.' It says 'Villian.'"

"I know. I spelled it wrong—"

"What?"

"*They* spelled it wrong."

This wasn't quite true. Jimmy had gone to Inkredible Tattoos in Caribou not long after Sandrine had disappeared on him. And he had brought Liv, one of the tattoo artists there, a printed image of what he wanted his tattoo to be.

And the image was supposed to be the word "Villain" in an Old English font. But—the printed image Jimmy had presented to Liv was spelled wrong. Because Jimmy had spelled it wrong when he had typed it up. And instead of "Villain," it read, "Villian."

But Jimmy's eye corrected the mistake every time he read it, so he only ever saw "Villain."

But Liv saw "Villian." And figured it was the name of someone who was very special to Jimmy. And she showed the image on the printout to him to make sure it was what he wanted his tattoo to be.

And Jimmy confirmed that it was.

Because his eyes only ever saw "Villain," and not "Villian."

So Liv proceeded to emblazon "Villian" on the inside of his right forearm.

And, a couple of hours later, she was bandaging Jimmy up. And after giving him instructions on post-tattoo care, she asked, "So, who's Villian?"

Jimmy looked confused. "Huh?" he asked.

"Who's Villian?" Liv repeated, pointing to her handiwork—which was covered by the bandage.

"Huh?" Jimmy repeated.

"Villian—your tattoo—who is she?" Liv asked again, handing him the printout he had given her.

Jimmy took the printout. And finally saw what was actually on it: "Villian."

And he turned the color people turn when they're about to puke.

"You okay, pal?" asked Liv.

"Yeah . . ." Jimmy broke into a cold sweat.

"So, who is she?" asked Liv, all smiles.

Jimmy managed to lie to cover for his mistake. "She's . . . she's my girl."

"I figured." Liv smiled. "That's sweet. I like her name."

Jimmy smiled and nodded and got all hot and embarrassed.

"You must really love her—to get a tattoo of her name!"

"Yeah." Jimmy was drowning in embarrassment.

"You're all embarrassed. So cute!"

"Oh. Yeah."

Jimmy was embarrassed. Not because he loved a girl so much that he had gotten a tattoo of her name on his arm, but because he had spelled the word he wanted to get tattooed on his arm—wrong.

And now he was embarrassed all over again, because Sandrine had spotted his misspelled tattoo and was asking, "Who spelled it wrong?!"

"The girl who did my tattoo," lied Jimmy.

"Well," Sandrine scoffed, "you shoulda made her fix it!"

"Yeah."

Sandrine could not believe what Jimmy had done to himself. And had to ask, "Jimmy, why did you want a tattoo that says 'Villain'?"

Jimmy didn't really want to answer, because the song about the guy who liked big butts had ended and there was no music playing, so the bar seemed quiet, and he worried that people might hear their conversation—even though the place was still jumping and no one would have heard them over all the chatter of the Moose Paddy patrons. So he just shrugged and said evasively, "'Cause."

Jimmy's evasion made Sandrine hungrier for an answer. "'Cause *why*?"

"Just 'cause," said Jimmy, turning away from Sandrine.

"Just 'cause *why*?"

"Just 'cause . . ." Jimmy looked like he was gonna cry again, but he didn't, and finally confessed. "'Cause when a guy's got a girl like you . . . well, I just think that losin' a girl like you, drivin' a girl like you away—"

"Jimmy, you didn't drive me away."

"Well, I musta done somethin'! 'Cause you just disappeared on me." Jimmy wasn't crying, but it seemed like he was. "And whatever I did to drive you away—that's a crime. And it should be punished. So I punished myself. I marked myself a villain so girls would stay away. So I'd never have to go through what I went through with you. Again."

Sandrine was still. And silent.

She knew she had done Jimmy wrong.

But she didn't realize what that wrong had done to him.

Suddenly, Jimmy desperately asked, "Can I kiss you?"

Sandrine winced and said, "No." And then looked at the floor.

And Jimmy looked at the floor, too.

And there Jimmy and Sandrine stood, looking at the floor.

And they didn't say anything for a while. And felt like they were standing in silence even though people were chattering and laughing and billiard balls were clattering and glasses were clinking.

And then Sandrine looked around her to see who might see what she was about to do. And when she felt like no one was watching, she leaned in and tenderly kissed Jimmy on the cheek.

She didn't quite know why she had felt the need to do so. Maybe it was the only way she knew how to apologize. Or maybe it was her way of thanking him for letting her go—with his blessing.

Whatever it was—she immediately wished she hadn't done it. Because Jimmy tried to turn Sandrine's kiss on the cheek into a kiss on the mouth, and Sandrine pulled away and said, "Hey!" to let him know he was out of line.

"Sorry." And Jimmy just stood there in the mess he'd made.

And then an old pop song about girls wanting to have fun started playing on the jukebox. And a bunch of girls from the bachelorette party whooped it up on the dance floor, hopping and bopping and singing along.

And then Sandrine realized she needed to get back to them, and she stroked Jimmy's tattooed forearm and said, "You can get that undone, you know."

"Yeah . . ." But the closest tattoo-removal places were one hundred sixty-four miles southeast in Fredericton, New Brunswick. Or in Bangor—which was one hundred sixty-nine miles south. And Jimmy would have a hard time finding the time to go to either place, because work was too busy.

"Oh," said Sandrine. And she felt terrible that she had made Jimmy want to mark himself a villain—because of her. She had no idea that she had hurt him as much as she had when she disappeared on him. Maybe because she didn't think much of herself when she was dating Jimmy. And people who don't think much of themselves are surprised by the damage they can do to people who think the world of them.

But on the Friday night when all the extraordinary things did or didn't happen, Sandrine realized the damage she had done. And she apologized to him for disappearing on him.

Finally.

"Jimmy, what I did—the way I left—was just . . . it was wrong. And I'm sorry. I'm so sorry. I just never knew how to tell you that I wanted out. And—it wasn't you. It wasn't anything you did. I just didn't love you like I think you loved me. And that's just . . . not fair. So I just left. And I figured I'd explain why someday. And I never did. And I know that that's an *awful* thing I did. But I did it. And I'm really sorry. And . . . I know that saying I'm sorry isn't gonna make it right. But it's all I can do, so . . . I'm sorry." And Sandrine shrugged her shoulders. Because that was all she could say.

Jimmy didn't say anything.

And Sandrine didn't know if the apology had been accepted.

And it hadn't been. At first. Because what Sandrine had done was cruel. Leaving someone with no explanation is easy for the leaver. And torture for the one who's been left. Because all the one who's been left can do is wonder what happened. And so the one who's been left throws himself into his work. And goes a little mad. And gets really sad.

Sandrine didn't know what to do. Jimmy looked so sad. And kind of mad. And figured that it didn't matter if her apology was accepted or not. She didn't really deserve for it to be accepted. And so she decided the best thing she could do was leave. And she was about to say goodbye to Jimmy when he suddenly hugged her.

And Sandrine felt him accepting her apology with that hug.

And she felt him thanking her for finally explaining why she had disappeared on him with that hug. Even though he thought the explanation was a lousy one.

And she felt him saying goodbye with that hug.

And she returned the hug so she could say goodbye, too.

And Jimmy received the hug.

And they finally got to say goodbye.

And break up.

Officially.

Jimmy slowly pulled away and held Sandrine by the shoulders and said, "Thanks." The thanks were for the apology. And for the explanation. As belated as they were, they were exactly what Jimmy needed.

Because now he was free from wondering about what had gone wrong with Sandrine.

And he could move on.

And he let go of Sandrine. And let his hands fall to his sides. And Sandrine said, "You're welcome." And she waited to see if he had anything else to say. And he didn't. So she said, "Bye, Jimmy."

And Jimmy said, "Bye."

And they felt like it would probably be a good long while before they talked again. If they ever talked again. And Jimmy ached. And Sandrine felt relief. And she turned and started to go. She had taken only a couple of steps when Jimmy called to her. "Hey!"

Sandrine stopped and turned back to Jimmy.

And he said, "I'm glad you got found."

It took Sandrine a second to understand what Jimmy was saying. And when she did, she said, "Thanks, Jimmy." And laughed at the weird congratulations or blessing or whatever it was. "I am, too," she said. And then she almost turned to go but stopped and said, "I hope you get found, too." And then she shrugged and realized how corny that sounded. And she tried to make it less corny by qualifying it with, "If that's something you want."

Jimmy didn't know if he wanted to get found.

But he did know that he still wanted her.

But he wasn't ever going to have her, so he needed to get over that.

He just didn't know how he was going to do that.

Sandrine slowly turned and headed toward the front of the Moose Paddy and out onto the dance floor to be with the girls who had thrown her her bachelorette party.

And Jimmy was so sad. Because all that had been lost had been found—but lost again. For good.

Jimmy saw the girls welcome Sandrine back with a joyful roar. And they all hopped and bopped to the song about girls wanting to have fun and made Sandrine drink something purplish-pink. And she did. And the girls cheered. Jimmy witnessed all this joy from afar. And it washed over him and made him feel about as joyless as he had ever felt.

Then he sat back down in his chair and was about to finish his Bud when the waitress returned and said, "Hey! Sorry! Somebody said you were wavin' me down!" She was a bit out of breath. "I didn't see you," she continued, a little frazzled, "but it's so busy! Friday night! Whew!" Another round of joyful whoops emanated from the bachelorette party as the song about girls wanting to have fun faded out, replaced by a song about a guy who said he had friends in low places.

"God. That bachelorette party!" moaned the waitress, looking back at the girls. "Those *girls*! Good thing it's not 'Drink free if you're glad,' 'cause those girls are wicked glad." The waitress laughed and looked off toward the dance floor and marveled at all that gladness those girls were feeling. And she turned to Jimmy and cheered, "Good for them, huh?! Everybody oughta be glad like that, right?"

And Jimmy and the waitress watched the revelers swaying to the song about the guy who has friends in low places, and they both wondered if they'd ever be glad like that again in their lives.

And then the waitress smiled and turned back to Jimmy and got back to work. "Anyway—sorry if I forgot about ya for a second. Hoo—wee! I had to fight my way through to find ya again, way back here! But I did it! I found ya! So, what do you need? What can I do ya for?" She clapped her hands together once and put them on her hips, ready for whatever Jimmy might need her to get or do for him.

But Jimmy wasn't listening to her. He was watching Sandrine, the happy bride-to-be, and her girls, dancing and singing about having friends in low places.

He was happy for her. Happy she had found someone.

But also so sad. Because he was wondering if he'd ever find someone.

There weren't many single women his age in Almost.

Maybe he'd just wait till the first wave of divorces hit his age group.

It'd be comin' up soon, he thought.

And then he scolded himself for getting so sour.

And then his face just looked like pain as he gazed at Sandrine on the dance floor.

And his eyes started to look like tears were about to fall out of them.

And the waitress followed Jimmy's gaze. And saw all the girls dancing around Sandrine.

And she saw one of them put a tiara on her head.

And the waitress put two and two together and started to realize that the woman who she thought at first was Jimmy's date wasn't Jimmy's date at all.

She was the bachelorette.

And Jimmy wasn't her guy.

The waitress inhaled sharply as she understood what was going on and didn't breathe for a second as she tried to figure out what to do. "Oh, pal . . ." She finally exhaled. "Um . . . Oh, God. I am *so* sorry."

She desperately tried to figure out how to help Jimmy, because he needed help. Bad. "Oh, boy." She sat in the chair that Sandrine had been sitting in and tried to make the best of the terrible situation. "Um . . . Well, remember, like I said, Moose Paddy special: Drinks are free if you're sad. Okay? Just tell me you're sad, and you'll drink free."

Jimmy may have heard the offer. But he didn't respond. He just continued to let all the joy from the bachelorette party up front wash over him and turn into sorrow.

The waitress continued. "Just say the word. And you'll drink free. Let me know. 'Cause I know from sad, and you're lookin' pretty sad."

And Jimmy *was* lookin' pretty sad.

Tears were falling out of his eyes.

And snot was falling out of his nose.

But he didn't realize either of those things were happening.

The waitress slapped some napkins in Jimmy's hand, hoping he'd wipe his nose, and said, "Okay, well . . . I gotta get back to work, so . . ." She paused and gave him a chance to tell her that he wanted to drink for free. But Jimmy didn't take the chance. "Okay," she said, giving up on her sad customer. "Well, my name's Villian, if you need anything. Just ask for Villian."

And then she turned and left.

And Jimmy stopped breathing. And felt that strange lightness he had felt earlier—when he was about to walk into the Moose Paddy. And it made him feel like he had the glow of a thousand fired-up pellet stoves inside him. And like he had a thousand butterflies in his stomach. And he felt like he was levitating—even though he wasn't.

He couldn't believe what he'd just heard.

Had the waitress just said that her name was Villian?

Jimmy slowly lifted his head, dumbfounded, and watched the waitress walk away and called after her. "Villian?"

The waitress stopped and turned.

"Yeah?" she asked as she hustled back to Jimmy—who was just staring at her. "What's up?" she asked.

Jimmy continued to stare at the waitress.

"You okay, pal?"

"Yeah. I would just like . . . another Bud. That I'll pay for. Because I'm not sad."

"All right." Villian smiled and turned and was about to go get Jimmy another Bud.

"In fact I'm really glad right now!" called Jimmy.

"Okay," said Villian, turning back to the guy with the hangdog eyes. And then she smiled and turned and made her way back to the front of the bar.

And Jimmy hollered to her again. "Villian!!!"

Villian stopped and turned to Jimmy. "What?!?" she asked, a little exasperated as she made her way back to him.

"I've just . . . I've never seen you. Before. Around."

"Well, I just moved here. Couple weeks ago."

"Oh." Almost wasn't a place people moved to. It was a place people left. But Villian had read in a Maine lifestyle magazine that Aroostook County was one of the best places for a fresh start. And she needed a fresh start.

Villian turned and went to get Jimmy his Bud, but as she did so, Jimmy stopped her again and yelled, "Villian!"

Villian stopped. Again. She was getting annoyed. "Dude, I'm workin' here. What?!?"

"I'm just . . . I'm glad you found me."

Villian screwed up her face and wondered if this "I'm glad you found me" business was some sort of newfangled pickup line. Half-charmed, she said, "All right." And then she headed to the bar.

As she did, she mumbled, "I'm glad you found me," to herself. And really hoped it was a pickup line.

And then she felt a strange lightness inside her. It felt like a spark. And a tingle. And gave her a bounce in her step. And it took her breath away.

But she soon got herself breathing again and went to get Jimmy another Bud.

Jimmy watched Villian head toward the bar.

And then he looked down at his "Villian" tattoo.

And put his hand on it.

And squeezed it.

And tried to make sense of what had just happened.

And then stopped trying—because he couldn't make sense of it.

And he felt like something great was about to happen—extraordinary even.

Which is scary for someone who isn't used to having extraordinary things happen to them.

Because what if it doesn't happen?

6

As Ginette made her way past the Moose Paddy, she tried to ignore the guy and the girl who were laughing and hugging and kissing in the parking lot.

But she couldn't.

And she watched them make their way toward the Moose Paddy's entrance. They were holding each other close. And it looked like the guy was saying something in the girl's ear.

Ginette bet that the guy wasn't saying to the girl that, even though they were about as close to one another as they could possibly have been, they were actually about as far away from each other as they could possibly be.

And she continued on her way and wondered why Pete had shared his asinine theory on what it means to be close—at such an inopportune time.

And she was happy to be leaving the theory behind—but not the theorist.

At ten past eight, Ginette found herself approaching the Rec Center, which was about a quarter of a mile down the road from the Moose

Paddy. An A-frame sign illuminated by a clamp light was perched on a snowbank in front of the one-story brick building. It announced:

Country Swing!

Tonite!

5 bucks!

It seemed to Ginette that there was a whole lot of dancing going on in Almost on the night when all the extraordinary things did or didn't happen. And that irked her. Because she wished that she and Pete were at Country Swing, dancing.

But they weren't.

But Justin Legassie and Michelle Blackmore were—or they were about to be—or so they thought.

Michelle had just pulled her old black Buick LeSabre into the Rec Center parking lot. Because Justin had said that he wanted to go dancing. And he never thought he'd go dancing with Michelle again. Maybe because he never really thought he'd see her again. Because when he left Almost a couple of years ago, he had never planned on coming back.

But his uncle Clair had died a couple of days ago. And his uncle Clair and his aunt Belinda had raised him. And Justin loved his uncle Clair more than anyone in the world. So he was back in Almost for his funeral.

A couple of hours ago, going dancing was the last thing Justin thought he'd be doing on that Friday night when all the extraordinary things did or didn't happen. He had been stretched out on the couch in the living room, sometimes staring up at the vaulted ceiling of his aunt's A-frame house counting pine knots, and sometimes staring at his uncle's big plaid puffy chair, and sometime staring at his uncle's guitar, which was resting on its stand in the corner next to the TV—and which was the guitar Uncle Clair had taught him to play on.

Justin was now the guitarist in a band in Portland. And they were starting to do really well. The *Portland Press Herald* had done a big feature on them last fall.

"Justy?" Aunt Belinda was calling to Justin from the kitchen.

"Yeah?"

"Father Tom's gonna be coming over soon to talk about funeral stuff. Just so you know."

"Kay."

Headlights from a car that had pulled into Aunt Belinda's driveway flashed across the living room.

"I think he's here!" called Justin. And he hopped off the couch and made his way to his room so he wouldn't have to see Father Tom. Who was a good enough guy. Justin just didn't want to see him right then. He'd see him tomorrow at the funeral.

He heard a knock on the back door. And he heard Aunt Belinda answer. "Oh! Hey, kiddo!"

And he heard a voice say, "Hi, Aunt B," in that way people do when they're greeting someone who's lost a loved one.

Justin froze. The voice was Michelle's. And he hadn't seen her or been in touch with her since he left Almost. And not because she hadn't tried to see him or be in touch with him.

He heard Michelle say that she was sorry about Uncle Clair—and that she had brought over a nine-layer casserole.

"Ooh!" gushed Aunt Belinda.

Justin wondered what the nine layers of a nine-layer casserole were.

"Justy!" called Aunt Belinda. "Michelle's here! Come say hi!" And then she asked Michelle, "Can I freeze this?"

"Yeah," said Michelle.

"Great. I'm gonna put it out on the porch." Aunt Belinda brought the nine-layer casserole out onto the porch, where it joined a bevy of other casseroles and would be preserved by the cold for future consumption. (Porches become freezers in northern Maine in the winter.)

Justin had shuffled down the hall into the kitchen and said, "Hey."

Michelle looked even bigger than he remembered. She had been six feet tall since she was thirteen. But she had never been one of those lanky tall people. She had always been sturdy. But she was sturdier now.

"Hi," said Michelle. Justin looked skinnier than she remembered. And he probably was. Because he wanted to be. Being skinny made him feel powerful. So he smoked a lot and ate only a little.

Michelle bet she weighed close to twice what he did now. And she started to feel bad about her size, like she used to. But then remembered that she had found someone who liked her size. And she stopped feeling bad about herself.

"How ya doin'?" asked Michelle—and she immediately regretted asking the question, because nobody who's just lost someone they love is doing okay. And she said, "Sorry," meaning she was sorry that she had asked the question—and that she was sorry for his loss. "Listen," she almost whispered, "can we go somewhere? Talk?"

"Um—" Justin didn't want to go anywhere with Michelle. And he didn't really want to talk to her.

"I just wanna—" Michelle was about to tell Justin that she had something she wanted to tell him. But she wasn't able to tell him, because Aunt Belinda was returning from the porch. So she couldn't tell him.

"So, Michelle: love your haircut!"

"Yeah. I chopped it off."

"Cute! You see this one's hair?"

Aunt Belinda pulled her nephew's hood back and revealed his long black hair. It had a streak of bright blue in it.

"Nice," laughed Michelle. She had seen pictures of him since he had left, so she wasn't surprised by his black—and blue—hair.

"It is, isn't it?" asked Aunt Belinda. She genuinely liked Justin's hair.

"Yeah!"

"So, listen," said Aunt Belinda, "I hate to do this to you two, but if you wanna hang out, you can't do it here, 'cause Father Tom's comin' by to go over some funeral stuff with me for tomorrow, so why don't you get outta here and go do somethin' fun?"

"Huh?" asked Justin, wondering why his aunt would have wanted them to go do something fun the night before his uncle's funeral.

"For your uncle Clair," explained Aunt Belinda. "It'd make him so happy to know you two were out havin' fun somewhere the night before his funeral."

This was hard to deny. Uncle Clair was fun. And wanted people to have fun. And he wouldn't have wanted people to stop having fun just because he was dead. But Justin didn't feel like—and Michelle didn't feel right about—going out and doing something fun the night before his funeral.

But before they could say so, Aunt Belinda was giving Justin his uncle Clair's old parka. "So get goin'. And make sure he wears this, Michelle. He only had his hoodie on when I picked him up at the bus stop in Caribou. Warm enough for Portland, maybe, but not here."

"I'll make sure," said Michelle.

"I'll wear it," said Justin simultaneously, irked that Michelle and Aunt Belinda were talking about him like he wasn't there. He grabbed the parka and pulled it on. It smelled like Uncle Clair. And made him look tiny because Uncle Clair was a much larger man than he was. Just about all men were.

"Thank you," said Aunt Belinda. "Now go have fun. For your uncle Clair. Please." And she grabbed her purse and slid Justin a twenty to help them have fun and patted the old friends on the backs and practically pushed them out the back door and onto the porch and closed the door behind them.

And the next thing they knew, Michelle and Justin were on the porch, standing among all the casseroles, and taking them—and the cold, quiet northern Maine night—in. And then Michelle sighed and shrugged. "So, I guess we're gonna go have some fun tonight, huh?" And then she laughed. She was trying to make the best of an awkward situation. She always made the best of awkward situations.

"I guess." Justin shrugged back.

Justin and Michelle wondered why Aunt Belinda was so insistent that they go out and have some fun. They didn't know that she wanted Justin gone so she could have some time to be sad by herself. She had been putting on a brave face because she was more worried about her nephew than she usually was. Because he seemed sad— and not just because his uncle Clair had died. This was a different, deeper sadness. And she hoped that Michelle might be able to help him through it. Because Michelle had known him since he was a kid. And people who knew you when you were a kid remind you what you used to be. And not what you've become. And Justin needed to remember what he used to be. Because he used to be fun. And full of joy.

And now he wasn't.

Justin and Michelle made their way to Michelle's LeSabre. They had spent a lot of time in that car.

When Justin got in the old sedan, he was met with the royal pine smell from the little tree air freshener hanging from the rearview mirror. He hadn't smelled that smell since the last time he was in the LeSabre two and a half years ago.

Being in that car made him feel safe. And like he belonged. And he didn't feel like he belonged many places.

Michelle started the car. "So what are we doin'? For 'fun'?" she asked, quoting Aunt Belinda.

"I don't know." Justin had been so focused on his music and his band that he didn't have much time for fun. So he didn't do much for fun. And now he was wondering if he even knew how to have fun anymore. "You tell me."

"I don't know." She thought for a second and then offered, "Tool around? See where we end up?"

"Tooling around" was one of the most popular pastimes for young people in northern Maine. Especially in winter. Because cars were warm—and, more important, private. The things that get talked about in cars are honest and true. Maybe because the things that are said in cars can't escape into the world and be heard by anyone else. So what's said in cars can only be known by the people in the car.

And the thing that Michelle wanted to tell Justin was one of the things that was best said in the car. Because it was something she hadn't told anybody yet. And it was something she didn't want anybody else to know yet.

And Justin said okay to tooling around. Because it would give her a chance to talk to him. And he felt like he owed her a chance to talk to him. Because he hadn't let her since he left.

And Michelle pulled out of Aunt Belinda's driveway and turned right and headed east on the Road to Somewhere. Because it was much more likely that they'd find some fun if they headed toward somewhere instead of toward nowhere.

They passed Echo Lake, where they used to go skating and pretend they were an Olympic ice dancing team.

Then they passed the Rec Center, where they danced together at the talent show when they were thirteen and stunned the crowd with their skill. A lot of people thought they should have won the talent show that year. But they got disqualified, because one of the judges didn't like the way they danced.

Justin's dad didn't like the way they danced, either.

He didn't think it was right, the way Justin and Michelle danced.

And on the way home from the talent show, he told his son he didn't want him to dance anymore—with her. Or with anyone. And he said that it was time he started spending time with boys and doing the things boys ought to be doing. Like playing soccer and basketball and going hunting and fishing.

But Justin didn't like doing the things that his dad thought boys ought to be doing. And his dad hated him for it. And eventually kicked him out of the house. And Justin's mom sent him to live with her sister, Belinda, and her husband, Clair. Which turned out to be the best thing that could have happened, because Aunt Belinda and Uncle Clair encouraged Justin to keep dancing. With Michelle. Or with anybody he wanted to.

Unfortunately, Justin no longer wanted anything to do with dancing when he started living with Aunt Belinda and Uncle Clair—because it reminded him of what his dad made him feel like for liking dancing.

But his uncle Clair told him there were other ways to dance. And he taught him how to play the guitar. Which was like dancing—but with the fingers instead of the feet. And Justin was grateful that

Uncle Clair had introduced him to music. It gave him purpose. And saved his life.

In a couple of minutes, they passed the Rec Center. Michelle saw the big lit-up A-frame sign that was perched on the snowbank.

COUNTRY SWING!

TONITE!

5 BUCKS!

And she thought that maybe they could go dancing—that maybe that could be the fun thing they did. The last time they had danced was when they were kids. And Michelle wanted to feel like a kid again. Because she was feeling more like a grown-up than she had ever felt.

But then she realized that Justin probably wouldn't want to go dancing, what with his uncle's funeral being the next morning.

So she kept driving.

And they passed the Moose Paddy.

And Ma Dudley's.

And St. Mary's Church.

And the Old Gallagher Potato Farm.

And the observatory at Skyview Park. Which wasn't there the last time Justin was in town. "You heard about this Skyview observatory place?" asked Michelle.

"No." Justin had seen the platform on his way into Almost and wondered what it was but wasn't interested enough to ask his aunt about it.

"They're trying to get astro-tourists to come up here," snickered Michelle.

"Huh?"

"They're trying to get people—tourists—to come up here to look at the stars."

"Why?"

"'Cause it's a good place to see the stars. Which is true, I guess," Justin agreed. He had learned that Portland wasn't a very good place to see the stars. And he realized he missed them. "All seems a little desperate, to me," added Michelle.

And it was desperate. Because northern Maine was desperate to attract people. Because it was losing so many of them.

And then they didn't talk for a while as they headed east on the Road to Somewhere.

And then Michelle started filling Justin in on what the people they had grown up with were up to. Justin didn't really care what they were up to. But he didn't tell Michelle that. So he listened as she told him that Stan Day had moved to Stonington and was working on a lobster boat. And that Paulette Wolf was going to McGill University in Montreal. (She was really smart.) And Mike Hoggatt was a lineman for the power company in Presque Isle. And Penny St. John was in jail for making meth in some cars in the woods.

"Oh, and Renee Saucier died."

"Yeah?"

"Overdose."

Renee Saucier did not seem like the kind of person who would die the way a lot of people probably thought Justin was going to. "Wow," Justin mumbled.

"Yeah."

And they didn't talk for a while. And thought about Renee Saucier being dead. And that wasn't much fun.

When they got to North/South Road, Michelle stopped at the stop sign and had an idea. If she took a left and headed north, they would be in Canada in about forty-five minutes. And they'd be able to go to bars there. Legally. And that could be fun. "Ooh! Wanna go to Canada?" she asked.

"No." The last time Justin went to Canada, he got beat up. Canadians are not as nice as everyone thinks they are.

"All right."

Michelle stayed stopped at the stop sign at the intersection of the Road to Somewhere and North/South Road and thought about what else they could do for fun.

"Movies?" offered Michelle. There were movie theaters in Fort Kent and Caribou and Presque Isle.

"Nah."

"How about Last Gas?"

That could be fun, thought Justin. Last Gas was a general store in Portage, and it was the last place to get gas or food or supplies as you headed west into the North Maine Woods and the Allagash Wilderness.

"All right," said Justin.

Michelle pressed on the gas pedal and turned right and headed south onto South Road.

She turned on the radio, which was tuned to the classic rock station out of Presque Isle. "Stairway to Heaven" was playing. Because "Stairway to Heaven" is always playing on classic rock stations.

Uncle Clair loved that song. And had taught Justin how to play it on the guitar.

And Justin missed his uncle so much. And hoped he was climbing the stairway to heaven.

And then he couldn't believe he had thought something so hokey. He didn't even believe in heaven.

"How'd he die?" asked Michelle, saving Justin from his

mawkishness. "Stairway to Heaven" had made her wonder if Uncle Clair was going to heaven, too.

"Heart attack." A widow-maker heart attack, technically. The left anterior descending artery in Uncle Clair's heart had become completely blocked. And that blockage is almost impossible for doctors to detect. And it's often fatal. And strikes far more men than women. And when it is, wives become widows. Hence the name.

"Oh."

And then Justin and Michelle didn't talk for a little while.

And thought about Uncle Clair being dead.

And that wasn't fun.

And then something really creepy occurred to Justin and he asked, "Where do you think they're gonna store him?"

"Huh?"

"Uncle Clair. Where'll they store his body, after the funeral?"

"I don't know." Michelle didn't really want to think about that.

"'Cause the funeral service is tomorrow," continued Justin. "But the burial service isn't till May or June." In northern Maine, if you die in the winter, you have to wait until May or June to be buried. Because that's when the snow melts and the ground thaws enough to dig up the earth and plant crops and bury the dead. "Where will they store him from now till May? Or . . . June?"

"I don't know," Michelle said again. She shuddered a little at the thought and then offered an obvious answer. "Storage, I guess?"

"Storage?" winced Justin.

"Yeah."

"Where?"

"I don't know," shrugged Michelle. "Funeral home?"

And they thought about Uncle Clair's dead body being in storage. At the funeral home. Or wherever.

And that wasn't fun.

And, even though he had no intention of ever living in a place where a body had to wait till May or June to be buried, Justin decided then and there that he was going to be cremated.

At about seven, they arrived at Last Gas, and Michelle pulled into the parking lot. And they went inside and soon stopped thinking about Renee Saucier and Uncle Clair—and when he was going to get buried. And they had some laughs as they looked at all the useless stuff that hikers and fishermen/women and hunters and campers from away would buy as souvenirs. Stuff like tobogganing bear figurines and plastic moose-shaped candy dispensers that poop chocolate pellets and T-shirts that say "I ❤ ME." Which were so annoying, Justin thought. Anyone who wore one of those shirts looked really conceited, because not many people know that "ME" is the postal abbreviation for the state of Maine. So if you're wearing one of those shirts, people just think that you're announcing to the world that you love yourself.

Then they played a couple of classic video games in the arcade corner.

And then they checked out the clothing and camping and survival supplies.

And then they looked at some watches and compasses and knives and guns—which were all locked away behind glass.

And then they headed over to the café section and checked out the pizza carousel and the hot dog broiler and the bakery case and the beverage refrigerator.

Justin got himself a cream horn (a flaky pastry tube filled with sweet, fluffy cream) and a Yoo-hoo—which was chocolate not-milk. And Michelle got herself a slice of pizza and a Moxie, a sweet and bitter cola made in New England that people either loved or hated.

When they went to pay, the middle-aged woman at the counter looked up with a smile and said hi. But her smile quickly became a scowl when she saw Justin's midnight-blue nails. And his long black hair with the blue streak in it.

Her scowl made Justin remember that someone like him really stuck out in places like northern Maine.

Justin paid for their food with the twenty Aunt Belinda had given him and got a five-dollar bill and four ones and a nickel for change. Then he and Michelle sat down at a table in Last Gas's café section.

"So . . . what's life like for Justin Legassie, rock star?" asked Michelle.

"It's Legacy now."

"Huh?"

"I go by Justin Legacy now."

"Oh. Is that like—a stage name?"

"I guess. Maybe. Mostly I just hate 'Legassie.' It's ugly."

Michelle couldn't deny this. Legassie is a French name, but, like many surnames in northern Maine, it's often pronounced in an anglicized way: "luh-GAS-ee." Which made Justin the butt of a lot of fart jokes growing up.

"All right. Well then, what's life like for rock star Justin *Legacy*?" said Michelle, teasing Justin a little for changing his name.

"I'm not a rock star. I'm just in a band," said Justin seriously.

"I know," Michelle said, letting him know she was just having some fun.

Michelle took a bite of her doughy pizza. (It was "America's Favorite," according to the pizza carousel.) And then took a swig of her

Moxie. And watched Justin eat his cream horn, which was dropping flaky pastry crumbs all over him. And then said, "I love the name."

"Huh?"

"Of your band. No Kill Shelter. Awesome."

"Oh. Thanks." Justin liked it, too. He had come up with it. And he was glad Michelle liked it.

"Sounds tough."

Justin smirked. "Well . . . it's not."

"Huh?"

"It's not. Tough. At all. If you think about it."

Michelle thought about it. And still thought the name sounded tough. And shook her head, seeking an explanation. So Justin explained. "No-kill shelters don't kill the animals they shelter. They keep them alive. Until they find homes for them."

"Oh," laughed Michelle.

She didn't know just how appropriate the name was. Justin and his bandmates had all struggled with staying alive—and the band had kept them alive. And it—and music—had given them a home.

"I wanna hear you someday," said Michelle. But a part of her felt like she never would. Because her life was getting complicated. "Before you get too big," she added. "Because it looks like you're getting big."

It meant a lot to Justin that Michelle knew that his band was getting big. Because they were: they had played a couple of gigs in Boston and their new manager had gotten them one in New York in February.

Michelle leaned over and brushed some pastry flakes off Justin. And hoped he would ask her what she was up to so she could maybe talk to him about the thing she wanted to talk to him about.

But he didn't. Which wasn't all that surprising. He was a pretty self-centered guy. And he needed to be. He had a lot he needed to figure out.

So Michelle asked, "You singin' at the funeral?"

"Yup," he answered.

"Good. What're you gonna sing?"

"Somethin' I wrote."

"Awesome." Michelle was surprised by how happy she was that he had written a song for his uncle.

"You sung it for anyone?"

"No."

Michelle smiled and said, "Sing it for me." And she motioned toward a small stage in the corner of the café section of Last Gas. It had an electric keyboard set up. And a guitar. And a microphone. Last Gas was trying to rebrand as a coffee house and had open mic nights from time to time. Which meant that anyone could get up and sing a song. Or recite some poetry. Into the mic. If it was open.

And, on the Friday night when all the extraordinary things did or didn't happen, it was open.

So Justin got up.

And picked up the guitar.

And tuned it.

And adjusted the amp.

And tested the mic.

And a couple of customers and the couple of people who were working at Last Gas sidled into the café section to see who was about to play—including the middle-aged woman who worked the counter and had scowled at Justin's hair and fingernails.

And then Justin sang the song he had written for his uncle.

It was about how, when you're a kid, all you want to do is grow up. And then you reach a point when all you want to do is stop growing up. Because growing up means having to say goodbye to people you love.

His singing was light but earthy. Sweet but scarred. Pained but hopeful.

When he finished, people clapped. And some were crying. And someone asked him to sing another song. And Justin looked to Michelle to see if she was okay with him singing another one. But she was leaving—in a hurry.

Justin put the guitar on its stand and thanked everybody, but said he needed to catch up with his friend. And as he made his way toward the exit, the woman at the counter seemed to have changed her opinion of him and told him to come on by and play anytime. And Justin said, "Sure," even though he knew he'd never play there again.

And he headed out to the car. And found Michelle sitting at the wheel. Justin got in the LeSabre and joked, "That bad, huh?"

But it wasn't a good time to be joking. Because Michelle was crying. Hard. Not from sadness. Just from too much feeling. "No. It was so good. That's a *good* song."

"Thanks." Justin was glad his songs still made her cry. But he didn't want them to make her cry as hard as she was crying.

"Sorry—just—growing up *is* hard," she said, referencing Justin's song. "That really got me," she heaved. "I guess 'cause it's happening so fast—to me—right now. But—not because I had to say *goodbye* to anybody. But because I'm about to say . . . hello to someone."

Michelle looked at Justin. And Justin looked at Michelle. Because he felt like she was giving some kind of clue. And she was. But it wasn't a very good clue. So she just told him the thing she wanted to tell him.

"I'm gonna have a baby."

There are things people tell you that make you grow up fast. Things like your dad telling you that you need to find another place to live. And your aunt telling you that your uncle who raised you like a son has died.

And your old best friend telling you that she's going to have a baby.

Michelle didn't breathe for a while, because she was waiting to hear what Justin would think of her news. And, while she waited, she felt a strange lightness fill up her insides. It made her feel like she had the light of a new day dawning inside her—which she did. And it made her feel giddy with excitement, because she had finally shared—with her best friend—a wonderful secret, a secret that only she and the father of her unborn child knew, a secret that would soon reveal itself to the world. And she felt like she was floating through the air, like a ballerina mid-lift. She had always wanted to be a ballerina. But her body had gotten too big too fast for her to ever get to dance ballet.

When Michelle finally started breathing again, she sounded like she had just run a sprint. And snot was rattling around in her nose and throat. "And," she continued, her breathing labored, "the crazy thing is—I'm happy. 'Cause I wanna have a baby. Because I love the guy. And he loves me."

And then she shrugged. And then laughed through some tears and said, "And I never thought I'd love anyone like I loved you."

And she shrugged again and said, through some more tears, "And I never thought I'd find a guy who would ever love a girl like me." And then she smiled and said, "But I did. And I'm real happy about it."

And then she leaned her head against her window and thought about what it was going to be like for her when her family and friends found out she was going to have a baby. And said, "But I'm afraid everyone's gonna make me feel like I should be sad about it."

Michelle turned to Justin, who was staring at the glove box. "Do you think I should be sad about it?" she asked.

Justin didn't say anything. For a while. Because he was trying to figure out what he thought about what Michelle had just told him.

Which made Michelle think that he thought she should be sad about it.

And they sat in the kind of silence that wasn't comfortable—but that talking would make less comfortable.

A rap on the passenger-door window interrupted the silence. Michelle and Justin jumped a little, and Michelle made sure she didn't look like she had been crying, and Justin grabbed the crank handle down by his knee and rolled down his window. A large woman in a forest-ranger uniform was peering into the LeSabre. In northern Maine, forest rangers could act as the police. Most didn't. But this one did.

"Evenin', kids," said the forest ranger.

"Hi," said Justin.

"Everything okay in here?"

"Yes, ma'am," said Justin.

"Okay," said the forest ranger, and she pointed toward the entrance to Last Gas and said, "No loiterin', okay?"

"Huh?" asked Justin.

The woman pointed harder. And Justin and Michelle saw a NO LOITERING sign above the entrance. "You've been sittin' out here for long enough that you're loiterin'. So, time to move on."

"Oh. Yes, ma'am," said Michelle and Justin.

The forest ranger rapped on the roof of the LeSabre and headed inside Last Gas for a coffee. And probably a doughnut.

And Michelle started her engine and pulled out of the parking lot and headed north on North Road.

"What was *that*?" asked Justin.

"I don't know."

"*Who* was that?"

"I don't know. She was probably just makin' sure we weren't drinkin'."

That's exactly what the forest ranger was doing.

And they drove for a while, the residue of their earlier conversation sticking to their thoughts.

But they didn't talk.

Michelle wanted to know what Justin thought of her news.

And she wanted him to be happy for her.

But she didn't dare ask him what he thought—because she sensed that he wasn't happy for her.

And he wasn't.

At all.

He was actually angry at her.

Because she had found someone.

And that made him feel like she wasn't his anymore. And it made him feel like she wasn't going to be there for him whenever he needed her, like she always had been. Which meant that he couldn't rely on her to be his girlfriend like he did in high school so people wouldn't wonder about him. And he couldn't tell people in Portland that he had a girlfriend named Michelle so he wouldn't have to go on dates with the guys and the girls who asked him out.

Because Michelle had a real boyfriend now—someone she loved. And who loved her. And Justin had to face the fact that he and Michelle—in spite of how much they had always loved each other—

had never been—and never would be—what Michelle and her new boyfriend were.

And that made Justin feel utterly alone.

Because he didn't think he was ever going to find someone.

Maybe because he wasn't sure he even *wanted* to find someone.

Because he had things he wanted to do with his life. Big things.

And he wished Michelle wanted to do big things with her life, too. And then he suddenly asked her, "Don't you have things you wanna do with your life?"

Michelle was taken aback—and a little irritated—by the question. And she scoffed. And then sneered and then said, "Yeah, I wanna 'do things with my life.' I just told you: I wanna have a baby. And a family."

Justin didn't say anything. Because he didn't understand people whose only goals in life were to find love and have a family.

"And I know I'm supposed to want more," admitted Michelle, softening. "But right now, I don't." Justin didn't know how to respond to that, so he didn't. "Anyway," continued Michelle, "I want you to be the godfather."

Justin winced.

He couldn't even take care of *himself*. How in the world could she count on him to be the person she trusted her kid with if anything happened to her and the kid's father?

And he ignored Michelle's wish that he be the godfather.

And turned on the radio.

Michelle immediately turned it off. Because she wasn't going to allow Justin to escape into his music like he always did. She was going to force him to be right there in the real world with her.

"Hey!" she said sternly, glancing over at him. "I just asked you to be the godfather to my kid. Is that something you wanna do or not?"

Justin couldn't bring himself to answer the question.

Michelle scoffed. "Well, I'd like for you to be godfather. To my kid." She glanced over at Justin. "And I'd like for you to be happy for me. 'Cause I'm happy!" she snarled. And then she waited for Justin to say something. And he didn't say anything. So she said, "But it doesn't look like you wanna be either of those things."

And then they didn't talk anymore.

They just thought.

And eventually Michelle turned left onto the Road to Nowhere.

And they passed the observatory at Skyview Park.

And then East's house.

And then St. Mary's.

And then Ma Dudley's.

And then the Moose Paddy.

And Echo Lake.

And, at about 8 p.m., they pulled into Aunt Belinda's driveway.

And Michelle figured Justin would get out of the car. And they'd never see each other again. Which is exactly what had happened the last time they saw each other, on the night they graduated. Michelle had come over to say goodbye. And they went tooling around one last time. And Michelle told Justin that she didn't know what she was going to do without him—and that she loved him. And Justin told her to take him home. And she did. And Justin got out of the car and went in his house. And Michelle never saw him—or even heard from him again. Until the Friday night when all the extraordinary things did or didn't happen.

But this time, Justin didn't get out of the car.

He just sat there.

And Michelle thought he was going to say something.

But he didn't.

So Michelle said something.

"You know, you're just like everybody else," she scolded. "You wanna think you're not. But you are."

If only she knew how untrue that was.

"'Cause everybody else is gonna tell me I should be sad about this. Like you just did."

"I didn't say that you should be sad about it," muttered Justin.

"You said, 'Don't you have things you wanna do with your life?' Which doesn't make me think you're too happy about it. But I am. I'm happy I'm gonna have a baby."

Neither of them said anything for a while.

And then Michelle said, "And, you know, just because you're sad doesn't mean everybody else has to be, you know. And just because you don't need love doesn't mean other people don't."

Justin didn't say anything and just listened. And stared straight ahead of him. For a while.

And then finally said, "I don't know if . . . I can be a godfather."

"Sure you can!"

And then Michelle felt like Justin was crying even though he didn't look like it.

"No. I can't. I have too much I gotta figure out."

"Who doesn't?" retorted Michelle.

"No—I have more. To figure out. 'Cause . . ." And he emitted a deep, single, heaving, moaning sob that sounded like a couple of decades of untold pain.

"Hey—what's wrong?" asked Michelle. The sound Justin had made seemed like it came from a place inside him that was farther away than the outer reaches of the universe. And he almost started crying—but didn't. And pulled himself together. And became his stoic self again. And calmly said, "I don't think I'm a him."

"Huh?" Michelle had heard Justin. But didn't quite understand what he had said.

"I don't think I'm a—"

"Oh," interrupted Michelle, understanding what Justin was saying.

"—him," he finished.

"Okay." Michelle nodded her head a little too vigorously, in the way that people do when they're trying hard to be supportive.

And then they sat in a northern Maine silence for a while.

And then Justin said, "But I don't think I'm a her, either."

"Okay." Michelle nodded her head a little too vigorously again. And didn't say anything else and just looked at Justin and waited for him to elaborate. Which he eventually did.

"I thought I was. A her. When we were little. Because I felt like a girl. More than I felt like a boy. But then I started feeling like a boy, too, as I got older."

"Okay." Michelle nodded her head a little too vigorously again.

"And then I felt like both a him and a her for a while."

"Okay." Michelle nodded her head a little too vigorously again.

"And I thought that I couldn't be both. And that I was gonna have to . . . pick. One or the other."

"Okay." Michelle nodded her head, but a little less vigorously.

"But then," Justin continued, "I figured out that I didn't have to pick. I could just be what I am. I could just be"—Justin looked at his body and then finished his sentence—"this." And then he looked over at Michelle and said, "So . . . I'm just gonna be"—Justin looked at his body again and repeated—"this."

And then he looked over at Michelle again.

"Okay," said Michelle, nodding her head, less vigorously still.

"Whatever 'this'"—Justin looked at his body again—"is."

"Okay." Michelle wasn't nodding her head anymore. And she grabbed his hand and squeezed it.

"And I've always known. Deep down. I always knew something was different . . . but I tried not to know—I didn't *want* to know— but I knew I was gonna need to figure it out. But I felt like I wasn't going to be able to really figure it out till I left."

Northern Maine can be a hard place to figure out things like what Justin had been trying to figure out.

And Justin thought it would be an easier thing to figure out in Portland. And it was—a tiny bit easier. A tiny enough bit that he was able to figure it out.

Michelle suddenly leaned across the front seat of her LeSabre and hugged Justin as well as you can hug someone who's sitting next to you in a car.

And that's when Justin cried.

And Michelle had never seen him cry.

Not when his dad kicked him out.

Not when he got beat up at school.

He hadn't even cried when he found out his uncle Clair had died.

But he was crying now.

Because Michelle had been kind to him. And he desperately needed kindness.

Michelle held Justin while he cried. And Justin held Michelle.

And it wasn't long before he was cried out.

And he pulled away from Michelle.

And Michelle moved herself back to over to the side of the car. And then leaned back and let herself slouch down in her seat until her head was where her back usually was and her shins were up against the dashboard.

And Justin collected himself and leaned back in his seat and let himself slouch down in his seat until his head was where his back usually was and his shins were up against the dashboard.

They say the truth will set you free. And it had in this case.

Because Justin and Michelle felt free.

Free from hoping that one day they might love each other the way the world had told them they were supposed to love each other.

Free from trying to be what the world told them they were supposed to be.

And they could just be what they were. And what they wanted to be.

And they could love each other the way they knew how to love each other—as friends.

The closest of friends.

That's how they were loving each other when they were sitting in the LeSabre in Aunt Belinda's driveway on the night when all the extraordinary things did or didn't happen.

"Whew!" whooped Michelle.

And she laughed. And Justin did, too.

They felt like they had just completed some great physical feat—or had surmounted an insurmountable obstacle—or had just survived a close call of some kind.

And Justin felt a strange lightness fill up his insides. It made him feel like he had a spotlight shining inside him. And like someone had taken a heavy backpack he had been carrying around—for as long as he could remember—and had started carrying it for him. And that backpack had been heavy with a secret—a secret that couldn't be kept. Because it wasn't a secret. It was a truth. And, while a secret *has* to be kept, a truth can't be. Because when the truth is kept in, it can get heavy. Too heavy to bear. But when the truth is told, it can make the teller feel the lightness that Justin was feeling.

And that lightness can make a person feel like he or she can do anything.

Like go dancing at Country Swing. At the Rec Center. With his best friend.

Justin turned to Michelle. He was smiling. And he didn't smile very often, so smiling didn't quite suit him.

"What?" asked Michelle, creeped out by his weird smiling face.

"Wanna go dancing?"

Michelle looked over at Justin and said, "What?!?"

"They got Country Swing at the Rec Center. They had a sign up outside."

"You saw that?"

"Yeah."

"I almost asked you to go but thought you wouldn't wanna, 'cause—I mean, you're not home to go dancing."

"I'm not. But Uncle Clair would be happy if we went. And danced. Like we used to."

"You sure?"

"Yeah." Justin felt bold. "Let's show 'em all how it's done!"

Michelle laughed. Because they *would* show them all how it's done.

"Unless you think you don't have what it takes anymore," teased Justin.

"Oh, I have what it takes. All you gotta do is follow me," said Michelle.

"Are you disrespecting following?" countered Justin.

"I am! I have to do all the work, throwin' you around."

"Yeah, and I'm not sure you can handle it. You're pregnant."

"Barely. And you weigh nothin'."

Michelle put the LeSabre in reverse and pulled back out onto the Road to Somewhere. She made the old car go as fast as she dared to make it go.

It was 8:10 when they arrived at the Rec Center. Michelle pulled into the parking lot and found a space in the back between a filthy white minivan and a snowbank.

She killed the engine and looked over at Justin.

He was far, far away.

"You okay?" she asked.

Justin looked at Michelle and said, "I'll be the godfather. Or god-mother. Or godperson. Or—whatever."

Michelle smiled. "Awesome. Thank you."

"And—you're gonna be a really good mom. 'Cause you know how to take care of people. And make them feel okay." He was speaking from experience. "And," he added, "I'm happy for you."

"Thanks," said Michelle. She was so glad that Justin was happy for her. Because she cared about what he thought of her more than just about anyone. "And just so you know," added Michelle, "he's a good guy. Neil is his name. He works at the university—he's the facilities manager. And he wants me to finish up my degree because he doesn't want me to give up on my . . . other dreams."

"And what are those?" asked Justin.

"Um . . . I don't know."

Michelle just wanted to be a mom. And raise her kids while she was young. And could figure out her other dreams later.

"It's harder for girls, you know," said Justin.

"Huh?"

"It's harder for girls. To dream. Boys have been taught to dream forever. Girls haven't. I know. I'm kind of both. Being a boy is easier. People expect boys to dream. But not girls."

Michelle started nodding her head again. And didn't know if that was true or not. And just took his word for it.

And then Justin took a deep breath and said, "You ready?"

And the old friends got out of the LeSabre and made their way through the parking lot and to the Rec Center entrance.

If they had been in a movie, their walk to the entrance would have been in slow motion.

They trotted up the few steps and pulled open the large brick building's big brown double doors and were immediately greeted by warm air and some rockabilly music—and Dana Doughty, who was the assistant to Gayle Pulcifer, who ran the Rec Center. Dana was sitting at a check-in table and was wearing more plaid than usual. "Hi!" she beamed. "Welcome to Country Swing! Bean supper's all done, sorry!"

"No problem," said Michelle, as Justin said, "That's okay." They were not at all sad that the bean supper was done.

"But everybody's dancing!'" continued Dana. "And Lalaine can give ya lessons on the fly if you need 'em!"

"We're good," said Michelle. She and Justin definitely did not need lessons.

"Okay, great, so . . . two?" asked Dana. She had a roll of tickets in her hand and a gray metal cashbox in front of her on the table.

"Yup," said Michelle. She was about to pull some money out of her pocket to pay when Justin started backing away from the table and said, "No." Michelle turned and looked at him and he looked like he was in a horror movie. And he turned and ran out of the building and down the steps and back to Michelle's LeSabre.

Because he and Michelle couldn't dance there. Because the

people at Country Swing weren't ready to see Michelle and Justin dance the way they danced. Because Michelle danced what was traditionally the man's part, because she was the bigger, stronger one, and she could do the lifts and the throws. And Justin danced what was traditionally the woman's part, because he was the one who was small enough and flexible enough to be lifted and thrown. And that was why that judge had disqualified them at the Rec Center Talent Show all those years ago. And why Justin's dad hated what he saw when Justin and Michelle danced at the Rec Center Talent Show all those years ago. Not only did his son dance—he danced as the girl.

Michelle called to Justin as he left the Rec Center. "Justy!" And she followed him down the stairs and out to the parking lot and got back in the car. "What's up?" she asked, breathing heavily from trying to catch Justin.

"We can't go dancing. Here. The way we danced. We can't."

"Okay." She knew he was right.

"People aren't ready for that here. And I thought I was. But I'm not. Not here."

"Okay." Michelle put her hand on Justin's knee and squeezed it to comfort him.

The lightness Justin had been feeling was gone and had been replaced by the heaviness he usually felt. And he missed the lightness. Because it made him feel good. It was hard to let go of feeling good. Because he felt good so rarely.

Michelle took her hand off Justin's knee and dug her keys out of her pocket and asked, "Wanna go?"

"Yeah," said Justin, leaning his head on the passenger-door window.

Michelle started the car and pulled out of the Rec Center parking lot and headed back to Justin's on the Road to Nowhere.

Justin turned on the radio and Michelle let him escape into some classic rock. A song about becoming comfortably numb came on. Justin was feeling *un*comfortably numb. And wished he felt comfortably numb. He had some stuff that would make him comfortably numb and wished that he could use some of it. But he couldn't. At least—not at Aunt Belinda's.

When they got back to the house, the lights weren't on.

And Aunt Belinda's Honda wasn't in the driveway.

Michelle had barely put the LeSabre in park when Justin got out of the car and headed inside. Michelle wondered if he wanted to be alone. Or if he needed to be alone—with someone. And she decided that he needed to be alone—with someone. So she cut the engine and followed him inside.

When she entered, she found Justin had finished taking off his black Chuck Taylors and was reading a note he had found on the kitchen counter. "They went to the Moose Paddy to get a beer," he said, relaying the contents of the note.

Justin didn't know how he felt about Aunt Belinda getting a beer with Father Tom at the Moose Paddy.

"Oh," said Michelle.

Justin went into the living room and turned on the radio, which Aunt Belinda had tuned to the country station out of Presque Isle. An up-tempo number about what people do in small towns on Friday nights was playing.

Justin immediately turned the dial to the classic rock station.

"No! Wait!" Michelle had kicked off her boots and was hurrying into the living room. "I love that song!" And she went to the radio and put it back on the country station and listened to the song about what people do in small towns on Friday nights. And one of the things the song said people do in small towns on Friday nights is dance.

And Michelle looked at Justin and pointed at the radio.

"What?" Justin asked.

"Yeah!" said Michelle, still pointing at the radio.

"Huh?"

"The song says that one of the things people do on Friday nights is dance. So come on!"

"No," said Justin, and he plunked himself on the couch.

"Yeah! Just you and me! Come on!" Michelle took off her jacket and threw it on Uncle Clair's big plaid puffy chair.

And then she went to the couch and stood over Justin. And Justin thought she looked so young—too young to be a mom. And he worried about her. Because his mom was Michelle's age when she had him. And her life was his dad's life. And nothing more.

"Please. For me," said Michelle. And she held her hands out to Justin. "We can really do it in here, too." She looked up at the vaulted ceiling of Aunt Belinda and Uncle Clair's A-frame house. Justin followed Michelle's gaze upward and saw that there was plenty of room for them to execute the lifts and jumps they used to do.

And then Justin looked at Michelle. And she held out her hands to him again.

And Justin gave Michelle his hands. Because—even though he didn't want to—Michelle needed to dance.

Michelle pulled Justin up off the couch and onto his feet.

And she started moving to the music.

And Justin started moving with her.

And they let their bodies remember how they danced. And did some simple steps and spins.

And then Michelle started moving some furniture around.

She pushed the oak coffee table Uncle Clair had made up against the fireplace.

And she pushed the couch up against the back wall.

And she moved Uncle Clair's big plaid puffy chair into the corner.

And Justin moved the honey-stained maple end tables into the other corner.

And they rolled up the red-and-black checked rug and pushed it up against the wall so the polyurethaned pine floor could be their dance floor.

And then another song about private conversations came on. It was a rockabilly up-tempo number—perfect for the kind of dancing they did.

And they took off their socks so they'd have some traction.

And Michelle and Justin started dancing—really dancing—like they did when they were kids, back before anyone cared about how they danced. They took hands and did the cuddle into a pretzel spin and then Michelle rolled Justin over her back and then swung him through her legs and then helped him moon-flip over her head. And it was spectacular.

If they had danced that night at the Rec Center the way they were dancing at Justin's house, some people would have cheered, no doubt, like they had at the talent show seven or so years ago.

But some people would have thought it wasn't right.

But how else could Justin and Michelle have danced?

Justin could never have flipped and tossed Michelle.

And Michelle didn't have Justin's grace and had no idea how to be tossed and flipped.

So they danced the way they were meant to dance.

And after some fast and furious and fancy footwork, Justin dove sideways into Michelle's arms like he was a plank of wood and Michelle spun him around her hips and then flipped him up onto her shoulder into an angel lift, and, as she slowly turned in a circle, Justin stretched his arms out like a bird as if he were flying.

And he felt the lightness fill up his insides again. It made him feel like a star. And like gravity had no effect on him—and it didn't for a while.

Because Justin and Michelle were dancing on air. And had been for a while.

They didn't know it.

But Aunt Belinda did.

She had just pulled into the driveway unbeknownst to Justin and Michelle. And saw them dancing through the living room picture window.

And she was so happy they had found something fun to do.

And she got out of her Honda.

And watched them dance.

And then she watched them elevate. Slowly. While they were dancing.

And she blinked a couple of times—hard—to make sure she was seeing what she thought she was seeing.

And she wondered if maybe she shouldn't have had that beer with Father Tom.

Because what she was seeing—Justin and Michelle dancing in the air—in her living room—was impossible.

Aunt Belinda was so mesmerized by the miracle she felt like she was witnessing that she didn't see the northern lights in the sky above.

And she just watched Michelle and Justin dance—on air.

And then, eventually, on the polyurethaned pine floor again.

And Justin and Michelle kept dancing—unaware that they had been dancing on air.

They just felt like they had been dancing.

And they were having fun.

So much fun.

Like Uncle Clair would have wanted.

7

As Ginette passed the Rec Center, she thought about how much her mom and dad used to love to dance. She remembered them going to Country Swing when she was little, and they'd always come back laughing and loving each other.

And she wished they still laughed and loved each other.

And then she hoped that her mom would maybe find someone else to take her to Country Swing someday. And that maybe they'd laugh and love each other.

And then Ginette wondered if she'd ever find somebody to laugh with and love.

She thought she had with Pete.

A little over an hour ago, they had told each other that they loved each other. And then they laughed and loved with each other for a few minutes. And those few minutes were the best few minutes Ginette had ever experienced.

But they were in the past.

And it seemed so wrong that all that laughing and loving was a part of their past.

It should have been a part of their present.

But it wasn't.

And Ginette realized that the farther and farther away she got from Pete, the less and less likely it was that she and Pete would ever laugh and love—or do much of anything—together again.

At 8:15, Ginette found herself approaching Lendall Tardy's house, which was about a quarter of a mile down the road from the Rec Center. Lendall was the guy you called if you wanted your kitchen remodeled, or if you were building a garage, or if you were painting your house. He had worked on just about every house and building in Almost, so everyone knew him. But no one knew him well. He was a quiet guy.

But Lendall's girlfriend, Gayle Pulcifer, was not quiet. She was a dynamo and ran the Rec Center, so everyone knew her, too—and she had a magical way about her that made everyone feel like they knew her really well.

Gayle had done wonders for Almost. Thanks to a grant from the Burby Foundation, she had transformed the Rec Center building—which had almost been abandoned years ago—into a bustling community center that offered programming for everyone in Almost.

For kids, there were arts and crafts classes and all kinds of board game tournaments and intramural basketball leagues and Nerf dodgeball leagues and free gym time to help young people fight off cabin fever during northern Maine's long winters.

And, because adults in northern Maine need help fighting cabin fever as much as kids do, there was plenty of programming for grown-ups. There were yoga classes, CPR classes, cooking classes, a gentlemen's basketball league, cribbage and bridge tournaments, AA meetings, and a painting class taught by an artist named Merle Haslem from Allagash.

And the Rec Center offered plenty of all-ages activities, like

Saturday morning nature hikes and movie nights and game nights and dance socials—like the Country Swing night that had been underway for a while on the night when all the extraordinary things did or didn't happen.

Ginette figured that Gayle must have been at Country Swing, supervising. And that Lendall must have been there with her, dancing with her and helping her make sure that everything was going smoothly, because he was always there for her. And she was always there for him.

They were such a cool couple, Ginette thought. They had been together forever—but they weren't married. And Ginette had always wondered why. And not long ago she asked her mom if she ever thought they were going to get married. And her mom said it was none of her business. And that it didn't matter if they were going to or not. What mattered was that they were happy.

And they sure seemed happy.

But Gayle wasn't happy on the night when all the extraordinary things did or didn't happen. She was sitting in her old red Jeep in Lendall's driveway. And feeling pretty sad.

Because she was about to break up with her boyfriend of eleven years.

Because she had just figured out that he didn't love her anymore.

She had had a hunch for a while that this was the case. And, a little over an hour ago, her hunch had been confirmed—at Sandrine St. Pierre's bachelorette party—which Gayle had shown up late to, because she needed to get the Country Swing event at the Rec Center set up and running. Unfortunately, there had been a hiccup in the early part of the evening: a young woman had suffered a bad fall while she and her dance partner were taking a lesson. Lalaine Deshain had encouraged them to try an over-the-shoulder throw that was way beyond their abilities. And the next thing everyone knew, the young woman was on the ground holding her face, keening, and bleeding profusely.

But the young woman's date had taken her to the hospital, and Lendall cleaned up the blood, and everything settled down. And Gayle's assistant, Dana Doughty, said she had everything under control, so Lendall went home, and Gayle headed over to the Moose Paddy to make an appearance at Sandrine's bachelorette party.

When she arrived, Sandrine was holding court with her unbetrothed attendees, offering unsolicited advice on how they could get their men to put rings on their fingers. And Sandrine asked Gayle how much longer she was going to have to wait before Lendall put a ring on her finger. And Gayle said that she and Lendall had a good thing going and that she didn't think having a ring on her finger would make it better, and Sandrine said, "Okaaay," in a way that made everyone know that she did not think it was okay.

And then Narda Smith announced that she needed some relationship advice—which Sandrine loved to offer—and said that she had recently had her boyfriend, Chuck, over for a pot roast. And while they ate it, she asked him what he thought about getting married. And he didn't answer. He just got quiet. And then asked what was for dessert.

The girls groaned and exchanged concerned looks.

"What?!?" cried Narda, fearing the worst.

And Sandrine said, "It means he wants out."

"What? No!" protested Narda, laughing but feeling like she was going to cry.

"Yeah," grumbled the girls in unison.

"It means he doesn't love you," said Sandrine.

"No!" gasped Narda.

"Yeah. Trust me. And I know," said Sandrine. "'Cause I've been there. Well—not on your end. But . . . on Chuck's end—with Jimmy. Remember Jimmy?"

"Yeah," they all moaned, because they remembered Jimmy. He was sweet. But just not right—not for Sandrine, anyway.

"Well," continued Sandrine, "he asked me one night what I thought about getting married."

"He did?" asked Narda. This was news to everyone and caused quite the kerfuffle.

"Yeah," answered Sandrine.

"And . . . ?" asked Narda, on everyone's behalf.

"And . . . I got quiet. For a long time. Because I realized that I didn't love him—at least, not as much as he loved me. And I had to let him know that I didn't wanna marry him."

"Oh," said Narda.

"So I did. And—I ended it with him—sort of—in my own way. And now you're gonna end it with Chuck. In your own way."

"Okay," whimpered Narda. And the girls comforted her. And then the waitress came up to the bar and said that they all needed to start thinking about moving into the banquet room, because dinner was going to be served soon.

So the girls started moving toward the banquet room.

And Gayle said she'd be right with them all, after she used the restroom. And she made her way to the back of the Moose Paddy, and, instead of going to the restroom, she slipped out the back door, and her heart started racing as she made her way to her Jeep.

And once she was in her Jeep, her heart stopped racing and just sank.

Because she had had Lendall over for dinner a couple of weeks ago and asked him what he thought about getting married.

And he got quiet.

So quiet.

And she had been wondering ever since what that quiet had meant.

And now she knew. Thanks to Sandrine. And Narda.

And now she had to end things with him. In her own way. Because he didn't love her anymore.

And she took a deep breath and started her Jeep and was about to pull out of the Moose Paddy parking lot and go end things with Lendall—when she realized that she needed to go back to her place first and gather up all the things that he had at her house so she could bring them back to him.

And then she'd end things with him. In her own way.

And then she'd get from him all the things she had at his house.

And then she'd leave.

And they'd be done.

So she pulled out of the Moose Paddy parking lot and turned left onto the Road to Somewhere and headed to her house so she could gather up all of Lendall's stuff. And give it back to him.

She passed Ma Dudley's Boardinghouse.

And St. Mary's Church.

And the old Gallagher Potato Farm.

And Skyview Park.

And, as she drove, she wondered what she was going to say to Lendall when she saw him.

Ten minutes later, she was at her house gathering all the stuff she needed to return to Lendall: some clothes, a toothbrush, deodorant, some tools, some boots, and some *American Rifleman* and *Popular*

Woodworking magazines. And she shoved all his stuff into his old army duffel and slung it over her shoulder and was about to leave when she realized that she had almost forgotten the most important thing she needed to return. And she gathered it up and shoved it into garbage bags—lots of garbage bags. And then she shoved the garbage bags into the Jeep. They barely all fit, but she managed to squeeze them all into the cargo area, and into the backseat, and she even had to put some of them on the passenger seat. And then she plunked Lendall's old army duffel on the floor in front of the passenger seat. And then she got in her Jeep and started it and headed back toward down-township Almost to Lendall's house, which was located about a quarter of a mile past the Rec Center.

As she drove, Gayle tried to work out what she was going to say to Lendall when she saw him. And then happened to glance in her interior rearview mirror, as good drivers do. And all she could see were all those garbage bags full of what she had to return to him— and she had a revelation. And suddenly knew exactly what she was going to say to Lendall when she saw him.

And soon, she was passing Skyview Park.

And the old Gallagher Potato Farm.

And St. Mary's Church.

And Ma Dudley's.

And the Moose Paddy.

Then she passed the Rec Center—and hoped Dana still had everything under control. And then, just before she got to Lendall's, she saw the beam from a flashlight shining up ahead.

Someone was out walking on the Road to Nowhere.

Which was a bit unusual, because it was after dark.

Gayle's first instinct was to check to make sure that whoever it was was okay. Even though she really didn't want to make sure they were okay—because she didn't want to get sidetracked.

But she had to see if everything was okay, because that's what people from Almost, Maine, do. They check in on each other, because if they don't, who will?

As she got closer to the flashlight beam, she slowed down.

Ginette bristled as she heard Gayle's Jeep slow down and start creeping along behind her. She didn't want to be seen out walking by herself on the Road to Nowhere after dark. Because she didn't want people wondering if anything was wrong. So she kept her head down and walked faster, hoping the decelerating vehicle would just accelerate again and pass her by.

But it didn't.

Instead, it rode along beside her.

Gayle rolled down her window and asked, "Everything okay?" and tried to figure out who she was talking to.

Ginette recognized Gayle's voice and turned to her, a sheepish smile on her face.

"Hi, Miss Gayle."

"Oh! Ginette! Hi!"

"Hi."

"What's goin' on? Where ya headed?"

"Home," Ginette said.

"Oh. Need a ride?"

"No. Thanks, though."

"Everything okay?"

"Yup," said Ginette, still walking. "I just wanted to go for a walk."

"Okay." Gayle could sense that everything wasn't okay. But decided to let it go. Because she didn't want to pry. So she said, "Well, be careful."

"I will."

"Bye."

"Bye."

Gayle rolled up her window and drove off.

As she did, Ginette hoped that Gayle wouldn't mention to her mom that she had seen her daughter out walking alone after dark. Because then her mom would ask questions—questions Ginette didn't want to answer.

But Gayle had no intention of mentioning anything to Ginette's mom. She figured that Ginette was out walking because she had something she needed to work out on her own. And no one— including her mom—needed to know anything about it.

So Gayle forgot that she had even seen Ginette, and she pulled into Lendall's driveway so she could do what she needed to do.

She parked near the side stairs that led to the front porch. And then killed her engine and the lights.

Then she went over what she wanted to say to Lendall one more time. And how she was going to end things with him.

And she felt good about her plan.

And then had second thoughts—and wondered if she really wanted to do what she was about to do. And she sat in her Jeep and waffled—for a good fifteen or twenty minutes. Because, while what she was about to do felt absolutely right, it also felt absolutely wrong. And she almost lost her nerve.

But then she remembered how quiet Lendall had gotten when she asked him what he thought about getting married.

And what Sandrine had said that that quiet meant.

And she found her nerve again. And she got out of her Jeep and started to make her way up the driveway to Lendall's house to do what she needed to do—when she stopped.

And remembered something.

She had left her keys in the ignition—which she always did when she was in Almost.

And she needed them.

Or—one of them: the one to Lendall's house.

She needed to give it back to him.

So she made her way back down to the Jeep, opened the driver's side door, and reached in and pulled the ignition key out of its slot—which was on the same ring as her house keys and her dad's keys and the keys to the Rec Center. The jumble of keys jangled as Gayle searched for the key to Lendall's house—a key she had never had to use, because Lendall never locked his door. No one did in Almost.

Once she had found it, she removed it from the ring, shoved it into her jeans pocket, tossed the rest of her keys on the driver's seat, and closed the Jeep's driver-side door.

Then she looked up at Lendall's house. And saw a dull blue light flickering inside.

The TV was on.

Lendall was probably watching hockey. Or—had been watching hockey. He had probably fallen asleep.

So she was going to have to wake him up.

So he'd be out of it at first.

So she was going to have to be really clear.

And she would be. She had gone over what she was going to say to him in her head several times. She thought her arguments were irrefutable. And her reasoning sound.

She started making her way up the driveway again.

And then climbed the steps onto the porch where she and Lendall had spent who knows how many lazy Sunday afternoons together in the summertime.

She went to the door and was about to barge inside—when she realized that she didn't want to do what she needed to do inside. She needed to do it outside, on the porch—in more neutral territory.

So she gathered up all her gumption and went to the door—and suddenly realized that she was really mad at Lendall. And she pulled open the white aluminum storm door and pounded on the wooden main door—at least five times—and yelled, "Lendall!"

Then she listened for a response. And waited for him to come to the door.

But Lendall didn't respond. Or come to the door.

Gayle figured he must not have heard her.

He was definitely sleeping.

So she pounded again—three times—and yelled, "Lendall!"

This time, Lendall heard Gayle and jumped a little as he woke up. Gayle was right: he had fallen asleep in his La-Z-Boy, watching the Bruins game.

Lendall checked the time. His watch said it was 8:39.

He wondered why Gayle was there. He had kissed her good night after Gayle got Country Swing up and running, and then Gayle headed over to Sandrine's bachelorette party, and Lendall headed home, because he had to be up early. He wanted to get a couple of hours of work in on Marvalyn and Eric's roof in the morning, because the rest of his Saturday was going to be taken up with Clair Gudreau's funeral and the St. Pierre/LaFerriere wedding. So he was planning on falling asleep early with the Bruins game on.

Gayle pounded on the door twice more and yelled, "Lendall!" and Lendall wondered why she was pounding on the door. "Gayle, just come in!" he called as he tried to get out of his chair—which took some effort. Lendall was thirty-seven and all the years he had worked in construction were taking their toll.

While he worked on getting himself up and out of his La-Z-Boy, Gayle waited on the porch, facing the door, her hands on her hips. And then she pounded on the door five more times and yelled louder, "Lendall!!!"

Lendall wondered why she was being so loud. The closest neighbors were far enough away that none of them would hear. But—still.

"Gayle! Just come in!" called Lendall again, a little irked that Gayle was making him get up and let her in. They didn't live together, but his place was hers and her place was his. So she could just let herself in like she usually did.

When he finally managed to extricate himself from his chair, he shook off his drowsiness, turned off the TV, and switched on the lamp on the end table by his La-Z-Boy.

Gayle pounded on the door again and yelled, "Lendall!!!"

Worried that something was wrong, Lendall hustled over to his front door. He usually used his back door, but he had been remodeling his kitchen for the past three years, and the back door was inaccessible. Contractors have to meet deadlines for their customers, so they never meet them for their own projects. Plus, the last thing they want to do in their spare time is what they do for a living.

Gayle pounded again as Lendall flicked on the porch light. And then the seal of the weather stripping popped as he pulled open his front door. Gayle folded her arms and started pacing as Lendall pushed the white aluminum-and-glass storm door open and asked, "What? What's goin' on? What's wrong?"

Gayle stopped pacing and turned to Lendall.

She was not what you would call a low-strung person. But Lendall had never seen her quite so high-strung.

And she had a look in her eyes that Lendall had never seen before.

"You okay?" asked Lendall, starting toward the woman he loved, but stopped. Gayle pulled away from him, not allowing him to touch her. "Hey. What's up? What's wrong?" Lendall asked gently as the storm door swung shut.

Gayle inhaled sharply and said, "Lendall . . ." And then she held her breath and grimaced in a combination of pain and disappointment and anger and confusion. And she almost lost her nerve again.

"Gayle—what's wrong?" asked Lendall, concerned.

Gayle exhaled loudly and her face relaxed, and then she inhaled sharply again and remembered how she had planned to do this. And then found her nerve again. And looked Lendall dead in the eye. And calmly stated, "I want it back."

Lendall scrunched up his forehead and asked, "Huh?"

"I want it back," Gayle repeated.

Lendall scrunched up his forehead some more and jutted his neck forward and wondered what she wanted back and asked, "What?"

"All the love I gave to you: I want it back. Now."

Lendall tried to figure out what Gayle was saying. And couldn't. And scrunched up his whole face and asked, "What?"

Gayle was irked by the question and had no patience for Lendall's confusion. Because she couldn't have been clearer. And, besides, she had already had this conversation with him many times in her head—since she had left the Moose Paddy.

Unfortunately, she had forgotten that Lendall hadn't been in her head. So he had no idea what she was talking about. Or what her intentions were. This was all new to him.

Nevertheless, she still expected him to follow what she was saying. And she continued, "I've got yours in the car."

"What?" asked Lendall, looking toward Gayle's Jeep, completely at a loss.

"All the love you gave to me: I've got it in the car."

"Why?" asked Lendall, turning back to Gayle.

"I don't want it anymore."

"What?!?" Lendall was starting to understand what Gayle was saying. And he felt his insides get heavy and knotty.

"You heard me. I don't want it anymore. So I've brought it back." Gayle nodded toward her Jeep and added, "It's in the car."

"What do you mean you don't want it anymore?"

"I've made a decision: We're done, and so—"

"Whoa, whoa, whoa. What do you mean we're done?"

"Just what I said. We're done, and so, I've brought all the love you gave to me back to you. It's the right thing to do."

"Gayle, what're you talking about?"

"It's in the car," repeated Gayle, ignoring Lendall's question.

Perplexed, Lendall turned toward Gayle's Jeep. And then back to Gayle. And was about to ask why she wanted all the love she had given him back, but before he could, Gayle interrupted him and offered, "I can get it *for* you . . . or *you* can go get it."

"Well, I don't want it back," said Lendall, scared of where this was going.

"Well, I don't want it!" exploded Gayle. "What am I supposed to do with all of it now that I don't want it anymore?"

"I don't know," grumbled Lendall, at a loss.

"Well, under the circumstances, it doesn't seem right for me to keep it."

"Under what circumstances?" demanded Lendall.

Gayle ignored the question and continued, "And since I don't want it anymore, I'm gonna give it back."

And, with that, Gayle headed down the steps of the porch and up the driveway to her Jeep to get all the love Lendall had given her so she could give it back to him.

"Hey! Gayle! Wait—I don't understand," called Lendall, following the woman he expected to spend the rest of his life with. "What are you sayin'?"

"It's not complicated, Lendall!" called Gayle. "I'm getting all the love you gave to me and I'm giving it back to you."

"Well, I told you—I don't want it back." Lendall had followed Gayle down to the driveway. And Gayle opened the rear hatch to her Jeep.

And Lendall stopped short, because the Jeep's interior light revealed that the vehicle was stuffed to the gills—with full garbage bags.

Lendall watched Gayle as she unloaded the Jeep.

She removed a couple dozen garbage bags from the cargo area.

And she removed a dozen from the backseat.

And a half dozen from the front seat.

And she tossed all the bags out onto the icy driveway.

Gayle would have liked to chuck the bags across the driveway and at Lendall.

But they were shapeless and soft and almost weightless. So they were completely unchuckable.

Once she had emptied the Jeep of all the garbage bags, Gayle grabbed Lendall's army duffel from the floor of the passenger seat and unceremoniously tossed it out onto the driveway. Whatever was in the duffel bag was much heavier than whatever was in the garbage bags, because it landed with a satisfying, chafey thud.

When Gayle had finished the more-Herculean-than-expected task of unloading the Jeep, she slammed the passenger door closed with a flourish, folded her arms, and waited for Lendall to take what was rightfully his into his house, and then bring out to her what was rightfully hers.

But Lendall wasn't doing anything—except staring at all those garbage bags. There was something otherworldly about them. They barely seemed earthbound.

Irritated by Lendall's inertia, Gayle gathered a bunch of the light, shapeless, bulky garbage bags and decided that she would bring them up onto the porch herself and just leave them there for Lendall to deal with.

And she blew past him and climbed the steps and dumped the first batch of bags onto the porch.

As she did, she thought about all the sweet summer days and nights she and Lendall had spent on that porch, laughing, playing cards, and listening to music. And she almost started to doubt her decision to end things with him. But only almost.

And then she made another trip to the Jeep to retrieve more of the bags.

And she brought them up onto the porch.

And then made a third trip.

And then a fourth.

And then a fifth.

And then a sixth.

And then a seventh.

Lendall made his way up the steps and onto his porch while Gayle shuttled back and forth. And when she dropped off the last of the bags, Lendall asked Gayle, "So this is . . ."

"All the love you gave me, yeah."

Lendall opened one of the bags.

Sure enough, it was the love he had given her.

Lendall took in the massive pile of shapeless, almost weightless bags that had accumulated. And was maybe a little proud of how much love he had given Gayle. And observed, "This is a lot."

"Yup," said Gayle curtly, and she turned and made one last trip to the driveway.

"A whole lot," called Lendall.

"Yup," replied Gayle, and she grabbed Lendall's old army duffel. And dragged it up the steps and onto the porch and dumped it in the old Adirondack chair Lendall sat in when the weather was nice.

And it landed with a thud—on the chair. And in Lendall's heart.

Lendall looked at his old army duffel. And presumed that it was full of all the stuff he had been keeping at Gayle's—other stuff that Gayle was returning.

And he realized that Gayle was serious about being done.

And he had no idea why.

And he needed to find out why.

But before he could ask her why, Gayle said, "And now, I think it's only fair for you to give me mine back, because . . . I want it back."

Lendall felt his chest tighten. And his breath got shallow. And he felt like he might throw up a little. Because he didn't want to give her back all the love she had given him. At all.

"So go get it," ordered Gayle.

"Gayle—why?"

"I told you: we're done."

"But I don't wanna be done!"

"Well, it seems like you do, and—"

"I don't!"

"Well, I do!"

"Why?!?"

Gayle ignored the question and went on. "So don't make this harder than it has to be. Go get what I came for. Now."

Lendall held his arms out, palms up, and shrugged and started to plead with his longtime love. "Gayle—"

"Please, Lendall. Go get it," snapped Gayle, not entertaining Lendall's plea.

Lendall dropped his arms and shoulders in defeat. Because Gayle was giving him no choice but to do what she had asked. Because she had decided that they were done. And the subject was not up for discussion.

Lendall wondered what he had done to make Gayle want to be done.

He couldn't think of anything.

But he must have done something that had hurt her in some way.

And he almost asked for her forgiveness for whatever he had done.

But what if he hadn't done anything—and she just wanted to be done?

His heart sank. And he ultimately decided that maybe the best thing he could do was honor Gayle's request. And get what she had come for. Maybe if he did that, she'd calm down and help him understand why she wanted to be done. And then maybe she'd give him a chance to make right whatever he had made wrong. Or fix whatever he had broken. Or plead his case. And then maybe she'd give him a chance to make her understand just how much he loved her—and maybe he'd be able to change her mind about wanting to be done.

Resigned and defeated, Lendall finally said, "Okay." And he pulled open the storm door and pushed open the main door to his house so he could go get what Gayle had asked for.

And he started inside.

Before the aluminum storm door swung shut, he caught it and pushed it open and asked Gayle if she wanted to wait inside.

And she said, "Nope. I'll wait out here. Thanks." She was afraid the warmth of Lendall's living room would melt her resolve.

"It's cold."

"No, it's not."

"Okay," said Lendall. Gayle was right. It wasn't cold. It was above average for the time of year. Nineteen degrees, according to the big round Agway thermometer on the porch.

Lendall headed inside and closed the door behind him to keep the heat in and the cold out. And started making his way across his living room and down the hallway to his bedroom to do what Gayle had asked him to do.

As he walked, he got anxious. And he wasn't the kind of guy who got anxious. But giving Gayle back all the love she had given him was going to change their lives forever.

And Lendall didn't know if that change was going to be for the best. Or for the worst.

As he dragged his feet into his bedroom, it felt like it was going to be for the worst.

Gayle, on the other hand, was convinced that getting back all the love she had given Lendall was going to be for the best. And she plunked herself down in the Adirondack chair she sat in when she and Lendall would sit on his porch and enjoy the sweet summer days and the cool summer nights that only places like northern Maine have.

And she looked out across Lendall's yard and across the Road to Nowhere and into the Norsworthys' broccoli and potato fields.

And waited.

When Lendall got to his bedroom, he felt a strange lightness fill up his insides. It made him feel like he had the light from a campfire dancing around in his belly. And it made him feel like what he bet the astronauts must have felt when they walked on the moon.

And it made him feel like something wonderful was about to happen.

Even though what was actually happening was really awful.

He went to his dresser and opened its top middle drawer, which was where he kept his wallet and his keys and his Skoal and his nail clippers and his change and some Big Red gum and some Tums and—for the past couple of weeks—something else he had been meaning to give Gayle: a small maroon velvet pouch.

He picked up the pouch and closed his fleshy hand around it. And then took a moment to hope and pray that all would be okay.

And then he closed the drawer and exited his bedroom and started walking down the hall. The lightness he had been feeling had dissipated. And Lendall felt like his big, heavy self again as he walked.

When he got to the front door, he paused. And really hoped that Gayle would accept what he was bringing her—in the way he wanted her to accept it.

While Gayle waited for Lendall, she had settled into a strange position in her chair. Her feet were outstretched, her butt was resting on its front edge, her hands were jammed in her pockets, her shoulders were up around her ears, her face was sunken into her jacket, and the back of her head was pressed up against the back of the chair. She looked like a plank of wood. And did not look comfortable.

Lendall pulled the front door open, and the sound of the weather stripping unsealing made Gayle sit up in the chair. Then he pushed the storm door open and made his way onto the porch again. And it seemed like all the garbage bags full of all the love he had given Gayle—and that Gayle had returned—were taking up more room on the porch than they had been before he had gone inside.

He saw Gayle sitting in her chair—the one she sat in the summertime. And he hoped she'd still be coming by to sit in that chair next summer—and for many summers to come.

And Gayle looked up at Lendall.

And was not happy.

At all.

Because it seemed that Lendall had come out onto the porch empty-handed.

Gayle dropped her head and shook it disapprovingly. And scoffed. And rolled her eyes. And then looked back up at Lendall and was about to chew him out for not doing what she had asked—when she saw that Lendall had stretched his arm out toward her and was holding a small maroon velvet pouch in the palm of his hand. And when he was sure he had her attention, he turned his palm down and let the little pouch drop. His ring finger was looped through the drawstring of the pouch, so it only dropped a few inches. And then swung back and forth in the porch light.

Gayle did nothing but stare at the pouch for a few moments.

Lendall couldn't tell if she was disappointed or mesmerized by it.

And when it seemed like she was more mesmerized than disappointed, Lendall placed it on a small table next to Gayle's chair.

And Gayle continued to stare at the pouch.

And then she looked up at Lendall.

And then glanced back down at the pouch and then back up at Lendall and sneered. "What is that?"

"It's all the love you gave me." And it was all the love she had given him.

And then his heart fluttered and he felt that strange lightness again for a moment—and it made him feel like something wonderful was about to happen—again.

"What?" asked Gayle in disbelief. "That's not—there is no way— that is *not* all the love I gave you!" And then she laughed derisively. And then, all of a sudden, seemed to be crying.

"Hey," said Lendall, going to Gayle to comfort her.

But Gayle didn't want Lendall's comfort, because she didn't want it to weaken her resolve, so she hopped up out of the chair and didn't let him near her.

"Gayle, come on," Lendall pleaded. "Tell me what is goin' on?"

"I told you: we're done."

"Why do you keep sayin' that?"

"Because . . ." Gayle took a moment to collect her thoughts—and herself—and when she and her thoughts were collected, she went on. "Because when I asked you what you thought about us getting married—remember when I asked you that?"

Lendall remembered very well when Gayle asked him what he thought about them getting married. Because the question had confused him. Because Gayle had said a long time ago that she didn't want to get married. Because her parents hadn't exactly set the best example of what a marriage could be. And she didn't feel like she and Lendall needed God or the state to validate their commitment to one another.

But a couple of weeks ago, Gayle had had a change of heart.

Maybe because she was watching a lot of her friends—like Sandrine—get married. Or maybe because the anniversary of their first date was coming up. Or maybe because she finally trusted that Lendall wasn't going to limit her the way so many of her friends' husbands had limited them.

Whatever the reason, she had decided that she wanted to get married. And when she told Lendall this, he got quiet.

Like he was being just then.

"Lendall!" hollered Gayle, sick of all his quiet.

"What?" asked Lendall, wondering why she was hollering.

"Yes or no: Do you remember me asking you what you thought about us getting married? It was snowing? I made a pizza?" Gayle made very good pizza.

"Yeah," Lendall finally managed to answer.

"Yeah, well, when I asked you . . . *that*, you got *so quiet*. And I know you're a quiet guy. But the way you got quiet when I asked you what you thought about us getting married—it was a different kind of quiet. And it made me realize some things. And one of those things is that you don't love me."

"What—whoa—wait—no!" Nothing could have been further from the truth. Lendall loved Gayle—her whole heart and mind and body and soul—more than anything or anyone he had ever known. "That's not why I got quiet!"

Gayle shushed Lendall because she didn't want to hear what he had to say, and went on. "And I have been trying to fix that, I have been trying to *make* you love me by giving you every bit of love I ever had—which is so stupid, because I can't make you love me if you don't!"

"But, I do!"

"No. You don't. I've decided. And since you don't, well, then, I think the best thing we can do right now is return the love we gave to each other, and call it . . ." Gayle looked at the three or four dozen garbage bags that contained all the love that Lendall had given Gayle and then looked at the single small maroon pouch that supposedly contained all the love that she had given Lendall and whimpered, ". . . even."

But it wasn't even at all.

"Oh, Jeezum Crow," said Gayle, looking up at Lendall and indicating the small maroon pouch that was sitting on the table. "Is that really all the love I gave you?"

That was a tough question to answer. Because it was—and it wasn't.

"I mean," sighed Gayle, spiraling into self-doubt, "what kind of person am I if that's all I gave you?—Wait—no!" She knew that she had given him more love than what could possibly have been in the small maroon velvet pouch and instantly stopped doubting herself. "No. No, no, no. I *know* I gave you more than that, Lendall, I know it!"

"Gayle—" Lendall wanted to tell her to take a look at what was in the small maroon velvet pouch before she got upset again but didn't get a chance to, because Gayle wasn't done.

"Did you *lose* it?" she half asked and half accused.

"What? No!" Lendall was surprised to find himself raising his voice.

"Did you lose it, Lendall? 'Cause I *know* I gave you more than that, and I think you're pulling something on me, and this is not a good time to be pulling something on me!"

"Gayle! I'm not pullin' somethin' on you! I wouldn't do that to you! Jeez!" Lendall was really mad. And he was surprised by how mad he had gotten. And by how mad Gayle had gotten. And by how loud they had both gotten.

And so was Gayle.

And it was quiet for a moment. And then Lendall pulled himself together and said calmly, "Gayle, I don't like the way you're talkin' to me right now. And I don't like the way I just talked to you right now. And—I'm sorry—but—I'm mad. Because I don't think you get to just decide that 'we're done' out of the blue without talkin' to me about it first. But since you seem to think that you do get to decide— for both of us—that 'we're done'—out of the blue—without havin' all the facts—" Lendall gestured toward the small maroon velvet pouch he had given her—"then I guess maybe you should just take what you came for . . . and I guess we'll be done."

And with that, Lendall went back inside his house and slammed the door behind him.

The storm door haltingly danced its way shut with a dull metallic thud a few seconds later.

And then it was quiet.

More quiet than it had gotten when Gayle asked Lendall what he thought about them getting married.

And more quiet than Gayle ever remembered it being in Almost—and Almost was a pretty quiet place.

Gayle stood on the porch with all the quiet, facing the door that Lendall had just slammed—and was stunned. Because she had come over to end things with Lendall.

And he had beaten her to it.

And a wave of rage surged through her body. And she punched the aluminum storm door with the outside of her fist. And then kicked it.

Because this breakup was not going as planned.

Lendall was standing on the other side of the door, also stunned—and a little sick to his stomach—that he had just ended things with Gayle.

He jumped when Gayle punched the door with her fist. And again when she kicked it.

And then he felt a wave of anger surge through his body. And it made him do something he hadn't done in who knows how long: he locked the door.

Gayle heard the cylinder of the deadbolt click into its locked position.

And she gasped.

And stared at the door.

And wondered if Lendall had just locked her out.

She opened the storm door and grabbed the knob of the main door and tried to open it.

But couldn't.

Because Lendall had locked her out.

Which wasn't a big deal, because Gayle had a key to Lendall's house. And Lendall knew she had the key. So locking the door was merely a symbolic gesture.

But—an effective one.

"Lendall?" called Gayle weakly.

Lendall heard Gayle. And was so irritated with her that he slapped the switch to the porch light off.

Which left Gayle stunned and alone and locked out (kind of) and in the dark.

Lendall couldn't believe that he had ended things with Gayle.

And he couldn't believe that he had locked the door—and turned out the light.

But he didn't know what else he could have done.

All Gayle seemed interested in doing was being angry at him. And being done with him.

And now Gayle and Lendall were done.

And Lendall didn't want them to be done.

Because he felt like they were just about to get started.

Oh, if only she would look inside the small maroon velvet pouch he had given her, maybe she wouldn't be so mad at him.

Maybe she'd be happy with him, even.

"Lendall?" Gayle called gently. She was leaning her forehead against the wooden door, hoping Lendall would answer her. But he didn't. "Lendall?" she repeated.

Lendall went to the door and almost unlocked it and went back out onto the porch to comfort Gayle.

But then didn't. And just stared at the door.

Gayle stared at the door, too.

And then she turned and went to the porch railing and leaned on it and looked out over the starlit potato fields of Norsworthy's Potato Farm toward the horizon.

And she sighed.

And thought.

And then turned and took a few steps toward the door.

Which Lendall was still standing on the other side of, trying to figure out what Gayle was doing.

And when he heard those few footsteps coming toward him, he hoped that Gayle was going to ask him to let her in. Or maybe use her key to let herself in so they could talk and make right whatever was wrong.

But Gayle didn't think that what was wrong could be made right.

So she took Lendall's house key out of her jeans pocket.

And bent down and laid it on the doormat.

And then stood back up.

And took a breath.

And started to go. But stopped. And remembered the small

maroon velvet pouch Lendall had brought to her. And figured she'd take it. It was hers, after all.

She went to it. And Lendall heard her footsteps and wondered what she was doing and pressed his ear up against the door.

But he heard nothing more, because Gayle had stopped. And was staring at the pouch—which she was able to see thanks to the faint light that was spilling out onto the porch from from the lamp on the end table in Lendall's living room.

Gayle remembered Lendall pointing to the pouch and saying something about her not having all the facts yet—before he stormed into his house and slammed (and locked) the door behind him. And she wondered what was in it. So she leaned down and picked up the small maroon velvet pouch from off the small table between their Adirondack chairs.

She could tell that it contained something small and solid—a little box, it felt like.

She shook the pouch a bit, trying to gather more information. And sat back down in her Adirondack chair and opened it—but couldn't quite see inside, because there wasn't enough light.

Because Lendall had turned off the porch light.

Which was really childish, she thought.

And then she reached inside the pouch and her fingers found a small box—which she pulled out.

The box was fuzzy, like the little pouch.

And Gayle wondered what it was.

It definitely wasn't what she had asked Lendall to bring her.

"Lendall!" she called. And she got up out of her chair and rapped on the storm door and asked, "Lendall, what is this?"

Lendall felt that strange lightness fill up his insides again. Gayle must have been looking inside the pouch he had given her.

"What the heck is this, Lendall?"

Lendall flicked the porch light on—which allowed Gayle to see that the box she was holding was the same color as the pouch it had come in.

And then the seal of the weather stripping popped as Lendall slowly pulled open the main door. And Gayle looked up and saw Lendall push open the aluminum storm door, and she asked again, "Lendall! What is this?"

It was pretty obvious what Gayle had in her hand.

But she was so fixated with what it wasn't that she was unable to comprehend what it was.

"It's a ring, Gayle," said Lendall gently as he stepped out onto the porch, pulling the wooden front door closed behind him.

"What?!?" Gayle winced.

"It's a ring," repeated Lendall. The storm door swung shut behind him.

"Wha—?!?" Gayle looked up at Lendall. And then at the maroon velvet box. And then back up at Lendall. "Noooo," she whispered.

"Yeah," Lendall gently refuted.

And then Gayle realized what she was holding in her hand.

And she began to understand what was happening.

And she felt a strange lightness fill up her insides. It made her feel like a light bulb had just been switched on inside her. And like she might start rising like a helium balloon.

"Lendall." Gayle looked up at Lendall for a long time. And finally asked, "Is this a *ring*?"

Lendall nodded in the affirmative.

"Yup."

"Oh, no," she croaked.

And Lendall got a little nervous. Why had she just said, "Oh, no"?

And then Lendall watched Gayle crumple into her Adirondack chair.

"Whoa—you okay?"

"Yeah. No. I don't know," said Gayle, staring at the box.

Which she then opened.

And when she did, she saw a small, simple, perfect diamond ring.

And she gasped.

And Lendall got less nervous.

Because her face looked like it liked what she was looking at.

But, as Gayle made sense of what was happening, she realized that what she was holding in her hand—wasn't what she had come over to get. "But—wait—all the love I gave you—where is it?"

"It's right there, Gayle," said Lendall, pointing to the ring.

"But—"

"It's right there."

"But—" Gayle looked at the small ring and wondered how it could possibly have contained all the love she had given Lendall. "How could it all be . . . in here?"

"I don't know. But it's all in there. I mean, that's not where it's always been. I've been keepin' some of it in the attic, and I had to put some in the shed, 'cause you've given me so much of the stuff over the years." And he wasn't going to say how many years they had been together, because he didn't want to make her feel bad for making him wait so long for her. But then he decided that maybe he did want to make her feel a little bad about how long she had made him wait for her, and added, "It's been eleven years, you know."

"I know," conceded Gayle, quite aware of how long she had made Lendall wait.

"Yeah. Anyway—when you asked me what I thought about us

gettin' married a couple of weeks ago, well, there was more of it than ever comin' in, and so I asked my dad if he had any suggestions what to do with it all, and he said, 'You get her a ring yet?' and I said, 'No,' and he said, 'Get her one. It's time. When there's that much of that stuff comin' in, that's about the only place you can put it.'"

Lendall looked at the ring and added, "He said it'd all fit." And then Lendall looked at Gayle and said, "And he was right." Lendall looked at the ring again and said, "That thing is a lot bigger than it looks."

"Yeah." Gayle nodded, supposing that was true.

And then she and Lendall stared at the small, simple, perfect ring.

"So there it is," said Lendall, still looking at the ring. "All the love you gave me. Just . . . not in the same form as when you gave it." Lendall looked at Gayle, who was looking at the ring. And then he asked, "You still want it back?"

"I do."

"Well then, take it."

Gayle started to take the ring out of the small maroon velvet box—but stopped. And looked at the huge pile of garbage bags that were full of all the love that Lendall had given her and asked, "Can I keep all this?"

"It's yours," laughed Lendall, happy that Gayle wanted to keep it.

"Thank you." And Gayle looked at all the love Lendall had given her. There seemed to be even more of it than when she looked at it seconds ago. And she wondered how she could have ever thought that Lendall didn't love her.

And then Gayle took the ring out of the box. And admired it.

And then neither she nor Lendall quite knew what to do.

Because they had almost broken up. And now Gayle had an

engagement ring. Which Lendall realized wasn't on Gayle's finger yet. So he did something very traditional. Or—since Lendall and Gayle weren't very traditional—maybe it was actually quite radical: he got down on one knee, held out his left hand, and motioned for Gayle to place the ring in it. Which she did.

And then he took the ring and held it between his thumb and index finger.

And then he took Gayle's left hand and held it in his.

And he put the ring on her ring finger.

And said, "Gayle Pulcifer: Will you marry me?"

And Gayle said, "Yes," through a few tears.

And then Lendall helped his one and only up onto her feet.

And then he hugged her. And said, "I'm sorry," while he did.

Gayle broke from the hug and looked into Lendall's eyes. "For what?"

"For getting so quiet."

"Oh. Yeah. Well . . ."

"It's just—when you asked me what I thought about us getting married a couple weeks ago . . . well, you surprised me. And I just needed to figure some things out. And take care of a few things."

The main thing Lendall needed to figure out was whether or not he still wanted to get married. He had long since given up on marrying the love of his life. So when Gayle asked him what he thought about getting married the Saturday before last, he was completely taken aback, and it took him a second to figure out what he thought about it—but only a second, because he had been wanting to marry Gayle pretty much since the day he had met her on a snowmobile excursion to Quebec City almost eleven years ago.

And once he had figured out what he thought about them getting married, he realized that he needed to take care of a few things—like meet up with Gayle's dad and ask for his blessing. And call Gayle's mom (she lived in Connecticut) and ask for her blessing.

And then he needed to get her a ring.

And then he needed to decide when he was going to give it to her.

But he didn't tell Gayle what all he had needed to figure out or what all he had needed to take care of after he proposed to her on the night when all the extraordinary things did or didn't happen. He could tell her all that another time. So instead he said, "And you know that I get quiet when I need to figure things out and when I have things I need to take care of."

"I know," said Gayle. "Just . . . maybe you could try being a little less quiet. In the future. So I know what's goin' on."

"Maybe I could," admitted Lendall. And then he hugged Gayle again. Maybe to complete his apology.

And Gayle looked at the ring on her finger. And then pulled away from Lendall and hung her head in shame and said, "You know, you didn't have to get me a ring. That's not what I was asking—"

"Yeah, I did." Lendall got up on his feet again. "'Cause you wanna get married." Lendall took Gayle around the waist and pulled her close. "And so do I. Always have."

And they smiled into each other's eyes and started swaying to some music that only they could hear.

And then Gayle collapsed a little into Lendall's chest and said, "I'm so sorry. About tonight. It's just that—Sandrine and Martin haven't even been together for a year and they're already gettin' married." Gayle scowled at herself, because she hated that she had let Sandrine make her doubt her relationship with Lendall. "And, you know," she continued, "it's our anniversary comin' up . . . " Lendall was well aware of this and almost told Gayle that he was planning on proposing then—but then decided not to tell her that just then, because it didn't seem like that would help anything. "And," added Gayle, "I think all that stuff made me wonder what's goin' on with us. And—I don't have to wonder what's goin' on with us. I know what's goin' on with us. And I like it, what's goin' on with us. Always have."

"I'm glad. Me, too." Lendall pulled Gayle close. And gave her a kiss.

And they both felt that strange lightness grow inside them.

And they looked into each other's eyes and started swaying again because the music that only they could hear was playing again.

And all the love that Lendall had given Gayle was all around them—and taking up even more room than ever on the porch.

And all the love that Gayle had given Lendall was in the ring on her finger.

Gayle held up her hand so she could see the diamond sparkle in the porch light.

As she did so, she thought she might have caught a glimpse of the northern lights in the sky out over the Norsworthys' potato fields across the Road to Somewhere/Nowhere.

And she had. Because they had started dancing around in the sky when she opened the small maroon velvet box and saw the ring.

Gayle was disappointed she had only caught a glimpse of the northern lights.

And was then disappointed in herself for doubting something as undoubtable as Lendall's love.

And then she realized that she and Lendall had to go to Sandrine's wedding tomorrow—and Clair Gudreau's funeral.

And she wondered what she was going to say when everyone asked about her ring.

Because they'd see it.

And they'd ask Gayle to tell the story of how they got engaged.

And Gayle decided that she was going to have to make up a story.

Because there was no way she was going to tell the story of what had actually happened.

Because she would look like the biggest jerk in the world if she told people what had actually happened.

And—anyway—who would believe her if she told them?

8

As Ginette passed Lendall Tardy's house, she thought about how happy Lendall and Gayle seemed.

And how they had been together forever.

And then she thought about how she felt like she and Pete were going to be together forever after they had confessed their love for one another on the bench at Skyview Park.

But now—they weren't together at all.

They were far away from each other. And getting farther away with every step Ginette took.

Although—according to Pete and his theory on what it means to be close—every step Ginette took was bringing her *closer* to Pete.

But it was also bringing her closer to home, which was another few minutes' walk down the Road to Nowhere.

And she was looking forward to being home. And going to bed.

She was tired.

Telling someone you love them for the first time takes a lot out of you.

Having them tell you that they love you back—for the first time—takes more out of you.

But having them say that you aren't close to them at all—when you're sitting right next to them—after confessions of love have been made—takes just about everything that's left out of you.

It was 8:20 when Ginette passed Echo Lake Park, a wooded expanse that linked up with the North Maine Woods and the Allagash Wilderness and separated the two westernmost potato fields of Norsworthy's Potato Farm. Nestled among the evergreen forest was the park's main attraction, Echo Lake, one of Maine's six thousand lakes and ponds. Echo Lake's waters were fed by Echo Lake Brook, which was linked to a chain of streams and lakes and rivers that were home to landlocked Atlantic salmon, Arctic char, and the largest population of native brook trout in the United States.

Ginette had spent a lot of time at Echo Lake, swimming and fishing and kayaking and canoeing in the summer, and skating in the winter.

Marci and Phil Pelkey used to spend a lot of time at Echo Lake, too, swimming and fishing and kayaking and canoeing and skating. But life and its complications and responsibilities—like work and family obligations—had made it more difficult for them to find the time to go swimming, fishing, kayaking, canoeing, or skating—or do much of anything for fun—anymore.

But on the night when all the extraordinary things did or didn't happen, Marci had managed to get Phil to go skating at Echo Lake. For fun. Like they used to. And Phil didn't really want to go, because it was going to be more work than it was worth, he said, to clear the ice of all the snow that had fallen earlier in the day. So he asked his wife if she wanted to go to the Snowmobile Club up in Eagle Lake for a nice dinner instead of going skating.

And Marci said no, that she wanted to go skating—and that their son, Jason, and his buddies had cleared a hockey rink–size patch of ice on the lake and had been playing hockey there all afternoon. So there would be no snow to clear.

Besides, it'd be romantic, she said. Because they'd probably have the whole lake to themselves, because Country Swing was going on at the Rec Center.

And Phil said that, if she really wanted to go, then they should go.

And Marci said she really wanted to go.

So Phil grabbed a hockey duffel and loaded it up with their skates and a couple of flashlights and a couple of towels and some blankets and some extra winter clothing, and Marci loaded up a large L.L.Bean tote with a thermos of hot chocolate and a couple of Coleman lanterns and a box of wooden matches, and they hopped into Phil's GMC Sierra and headed west on the Road to Nowhere to Echo Lake so they could go skating.

As Phil drove, Marci talked about how maybe they needed to get Jason a math tutor. Geometry was killing him.

And then she talked about how she couldn't believe Missy would be heading off to college next fall. And said that people at school were telling her she had a really good a shot at getting into Bowdoin—and that that was pretty exciting.

And then she asked if maybe they could have Lendall Tardy come by and give them a quote for the kitchen. Marci wanted to knock down the wall between the dining room and the kitchen and get new cupboards.

And Phil wondered if maybe they could wait and see if Missy got into a fancy college like Bowdoin before they committed to remodeling their kitchen.

And Marci said that, now that she was working again, they'd be able to handle both the college and remodeling expenses.

And Phil shrugged and said, "We'll see," and seemed irked.

And Marci asked him if he was okay.

And he said he had a lot on his mind.

And neither of them said anything else as they came into down-township Almost.

They passed Skyview Park.

And the old Gallagher Potato Farm.

And St. Mary's Church.

And Ma Dudley's Boardinghouse.

And the Moose Paddy.

And the Rec Center.

And at a little after eight, they arrived at Echo Lake.

They turned left onto Echo Lake Road, which wended through the woods for about a quarter of a mile and then deposited them in the parking area—which was, as Marci had predicted, deserted.

Phil parked the Sierra and cut the engine and they got out of the truck. He grabbed the hockey duffel from the backseat and pulled one of the flashlights out of it, while Marci grabbed her tote bag. Phil's flashlight guided them down to the picnic tables—which had been dragged up to the edge of the frozen lake so skaters would have somewhere to sit while they changed into their skates.

Marci dropped her tote bag on the middle picnic table and removed the Coleman lanterns from it and placed them on the table. Then she primed them and got the box of wooden matches from her bag, struck one, and lit the lanterns' mantles, which began to glow white hot.

Phil clicked off his flashlight now that the lanterns had been lit and placed it on the picnic table.

Then Marci and Phil sat down on the picnic table bench, and Phil pulled their skates out of his hockey duffel.

Phil took off his Red Wings and slid his old black CCM hockey skates on and laced them up.

And Marci kicked off her new black waterproof slip-on faux-suede winter shoes that Phil's mom had gotten her from L.L.Bean for Christmas, and she slid her old white figure skates on and laced them up. When she was ready to skate, she hopped up and said, "Come on!" And she grabbed one of the Coleman lanterns and skated to the center of the rink that had been created by Jason and his hockey buddies earlier in the day, and set the lantern down so the makeshift ice rink was illuminated.

"I'm comin'," said Phil. He finished tying his skates and watched his wife of twenty-three years hit the ice. He had forgotten what a good skater she was. She had grown up in Presque Isle, where they have an indoor ice rink called the Forum, and she had taken figure skating lessons there when she was younger.

As Phil watched Marci, he felt like he still loved her.

"What are you doin'?" called Marci. She could make out his silhouette against the light from the lantern on the picnic table—and it wasn't moving. "Come on!"

Phil got up and joined Marci on the ice.

And they skated for a while. And Marci started singing an old rock song about being on the edge of seventeen that they always used to hear at the Forum in Presque Isle when she'd take Phil to Public Skate when they were in high school. The song reminded Phil of better times. Or of times when he felt like he was better. Or something. So he started singing along.

And he and Marci almost had fun. But not quite. Maybe because Phil felt like Marci was trying to force the fun. Which was what she always seemed to be doing lately.

And that irritated him.

And then Marci tried to get Phil to dance with her. And that irritated him some more, and he abruptly shrugged his wife off and skated off by himself.

And Marci watched Phil skate off. And sighed defeatedly. Because Phil was irritated with her. And had been for a while. Which seemed fair, actually, because she had been irritated with him for a while, too.

But on the night when all the extraordinary things did or didn't happen, she wanted to see if maybe they could become a little less irritated with each other.

And she gently called to her husband and asked him if he was okay and said that he seemed on edge.

And Phil apologized and said he *was* on edge. Because work had been a lot lately. There was a lot going on—and wrong—at Aroostook Pellets, the wood pellet plant in Masardis that Phil owned and ran. The company was still rebuilding from a fire last summer that had destroyed one of the storage silos. And oil prices were low—cheaper than pellets, currently. So wood pellets weren't as popular a fuel source as they had been, so sales were down. Way down. And Phil was starting to worry that the business he had built was going to fail.

"Well, try to just . . . you know, be here now," said Marci gently. "And let that all go for a little while. So we can have some fun."

"Yeah."

And then Phil apologized for thinking about work so much lately.

And then he apologized for being late for their date—he had gotten hung up at work, as usual. And Marci told him not to worry about it and said that she understood and then skated away from him, because she really didn't understand. But now wasn't the time to let him know that she didn't understand. And she wondered if there would ever be a right time to say that she didn't understand. Because there was so much she didn't understand lately.

Phil watched Marci skate away. And really wanted to smoke a cigarette. But he didn't have any cigarettes, because Marci had made him quit.

So he just watched his wife skate for a while.

And then he found himself staring out across the lake, past the illuminated makeshift ice rink, and into the darkness. He was lost—not in thought (because he wasn't thinking), but in time and space. So he didn't hear Marci when she called to him.

"Phil!"

Phil was looking her way but he wasn't responding.

"Phil!" Marci called again.

"Huh?" asked Phil, shaking himself out of his daze.

"What are you doin'?"

"Oh, just . . ." And he didn't finish his sentence, because he didn't know what he had been doing. And he started skating over to his wife. "I don't know."

"Well, did you see that?" Marci was asking Phil if he had seen the impressive spin and jump that she had just done.

"What?"

"I just did a single axel!" A single axel is a jump in figure skating that requires a skater to jump up while skating forward, rotate one and a half times in the air, and then land skating backward. Marci used to be able to do double axels—but she hadn't skated in years. So she was pretty happy she was able to execute a single axel. "I still got it, baby!" she boasted. "Did you see me?" she asked, skating over to Phil.

"Aah, sorry, I didn't."

"Oh." Marci was surprised by how disappointed she was that Phil had missed her single axel.

"But that's awesome!" cheered Phil a bit too enthusiastically.

"I haven't done one of those in . . . who knows how long," said Marci, enthused but rueful.

"Awesome!"

"I thought you were watching—it looked like you were watching."

"I was," lied Phil, without meaning to.

"Well, obviously you weren't. What were you doing?"

"I don't know." Phil really wished he had just lied and said he had seen his wife's single axel. "I guess I was just . . . thinkin'. About work," he said, lying again. He hadn't been thinking about anything. But he knew she'd believe him if he said he was thinking about work. Because he was always thinking about work lately. "Sorry."

"Well, just try to be here now, you know."

"Yeah. Sorry," said Phil, wanting a cigarette again. And then he tried to make up for missing Marci's single axel and said, "Hey! Why don't you do another one! I'll watch this time."

Marci laughed and said she didn't know if she could pull off another one. And then changed the subject and asked, "Want some hot chocolate?"

"Sure."

And Marci and Phil skated back to their picnic table, and Marci pulled a thermos out of her tote bag and cracked it open and poured a couple of mugs full of hot chocolate, and they sat and sipped.

"Mmm. This is good," said Phil.

"Thanks. I made it the way people used to make it. With actual melted chocolate."

"It's good."

Marci was still excited that she had executed a single axel jump. And started talking about how maybe she should take skating lessons again. Just for fun. Her work brought her to Presque Isle a few days a month. Maybe the next time she was there, she could swing by the Forum and inquire about lessons.

Phil wasn't really listening to his wife because he was actually thinking about work. It looked like Aroostook Pellets might be losing its largest single contract, the University of Maine at Fort Kent, because the university had started installing biomass boilers. And now Phil was worried that biomass was going to become the university's preferred heating fuel.

"Phil!"

Phil jumped a little and wondered why Marci was practically yelling at him. He didn't know that she had asked him—twice—what he thought about her taking skating lessons.

"What?" he asked, irritated—because his wife seemed irritated.

"Where are you? Where'd you go?"

"Oh. Sorry—just . . . we may be losing the university in Fort Kent—and . . . we're gonna have to lay people off if we do. And that's . . . not a good feeling."

"Oh. Sorry." Marci didn't realize how grave the situation at Aroostook Pellets was and wanted to comfort her husband—but didn't know how to.

And then Phil started unlacing his skates. Because he was done skating. And never wanted to go in the first place.

And Marci forgot about wanting to comfort Phil. "What are you doing?" she demanded.

"I thought we were done."

"We're just having a hot chocolate break, Phil," said Marci, exasperated. "We haven't even been here twenty-five minutes! And you told me to do another single axel—so you could see!"

"Oh." Phil had forgotten that he had said that he wanted to see his wife do another single axel.

But he couldn't bring himself to re-lace his skates.

Because he didn't want to see her do another single axel. And he didn't want to be at Echo Lake.

Marci saw Phil make no effort to lace his skates back up.

So she started undoing her skates—and made sure that he knew she was angry as she did. Because she didn't want to leave. "I mean," she griped, "we just got here."

"You're right. Sorry," said Phil. And he started reluctantly lacing his skates back up.

"No. Forget it. Let's go."

"Sorry—it's just . . . my mind's not here."

"Yeah, I know."

"And I'm kinda cold," groused Phil. Marci looked at her husband and wanted to say, "Liar." Because it wasn't cold. It was nineteen degrees. And Marci wasn't cold yet. And if she wasn't cold, there was no way that Phil was cold.

He just didn't want to be there. And Marci knew it.

"Okay. Fine," said Marci, in a way that made Phil know it wasn't fine.

And, even though he knew it wasn't fine that he wanted to go, Phil couldn't bring himself to make any effort to stay.

So he and Marci unlaced their skates. And the air got heavy with disappointment and dissatisfaction as they did. It felt like what the air in their house felt like when they had been arguing. Or like when they were just about to argue. It was a feeling similar to when the barometric pressure changes before a storm comes.

But they hadn't been arguing.

Maybe that was just what the air around them was like now.

"I mean, if you really wanna stay, we can stay," offered Phil half-heartedly, trying not to seem like the bad guy.

"It's okay, Phil."

"Well, I feel like it's not okay. I feel like you're mad."

"I'm not mad!"

Phil wanted to say, "Then don't act like you're mad," but wisely did not. And, instead, just said, "Okay."

And Marci and Phil unlaced their skates in silence.

And soon, Phil had taken off his old CCMs and had put his Red Wings back on. And he took one of the towels from the old hockey duffel and wiped the snow and ice off his skate blades so they wouldn't rust, and then slid his skate guards on them to protect them. Meanwhile, Marci had pulled off her skates. And she slid on one of her new black waterproof slip-on faux-suede winter shoes. And then went to slide on her other new black waterproof slip-on faux-suede winter shoe.

But she couldn't find it.

She looked underneath where she was sitting.

And she looked around her.

But it was nowhere to be found.

Which was weird.

Because it had to be there. Somewhere.

She was just about to ask Phil if he had seen her other shoe when he said, "We don't have to go."

"Phil, you don't wanna be here, so let's go."

"Well, I feel like you're gonna be mad at me if we go."

"I'm not."

"But I also feel like you're gonna be mad at me if we stay, so—"

"Phil, I'm not mad!"

"Well, it feels like you are. Or—were."

"I'm not mad, Phil," she said, realizing that she may have sounded mad. And she tried to assure Phil she wasn't. "I was having fun," she said almost brightly. "I had fun, skating. Did you?"

Phil wanted to say no. But he didn't. He just nodded yes.

Phil and Marci had learned, like many educated and successful people, how to not quite tell the truth about their feelings in that way that only educated, successful people know how to do.

"Good," said Marci, happy that Phil had had fun. She wanted to stroke his hair. Which was so gray now. And thinning on the top. And so cute, she thought. But she didn't touch him. Because she and Phil hadn't touched in a while. And the longer you go without touching the person you love—or once loved—the harder it is to touch them. Or be touched by them.

Marci looked again for her other new black waterproof slip-on faux-suede winter shoe.

But still couldn't find it.

Anywhere.

Phil didn't know that his wife was having trouble finding her other shoe. But he did know that she was mad. At him. And he thought he knew why. So he tried to defend himself. "I mean, I'm sorry I missed your jump out there—"

"It was a single axel."

"I'm sorry I missed your single axel jump, and—"

"It's okay—"

"And I'm sorry I was late getting home tonight—but we're trying to figure out how to . . . stay in business. It's serious, you know."

"I know."

"I don't think you do," retorted Phil.

Marci was still looking for her other new black waterproof slip-on faux-suede winter shoe and said, "Phil—I'm not mad at you. You had to stay late. You've got a lot goin' on."

"I do!"

"I get it."

Phil was about to say "I don't think you do" again when Marci preempted him and said, "Phil, where's my shoe?"

It took Phil a second to process the off-topic question, and asked, "What?"

"Where's my shoe? I can't find it."

"Well . . ." Phil scanned the area. And saw no sign of Marci's other shoe. Which was odd. "It's gotta be here," he said, puzzled.

"Where is it?!?" Marci asked again, flummoxed.

"I don't know."

"Well, it's black. Like this one." Marci held up her left foot and showed Phil the new black waterproof slip-on faux-suede winter shoe that was on it. "So it oughta show up in the snow, right?"

"It oughta." Phil grabbed one of the flashlights he had brought and searched the area for a moment. And then asked, "Is it . . . buried?"

Phil started kicking at the fresh snow around him to see if Marci's other shoe would materialize.

And Marci grabbed the Coleman lantern and searched the area around her to see if she could locate her other shoe.

And then she stopped searching and turned to her husband and asked—with a little sass—"Is this you being funny?" She hoped that Phil was being funny. Because Phil used to be funny. So, so funny. And fun.

"No!" said Phil, defending himself.

"'Cause it's not funny," scolded Marci. "I'm cold!" And she actually was, now. And her stocking foot was colder.

"Well, you're the one that wanted to go skating!"

"Well, if you didn't want to go, you should have just said."

"I did say! I said, 'Wanna go to dinner at the Snowmobile Club instead?' But you said you wanted to go skating. And I said that if you really wanted to go, then we should go."

"Yeah, well, I really wanted to go."

"Yeah! And we went! We're here!"

"Yeah." They were there. At least she was. But he wasn't. She felt like Phil wasn't really ever anywhere that she was anymore. And she almost laid into him and told him so, when her better nature suddenly took over. And made her say, appreciatively, "And I'm glad we're here. Thanks for going with me."

"Sure," said Phil. And he felt like everything was okay for a second.

Marci also felt like things were okay for a second.

And then Phil got back to work looking for Marci's shoe.

And Marci put the Coleman lantern back on the picnic table and put her skate back on, so she could be more mobile—and to warm up her stocking foot.

And then, with one skate on and one shoe on, she grabbed the lantern and joined Phil in the search for her other shoe.

After a few seconds, she stopped searching and turned to Phil and said, "You know . . . we used to do this all the time."

"Look for your other shoe?" asked Phil, being funny.

"Ha-ha, no. Go skating." She was hoping hard that he would understand why she wanted to go skating so badly. "Why don't we come here anymore?"

"I don't know."

"It's fun."

Phil didn't quite agree that skating was fun. But didn't say so.

And then Marci realized that it had been a really long time since she and Phil had done anything fun.

And she wondered why that was and asked, "Why do people stop doing the things they used to do for fun, huh?"

"I don't know. They get busy, I guess."

"Well . . . that's no reason to stop doing fun things."

Phil shrugged. And didn't know what else to say about why people stop doing the things they used to do for fun. And he really wasn't interested in thinking about why he and his wife didn't have fun anymore, so he changed the topic and got them back on task and asked, "Where the heck is your shoe? It's gotta be here."

Marci watched Phil as he resumed his search for Marci's other shoe—which he was expanding to include the entire picnic area.

And then she felt like she needed to extend an olive branch—maybe to preempt the fight that she felt was coming. "Phil," she said tenderly, "I'm not mad. I was never mad."

Phil stopped searching and turned to his wife and felt like Marci was about to apologize for being so hard on him lately. But instead she said, "I just . . . I thought you'd be more excited about bein' here tonight."

"Marce, I'm sorry, but I told you, work's been—"

"I know! Work's been rough. And I thought you needed some fun! And I thought it would be fun—to come here. Help us forget all the . . . stuff. Get us away from the kids, get us back to where we used to be. We went skating, you know, the first time you kissed me. On a Friday night just like this one. 'Member? Right here. Echo Lake."

Marci had made her way over to Phil and reached out and linked her pinkie finger in his, hoping Phil would remember. And he did. He had met Marci in high school at a party in Presque Isle. He had arrived with Lori York and left with Marci McCrumb. And they started dating. And Phil had to convince Marci's parents that a boy from the hick non-town of Almost was worthy of their daughter. And that took some doing. But he did it.

And on their third date, he took her to Echo Lake.

And they kissed.

And knew that they loved each other.

And they promised to always remember the way they felt on that night. And Marci linked her pinkie finger in Phil's.

But when Marci linked her pinkie in Phil's on the night when all the extraordinary things did or didn't happen, Phil pulled his pinkie—and all of himself—away from her and grumbled, "Where the heck is your shoe?"

Marci was stunned by her husband's rejection.

"Maybe it's in the truck," reckoned Phil. And he scanned the picnic table area again with his flashlight and started toward the Sierra.

"It's not gonna be in the truck, Phil," mumbled Marci. And she made her way back to the picnic bench and put the lantern back down on the picnic table and sat down and stared into the blackness beyond the illuminated patch of ice they had been skating on.

She heard Phil open the truck's passenger-side front and rear doors. Then she heard nothing as he searched. And then she heard him close the passenger-side front and rear doors.

And then she heard the scrunch of footsteps in the snow as Phil walked around to the driver's side. And then she heard him open the driver's side front and rear doors. And then she heard nothing while Phil searched.

Marci shook her head. She knew he wasn't going to find her shoe. Because she hadn't taken it off in the truck. She had taken it off at the picnic table, with him.

And besides, he was never going to find it, because he couldn't find things.

She looked up at the sky as if it might tell her what was going on with her husband of nineteen years.

And then she closed her eyes and prayed that they would be okay.

And that things at Aroostook Pellets would be okay.

And that Phil would be okay.

Her prayers were interrupted when she heard Phil slam the doors to the Sierra, having thoroughly searched it for Marci's other shoe.

And she opened her eyes, still looking at the sky. And heard him make his way back to the picnic table.

"Well, it's not in the truck," conceded Phil, dropping his flashlight on the icy picnic table and sitting down. "I wonder—"

Marci suddenly jumped up, interrupting Phil and shushing him. "Oh-oh-oh! Shh-shh-shh! Shooting star, shooting star!" she cried, and she sat back down and closed her eyes and wished on the streak in the sky she had just seen as if her life depended on it.

Phil looked up, excited. "Wha—where, where?!?" But he was too late to see anything but the regular stars. "Where?" Phil asked again, disappointed he had missed the shooting star.

Marci's eyes were still closed. "Shh!! I'm wishing, I'm wishing!"

Irritated that his wife had just shushed him, Phil searched the sky for the shooting star. And then stopped feeling disappointed that he had missed it, because all he had actually missed was a piece of falling space debris. Because that's what shooting stars are. Falling bits of rock that are burning up in the atmosphere. "Oh, well," he said. "I missed it."

Marci finished wishing and looked over at her husband, her eyes resigned and a little dead. "Yeah, you did," she said, in a way that made it difficult for Phil to determine whether she was agreeing with him or berating him.

It felt more like she was berating him—and like she was spoiling for a fight.

So Phil got ready to fight. "What's that supposed to mean?"

"Nothing. It's just . . . not really all that surprising," she said. And she let just enough disdain color her response that Phil could tell that she, too, was spoiling for a fight.

"What's not surprising?" asked Phil.

"That you didn't see it." Marci waved her arm up at the sky to let him know that by "it," she meant the shooting star.

"Why is that not surprising?"

"You don't pay attention, Phil."

Phil smiled angrily and shook his head and said, "See, when you say things like that, I feel like you're still mad."

"I'm not mad!" Marci truly thought she was telling the truth.

"Marce—"

"I wasn't mad!" And then she exploded, "*Where the heck is my shoe?!?*" And she got up and grabbed the flashlight and angrily searched the area around the picnic table.

Phil didn't quite know how to respond to Marci's explosion. Because he didn't understand why she was so upset that she had lost her shoe. Because he didn't understand that she was angry about a lot more than not being able to find her other shoe.

"Maybe it *is* in the truck," muttered Marci, mostly to herself. And she started hobbling up to the Sierra—even though she knew her other shoe wasn't in the truck. She just wanted to get away from Phil. Because she was angry at him. And she couldn't figure out how to tell him why.

"It's not in the truck," said Phil—mostly to himself. And he watched her go. She looked so ridiculous, limping along with one skate on and one shoe on.

And then he turned and looked out past the illuminated patch of ice they had been skating on and into the darkness and thought about how much he hated it when people pointed out shooting stars to him. Because he never saw them.

He hated it even more when people pointed out the man in the moon. He bet that most people—like him—had never seen the man in the moon and were just too afraid to admit it. Well, he was admitting it: he had never actually seen the man in the moon.

He looked skyward for the moon so he could prove that he couldn't see the pareidolic image.

But there was no moon in the sky on the night when all the extraordinary things did or didn't happen. Because it was a new moon. So he couldn't prove anything.

As he scanned the sky looking for the moon, the Milky Way overwhelmed him. It was so deep. And mesmerizing. And he got a little dizzy—and felt like he might fall up into it.

But then he steadied himself when he heard Marci opening and closing all the doors to the truck, searching for her other shoe in all the same places Phil had searched. And he figured she'd find it. Because Marci always managed to find all the things her son and her daughter and her husband couldn't find.

"This is so weird," Marci called down to Phil. "I know I didn't put my skates on in the car, 'cause the shoe I have on was out there, under the picnic table bench. 'Cause I put my skates on out there with you, right?"

Phil didn't answer, because he was staring out across the illuminated makeshift ice rink and out into the blackness.

"Phil?" Marci repeated as she made her way back down to the picnic table. "I put my shoes right next to yours after we put our skates on, but it's not . . . there. This is the weirdest thing."

Phil dropped his head in his hands and pressed his palms against his eyes. And wondered how he could be so angry with someone he used to love so much. And he couldn't breathe for a moment—because he had never thought of Marci as someone that he used to love.

"It's not in the truck," continued Marci. "I mean, I'm not gonna put one skate on in the car, the other one on out here—" Marci interrupted herself when she returned to the picnic table, because she saw Phil hunched over, his head in his hands. "Hey—you okay?"

"Huh?" Phil wasn't okay. He was so sad. But he sat up quickly and did his best not to look sad.

But Marci could tell something wasn't right. "What's wrong?" she asked.

"Oh . . ." Phil tried to cover up his sadness and lied, "Nothin'." And then he looked up at the sky and he lied some more. "I'm just makin' a wish of my own, on a regular one."

"Oh." Marci looked up at the stars.

"Wanna wish on it with me?" offered Phil.

"Yeah," said Marci, touched by the offer. "Yeah, that'd be nice," she said, sitting down next to her husband and asking, "Which one?"

"Umm . . . see Shepalojo Mountain?" asked Phil. Marci looked across the lake and could make out the silhouette of Shepalojo Mountain against the starlit sky. Shepalojo Mountain wasn't even sixteen hundred feet high, so it really should have been called Shepalojo Hill.

"Uh-huh," said Marci. She and Phil were talking to one another familiarly and kindly. And they hadn't done that in a long time. And they both liked it.

"Go straight up, right above it," continued Phil, pointing directly above the mountain to the brightest object in the sky.

Marci followed the line of Phil's arm to make sure she was looking where Phil was looking and asked, "The bright one?"

"Yeah."

"That one?" asked Marci, making sure Phil could see which star she was pointing at. She seemed irritated, which confused Phil.

"Yeah, what's wrong?"

Marci took Phil's arm and used it as a sight just to be sure she was looking where her husband was pointing. "The reddish one, right there?" she asked, seeming more irritated.

"Yeah, what's wrong?"

"Phil?"

"Yeah?"

"That's a planet."

"What?"

"That's a planet. You're wishing on a planet."

"That's a—?"

"A planet, yeah."

"Well, how do you know?"

"And it's . . ." Marci started singing, 'When you wish upon a *star*,' not 'when you wish upon a *planet* or *Jupiter*'!"

"How do you know it's a planet?"

"Jupiter's the brightest object in the sky this month. They've been sayin' it on the weather all week. And your wish is never gonna come true if you're wishing on a planet."

"Well—"

"You gotta pay attention," chided Marci.

"Why do you keep sayin' that?"

"What?"

"That I gotta pay attention?"

"'Cause you don't."

"What are you talkin' about?"

"Phil." Marci looked right at her husband and said, "Happy Anniversary."

Phil stopped breathing.

And tried to make sense of what his wife had just said.

And when he had made sense of it, he realized that he had forgotten their anniversary.

And his stomach hurt.

And he grimaced and weakly asked, "Huh?"

"Happy Anniversary," repeated Marci. "That's what I'm talkin' about."

Phil knew he was in trouble.

He knew he was in the wrong.

And he knew he needed to say he was sorry.

And he almost did. "I'm . . ."

But then he didn't.

And instead of saying he was sorry, he said, "I knew you were mad."

Phil's response to Marci's revelation was not at all what Marci was expecting.

She was expecting him to say, "I'm sorry."

Or, "Happy Anniversary to you, too, honey."

Not, "I knew you were mad."

"What?!?" squeaked Marci, glaring at Phil.

"I knew you were mad," repeated Phil.

"I heard you!" snapped Marci, sighing in disbelief and glaring at her husband. "I'm not mad, Phil!"

"Yeah, you are! You're mad at me, and pretty soon, outta nowhere, it's gonna get ugly!" It had already gotten ugly. Phil was a good man, but he had a temper. And it was flaring.

Marci knew how to handle Phil's temper and calmly stated, "Phil, hon, I'm not mad, I'm—"

But it was too late. The gasket had been blown. "I mean, Marce:

I'm *sorry*!! I know I missed some things, but I gotta *work*! The company's in trouble. The plant could close. And everything I've worked for might be gone."

"I know, I know—"

"No, you *don't* know. If it fails . . . what'll we do?"

"We'll figure somethin' out—"

"What? What'll we figure out?"

"I don't know—"

"Yeah! That's why I gotta be there so much. I gotta work to keep it goin', and you can't get mad at me for that, for wanting to be able to pay for our lives!"

"Phil! I'm not mad at you for that. I understand all that. What I don't understand . . ." Marci's throat closed up in the way throats do before tears fall. But she managed to keep the tears at bay and said, "What I don't understand is . . . why I'm lonely. I got a husband and a coupla great kids. And I'm lonely."

Living in Almost, Maine, had always been lonely for Marci. Because she was a city girl. From Presque Isle. So she was from away. And would always be from away.

And she was the girl who had nabbed Phil Pelkey, much to the dismay of the other girls in Almost who had hoped to nab Phil Pelkey.

And she and Phil had money. And a nice house. Unlike most people in Almost.

And she had had her kids later in life. So Marci was ten years older than the moms of her kids' friends.

And she had gone to Bates College—one of those fancy, expensive colleges.

And she ran the Burby Foundation and wanted to help people in northern Maine. And many people in northern Maine didn't like people who thought they needed help. Even though Almost had benefited tremendously from the work the foundation did. Marci had recently awarded grants to Gayle Pulcifer at the Rec Center so she could expand her programming, as well as to a bunch of dark-sky enthusiasts so they could build the observatory at Skyview Park.

So Marci had always felt like the outsider since she had moved to Almost. And that had made her feel lonely.

But the lonely she was feeling right now was a different kind of lonely. It was the kind of lonely that only people who have been married for a while can understand.

Phil had no idea what to say. He had had no idea that his wife was lonely.

"And, you know," continued Marci, "I shouldn't be lonely." She shook her head, and a few tears fell out of her eyes.

It killed Phil to see Marci so sad.

But he didn't know what to do to comfort her.

And it killed him that she was lonely.

But he couldn't bring himself to make her less lonely.

"You just . . ." Marci took a second to pull herself together and went on. "You don't pay attention anymore. And—I know you're busy. I'm so proud of you and what you've made, but . . . you're never here. With me. Anymore. You go away. Somewhere where you can't pay attention, and you miss Jason's first varsity basketball game. And you forget Missy's birthday."

"Honey . . ." Phil wanted to defend himself. But he couldn't. So he didn't.

So Marci added, "And you forget your anniversary."

Phil felt like the biggest jerk of all time for forgetting their anniversary. And he was about to say he was sorry, because he thought Marci was finished. But she wasn't. "I mean, I brought you here hoping you'd remember—about us. About . . . what we used to be. Before we got to where we are now."

She paused. And sighed. And looked out onto the lake, past the illuminated makeshift ice rink and into the blackness.

And then said, "But you didn't. Remember."

And then she was still. And seemed defeated.

But then she took a deep breath and turned to Phil and hissed, "And that makes me *so mad* that . . . I don't know what to do anymore."

Phil winced at the rage Marci had unleashed.

But then realized how happy he was to finally have some truth.

Because Marci never told him the truth anymore.

So he gave her some truth right back.

"You lie," he said.

"What?!" she rejoined. Phil's response was so far afield of what she was expecting, it was almost absurd.

"You lie so bad."

"*What?!?*"

"You're mad at me. But you don't *tell* me—even when I ask you over and over."

"Because I'm only just figuring all this out!" cried Marci.

"No! No! No!" yelled Phil, springing to his feet. "You figured it out a long time ago! You've been mad at me—and disappointed in me—for a looooong time. But you don't tell me you're mad or disappointed. You just expect me to figure it out. So I'm always wondering how I'm doin'—as a husband, as a dad. So I just have to wonder and wonder and wonder where I am, where I stand with you." Phil took a moment to breathe. And then added, "Maybe that's why I go away. So I can know where I am for a second." Phil stewed and paced for a moment and then stopped and turned to Marci and snarled, "And you know what? It's lonely there, too, where I go. And you sent me there. You went away a long time before I did."

"I didn't go anywhere!"

"Yeah, you do. You go . . . wherever *I'm* not! Everything you do is for the kids! And now—with your new job—for *other* people! And *their* kids! And there's nothin' left for me! And you go around *lyin'* like you like me and like we're so happy—"

"I don't go around lying!"

"Yes, you do! You say you're not mad, but you're mad! You say you have fun, but you don't! You didn't have fun tonight, did you?"

"No."

"But you kept sayin' you did."

"I didn't. I didn't have fun, Phil. I don't have fun with you anymore."

Phil started nodding as he took in the truth Marci had spoken. And it hurt. But it was refreshing. And then he started laughing and said, "Well, I don't either."

And there it was. The truth. From both of them. For the first time in a long time.

"Well, then . . ." Marci smiled, even though her heart was heavy and achy. She was good at smiling when she didn't mean it, and then asked, "What are we doin'?"

And Marci and Phil looked—really looked—at each other for the first time in a long time.

And neither of them much liked what they were looking at.

So they looked out onto the lake—past the illuminated make-shift ice rink and out into the darkness.

And they sat in the stillness. And felt . . . nothing. A winter night in northern Maine can make you feel nothing. Because it can make you feel senseless. The cold can numb your hands and feet, so you can't feel them. Cold air is practically odorless, so you can't smell anything. And it's so dark, you feel like you can't see. And it's so quiet, you feel like you can't hear.

So none of your senses feel like they work.

And you feel senseless.

Numb.

Which was how Marci and Phil felt.

Phil sat down next to Marci at the picnic table.

And neither of them knew what to say.

And neither of them knew what to do.

And then—they both felt a strange peace. And a strange lightness filled up their insides—and made them feel like they had just been released of a heavy, heavy weight. And also—like everything was going to be okay, somehow. Eventually.

Marci turned to Phil and asked, "Phil?"

"Yeah?"

"I asked you a question: What are we doin'?"

"I don't know," answered Phil.

Marci didn't know what they were doing either.

"Well then . . . what are we waiting for?" asked Marci.

Phil didn't know what Marci meant by the question and was about to ask—when something fell.

From the sky.

Into the snow.

Right in front of them.

Phil and Marci jumped—Phil all the way up onto his feet. And they looked down in front of them to see what had fallen from the sky.

It had fallen far enough and fast enough that it had almost disappeared into the snow—into a hole of its own making.

Phil shone his flashlight on the hole as he went toward it.

Marci followed.

And Phil reached into the hole.

And dug out a shoe. A new black waterproof slip-on faux-suede winter shoe from L.L.Bean.

It was Marci's other shoe.

And it had dropped.

From the sky.

Phil and Marci looked at each other.

And then looked back at the shoe.

And then they looked up to see if maybe it had fallen out of a tree or something. But there were no tree branches above them. Just the sky—which was all aglow with the northern lights. Which normally would have elicited more awe from the Pelkeys. But the shoe that had fallen from above—from seemingly out of nowhere—was hogging all the awe.

Marci and Phil looked down at the shoe that Phil was holding.

And then looked back up at the sky. Which was still full of the northern lights.

And then they looked back down at the shoe.

And tried to figure out where it had come from.

But couldn't.

And then Phil held the shoe out to Marci.

And Marci took it.

And looked at it.

And then looked at her husband.

And then looked back up at the sky.

And then looked back at her husband.

And then looked back at the shoe.

And then sat down on the picnic bench and pulled her skate off.

And checked the sky one more time.

And looked at the shoe one more time.

And then slipped it on.

And looked back up at the sky.

And then looked to her husband.

And wondered what in the world was happening.

And then she slowly stood up and started gathering their things—her skates, Phil's skates, the thermos—and shoved them into the hockey duffel bag. Then she shouldered the duffel, grabbed her totebag and the Coleman lantern, and made her way up to the Sierra, and tossed the duffel bag and her tote onto the backseat of the truck. Then she switched off the lantern and watched the flame die and set it on the floor in the backseat.

And then she got in the truck and waited for Phil to join her so they could go home.

But Phil didn't join her.

She rolled down her window and leaned out and called, "Phil."

And waited for an answer.

And didn't get one.

So she rolled up the window and grabbed a flashlight out of the glove box and made her way back down to the picnic table and shone her light on Phil. Who had been staring out across the lake, past the illuminated makeshift ice rink and out into the darkness.

"Phil. Come on."

But Phil didn't come on.

Instead, he took his keys out of his pocket and held them out to Marci without looking at her.

And Marci stared at them.

And she felt a heaviness in her stomach. And it made her feel awful.

But then that strange lightness filled up her insides again. And it made her feel hopeful. And brighter. And unburdened.

And she took the keys from Phil.

And made her way back up to the Sierra.

She stopped and turned to Phil and jangled the keys once to let him know she was going—and maybe to ask him if he really wanted her to go.

Phil didn't respond.

So Marci got in the Sierra, flicked off the flashlight and tossed it onto the passenger seat.

And then she started the truck.

The sound of the engine roaring to life filled the silent night. And the headlights flooded the ground and illuminated the spruce and hemlock and fir and pine trees. And Echo Lake Road.

Marci gave Phil one last chance to change his mind and join her in the truck.

But Phil was still staring out across the lake.

And not changing his mind.

So Marci revved the engine and drove up Echo Lake Road toward the Road to Somewhere/Nowhere.

And she took a right on the Road to Somewhere.

And headed home.

And the sound of the Sierra melted away into the silence.

And Phil felt the lightness fill his insides again. And it made him feel brighter.

Which was confusing, because he felt so sad.

But the lightness felt good. It made him feel unburdened. And hopeful, somehow.

He looked up at the sky.

And the northern lights were gone.

But he saw a shooting star.

His first instinct was to point it out to Marci.

But she wasn't there.

9

As Ginette passed Echo Lake, she wished that she had never taken Pete to the observatory at Skyview Park to see if they might see the northern lights.

Because the only thing there was to do at the observatory was sit. And look at the sky. And she wished she and Pete had gone and *done* something. Like—gone dancing. Or gone skating at Echo Lake.

They could have seen the northern lights just fine while they were out on the ice. And if they appeared, great. And if not, they would have at least been doing something fun.

And Ginette could have let whatever was happening between them just be what it was—and become what it was, in its own time, instead of trying to name what it was.

She cursed herself for forcing the issue with Pete.

And then she dreamed on how going skating with Pete would have played out.

They probably would have had to shovel a space to skate on, and Pete would have grumbled a little about how much work it would have been. Because he was a little lazy.

And then Ginette would have had to hold Pete's hand to make sure he didn't fall. Because he was a lousy skater.

And she would have felt so close to him while she held his hand.

And he would have felt so close to her.

And they probably would have felt exactly like they had felt when they were sitting on the bench at the observatory.

And then she thought that maybe she should go back to the observatory and just sit back down next to Pete on the bench and take his hand in hers and not talk about what had just happened.

And they could just be close again.

And they could start over.

And she almost turned and ran back to him—when she realized that she was home.

And decided that home was actually just what she needed.

And she crossed the Road to Nowhere and made her way into Spruce View Estates on Spruce View Lane.

Hers was the first mobile home on the right.

She headed up her driveway and remembered that her mom was at work, so she'd have the house to herself. So she could have a snack and watch something dumb on TV and fall asleep on the couch.

And maybe she'd see Pete tomorrow and try to pick up where they were before they had gone to Skyview Park—when they were holding hands in front of Pete's parents—before Ginette had tried to name what they were.

But then that strange lightness filled up her insides again. It was the same lightness she had felt earlier in the evening when she had held Pete's hand and told him she loved him, and when Pete had told her that he loved her, too.

And that lightness made her feel like something really wonderful was going to happen.

And it made her feel like Pete was a part of the wonderful thing that was going to happen.

And it made her turn around and head back down Spruce View Lane and back to the Road to Nowhere.

She was about to turn left and head east on the Road to Somewhere to go see Pete.

But that strange lightness made her turn right.

And head west.

Toward the edge of Almost and the wilderness of northwestern Maine.

It was 8:30 when she heard a car approaching slowly from behind her. And she hoped that whoever was driving wouldn't stop and check on her, like Gayle Pulcifer had. Fortunately, the vehicle passed Ginette by, and when it did, Ginette could see that it was a taxicab—and she had only seen a few taxicabs in her life. In Presque Isle. In Bangor. In Washington, DC, on a school trip.

But she had never seen one in Almost.

Who the heck, she wondered, would have been taking a taxi to Almost, Maine?

And where were they going?

The Road to Nowhere ended in less than a mile. And there were only two more houses on it: the Hardings' and Rhonda Rideout's—which was the last house in Almost before the wilderness began.

Ginette watched the taxi's red taillights shrink as they moved away from her. And then they stopped moving away from her. Because the taxi had stopped—about a quarter of a mile away at the Hardings' house.

Ginette walked more slowly and watched the taxi sit in front of the Hardings' for about a minute. And then it turned around and started heading back toward Ginette. And went by her.

Ginette wondered where it was going.

And then she wondered where she was going. And she stopped and almost turned and started making her way back home.

But just as she was about to turn back, she felt that strange lightness fill up her insides. And it made her keep walking.

Even though she had no idea where she was going.

At 8:35, Ginette reached the Hardings', which was about half a mile down the road from Echo Lake.

Mr. and Mrs. Harding had two daughters. Allie was a couple of years younger than Ginette and was really good at chess and wore the thickest glasses Ginette had ever seen. And Emma was a couple of years older than Ginette and had been wearing braces her whole life, it seemed, and liked to party.

The post lamp in the Hardings' front yard was on when Ginette walked by. And, against the light it threw, Ginette could see the silhouette of a very tall, slim woman. Even from her silhouette, Ginette could tell the woman had high heels on. And a short dress or skirt. And a coat with a large, fur-lined hood.

She must have been the passenger in the taxi. Because her silhouette told Ginette that she was definitely from somewhere else. But not from somewhere like Presque Isle or Caribou or Fort Kent.

She was from somewhere much farther away—in distance and in sensibility.

Ginette stopped to look at the woman, clicking off her flashlight as she did so she wouldn't be discovered. There was something so glamorous about her, Ginette could tell, even in silhouette. And she wondered why such a glamorous woman was at the Hardings'—the least glamorous people she knew.

And then she continued on her way, trying to not let her boots crunch too loudly in the snow.

And was surprised by how sad she was to realize that she'd probably never see the woman again.

Ginette had been right: the tall, slim woman was the passenger in the taxicab.

And she had come from far away—from the opposite corner of the country, actually.

When the taxicab driver dropped her off in front of the Hardings', he asked her if she wanted him to wait for her.

But the woman said no, that she was fine. And that she wouldn't be needing a ride back.

Because she was at the right house. And she was sure that the person she was there to see would be there. Because she had heard that he still lived there.

And she could tell that he was home. Because a warm, creamy light shone through the closed curtains in the front picture window.

As the taxicab drove away, the woman really hoped she had heard right.

She crunch-crunch-crunched her way up the recently plowed driveway and pulled her suitcase behind her by its telescoping handle. A thin crust of uneven snowy ice covered the driveway and made the suitcase totter and weave a bit—and the woman almost slipped, because she was wearing heels. And she wondered why in the world she was wearing them. They were useless in northern Maine, especially in the winter.

But she had come in such a rush that she had forgotten to dress properly. Or wear the right shoes.

After a few more steps, she stopped and looked at the house.

It was still green with white trim. And still tidy and well kept.

Suddenly, she felt a strange lightness fill up her insides. It was the same strange lightness she had felt that morning—when she was preparing for an early conference call with clients from the other side of the country—and saw the sunrise through the window of her corner office on the nineteenth floor.

The woman hadn't watched the sunrise in a while.

And it made her think of him.

And of something very important that she was supposed to have done nearly twenty years ago—at sunrise.

And she hadn't let herself think about him or what she was supposed to have done—since she had seen him last. Because she couldn't let herself think about him. Because thinking about him would have derailed the grand plans she had made for herself.

But that morning, as she watched the sunrise, she found herself thinking about him.

And as she looked out over the world from her high perch, she felt a deep, desperate dread that she might never find her place in it.

And she felt like she was going to throw up. Because she thought she had done all she could have done to find her place in this world. She had earned. She had accomplished. She had experienced. She had traveled. She had influenced and hobnobbed.

But she still hadn't found it.

And then a strange lightness filled up her insides. It over-whelmed her. And relieved her nausea. And made her feel like she had the warmth and light of the very sunrise she was watching inside her. And like she might levitate or something.

And she realized that she didn't need to find her place in this world.

Because she had already found it.

It was with him.

And she needed to see him.

Right then.

So she skipped out on her early conference call with her clients from the other side of the country.

And went to him.

Right then.

She got on a plane to Boston. And then to Bangor. And then she took a taxi to get to him.

And now, she was about to see him.

And it looked like he was home.

The lightness she had been feeling as she stood in his driveway gave way to another equally alien feeling—one of yearning. And it surprised her. Because yearning was something she had trained herself not to do. The people she associated with didn't yearn. For anything. If they wanted something, they got it. And if they wanted to accomplish something, they accomplished it. And if they wanted to be something, they became it.

The woman had learned well from them. And she had gotten really good at getting and accomplishing and becoming. She did it better than any of them.

And she didn't yearn anymore. Or—so she thought.

But there she was. In Almost. At his house. Yearning. Hoping.

But still absolutely certain that she'd get what she deserved.

A surge of anticipation—and maybe the cold, too—made her shiver.

She smiled at how right everything was about to be.

And she continued up the driveway toward the house.

Her shoes made the going rough. And made her feel like she wasn't from there anymore.

And that made her happy. Because she wasn't from there anymore. And she had worked hard to seem like she wasn't from there anymore.

Which may be why she hadn't been back to Almost since she went away to college. That—and her family had moved away shortly after they dropped her off at a university that no one from Almost, Maine, had ever gotten accepted to. So there was no reason to go back. Because there was nothing in Almost for her. Or so she had always thought.

The woman started toward the modest ranch-style house again, her heels crunching in the icy driveway. And she must have crossed some magical plane, because a motion sensor turned on the black outdoor post lamp that lit the path from the driveway to the front door.

And she froze, expecting him to answer the door at any moment. Because he must have seen the light go on.

But after a few moments, she realized that maybe he hadn't seen the light go on. Because he wasn't coming out to see what—or who—had triggered the sensor.

And she got nervous. Everything felt wrong all of a sudden.

And she decided that there was no way she was going to be able to go through with this, and she turned and started heading toward the road, pulling her wheelie suitcase behind her.

But then that strange lightness she had been feeling grew inside her. And made her relax. And believe. And she turned and faced the house so she could do what she was there to do.

And she made her way to the side door, because she had never used the front door of his house.

As she did, another motion sensor switched on the light by the door. The sudden illumination startled her a little, but she was happy for the light, because it helped her see the little cement set of stairs that led to the small back porch better.

The woman put down her suitcase.

And realized that she was exactly where she had been when she last saw him.

And she couldn't wait to see him again.

She walked up the three steps to the door.

And smiled at the promise of what was to come. And inhaled deeply. And then put her black-genuine-leather-gloved hands to her mouth and didn't exhale for a while. And maybe giggled a little as she dropped her hands to her sides. And then she shook off some nerves and *rat-tat-tatted* on the white aluminum storm door.

The *rat-tat-tat* on the door pierced the northern Maine quiet.

The woman waited, and the anticipation she was feeling made the quiet seem so loud.

After a moment, she knocked again. And in the middle of the second *rat-tat-tat* on the door, the kitchen light came on.

The woman suddenly hurried down the cement steps to give herself some space from him when he answered the door.

She heard the weather stripping make a squeaky, popping sound as it unsealed itself from the door frame. She hadn't heard that sound in a couple of decades.

As the main door squeaked open, the woman dropped her head into her leather-gloved hands and smiled and tingled all over. And when she heard the aluminum storm door pop open, she turned away from the man who had appeared on the stoop and started babbling: "I know this isn't going to be very easy, but I was in my office early this morning, and I saw the sunrise, and I just realized that what I did was wrong, and I wanted to make it right, and so I flew and I took a taxi to get to you, I just had to come see you, thank God you're here—"

The woman had finally looked at the man and suddenly stopped talking and actually gulped, because—the man wasn't the man she was looking for.

He was . . . someone she didn't know. A small man. An old man, maybe. In a bathrobe.

The woman looked like she had seen a ghost.

"Oh—wait—I'm sorry—you're not— I'm . . . I'm so sorry," she said, laughing a strange laugh. "Um . . . does Daniel Harding live here? I'm looking for Daniel Harding."

The small man seemed surprised and deliberately asked, "You're looking—?"

The woman finished his sentence to save time. She was very efficient. "Looking for Daniel Harding, yeah. He lives here. I thought."

The man stared blankly at the woman. He looked quite confused. Which made sense. He probably hadn't expected someone to be coming to his door at a little before nine on a Friday night in the middle of winter.

And he certainly wasn't expecting someone like this woman, in her high heels and fancy coat with its large fur-lined hood.

Then the woman realized that she was so sure that Daniel Harding—the man that she was looking for—was going to be there, that she hadn't even considered the fact that he might *not* be there. And she started to sweat. Even though she was cold. Because she was realizing that the man she had come to see no longer lived where he used to live. And she was completely shocked that he wasn't there. "Oh, no!" she gasped. "He doesn't live here, does he?"

Before the man could answer, the woman was talking again. "Oh, my God, I am so sorry!" She was frowning and smiling alternately. And sometimes laughing even though she felt like she was going to throw up.

He wasn't there.

Oh, God.

He wasn't there.

How could this be?

The woman turned away from the man and put her head in her hands. So she didn't see him pull the main door to his house closed behind him—which he did to keep the heat in and the cold out. And also so that no one inside would come out and wonder what was going on outside.

"Argh, I am so embarrassed!" said the woman in a voice that made her sound a little like a chicken. She turned back to the man and asked—as if she was giving voice to his thoughts—"Who is this woman and what is she doing here, right?"

And she laughed and then suddenly stopped laughing and almost cried, but then collected herself and said in all seriousness, "I'm sorry. I just honestly thought he'd be here. I always thought he'd be here. Always."

Then she took a few steps back so she could get a better view of the house—so she could make sure she was in the right place. And she was. She knew she was. "This is the house," she said to herself.

And then she looked at the man and was about to apologize for disturbing him when she had the strangest feeling that he might be able to help her somehow. And she took a step toward him and asked, "Do you know him?"

Before the man could answer, the woman was describing Daniel Harding.

"He's a big guy. Big, tall guy. Played basketball. All-Maine, center, strong?"

The small man in the bathrobe looked up at the woman. He was silhouetted by the porch light. So she couldn't see that he had a strange look on his face—like he didn't understand the question.

"Do you know him?" she asked again.

"Well—"

"Oh, don't even answer that. That was—*blech*—I know that's a horrible question to ask a person who lives in a small town, as if everybody in small towns knows everybody else, *argh*, can't believe I asked you that. I don't live here anymore, but when I did, I hated it when people assumed that I knew everybody in town just because it was small. It was worse than when they'd ask if we had plumbing, 'way up there?'"

The man laughed a little and nodded upon remembering the joke he and many other Aroostook County residents had endured many times in their lives.

And the woman was happy that she had made him laugh a little. He didn't seem like the kind of person who laughed much. And the woman was surprised to find herself pitying him for a moment.

"Anyway," she continued, "I'm sorry I presumed that you'd know him, because you know, people in small towns really don't know each other any better than people in big towns, you know that? I mean, you know who you know, and you don't know who you don't know, just like anywhere else."

The man had never thought about this, but supposed it was true. And nodded in agreement.

And the woman smiled and nodded back.

And was completely at a loss. Because this reunion was not going as planned. Probably because she had not been reunited with anyone.

And even if it had been the reunion she had hoped for, what was the likelihood that it would have gone as planned? How in the world could she have expected to show up in Almost and pick up with Daniel where she had left off with him?

But—while it was ridiculous of her to have presumed that she could just show up and pick up where she and Daniel had left off, it wasn't ridiculous for her to have expected to see him.

Because she had made sure he was still there—she had checked public records.

But—he wasn't there.

And she really needed to see him.

Because she had something very important to tell him.

But now it looked like she wasn't going to be able to tell him.

And that made her feel like she was going to cry.

But she didn't cry.

Because she had gotten good at not crying—by forcing herself to smile when she felt like crying.

So she smiled really hard at the man who stood before her so she wouldn't cry. And said sincerely, "I am so sorry to have bothered you." And then she bowed her head a bit and turned and grabbed the telescoping handle of her wheelie suitcase and started to go.

The man wanted to stop her. Because he really wanted to know why this woman was at his house. But he couldn't come up with anything to say to make her stay.

Fortunately, he didn't have to come up with anything to say. Because the woman had stopped herself and had turned back to the man and said *argh* in a voice that made her sound like a pirate-chicken. And then, in her own non-pirate-chicken voice, she continued, "I was just so sure . . ."

The woman didn't finish the sentence and the man wanted to know what the woman was so sure of and so he asked, "What?"

"Ugh," she grunted. "I was just so sure he'd be here. When his parents passed away, he kept the house, I heard. He lived here. He stayed here, I thought. He was one of the ones who stayed." The woman stared at the house and wondered where in the world Daniel was now. And then added, "I didn't stay. I went away."

"Most people do," said the man ruefully. And he was telling the truth. Intelligent, aspiring people like this woman had been encouraged to leave northern Maine. And bring their intelligence and aspirations with them. Which is too bad, because places like northern Maine could use the intelligence and aspirations that the people who went away took with them.

"Yeah," agreed the woman. "And I guess he went away, too. I never thought he would. I guess I lost track. I wish there was something you could keep people in for when you need 'em, you know?" She opened her purse and pointed inside. "Oh, there he is, perfect!" she said as if she were a Muppet or a cartoon character, hoping he'd think she was being funny and/or understand what she was saying.

But he didn't. Think she was funny. Or understand what she was saying.

Then she laughed, hoping he'd laugh.

And he didn't. Because he really didn't know what she was talking about.

And then it was quiet.

And the northern Maine quiet made the woman realize how much noise there was where she lived.

And how much noise there was in her head.

And she realized that she needed to get back to a place where there was more noise outside her head than there was inside her head. So she grabbed her wheelie suitcase and turned to go.

But something inside her made her stop. It was that lightness again. It made her feel like she needed to be there—with this man. So she slowly turned to him. And looked lost.

"Are you all right?" asked the man.

"Yeah," lied the woman. "It's just . . . cold."

The man actually thought it was pretty mild for a midwinter night in Almost, Maine. It was nineteen degrees. So he didn't agree with the woman. But he didn't tell her so.

"It doesn't get cold like this where I'm from," added the woman. And then she smiled. Even though she didn't feel like smiling.

"Oh," said the man. He could see the woman's odd smile, because she was front-lit by the same lamp that was backlighting him. And he didn't know what to make of that smile. Because it didn't match her sad eyes.

And then he felt like he should say more—because there was more he could have said. Much more. But he couldn't bring himself to say it. Because he was too interested in hearing what the woman had to say.

"I'm sorry I'm still here," said the woman, trying to figure out why she was still there. "It's just . . ." She suddenly dropped her shoulders and let her head fall back so her face was open to the sky. "I can't *believe* . . . ," she groaned.

The man wanted to know what the woman couldn't believe.

But the woman didn't say what it was that she couldn't believe.

So the man asked, "What can't you believe?"

"I—" The woman struggled to bring herself to say what she was about to say. Because what she was about to say was ridiculous.

And then she finally said it.

Because she felt like the man would understand, for some reason.

"I took a taxi here. From *Bangor*. To see him."

The woman looked down and shook her head a little. And kicked at some ice in the driveway. And then laughed at herself. And made that strange *argh* sound she kept making.

The man just stared at the woman.

And said nothing for a while.

And then finally stated the obvious.

"That's far."

"Yeah."

"That's a hundred and sixty-three miles."

"Yeah." The woman rolled her eyes. "This place is a little farther away from things than I remember."

And the man wondered why in the world the woman would have done something as extravagant as spend several hundred dollars on a taxi ride.

"Why did you do that?" he asked incredulously.

The woman made that strange *argh* sound again. And then inhaled deeply. And held her breath for a moment. And then said, "Because I could only fly as close as Bangor, and I couldn't wait till morning for the next flight to Presque Isle—because I needed to get to him as fast as I could."

"Why?"

"I . . . wanted to answer a question he asked me."

"Oh." The man was intrigued.

"The last time I saw him, he asked me a very important question, and I didn't answer it, and that's just not a very nice thing to do to a person."

"Well, that's bein' a little hard on yourself, don't you think?"

"He asked me to marry him," said the woman in a way that let the man know that she didn't think she was being hard on herself—at all.

The man nodded as he took in this information. And agreed that not answering a marriage proposal is, in fact, not a very nice thing to do to a person. And remarked, "Oh." And then, just to confirm that he had heard correctly, he asked, "And you . . . ?"

"Didn't answer him, no."

The man whistled. It was a whistle that meant, "Wow, how could you have done such a heartless thing?" It was full of judgment.

"Yeah," conceded the woman, mildly irritated by the tone of the stranger's whistle. She didn't need his judgment. She had already judged herself plenty for not having answered the question. And besides, she was there to make her wrong right, so she defended herself: "And that's why I'm here. To answer him. I mean, I didn't answer him in the first place because I didn't have an answer at the time. Because I was going to *college*—my dream school!—and *then*, the *night* before I'm about to go off into the world to do what I hope and dream, he asks me, 'Will you marry me?' I mean, come on! I was leaving in the morning. What was I supposed to do?"

The man thought the question was rhetorical. But the woman was looking at him as if she wanted an answer. So he answered her. "I don't know," he said with shrug.

"I mean, I told him I'd have to think about it, that I'd think it over overnight and that I'd be back before the sun came up with an answer. And then I left. I left him standing . . . right there . . ." The woman pointed to where the man was standing on the small porch. "And . . . then . . . I didn't make it back with an answer. Before the sun came up or . . . at all." The woman dropped her head as if in shame. And she saw her shoes and wondered again why she had worn them.

"Well, that sounds like an answer to me," reasoned the man.

"What?!? No!" The woman looked back up at the man and desperately wanted him to know that her non-answer wasn't an answer. And she passionately pleaded her case. "That wasn't my answer! I just went off into the world, and that's not an answer. And I think . . ."

The woman looked up at the sky and went to a sad, faraway place.

"What?" asked the man, bringing the woman back to where they were.

The woman looked at the man. And looked as young as she did when she left Almost. And said, "I think he thought I'd say yes."

The man scoffed. And wondered why someone who was clearly intelligent would say such a stupid thing.

"What?" asked the woman, wondering why the man had scoffed.

And the man said, "A guy's probably not gonna ask a girl that question unless he thinks she's gonna say yes."

The woman looked back up at the sky and marveled at all the stars in it for a moment and conceded, "Yeah." And then she looked at the man again and said, "And I'm just afraid that he waited up all night, hoping for me to come by." And she realized how much harm she must have done to Daniel by not answering the question he had asked. "And," she went on, "I just want to tell him that I know now that you just can't do a thing like not answer a question like the one he asked me. You can't do that to a person. Especially to someone you love."

The man couldn't quite believe that the woman had just shared something so personal with him. And asked, "You loved him?" just to make sure he had heard her correctly. Because how could a person who had not answered a marriage proposal have loved the person who had proposed?

The woman gasped a bit. Because she couldn't believe that she had just admitted something so private to a complete stranger. And then she tried to backpedal. "Well . . . I don't know if I loved him. I mean, we were kids," she said, waving away the confession she had just made.

And then she stopped trying to wave away the confession.

And realized she was lying.

And realized she didn't need to lie.

And she let the confession be what it was—the truth.

And she said, "No—wait—that's not true. I did. Love him. I do. Love him."

And the lightness she had felt when she decided to begin her epic journey to Almost filled up her insides again.

"And I feel like—by not answering him . . ." The woman paused, wondering why she wanted to share her story with this stranger, but also feeling strangely compelled to explain herself to him. "I just feel like I dashed his hopes and dreams."

The man rolled his eyes. He couldn't help it. And he couldn't believe he had done it. He hated it when his daughters did it. It's just about the most dismissive body language there is. It's judgmental. And lazy. And cryptic. And it doesn't help solve a problem or help people reach any kind of understanding. But it was the only response he had for the woman's arrogance.

"Oh, come on," chided the man. "You give yourself too much credit."

The woman was stunned by the stranger's response. "Huh?"

"I don't think you 'dashed' his hopes and dreams." The man started making his way down the cement steps. "At least—not all by yourself. His hopes and dreams were going to get dashed at some point. By you. By other people. Because that's what happens. When you're young. And that's all you need to get your hopes dashed: be young. And everybody starts out young, so everybody gets their hopes dashed."

The man was now standing in the driveway looking up at the woman. And the woman looked down at him—surprised by how small he was—and she supposed that what he had said was true.

"And, anyway," continued the man. "I don't think you really *dashed* his hopes and dreams. 'Cause if you dash somebody's hopes and dreams—well, that's kind of a nice way to let 'em down, 'cause it hurts . . . but it's quick. If you'd said no, *that* woulda been 'dashing' his hopes and dreams."

The woman dropped her head and folded her arms and held them tight against her body. And the man's kindly way gave way to something subtly unkind.

"But you didn't say no," he continued. His voice was low. And almost sounded threatening. "You said nothin'."

The man paused and made sure the woman was hearing him.

"You just didn't answer him."

The man paused again. And then added, "At all."

The man paused again. And then continued his argument. "And that's . . . killin' someone's hopes and dreams the long, slow, painful way. 'Cause they're still there, just hangin' on. They never really go away."

The man kept his gaze fixed on the woman, making sure she was hearing him. And when he was sure that she was, he went on: "And that's kinda like givin' somebody a little less air to breathe. Every day."

The man paused. And then concluded his rumination.

"Till they die."

The man's gaze remained fixed on the woman. She was looking at the ground, arms still folded tightly against her body.

And he felt like he had made his point. And he felt like she had heard him.

And the woman raised her head and looked down at the man. He was so small he almost looked like a little boy. A bald little boy.

And then she looked up at the stars.

And processed the extremely unhelpful information the man had just shared with her.

And then shrugged her shoulders and nodded her head and

didn't know what to say, because what the man had said was absolutely true, she supposed. She had never thought about what she had done to Daniel in such morbid terms. But, as morbid as they were, they were probably pretty accurate ones.

And then she wondered if she had killed Daniel in a long, slow, painful way.

And hoped she hadn't.

And suddenly felt like she was in a horror movie—and she was the monster.

And suddenly she felt unwelcome.

And felt like she needed to get out of there—and go back to where she had come from. So she said, "Okay, well . . . thank you," and took hold of the handle of her wheelie suitcase and started to go.

"For what?" called the man, asking the question as if it were a challenge.

The woman realized that she had only thanked the man out of habit. And that she didn't really have anything to thank him for.

"I don't know," she admitted, shrugging. And she continued down the driveway back toward the Road to Somewhere/Nowhere. And stopped when she realized she had no idea where she was going to go.

Maybe she could get a room at Ma Dudley's. It was nearly two miles away, though. Which'd be a long walk in those shoes.

She thought about asking the man for a ride there.

But she had imposed on him enough already.

So she started to go again. To Ma Dudley's, she guessed. And as she left, the man said, "Goodbye, Hope."

The woman stopped and turned to the man and said, "Goodbye." And was about to go again, but before she did, she said, "I am so sorry to have bothered you! I really am."

And she started to go again.

And couldn't believe how completely not-as-planned the evening had gone. She thought that she was going to come back and find Danny. And he would take her back, and they would live happily ever after. Which may sound romantic—but it actually isn't. It's sentimental. Because sentimentalists think everything's going to work out just fine. And romantics think everything is going to fall apart. Most people become romantics by the time they're as old as the woman was. Because most things fall apart. But not much in the woman's life had fallen apart. So the woman hadn't yet become a romantic. She was still a sentimentalist.

And the sentimentalist felt the need to explain herself to this stranger one last time. "It's just—I saw the sunrise this morning for the first time in a long time. And it made me realize what I'd done to him—to Danny—and I had been feeling like I didn't have a place in the world, you know? And then I realized that I *did* have a place in the world, and it was with him, and—"

The woman interrupted herself, because she realized that the man had called her by her name. "Wait a minute," she said, hurrying back to him. "You called me Hope." She went up to the man, who looked up at her, his hands in the pockets of his red and green and yellow and white and blue and purple plaid bathrobe, and she almost demanded, "How did you know my name?"

The woman suddenly felt like she knew the small man with whom she had spent the past fifteen minutes talking. And she was frustrated that she couldn't see him well—the porch light was illuminating him from behind, so he was still mostly in shadow. "Do I know you?" she queried.

The woman felt like the man was standing in a hole, because he was so small. She would have towered over him even if she hadn't been wearing her high heels.

She started to initiate a slow-motion do-si-do with him. She wanted to get the man's face in the light.

The man moved with the woman in the strange, slow do-si-do.

And when they had switched positions, and he was lit from the front, he weakly opened his arms and palms and shrugged ever so slightly to present himself to the woman.

The woman gasped and she felt like she was falling in slow motion as she recognized the man.

It was the man she had come to see.

"Danny?!?" she whispered in disbelief.

"Hello, Hope," said Danny sheepishly.

Hope felt like everything was spinning and like she might fall over, and the only words she could find to say were, "Danny . . . I didn't rec—"

"I know."

"I didn't rec—"

"I know."

"I didn't even recognize you!"

"I know."

"You're so . . ."

"I know."

". . . small."

"Yeah. I, uh . . . lost a lotta hope, I guess. That'll do a number on ya."

And then Danny and Hope just stood there staring at each other.

And couldn't figure out what to say.

So they said nothing.

And they tried to make sense of what was happening.

And the northern lights were hovering in the sky above.

Neither of them took notice. Because, as dazzling as they were on the night when all the extraordinary things did or didn't happen, they weren't nearly as dazzling as Hope was to Danny or as Danny was to Hope. (Even though Hope couldn't quite work out how such a robust young man had become so small and fragile.)

Finally, Hope managed to say, "Danny, I am so sorry I never came back—"

"Shh. It's okay," Danny interrupted gently.

Hope shook her head no, because she knew it wasn't okay.

"No—it is," reassured Danny. "'Cause you know something?"

"What?"

"You're early." Danny smiled.

Hope didn't understand what Danny was saying. "What?" she asked, wincing as she did.

"You're early. You said you'd be back with an answer to my question before the sun came up, and Jeezum Crow, the sun's not even close to being up yet. It only went down a few hours ago." Danny smiled bigger. And then added wryly, "Look how early you are. That's good of you."

Hope appreciated Danny's kindness.

Because they both knew she wasn't early.

She was late. So, so late.

And they stood under the vast northern night sky, overwhelmed by the reunion.

And then something troubled Hope. She wondered why Danny hadn't told her who he was when she arrived.

In the same moment, Danny realized that he needed to apologize for withholding his identity. So he did. "I'm sorry I didn't say anything when I came out on the porch and saw you. I was just so *surprised*. To see you. And happy. And then, when you didn't seem to recognize me, I guess I remembered what I had become. And I just didn't know what to do. So I didn't do anything. And I just . . . let you talk."

"Yeah." Hope wished she hadn't talked so much. Or had listened more. Or something.

"So," Danny said, smirking a little, and changing the subject. "You took a taxi all the way from Bangor?"

Hope nodded. "Yup," she said sheepishly. And proudly.

Daniel whistled another whistle that meant, "Wow."

And then asked, "How much did that cost ya?"

"A lot," she replied, embarrassed.

But Danny was impressed. She must have really made something of herself. Because she could afford to take a taxi from Bangor all the way to Almost.

And then he took a deep breath and asked the question he had been waiting all those years for an answer to. "So, what'd you wanna tell me?"

"Huh? Oh—"

"You said you came here to answer a question I asked you," he said, smiling eagerly.

"Yeah," said Hope, smiling sheepishly.

"So . . . what's the answer?" Danny felt a strange lightness fill up his insides as he asked the question. It made him feel like a dying ember inside him had become a roaring flame. And like he was about to be launched into space, like a rocket—but in slow motion.

And it made him feel like his life was about to change forever.

And Hope felt the strange lightness she had felt earlier in the day fill up her insides, too. And felt like her life was about to change forever, too. And she was about to give her answer and see what happily ever after was all about—when the seal of the weather stripping on the door popped and the door opened and the storm door opened a bit and a small round woman popped her head outside and asked, "Hon, what's goin' on? Who's here?"

Hope and Danny froze.

And Danny quickly turned toward the woman who had called to him and said, "Hey, honey!"

Hope felt the strange lightness leave her body in an instant. And it was replaced by a heaviness that she feared was going to bring her to her knees. But she managed to stay upright.

The same heaviness overcame Danny and replaced the lightness he had been feeling. And he felt more earthbound than he had ever felt. He moved toward the cement steps to the porch, trying to figure out how he was going to explain the situation.

"Everything okay?" chirped the woman.

"Yeah!" said Danny a little too loudly and clearing his throat a few times and chuckling oddly.

The woman had come out onto the porch. She smiled and waved to Hope. "Hi," she said.

"Hi!" said Hope, smiling. And not meaning it at all.

"This is, um . . . this is . . ." Daniel tried to introduce Hope to his wife, Suzette. But couldn't. And instead said, "This woman . . . just . . . needs directions."

"Oh. Is everything okay?" The woman chuckled, uncertain of what to make of the tall, slim woman in the tall shoes and the chic clothes and the coat with the fur-lined hood who was asking for directions at a little after nine o'clock at night. "It's a bit late for directions," she said skeptically.

"Yeah, listen, Suzette." Danny looked at Hope for a moment. And then back to his wife. And then back to Hope. And then he said to his wife, while looking in Hope's eyes, "I'll be right in, hon."

"Okay," cheeped Suzette.

"Thank you so much for your help, sir," Hope said to Danny, trying to make it look like she had gotten the directions she needed—and trying to cover for the emotional indiscretions that had been committed.

"Where are you headed, sweetie?" Suzette spoke to the tall, slim woman in the driveway like she was a girl, because she presumed that Hope was much younger than she was. She would have been sad to have learned that Hope was actually a few years older.

"She's just lost her way," said Danny, happy to speak for Hope.

"Yeah!" Hope smiled, happy to have Danny speak for her.

"Oh." Suzette didn't quite know what to make of the strange situation she had found herself—and her husband—and the strange woman—in. And figured she could ask Dan about it later when he joined her in bed. "All right, well, I hope you find your way! Bye-bye, now."

"Bye-bye," said Hope.

As Suzette started to go inside, she nagged her husband gently, "Allie said it's your move and she's got you in check and Emma just called and said she's gonna be later than eleven and you need to talk to her about that, because I said no later than eleven."

Hope felt the heaviness again when she learned that Danny had kids—who were old enough to be playing chess and staying out until eleven.

"Okay, I'll be right in," said Danny.

"Good luck," Suzette said to Hope. And she may have given Hope the once-over before she went back inside.

"Thanks," said Hope, smiling—and not meaning it.

Hope and Danny watched Suzette go back inside. And they

heard the weather stripping reseal itself as she pushed the door shut. And they watched the aluminum storm door slowly swing itself shut behind her.

They stared at the door.

And then Danny turned to Hope.

And he exhaled an apologetic smile.

Hope shrugged her shoulders and smiled. Even though she felt, like crying. Because she couldn't believe that it hadn't even occurred to her that Danny may have moved on. And gotten married. And had kids. At least one of whom was a teenager.

And she couldn't believe that it hadn't occurred to her that she was the one who hadn't moved on. Even though she thought she had. By trying to acquire and accomplish and achieve.

Danny inhaled sharply and seemed like he was about to say something.

But he didn't say anything.

"What?" asked Hope, desperate to hear what he had to say.

"I, um . . ." He looked up at Hope. And then up at the sky, where the northern lights had appeared moments earlier.

"What?" Hope smiled, hoping that maybe Danny was going to say, "Let's run away and start a life together." And she felt that strange lightness fill up her insides again, in anticipation.

But then Danny said, "I hope you find it, Hope. Your place in this world. Or whatever it is you're looking for."

And the lightness inside Hope disappeared. And became heaviness and darkness.

And then Danny said, "Bye."

And Hope said nothing as she watched the small man go up the stairs onto the porch and open the aluminum storm door and then the main wooden door and go inside.

She heard the door seal shut.

And she watched the storm door swing closed behind it.

"Goodbye, Danny," she said to herself. And to him.

And she stared at the door for a while.

And then—twenty years too late—she answered him.

"Yes," she called quietly.

Hope stared at the door for a while longer.

And then repeated, more quietly and more to herself, "Yes."

And she stared at the door for a while longer.

And then the porch light went off.

And Hope grabbed the telescoping pull handle of her wheelie suitcase and started to go.

She passed the post lamp in the front yard and her movement triggered its sensor and it flickered on.

And when she got to the end of the driveway, she turned and looked at the tidy home one last time.

She pictured Danny and Allie playing chess. And she wondered if Emma would be home on time. Or after eleven. And what would happen if she was home late.

And then the post lamp in the front yard flicked off.

And then she turned to go but couldn't see anything. Because it was so dark.

She waited for her eyes to adjust. And they did. But there was so little light.

She looked up and saw the stars.

And the Milky Way.

And couldn't remember the last time she had seen it.

And then she started walking.

She'd go to Ma Dudley's. And see if there was a room available.

Maybe Ma would be up. Or Sunny. And Hope could talk to them.

Ma and Sunny were good to people who felt like they had no place in the world.

As she walked, she hoped that Ma and Sunny would remember her.

And wished she hadn't worn those shoes.

10

As Ginette passed the Hardings', she wondered why that tall, slim woman was just staring at their house.

Maybe she was a prowler, and was about to burgle the place.

And then Ginette laughed at herself.

The woman was not a burglar.

She wasn't dressed to burgle.

And her shoes were not made for burgling.

And, if she was a burglar, she was terrible at being stealthy, because she was just standing in plain sight, illuminated by the post lamp in the front walkway, staring at the Hardings' house.

And, anyway, what kind of burglar would have taken a taxi to where they were going to burgle?

What was she actually doing there? wondered Ginette.

And where was she from?

She looked so elegant. Like maybe she was from Montreal. Or New York City. Or Los Angeles.

Ginette wondered if she'd ever get to visit any of those exotic places. And smiled as she thought about visiting them with Pete someday.

And then remembered that she probably wouldn't be visiting them with Pete.

Because they weren't Ginette and Pete anymore.

She didn't know what they were.

They had crossed a line and had become more than friends. And she wondered if they would ever be able to cross back. And be just friends again.

Would they still hang out? Or would it just be too awkward for them to be around one another?

Ginette continued on her way, wondering where she and Pete were headed.

And then wondered where she was headed—literally—at that moment, since there wasn't much left of the Road to Nowhere.

She had no reason to go to Rhonda Rideout's—which was the only place left to go before the wilderness.

And she didn't want to go into the wilderness.

And she almost stopped and turned around and headed home.

But she couldn't.

Because that strange lightness she had been feeling seemed to be compelling her to keep walking toward the woods.

So she just kept walking.

For a while.

And then she heard the yowl of a snowmobile engine in the distance—off to her left and behind her.

She turned toward the yowling sound and looked out into the potato fields that stretched from Echo Lake to the wilderness of northwestern Maine. And she saw a snowmobile's headlight speeding across the wide-open fields toward the woods.

It must have been Rhonda Rideout heading home, Ginette figured.

And she watched the speeding snowmobile slow down as it approached—and then disappear into—the woods.

And as she continued on her way, the potato fields on the south side of the Road to Nowhere gave way to a forest of primarily spruce, fir, hemlock, pine, and cedar trees. And Ginette felt so small next to them.

Ginette stopped and looked up at the trees—and felt a little claustrophobic. So she crossed the road so she could walk next to the potato fields on the other side of the Road to Nowhere, which made her feel a little less claustrophobic.

And then she heard the less robust yowl of another snowmobile engine coming from the same potato field that the last one had come from. And she turned and looked across the road and into the field and, sure enough, saw the headlights of another snowmobile not quite speeding across the open field.

Ginette figured it was Dave Bonenfant. And it was. He and Rhonda had been hanging out a lot lately.

And everyone in Almost was wondering if they were together or going out or something.

It was about 8:40 when Ginette made her way past the long driveway that led to Rhonda's cabin. This was just about the time that Dave made his way into the woods on his sled in pursuit of Rhonda, and the same time that Rhonda emerged from the woods and into her backyard. Her arrival made a series of lights on her property flick on. The lights were triggered by motion sensors, which Rhonda had recently installed so she'd be able to keep an eye on the black bears that often got a little too close for comfort when they visited her bee-hives in the spring, summer, and fall.

Rhonda eased her Polaris sled up onto its storage pallet next to her garage and killed the engine. And then she dismounted the machine and took off her helmet. And then she covered the snowmobile with a blue tarp and secured it with a bungee cord to protect the machine from the elements.

But soon stopped. Because she thought she heard the sound of a snowmobile approaching.

And, as the sound got louder, there was no doubt that another snowmobile was approaching.

And she waited. And wondered who was coming.

And soon Dave Bonenfant emerged from the woods on his old Arctic Cat and into Rhonda's backyard.

He pulled up to where Rhonda was standing.

And killed his engine.

And then took off his helmet and dismounted his sled.

"What's up?" said Rhonda, hands on her hips, wondering what the heck Dave was doing at her house.

"Um, well—I just . . ." Dave was anxious and couldn't seem to bring himself to tell Rhonda what was up. He seemed troubled.

"You okay?" asked Rhonda.

"Yeah. I just, uh . . . wanted to say . . ." Dave stopped breathing and realized that he didn't quite know how to tell Rhonda what he had come all the way out to her house to do, so he told her something else—something he just wanted to make sure she knew: "That was just fun tonight."

"Yeah. It was," agreed Rhonda. She and Dave had gone on a sledding trip to the Snowmobile Club for Trivia Night. And it had been fun. But Dave didn't have to come all the way over to tell her so.

"Yeah. It was," Dave reaffirmed. And then he just stood facing Rhonda and didn't say anything. And looked nervous. Or scared. Or sick.

"You sure you're okay?" asked Rhonda.

"Yeah. I just also wanted to let you know that . . ." Dave stopped breathing—again—and realized—again—that he didn't quite know how to tell Rhonda what he had come all the way out to her house to do. So he tried to think of something—anything—else to say. And finally came up with, "So that was fun tonight, huh?"

"Yeah," said Rhonda, wondering why Dave was stating the obvious. They always had fun when they went sledding on Friday nights.

"Even though you whupped my butt!" added Dave, laughing.

"Well, that's what you get for ridin' an Arctic Cat. You get your butt whupped," teased Rhonda. It was also what he got for taking on the Northern Maine Snowmobile Association's Snowmobiler of the Year, but Rhonda didn't say that because she didn't want to rub it in.

"Yeah," conceded Dave.

"And I whupped it!" she teased, giving Dave a playful kick in the butt.

"I know, I know, I'm not sayin' you didn't!"

Dave and Rhonda laughed. And thought about how much fun they always had together.

And then Rhonda looked at Dave, and she felt like he had a lot more to say than that he had had fun sledding, but he wasn't saying anything, so she said, "Look, dude, I'm workin' tomorrow—first shift. I gotta be up at the crack o' butt, so what's up?"

"Oh—sorry—um. I just wanna . . . can I, um . . ." Dave couldn't stop stammering and was about to give up on trying to do what he had come all the way out to Rhonda's to do when he felt a strange lightness fill up his insides—a lightness he had been feeling whenever he thought about Rhonda lately. And whenever he was around her. It made him feel like the blue flame from a gas burner on a stove was glowing inside him. And like he was about to be in zero gravity or something.

Rhonda waited for Dave to finish what he seemed to be having a lot of difficulty saying. And when it didn't seem like he was going to be able to finish, she asked impatiently, "Dave, come on! Can you *what*?"

The lightness Dave had been feeling suddenly seemed to fill him with courage, and it made him blurt out, "Can I come in?"

Rhonda was a little taken aback by the question and asked, "Huh?"

"Can I come inside?"

"Um . . ."

"Just for a second," added Dave. "I just—have somethin' I'd like to . . . do . . . in there."

"You got 'somethin' you'd like to do there'?" asked Rhonda.

"Yeah."

"In my house?" Rhonda was scowling.

"Yeah."

Rhonda looked at her house. And then at Dave, quizzically. And then asked, "Like what?"

Dave wanted Rhonda to stop asking him questions before he lost his nerve. Because he was losing his nerve. So he practically begged, "Just—can I come in?"

"Why? You gotta pee?" asked Rhonda.

"No."

"'Cause you can pee out here."

"I don't have to pee."

"Number two?"

"No—"

"'Cause you can do that out here, too. Got an old outhouse out back there."

Rhonda's cabin had originally been built as a hunting cabin with limited amenities, and there was an old outhouse in the woods not far from where they were standing. Not that Rhonda used it—her place had indoor plumbing and an impressive array of amenities.

"I don't have to go to the bathroom," groaned Dave.

Rhonda felt herself get hot in the ears and neck. Because the thought of Dave coming inside her house was making her really nervous for some reason. "Well, what do you gotta do?" she demanded.

"Nothin', just—"

"Nothin'?" mocked Rhonda. "You rode all the way out here so you could tell me you wanted to come inside and do nothin'?"

"No—not nothin'. There's just somethin' I gotta do—inside—that I can't really do out here."

"Um . . . ," stalled Rhonda. This was weird. Dave had never been over to her house before—even though they'd been seeing a lot of each other since they met playing horseshoes at SummerDaze at the Rec Center over the summer.

They'd gone over to Dave's a lot, though. Maybe because Dave was an excellent cook. (He worked in food services at Caribou High School.) So he made them dinner a lot. And after dinner they'd play cribbage and drink a little beer and maybe smoke a little smoke.

And they always had a great time hanging out at Dave's.

But they had never hung out at Rhonda's. Maybe because Rhonda never spent much time at her house. She slept there—but she spent most of her time out and about. She worked as much overtime as she could get. And she was the treasurer of the Northern Maine Snowmobile Club. And she was on the tribal council of the Aroostook Band of Micmacs.

All this to say—Rhonda had a big busy life. And she wasn't home much. So she didn't really hang out with people at her home.

And now it looked like she was going to hang out.

With a person.

At her home.

And that person was Dave.

And that made her uncomfortable.

"Rhonda?" asked Dave.

Rhonda had been in a daze and asked, "Huh?"

"Can we go inside?"

"Oh. Yeah, sure," she said, trying to be casual about Dave's request. And she gestured toward the back door of her cabin. And expected Dave to make his way inside.

But Dave didn't. Instead, he scooted over to the storage compartment on the back of his sled.

"What're you doin'?" asked Rhonda.

"I'm comin', I'll be right there, I just gotta get somethin'."

"Well . . . hurry up."

"I'm hurryin'!"

Rhonda turned and started toward her back door and stopped at the stoop so she could kick the snow off her boots. And then she turned back to Dave and called, "Before I change my mind, pal."

"I'm comin'!"

As Dave approached the back door, Rhonda could see that he was carrying a flat, medium-size, square package under his arm. It was wrapped in brown craft paper. And looked like it was a present.

Unsure of what to make of what was happening, Rhonda went up the stoop's two wooden steps and pulled open the silver aluminum storm door and then pushed open the wobbly wooden door to her small home and went inside.

Dave reached the stoop and kicked the snow off his boots and followed Rhonda up the steps and inside.

Rhonda flicked on the interior light and turned to Dave when he had barely stepped inside and said curtly, "Okay. This is it. You're in. You're inside."

Dave didn't quite agree. Because they weren't quite inside—they were on Rhonda's porch.

"This is the porch," said Dave, implying that he'd like to go farther inside.

"It's winterized," said Rhonda, shrugging, and letting Dave know that, as far as she was concerned, he was as far inside as he was going to get.

Dave wondered if Rhonda's porch actually was winterized. Because it wasn't much warmer on the porch than it was outside.

And then he looked around and saw pretty much what you'd expect to see on a northern Maine porch.

To his left was a pile of wood that had a pile of old newspapers stacked on top of it.

An old telephone bench sat by the door that led to the rest of the house, with old sneakers and shoes and boots piled underneath. Jackets for all types of weather hung on a coat rack above it, and a bin full of hats and scarves and mittens sat beside it.

Across from the bench was a wicker table with a dead plant and some tools on it. Some plastic chairs sat at the table.

And the rest of the space was full of everything from snowshoes to old *SnowGoer* magazines to an old hibachi.

Rhonda's porch was basically a giant closet.

While Dave took in his surroundings, Rhonda pulled off her neck gaiter and gloves and stuffed them in her snowmobile helmet, which she tossed into the bin full of hats and scarves and mittens.

And Dave pulled off his gloves and his balaclava and shoved them in his helmet and set his helmet down by the door near the woodpile.

As he did so, Rhonda couldn't take her eyes off the flat, medium-size, square wrapped package that he was holding under his arm. Impatient and a little irked, she asked, "So, Dave, what? What do you gotta do in here that you couldn't do outside?"

"Well, I got somethin', here, for ya, here."

Dave offered Rhonda the flat, medium-size, square wrapped package he had brought her.

Rhonda just stared at what Dave was offering and asked, "What's the heck is this?"

"It's just . . . well . . . we've been together now—"

"*Together?!?*" scoffed Rhonda.

"Um—well . . . ," stammered Dave, realizing for the first time that maybe he did think of him and Rhonda as being "together."

"*Together?*" repeated Rhonda.

"I just meant—"

"What are you *talkin'* about, '*together*'???"

Dave talked over Rhonda, because he didn't want to lose his mojo. "Well, we been *friends* now for quite a few months, and . . . well . . ." He struggled to find words to express what he wanted to say. And then gave up on trying to find words and just forced his gift into Rhonda's arms and mumbled, "Here," avoiding eye contact with her, because he was really nervous about what she was going to think of it.

And now Rhonda had in her possession what he had been wanting to give her.

And the strange lightness filled Dave's insides again. And it made him all tingly. And it made him almost smile. Because he couldn't wait for her to open what he had given her. Because he couldn't wait to see what she was going to think of it.

Rhonda slowly looked down at the flat, medium-size, square

wrapped package that had been foisted on her. And asked gently—but also in a way that let Dave know that what he was doing was not copacetic—"What are you doin', here, bud?"

"Just open it," said Dave, looking at the floor.

"Okay," said Rhonda skeptically. And she suddenly wished she hadn't let him in her house.

"Please," pleaded Dave, letting Rhonda know that he really just wanted her to open what he had brought her. Because it would say everything that he had been unable to say over the past few months.

"All right," grumbled Rhonda.

And she scowled at what Dave had given her.

And then started to open it.

As she did, she scoffed again. "Together. What're you doin', here, bud?"

"Just open it! Jeez!"

"I am!"

Rhonda opened the flat, medium-size, square wrapped package, wondering why Dave was being so weird. And why he was giving her a present. Because she and Dave were the best kind of friends—the kind that don't have to get each other presents.

Then she balled up the brown craft paper that Dave had wrapped the present in and chucked it into the corner near the woodpile and the old newspaper pile.

And then she looked at what she had unwrapped.

It was a large, square piece of stretched canvas—with something painted on the front.

Dave felt that strange lightness grow inside him, because Rhonda was about to see what he had painted for her, and he was hoping that she was going to love it and hug him and kiss him and that they'd live happily ever after.

But that wasn't quite what happened.

"What *is* this?" asked Rhonda, screwing up her face as she peered at the square piece of canvas.

Dave was a little hurt by the question. And by the expression on Rhonda's face. "What do you mean, 'What *is* this?'"

"Exactly what I said: What is it?"

"Well, can't you see what it is?"

"A paintin'."

"Yeah," Dave said. It was obviously a painting.

Rhonda propped the painting up against an old milk crate that had some old glass electrical insulators and a Nerf football and some softballs and some ball gloves and some Frisbees in it.

And she stared at the painting.

For a while.

And then she asked, "Where'd you get this, it looks homemade?"

Dave's painting *was* homemade. That's what made it special, he thought. But the way Rhonda said that it "looked homemade" made it seem like she didn't think it was very special. Or of any quality. And that hurt. "What do you mean it looks homemade?" Dave asked, trying not to whimper.

"It looks like someone really painted it."

"Well, someone really *did* paint it!"

Rhonda looked at Dave. And wondered if he was the someone who had painted it for her and asked, "Did you paint this?"

"Yeah."

"For me?"

"Yeah."

"Oh." Rhonda stared at the painting and asked bluntly, "Why?" Because she really couldn't understand why Dave would have painted something for her.

"Well . . ." Dave tried to answer Rhonda's question—but couldn't.

And Rhonda sensed that his feelings were hurt and tried to make him feel better and said, "I mean, thanks, thank you," and didn't much sound like she meant it.

"You're welcome," muttered Dave, hurt—but still eager to see what Rhonda thought of his painting.

"So, Dave," said Rhonda sardonically, "I didn't know you painted."

"Well, I do." Dave did a lot of things. He cooked. He played the piano. He gardened. He built ham radios. He read.

And he painted.

"I paint," continued Dave. "See, I'm takin'"—Dave interrupted himself and went over to the painting and turned it right side up, because Rhonda had propped it upside down when she had set it against the old milk crate. And then he continued, "I'm takin' this painting class on Tuesdays at the Rec Center—this artist from Allagash is teaching it—it's real good—and this is my version of one of those stare-at-it-till-you-see-the-thing things. You ever seen one of those?"

"A stare-at-it-till-you-see-the-thing thing?"

"Yeah, you've seen 'em, right?"

"No, I don't know what you're talkin' about."

"Yeah, you do, you know what they are."

"I don't think I do, Dave." Rhonda hated it when people—especially guys—decided what she knew and didn't know.

"Yeah, you do: You know those picture books with the illustrations that take up the whole page and just look like rows and rows of a bunch of little repeating images—like little stars or birds or umbrellas or whatever—anything, I guess? Anyway, if you don't focus on the little images and kinda cross your eyes and stare at the whole page for long enough, you can eventually make out a 3-D image that's hidden inside all the little repeating images. It'll appear to you—from out of the 2-D patterns you've been starin' at."

"Okay, yeah, I've seen those but—"

"Told ya!"

"I can never see what you're supposed to see in 'em!"

"Well, hopefully you'll see this one!" And then Dave wondered for a moment what he would do if Rhonda wasn't able to see what he had painted for her. And he almost lost heart for a second. But then that strange lightness that he had been feeling grew inside him and helped him find heart again, and he continued. "Anyway, these things are called stereograms, and that's kinda what I made, here, for ya. And—we learned that some of the old painters made somethin' like these with dots. They called it . . . oh, man, they called it . . . pointa-somethin'—I don't remember—but—it doesn't matter—anyway, we did it with little blocks of colors, see, and if you just look at the little blocks of colors, it's just colors, but if you step back and look at the whole thing, it's not just little blocks of colors—it's a picture of somethin'."

"Picture of what?"

"I'm not gonna tell you, you gotta figure it out." Dave grinned. He loved making people figure things out.

"Oh, come on, Dave, I had so much crap to figure out at work today, I don't wanna have to figure somethin' like this out. Just tell me what it is."

"No! I'm not gonna tell ya what it is! It'll take all the fun out of it!"

"Dave—"

"Now, it can take a little time. It can be a little frustrating."

"Well, why would you give me somethin' that's gonna *frustrate?*"

"No, no! I just mean . . . you gotta not *try* to look for anything, that's what'll frustrate you. You gotta just kinda . . . zone out at it. And look at it so it doesn't *know* you're lookin' at it."

Rhonda wondered how in the world a painting could know or not know if she was looking at it. "What're you talkin' about?!?"

"Here. Sit down." Dave pulled one of the plastic chairs from its place at the wicker table and set it in front of the painting and motioned for Rhonda to have a seat.

And Rhonda warily did.

And then he picked up the painting and said, "Now, I'm gonna hold the painting up real close to you—right in front of your face."

"Okay . . ."

Dave approached Rhonda, and when the painting was so close to Rhonda it was practically touching the tip of her nose, he said, "Now just stare at the center of the painting."

"Okay," said Rhonda.

"And keep starin'."

"K."

"And I'm gonna back away from you real slow."

"K."

"But try to keep your focus where it is—right here, right now—while I move away."

"K."

"Let your eyes cross. And don't let 'em focus on the painting." Dave slowly moved a few stops away from Rhonda. And stopped.

And Rhonda stared. And kept staring.

And she tried to keep her focus fixed on where it had been before Dave started moving away from her. And she tried to let her eyes cross. And she tried not to let them focus.

But she failed on all counts.

"See anything?" asked Dave.

"No. Do it again."

Dave brought the painting close to Rhonda again and offered a tip: "Try to make your eyes think that the painting is still right in front of your face, even as I move it away from you."

"K." Rhonda prepared to make her eyes do what doesn't come naturally to them as Dave started slowly backing away from her again. "And I'll give you a hint," said Dave as he moved. "It's a common thing. It's somethin' everybody knows."

Rhonda thought Dave's hint was a lousy one, and she tried not to focus on the painting so she would be able to see what Dave had painted for her. But all she could see were the blocks of colors Dave had painted. "Ugh," she grunted, "I can't *not* focus on it."

"Okay, no problem. Try again." Dave brought the painting close to Rhonda's nose again.

"No." Rhonda's frustration was mounting.

"Just try."

"No—Dave—I can't see these things, I told ya!"

And then Rhonda pushed the painting away from her, accidentally knocking it out of Dave's hands and onto the floor.

And they both froze. And hoped the painting was okay.

Fortunately it was.

And Dave quickly picked it up.

And Rhonda muttered, "Sorry."

"It's okay," said Dave.

And it really was okay—enough so that Dave had already moved on and had come up with another plan to help Rhonda see what he had painted for her: "Here, how 'bout try this: Trick it!"

"What?!?"

"Trick it!" repeated Dave, smiling a silly smile.

"What're you talking about?"

"You gotta trick it!" said Dave, all excited about his new tactic.

"How do you trick a painting?" asked Rhonda, looking at Dave like he was nuts.

"Well, you gotta not let it know that you're lookin' at it."

"How do I not let it know that I'm lookin' at it? It's a painting, Dave! It's not gonna know or not know if I'm lookin' at it!" razzed Rhonda.

"No—I just mean you can't look at it the way you usually look at things. You gotta change your perspective—'cause your brain's gettin' in the way—'cause it's looking for a solution—but not in the way it's used to gettin' a solution, so you gotta get your brain to look at it in a new way."

"Well, how do I do that?" asked Rhonda, irked.

"Well, you gotta teach your eyes to cross."

"I don't wanna teach my eyes to cross!" griped Rhonda.

"Well, then you're never gonna see it, are ya?" teased Dave.

"Come on! Why don't you just tell me what it is?"

"No! That'll ruin the fun!"

"Well—I'm not havin' fun, Dave, so there's nothin' to ruin."

"Okay. Sorry. That's no good. How 'bout let's just forget about it for a while and take a break." Dave set the painting on the wicker table, propping it up against the wall, and said, "And let's just do somethin' else. What do you usually do on Friday nights, after we hang out?"

"I have a Bud and talk to you on the phone."

"All right, then. Let's have a Bud. And we can talk. Not on the phone—but in person. Where's the kitchen?"

Dave started toward the door to the rest of Rhonda's house—where he presumed the kitchen was—when he suddenly found his path blocked by Rhonda. "No!"

"No what?" asked Dave, confused, because it seemed like Rhonda was preventing him from going inside her house.

"I'm outta Bud," said Rhonda, looking at the floor and trying to make it seem like it wasn't weird that she wasn't letting Dave inside her house. "I only got Natty Light."

"All right," said Dave. "Then, let's get us a coupla Natty Lights," and he started inside again.

"I'll get 'em," said Rhonda quickly, heading Dave off again.

And before he knew it, Rhonda had opened the door and closed it behind her and was inside her house getting her and Dave their beers.

And Dave was by himself on the porch.

And he wondered why Rhonda didn't seem to want to let him go inside her house.

Maybe she was a hoarder, he thought, and she lived in cramped, crowded squalor or something, like people he had seen on TV.

But then he decided that Rhonda wasn't a hoarder.

Because she didn't seem like she was a hoarder.

But neither did the people on TV who were hoarders.

And then he stopped wondering if Rhonda was a hoarder, because the porch was cluttered, but it didn't look like a hoarder's porch.

And he sat down in the plastic chair at the wicker table and was about to flip through one of the *SnowGoer* magazines that was on it when Rhonda emerged from inside with two cans of Natty Light.

She tossed one of them to Dave.

And Dave said, "Thanks."

And Rhonda said, "Sure."

And Dave cracked open his beer and took a sip.

And Rhonda sat back down in the plastic chair that she had been sitting in earlier and cracked open her beer and took a sip.

And they didn't talk.

And Dave wondered again why Rhonda didn't seem to want to let him go inside her house.

And Rhonda hoped that Dave wasn't wondering why she wasn't letting him go inside her house.

And then asked, "So . . . now what?" to distract him just in case he was wondering why she wasn't letting him inside.

"Huh?" asked Dave. "Oh—"

"You told me to do what I usually do around the house on Friday nights after we hang out, and I'm doin' what I usually do around the house on Friday nights after we hang out. Kinda. I mean, I'm outta Bud. So I'm havin' Natty Light. So that's not usual. And I'm talkin' to you in person, instead of on the phone, 'cause you're here. So that's not usual either, so . . . I'm not doin' what I *usually* do, you know."

"Well, I just mean—do normal things, like drink your beer and hang out with me, like you're doin', and just don't focus on tryin' to see the thing I painted for you."

"Okay."

"Just look at it once in a while, real casual-like."

"Okay."

"While we hang out and drink our beers."

"K."

And Rhonda and Dave hung out.

And drank their beers.

And Rhonda checked out the painting casually every once in a while.

And sometimes stared at it.

And Dave would tell her to let her eyes cross.

But she couldn't.

And it wasn't long before she was frustrated again, because she wasn't seeing anything but a jumble of little blocks of reds and blues and purples and blacks and grays.

And she said, "Dave—this is stupid. I'm not seein' anything."

"I told you—it can take a little time."

"Yeah, well, I don't have a little time, I gotta go to bed. I gotta work in the mornin', I told ya."

Dave really wanted Rhonda to see what he had painted for her, so he said, "Well, how about this? How 'bout just start guessin'—just look at it and just say whatever comes into your brain."

Rhonda was skeptical of Dave's latest scheme, but she really wanted to know what he had painted for her, so she gave his suggestion a shot and sat up and got ready to guess when she suddenly said, "Ooh!" because she felt like she may have actually seen something.

"What?" asked Dave, excited.

"I got somethin'!"

"Yeah?" Dave sprang to his feet and joined Rhonda, because he wanted to be close to her when she saw what he had painted for her. And, as he hopped up, he felt that strange lightness fill up his insides again. And he also got a knot in his stomach, because he wondered what she'd think of what she was seeing.

"Yeah! Yeah, yeah, yeah!" enthused Rhonda.

Dave's heart was swelling, because it seemed that Rhonda liked what Dave had painted for her.

And then she told Dave what she was seeing: "Roadkill."

The lightness inside Dave started to fade. And get heavier.

"What?" Dave winced.

"Roadkill."

"*What?!?*" Dave looked at his painting to see how Rhonda could possibly have been seeing roadkill.

Rhonda motioned toward the jumble of blues and reds and

blacks and purples and grays she saw on the canvas and said, "I see a road. And a dead raccoon in the middle of it."

Dave was dumbfounded. And a little aghast. He screwed up his face and looked at the painting, trying to understand why Rhonda would think that he would want to paint roadkill—and why he'd ever want to *give* her a painting that depicted roadkill. "What? No, that's not what it is!" he cried.

"Okay." Rhonda took another guess. "Um . . . then . . . how about . . . a dead bloody deer in the middle of the road!"

"What?!? No!!!" protested Dave.

"Okay! Relax!"

"It's not a dead deer in the middle of the road!!!"

"Okay, then moose!" Rhonda was now just kidding around. Because she had no idea what Dave had painted for her. It just looked like a splatter of paint on the canvas, to her—and not unlike roadkill, actually.

"*What?!?*" Dave didn't like Rhonda's guesses. And he didn't like that she seemed to be kidding around. Because he had worked really hard on his painting, and it seemed like she wasn't taking his efforts seriously.

"Yeah! Dead bloody moose in the middle of the road!" Rhonda motioned toward the painting again. "See? There's the road and a bloody mash of moose. And this could be the car that hit it."

Rhonda looked up at Dave, who was baffled by her guesses. "What?" he whined. "Are you serious? That's what you see?!?"

"I don't know! Relax!" she answered, finishing her beer and chucking the empty can in a bin full of returnables in the corner.

"No! I'm not gonna relax! 'Cause that's not somethin' I'd want to paint!!! That's not even close to what it is! Dead moose?!? *Come on!!!*" cried Dave.

"Well, that's what I see! I don't know what it is!" said Rhonda, wondering why Dave was taking his painting so seriously. "And don't get mad! At *me*! It's not my fault I can't see what *you* painted!"

"I'm not mad!" And Dave wasn't mad. He was just frustrated. And he went over to the painting, picked it up, and looked at it, pained that Rhonda thought it was roadkill. And then he asked Rhonda, almost defeatedly, "You really don't see what this is?"

"No," said Rhonda, feeling stupid for not being able to see what Dave had painted for her.

Dave genuinely believed that Rhonda wasn't seeing the image on the canvas he was holding in front of him. And he sighed. And said, "Well . . ." And he looked at his painting again. And then he looked at Rhonda again and gently asked, "Can I give you another hint?"

"Yeah!" said Rhonda, like she was saying "Duh!"

Dave kept looking at Rhonda. And started shifting his weight back and forth on his feet as he summoned the courage to do something he hadn't done in a long time.

And then he dropped the painting on the floor and walked straight toward Rhonda—who was still sitting in her chair. And he looked right at her. And that strange lightness filled up his insides again and seemed to compel him to go to Rhonda and give her his hint. And gave her his hint.

Which was a kiss.

And probably the shortest kiss two people have ever shared. Because not even a second after he started kissing her, Rhonda pulled away from Dave and got up out of her chair so quickly that it tumbled over backward.

And the strange lightness Dave had been feeling faded again and was replaced by an awful darkness and heaviness.

Because now he felt like something was wrong. Very wrong.

Because Rhonda's face was all turned in on itself. And she looked scared. And confused. And angry. And she hissed, "What are you doin'? What *was* that?!? Why did you *do* that?"

Dave gently answered, "'Cause I was givin' you a hint." And then he smiled weakly.

Rhonda scoffed and then inhaled sharply and then calmly and seriously said, "Well, you can't just do that to someone. Like that."

Dave realized that maybe he shouldn't have given Rhonda the hint he gave her. And he felt ashamed.

"And don't ever do that again! Ever!" hissed Rhonda. And she started pacing. And tried to figure out what to do next. She was not at all happy that Dave had just done what he had just done. It was too fast. Too soon. And she suddenly turned to him and roared, "And GET OUTTA HERE!!!" And she stormed into her house and slammed the door behind her.

Dave was stunned. And stood motionless. He felt like he had a boat anchor inside him.

And he tried to figure out what had just happened. And why Rhonda had gotten so angry at him. And why she had yelled at him.

The aftermath of the yell was the quietest quiet and the stillest stillness he had ever experienced.

And he realized that he hadn't breathed in a while.

And so he exhaled.

And wondered how long he had been holding his breath.

And then he scoffed. And laughed sardonically. And he didn't do much sardonically. Because he wasn't a sardonic guy.

And he faced the door that Rhonda had just retreated behind.

And he raised his arms up a little, palms open, and looked upward as if he was asking the universe or God or anyone who would answer what the heck had just happened.

But the universe didn't answer. And God didn't answer.

And Rhonda wasn't there to answer.

So he dropped his arms and his head and sighed, "Jeezum Crow," which was a euphemism for something his grandmother didn't like him to say.

And he grabbed his snowmobile helmet and his gloves and his balaclava. And was about to go when he stopped, turned, and looked at the door Rhonda had just slammed behind her—which she was on just the other side of, standing still, trying to make sense of what had just happened. And Dave thought about opening that door and going inside and apologizing and trying to make right what he had made wrong.

And he thought about going inside and apologizing to Rhonda and trying to make right what he had made wrong.

But then he figured he'd deal with everything another day when she was less upset, and he turned to go. And he pulled the wobbly wooden porch door open.

And then he pushed on the levered latch on the silver aluminum storm door, and when Rhonda heard it pop open, she almost called to Dave and told him not to go.

But didn't.

And Dave was just about out the door—when he stopped, because he realized that he wanted his painting. If Rhonda couldn't appreciate it, there was no reason for her to have it. So he went over to it and picked it up and was about to head out the door again when he got really hot inside. And—angry. And he wasn't the kind of guy who got angry.

And he suddenly strode up to the door Rhonda was standing on the other side of and facing, and yelled, "HEY, RHONDA!!!"

Rhonda jumped a little. And she wasn't one to jump. But she was surprised by how loud Dave had just been. And by how angry he seemed.

And his anger made her angry. Because *he* was the one who had crossed a line. *He* was the one who had kissed her out of nowhere. *She* was the one who was supposed to be angry.

So she roared back, "WHAT?!?" Dave was surprised to hear Rhonda's voice coming from so close to the door, and he jumped a little. Because Rhonda was louder than he was—which wasn't surprising. She outdid him at just about everything.

But what he had to say was important. And he wasn't going to let her cow him.

And he dug deep and found the strength and the courage to say what he needed to say.

"YOU KNOW," he yelled, "WE HANG OUT EVERY FRIDAY NIGHT LATELY!"

"YEAH?" Rhonda roared back. "SO?"

"WE GO SLEDDIN'!"

"YEAH, AND?"

"AND THEN I GO HOME!"

"YEAH!"

"BUT I DIDN'T WANNA GO HOME TONIGHT! I WANTED TO COME OVER! 'CAUSE I WANTED TO GIVE YOU SOMETHIN' I MADE FOR YOU . . . BECAUSE . . ." Dave felt the lightness grow inside him again. And it made his heart swell and it made him feel like someone else—someone braver—had taken control of his body and was making him say, "'CAUSE I LIKE YOU, YOU KNOW!"

Rhonda froze.

And she didn't know what to make of what Dave had just said. Because the words he had said were beautiful. But the way he had said them made them sound so ugly. So she didn't respond.

Dave didn't know what to make of Rhonda's non-response. And

it was too late to take back what he had said. Because it had been said. And it had definitely been heard. Because he had yelled it. And the only thing he could think of to do was yell some more.

So he did.

"AND I THINK WE OUGHTA BE TOGETHER! OR GO OUT! OR SOMETHIN'! AND—" Dave suddenly interrupted himself and realized that he didn't want to be yelling at Rhonda. Because he loved her. And he went to the door and rested his arm on it and leaned his head on his arm and said in a more civil tone of voice, "And that's why I kissed you." And then he pushed himself away from the door and just stared at it for a second. And then continued, speaking to the door as if it were Rhonda. "I just—I wanted you to know how I felt about you, and I didn't know how to tell you, so I just kissed you, and I'm sorry if—"

The door suddenly opened, interrupting Dave. And Rhonda moved into the doorframe and said quietly, sternly, "Then you shoulda just told me. How you felt." Rhonda stepped out onto the porch and pulled the door behind her. And Dave backed away from her as she did, because he didn't know what to make of her mood. Rhonda took a deep breath and thought and then looked Dave square in the eye and said in all seriousness, "'Cause you can't just do what you just did, you know." The reprimand came from somewhere deep inside Rhonda. And it froze Dave. Because the good guy had done something that wasn't so good. "You can't do that, Dave," added Rhonda.

"I know," said Dave simply. And that strange lightness he had been feeling disappeared again, and was replaced once more by the heaviness that made him feel like he had a boat anchor inside him. "I'm sorry. I just thought that you liked me the way I like you. I didn't mean to upset you." He was trying to defend himself—even though what he did wasn't defensible.

"Doesn't matter what you meant," said Rhonda.

Dave realized that Rhonda was right. It didn't matter what he had meant. The fact was, he had done her wrong. And he needed to make it right. But he couldn't figure out what to say or do to make it right. So he just said, "You're right. I'm sorry. I really am. I just— really like you. And if you don't, well . . ." Dave didn't finish his sentence, because there was nothing more to say. And so, he started to go. Because—what else could he do.

Rhonda watched Dave as he headed toward the door. And she felt a strange lightness start to grow inside her. It made her feel like she had fireflies dancing around in her stomach, lighting her up from the inside. And it seemed to make her heart swell. And it filled her with courage. And it seemed to commandeer her body and force her to blurt out, "I do," just as Dave reached the door.

Dave stopped. And turned to Rhonda and asked, "Huh?"

"I do. Like you. The way you like me."

"You do?" Dave felt that strange lightness fill up his insides again.

"Yeah," said Rhonda, looking at the floor.

And Dave started nodding. And then muttered, "Well, all right, then." And he looked at the floor, too.

And then he looked at Rhonda. Who was still looking at the floor. And he asked, "Um . . . so . . . do you . . . wanna . . . be together? Or go out? Or somethin'?"

Rhonda looked at Dave. And looked him over. And considered him. And the question. And then looked at the floor again and said, "I guess," as nonchalantly as she could—even though she was feeling anything but nonchalant about being together or going out with Dave.

"Well, all right, then!" Dave repeated. And then he just stood there smiling goofily and nodding his head up and down, waiting for Rhonda to make the next move.

But Rhonda wasn't moving.

She was standing stock still—looking at the floor still.

"So . . . um . . ." Dave ducked down and tried to move his face into Rhonda's field of vision. "Can—can I—um . . . I would like . . . to kiss you, if that's okay."

Rhonda didn't respond.

"Rhonda?" asked Dave.

Rhonda shook her head back and forth and continued to look at the floor and said, "It's not. Okay."

"Oh. Okay." Dave was crushed. And that strange lightness he was feeling was replaced by the strange heaviness again.

And he knew he needed to respect Rhonda's wishes. So he did so—the only way he knew how: He started to go. Again.

As he did, Rhonda said, "'Cause I don't know how."

Dave stopped and turned to Rhonda. "Huh?"

"I don't know how . . . to do what you just said you would like to do. I've never done it before."

Dave looked blankly at Rhonda. "What do you mean?"

Rhonda shrugged and said, "I've never kissed anyone before."

"What?" Dave was stupefied. Because what Rhonda had just said couldn't have been true. "No way!" he squawked.

"Yeah way. Never happened in high school. And then never happened at college." (Rhonda had gone to Northern Maine Community College and majored in precision machining technology.) "And then I started workin', and I got busy . . . And, I mean . . . I won arm wrestling at the Maine Potato Blossom Festival two of the past three years."

Dave was just about to ask Rhonda what any of this had to do with her never having kissed anyone before when Rhonda said, "And I work in oriented strand board." (Rhonda was a supervisor at Bushey's Lumber and Engineered Wood Products.)

Dave didn't understand what Rhonda working in oriented strand board had to do with her not having kissed anyone before either, so he said, "Yeah, so?"

"Dave, come on. Look at me."

"I'm lookin' at ya." And Dave liked what he saw. "And . . . you know," he continued, "I think you'd be surprised how many guys think you look . . . really good. I mean . . . *I* do."

Rhonda winced.

And then Dave realized something.

And he looked at Rhonda.

And thought about what else Rhonda may never have done if she had never kissed anybody. "Wait—So you've never . . . ?"

"No," said Rhonda flatly before Dave could complete his very personal question. "Not that it's any of your business," added Rhonda brusquely.

Dave felt bad for pressing the issue and was about to apologize when Rhonda continued, "And—I'm not really sad about it, you know. I'm happy bein' just me. I don't need to be with someone to be happy, you know."

"Oh, I'm not sayin' you're not happy," said Dave. "You're the happiest person I know."

"Yeah well . . . maybe I could be happier," said Rhonda, looking at the floor again, "if I was with someone like you."

Dave's heart swelled and the lightness filled up his insides again. "Yeah?" he asked, beaming.

"Yeah. I think . . . that's somethin' I'd be good with."

"Really?"

"Yeah."

"Well, all right, then," said Dave. And that strange lightness continued to fill up his insides. And it made him feel like he might burst—or like he was about to launch into space like a rocket ship. "So . . ." Dave was about to ask Rhonda again if he could kiss her, but wondered if maybe she wanted to be the one to initiate the kiss, and he asked, "Do you wanna try kissin' me?"

"I don't," said Rhonda quickly, quashing Dave's hopes.

"Okay," said Dave, genuinely accepting her answer, but still feeling that strange lightness.

And then Rhonda added, "I wanna do this." Rhonda pointed to the painting—which Dave had forgotten he was holding.

And had forgotten he had given her.

"Okay," said Dave, and he accommodated Rhonda by turning the painting around so she could hopefully see what he had painted for her. And, as he did, that strange lightness continued to grow inside him. And Rhonda felt it grow inside her again, too. This time it made her feel like she had even more fireflies dancing around inside her. And she felt bright—and light as air. And she started moving closer to the painting. And she wanted to know so badly what it was that Dave had painted for her. And so she started guessing again, and asked "Is it raspberries?"

"Nope."

"Apples?" Rhonda kept coming closer to the painting.

"Nope."

"A big open-faced strawberry rhubarb pie?"

"Nope."

Rhonda suddenly took the painting from Dave and looked at it. And then she looked at Dave and grabbed him and kissed him hard, letting the painting drop as she did. And it landed on the floor faceup. And Dave worried about it getting damaged for a split second but then realized he didn't care about the painting at all anymore, and he kissed Rhonda back.

And Rhonda pulled away from Dave for a second, gasping a little as she did.

And all the hearts and all the veins and all the arteries that were on the porch were pounding.

"Are you okay?" asked Dave, checking in with Rhonda.

"Shh," said Rhonda, not wanting to talk. And she grabbed Dave and kissed him again, hard and fast.

And then she pulled away again, her breathing labored.

"You sure you're okay?" asked Dave.

"Yeah," wheezed Rhonda, trying to catch her breath. But she couldn't. So she closed her eyes and bent over and pressed her hands against her knees and tried to regulate her inhalations and exhalations.

"Hey, easy," said Dave, rubbing Rhonda's back.

And then Rhonda opened her eyes—and realized that she was standing directly over the painting, and she gasped again.

"What's wrong?"

And Rhonda crumpled to the floor and picked up the painting as she did and cried, "I see it!"

Dave joined her on the floor and asked eagerly, "Yeah?"

"Yeah!" Rhonda inhaled sharply again, overwhelmed, and said, "It's a hhh . . ." The *hhh* sound she was making turned into laughter. Because she didn't have to say what Dave had painted for her, because Dave knew what he had painted for her. And what he had painted for her—was beautiful.

As beautiful, even, as the northern lights that were hovering in the sky above at that moment.

"I see it!" Rhonda said, her breathing starting to normalize.

"It's nice," she said, looking at Dave. "It's really nice."

"Thanks." Dave felt all hot. And light.

"It's good!" Rhonda said, looking at the painting. And then she looked at Dave and said, "You're good at this!"

"Yeah, well, *you* are good at *this*." And Dave kissed Rhonda again, the painting getting squished between their bodies as he did.

And Rhonda pulled away from Dave and confessed, "I thought it'd be . . . complicated—or hard to figure out how to do or somethin'." And then she kissed Dave again. And the painting got squished between their bodies again. And then she pulled away again and said, "But it's not."

"Nope," confirmed Dave, smiling goofily.

Rhonda kissed Dave again. And then she got up and rushed over to the old telephone bench by the door that led inside and carefully set the painting down on it. And then she turned to Dave and started hopping up and down, because she didn't know what to do with all the extra energy that was coursing through her body, and said, "And I feel like I wanna keep kissing you—for a long time, but I also feel like I wanna do something else, next." And then she suddenly stopped hopping and stood still and faced Dave and asked, "But I don't know what that is."

Dave got up off the floor and raised his right hand as if he were taking an oath or letting a teacher know that he knew the answer to a question and said, "I do." And then he slowly approached Rhonda. And reached out and took the zipper to her partially unzipped purple, red, and gray Polaris snowmobile jacket. And unzipped it. And then helped her take it off.

And then he unzipped his black, neon green, and white Arctic Cat jacket and took it off.

Rhonda and Dave stared at each other, hearts racing and their breathing audible.

And then Dave undid the Velcro on the not-quite-snowmobile-but-close-enough boots he got at Walmart in Presque Isle and pulled the left one off, tumbling onto the floor as he did. While he was down there, he pulled the right one off, too.

Rhonda laughed when Dave fell. And then followed his lead and started undoing the Velcro—and then the laces—of her black and gun-metal gray Polaris snowmobile boots. And then she tried to pull her left boot off, hopping all around and struggling to stay upright as she did. And she eventually tumbled onto the floor as she finally freed her foot from the boot's stiff, waterproof confines.

And Dave was there to help her finish pulling her right boot off.

They laughed and then got back up on their feet, eyes locked, their hearts still racing and their breathing still audible.

And Rhonda waited for Dave to show her what was next.

And Dave did.

He unbuttoned and unzipped his black ski pants that worked well enough as snowmobile pants and started peeling them off.

And Rhonda did the same thing. Except her pants were actual snowmobile pants—Polaris brand—and they were gun-metal gray.

Their pants swished and swooshed as they peeled them off, and when they kicked their feet out of them, they stood facing one another again, hearts racing, breathing audible.

And then Dave unbuttoned his Scotch plaid chamois shirt.

And Rhonda stripped off her green NMCC Falcons sweatshirt.

Then Dave whipped off his Boston Red Sox long-sleeve T-shirt.

And Rhonda whipped off her "I'm a trout's worst nightmare" T-shirt.

And then Dave unbuttoned his Wrangler jeans and peeled them off.

And revealed some cream-colored cotton long johns.

And Rhonda peeled off her Lee jeans.

And revealed some sky blue wool long johns that her mom had gotten her for Christmas.

And Dave and Rhonda stood facing one another.

And then they laughed.

And then Dave suddenly got a little self-conscious about what he looked like. He wondered if Rhonda would think he looked okay without many clothes on. He was a little doughy and tried to hold his belly in.

But there was a little too much of it to hold in.

But Rhonda didn't seem repulsed by it. Or him.

So he stopped worrying about what he looked like and instead looked at how beautiful Rhonda was in her long johns.

Rhonda liked how Dave was looking at her. It made her feel beautiful. And she didn't usually feel beautiful. But on the night when all the extraordinary things did or didn't happen, she did. Because of Dave.

Rhonda looked at Dave the way he was looking at her. And Dave liked the way she was looking at him and asked, "So . . . do you wanna know what comes . . . next?"

"Yeah," said Rhonda, nodding.

"Well, why don't we go inside. And I'll show you."

"All right." Rhonda walked past Dave and said, "Well, then why don't you go on inside and show me what's next!" And she opened the door and showed Dave the way.

"All right!" yowled Dave and the lightness he had been feeling expanded inside him even more and made him feel brighter and lighter than he had ever felt, and he pushed open the door to the rest of Rhonda's house and bolted inside.

Rhonda heard something crash.

And she heard Dave whimper.

"Light switch on the right as you enter!"

"Thanks!"

The lights in the living area and kitchen of Rhonda's house went on.

And she looked down at the old telephone bench by the door—and at the painting Dave had given her.

And she was glad she had finally been able to decipher the image.

It was a heart.

An anatomically correct heart. That looked like little blocks of red and purple and blue and gray and black when you looked at it one way—but like a human heart when you looked at it another.

Rhonda gazed at the painting. And really couldn't believe how good it was.

And Dave wondered why Rhonda hadn't joined him inside yet and yelled, "Hey, Rhonda! Let's go!"

But Rhonda didn't move.

And after a while Dave called to her again. "Rhonda!"

And Rhonda went toward the door to go inside.

And then stopped.

And Dave came back out onto the porch and asked, "What's up?"

"Um . . ." Rhonda went to the old telephone bench and picked up the painting and stared at it—and seemed unsettled.

"You okay?" asked Dave.

"I'm just . . . I really like this," Rhonda said, indicating the painting.

"Good."

"And I really like you."

"Good! I really like you, too!"

"And I really like kissing you."

"Good! I really like kissin' you, too!"

"But . . ."

Dave's heart started to sink, and he waited to hear what the "but" was.

But Rhonda wasn't saying what the "but" was.

So Dave asked, "But what?"

Rhonda looked scared and sad, and Dave couldn't figure out why. "I—I just," stammered Rhonda. "I just don't know if I'm ready for what comes . . . next."

"Oh. Okay. That's okay," Dave said accommodatingly.

"Is it?"

"Yeah," assured Dave.

"Really?" asked Rhonda.

"Yeah."

And Rhonda was glad Dave had told her it was okay.

And she looked at the painting again. And said, "Um . . . would it be okay if . . . we just look at this for a while? 'Cause I just . . . wanna look at it for a while."

"Yeah. Sure," said Dave.

"'Cause it's really good."

"Thanks."

And Rhonda sat on the old telephone bench. And looked at the painting. And loved it.

And Dave joined her on the bench.

And looked at the painting with her. For a while.

And then Rhonda said, "You're a good guy, Dave."

"You're better," said Dave.

"True," admitted Rhonda.

And they laughed. Because Rhonda was joking. But they both knew it was no joke that Rhonda was the better person.

And then Rhonda shivered a little. Because her porch wasn't fully winterized. It had screens instead of windows. But it wasn't heated. So it was cold. Maybe not nineteen degrees, like it was outside. Maybe more like twenty-seven, thanks to the ambient heat from the house. Which is cold when you're only wearing long johns.

Dave grabbed his jacket from off the floor and put it around

Rhonda to warm her up. And Rhonda smiled—even though Dave had just draped an Arctic Cat jacket around her.

And she felt the lightness fill her insides again. It made her feel like she had even more fireflies inside her. And like she might levitate.

And she took Dave's hand.

And held it tight so she'd have something to hold onto just in case she did.

11

As Ginette passed Rhonda Rideout's, she wondered if Rhonda and Dave were together or going out or something. She knew her mom didn't like it when she wondered about things that were none of her business, but everyone in Almost had been wondering about Rhonda and Dave lately. So why couldn't she?

And all the wondering that people were doing about Dave and Rhonda made Ginette wonder if people had been wondering if she and Pete were together or going out or something. Because they had been hanging out a lot lately, too.

And then Ginette hoped people weren't wondering about her and Pete, because there was nothing to wonder about.

Because Ginette and Pete weren't together. And they weren't going out.

And they were not "something."

They were nothing.

Because of Pete and his stupid theory of closeness.

Ginette wondered what Rhonda would have done if Dave had ever said something like what Pete had said to her earlier—about being as far away from someone as you can possibly be when you're sitting as close to them as you can possibly be.

And then she realized it didn't matter what Rhonda would have done, because Dave would never had said anything so convoluted. Because Dave wasn't a convoluted person.

But Pete obviously was.

And Ginette was done with his convolutedness.

And she was done with the strange notions that meandered through his mind. Notions like . . . that you can be far away from someone when you're sitting right next to them.

And she walked faster as if she were trying to distance herself from Pete and his nonsensical notions.

But then she suddenly stopped and ached and almost gasped and realized she wasn't ready to be done with Pete's convolutedness.

And she wasn't ready to be done with the strange, nonsensical notions that meandered through his mind.

This latest one, though—well, she just didn't understand it. She understood its meaning—she just didn't understand why Pete had shared it when he had.

And she wondered if maybe she should go back to the observatory at Skyview Park and see if Pete was still there and ask him to explain himself—and his bad timing.

But—no, she thought. He needed to come and find her if he was going to explain himself.

She would not be going to him.

So she continued on her way to Nowhere.

But she stopped again after a few steps. Because she had the strangest, strongest feeling that Pete was coming after her—because he wanted to explain himself. She whirled around and shone her flashlight down the Road to Somewhere, half expecting and half hoping that she'd see Pete running toward her, maybe in slow motion—like in a dumb movie—with his arms outstretched, apologizing all over the place for ruining the best evening that either of them had ever had.

But she didn't see him.

Because he wasn't running toward her.

He was probably still just sitting on the bench, nerding out over his theory, she thought.

But that was not, in fact, what Pete was doing. At least not just yet.

He had finally overcome the heaviness that had paralyzed him when Ginette left. And he had stood up. And was now staring off in the direction Ginette had headed when she left Skyview Park.

And he wasn't nerding out over his theory. He was worrying that he had made a big mistake by sharing it with Ginette. Because Ginette was gone. Long gone. She had left him at 7:45. And it was just about 9 p.m.

And then he started wondering if Ginette had taken his theory literally. He certainly hadn't intended for her to. He was just musing. About geography. And the distance between two points. And the enormity of love.

But what if Ginette had taken his musings seriously? What if she was walking around the world to get close to him again?

She couldn't possibly have been attempting to do something so Herculean.

She was probably just heading home.

But—she was the most remarkable person he had ever met.

And he wouldn't have put it past her to try to do something so Herculean.

And that was when he started nerding out over his theory. And he tried to figure out how long it would take for Ginette to return to him—and be (actually) close to him again—if she were to keep walking west and go all the way around the world.

The Earth, he knew, has a circumference of 24,902 miles at the equator.

And say Ginette walked at a pace of three miles per hour.

And say she walked eight hours a day.

That'd be twenty-four miles a day she could cover.

And 24,902 miles divided by 24 miles per day equals—Pete rummaged through his bag and pulled out a calculator and discovered the answer: 1,038.

1,038 days.

That's how long it would take for Ginette to circumambulate the globe.

That was almost . . . Pete divided 1,038 days by 365 days in a year, and his calculator revealed an answer of 2.84 years.

Pete didn't know if he could be without Ginette for 2.84 years.

But maybe it didn't have to be 2.84 years, because, he bet, some days Ginette would be able to put in ten- or twelve-hour days walking.

Plus, she walked fast, so she could probably cover more than three miles in an hour.

And she'd be able to run sometimes.

So maybe her pace would be more like three and a half miles an hour.

Okay. So if she walked at a rate of three and a half miles an hour for an average of ten hours a day, that would mean she'd cover thirty-five miles a day.

And 24,902 miles divided by 35 miles per day equals 711 days.

And that, his calculator told him, was not even . . . 1.94 years!

Which was still a long time to be without the girl he had just confessed his love to.

But wait! Pete just realized something! She wouldn't be walking at the *equator*. She'd start out walking along the Road to Nowhere, which was at the forty-seventh parallel north. And if she followed the forty-seventh parallel north, that would make for a shorter distance than she'd be walking if she were at the equator.

And Pete had learned—for fun, while he was working on his map projection project for science class—that the circumference of the Earth at any particular latitude could be calculated by using the formula $2\pi r(\cos\theta)$, where r is the radius of the Earth at the equator—or 3,963 miles—and θ is the relevant degree of latitude, in this case, 47. And the math revealed that the circumference of the Earth at the forty-seventh parallel was 17,622 miles.

And 17,622 miles divided by 35 miles per day, his calculator told him, equals 503.

Which is 1.38 years.

Which is still a long time to go without the girl you love.

But better than 1.94 years.

And better than 2.84 years.

Heartened, Pete imagined what Ginette's trip along the forty-seventh parallel north would be like. She'd start out on the Road to Nowhere and head into the North Maine Woods and into the Allagash Wilderness and into Canada and through Quebec City and maybe she could just pick up the Trans-Canada Highway when she got there and hitch rides from time to time.

No—probably not the safest thing.

She could just walk.

Along the Trans-Canada.

All the way across Canada.

And when she got to the Pacific Ocean, she could keep walking and go north along the coast of British Columbia and into Alaska—which she had to see, because Pete's dad had worked on a fishing boat there once and said Alaska was like a supersize version of Maine.

And once she crossed Alaska, she could take a boat across the Bering Strait and then she'd be in Russia. On the continent of Asia.

Wow.

She'd be up by the Arctic Circle by then, so that would really shorten the journey, because that would be the sixty-sixth parallel north—and maybe she'd be there in the summer and it'd be light all the time and she could really rack up the miles—because she could walk all day.

And then, eventually, she'd get to Europe where she could visit all the great cities and cathedrals and monuments that Mr. Smith had taught them about in seventh grade, and then maybe she could hop a boat to Great Britain, and then hop another one to Ireland, and then hop another one to Iceland.

Oh! Iceland! Pete had read about—and seen pictures—of Iceland in his *National Geographic*s and he'd want to hear all about the geysers and the hot springs and the glaciers.

And then, after Iceland, she could take a boat to Greenland, and then a boat down to Labrador, and into Quebec again. And then she'd need to catch a boat across the Gulf of St. Lawrence to the Gaspe Peninsula, where his mom and dad had taken him and his sister, Gwen, camping once when they were little.

And then she'd go through New Brunswick, and before she knew it, she'd be back in Maine again.

And in Almost.

And at Skyview Park.

At the observatory.

On the bench.

And she'd be close to Pete again.

Hopefully.

But then he remembered it would take Ginette 1.38 years to make such a journey—at best.

And he didn't want to be without Ginette for 1.38 years.

He didn't want to be without her for even 1.38 days.

Or 1.38 hours.

Pete stared off to the west toward down-township Almost, Maine, and into the wilderness of northwestern Maine.

And he wondered if he had lost her.

And if he'd ever see her again.

And there Pete was, looking to the west for Ginette.

And there Ginette was, looking to the east for Pete.

And they didn't know this—because they were over two and a half miles apart—but, at that moment, they were facing one other.

And they were both wondering how they could make right what seemed to have gone so wrong.

Pete thought about running after Ginette and catching up with her so he could explain his theory on what it means to be close—and tell her why he had shared it with her.

It was an epiphany—one that had come to him because Ginette had told him that she loved him. When she told him that, Pete felt like he had been whooshed away from her all of a sudden. And he felt farther away from her than he had ever felt—but also closer to her than he had ever felt, both at the same time.

And when he told Ginette that *he* loved *her*, he felt like he had been whooshed even *farther* away from her. But he also felt even closer to her than he had ever felt.

He wondered if maybe he should have just said *that*—that, after they had professed their love to each other, he felt farther away from her—and closer to her—than he had ever felt.

She probably would have understood that.

And she probably would have stayed, if he had said that.

But that wasn't what he had said.

Instead, he had said—when Ginette was sitting right next to him with her head upon his shoulder—that she wasn't actually close to him at all; that she was actually about as far away from him as she could possibly be.

And that seemed to have driven her away.

Which was understandable.

Pete shook his head sadly and sighed and checked his watch. It was a Timex. With a Twist-O-Flex band. It used to be his dad's.

It said 8:43.

Ginette had left him just over an hour ago.

She was home for sure.

Pete thought about going home himself.

But then that strange lightness filled up his insides again and seemed to compel him to stay where he was.

So he sat back down on the bench. And stayed.

Even though he knew he wouldn't be able to sit there for 1.38 years.

And Ginette turned around and kept walking, annoyed that she had let herself hope she'd see Pete rushing toward her to explain himself and his kooky theory.

And that strange lightness inside her compelled her to keep going west—even though her mind kept telling her to stop and go home.

It was a little before 9 p.m. when the potato field she was walking beside gave way to the woods.

A homemade sign welcomed her to the wilderness: PAVEMENT ENDS. FUN BEGINS.

Ginette had always wanted to meet whoever had made that sign.

And she left the well-plowed, paved road behind.

And went into the woods.

As she did, she was overwhelmed by the lightness inside her, which was still compelling her to go west.

She walked for a while through a tunnel of evergreens. Fir, spruce, cedar, pine, and tamarack trees stood sentry along the Road to Nowhere, as if they were escorting her to wherever she was going.

It was so dark in the tree tunnel.

She looked up and saw a narrow swath of night sky above, the Milky Way perfectly framed by the treetops.

A few steps later, her flashlight died, which was really annoying, because she couldn't see a thing. She clicked the flashlight's switch to the off position and then waited a few seconds and clicked it on again. The flashlight tried to beam—but couldn't. Its batteries were dead, Ginette figured. Which was an easy enough fix. She always carried a couple of extra D batteries in her backpack, which she swung off her shoulders and onto the snowy ground. She felt for the zippers that opened the main compartment, opened the pack and rummaged through its contents and felt her space blanket and the granola bars and the matches and the utility tool and the water filter straw and the mini first-aid kit and the thermos of water.

But no batteries. Because there weren't any in her pack. Because her mom had borrowed them a couple of weeks ago for her own flashlight—because the battery drawer at home was all out of size D batteries. And her mom had replenished the drawer with a twelve-pack last Sunday after she had done her Walmart run in Presque Isle after she hit the craft fair at the Methodist church. But she had forgotten to replenish her daughter's backpack with her backups.

In all fairness, Ginette had forgotten, too, and now, there she was in the woods, all alone on a Friday night with no flashlight. She cursed herself for not being prepared—and maybe cursed her mom a little, too, for forgetting to replace her backups. And started to panic for a second because she really couldn't see anything without her flashlight.

But her pupils were dilating, allowing her eyes to take in what little light there was from the stars above. As they did, she was able to make out the road in front of her and the bluish glow of the snowbanks that rose up next to her and the black silhouettes of the trees that were watching over her.

Ginette felt like her ears were dilating, too, as they tried to take in as much information as possible now that her eyes had become less useful. But there wasn't much for them to hear in the silent night—except the sound of her own breathing.

And then she wondered if she was scared.

And decided that she wasn't.

The forest is a dark place. And bad things can happen in the dark.

But bad things can happen in the light, too.

And she bet that far fewer bad things happened in the darkness of the woods of northern Maine than in the bright lights of cities like Montreal and New York and Los Angeles.

Maybe because there aren't very many people where she was.

And there might just be too many people in those places. Which may have something to do with why the bad things happen in them.

Ginette stood still in the darkness for a moment.

And felt a great peace overcome her.

And then felt that strange lightness fill up her insides again.

And it seemed to force her to look skyward.

And she did.

And when she did, she saw the narrow swath of stars framed by the pointy treetops.

And—she saw the northern lights.

Which were what she had told Pete she wanted to see after they had shown his parents what they were doing their science projects on.

And she was in awe as she watched the aurora dance in the sky—yellow, red, white, and green. And even blue and purple.

And then the lightness inside her—which seemed to be one and the same as the lightness above her—compelled her to continue on her way to wherever she was going.

And when she redirected her focus from the sky to continue on her way—she realized that she wasn't where she had just been.

She wasn't in the woods anymore.

She was in a snowfield.

Facing the observatory.

At Skyview Park.

And she was on the trail that she and Pete had taken when Ginette had taken Pete to Skyview Park to see if they could see the northern lights—after Pete had held her hand in front of his parents.

And she wondered how this was possible.

A tesseract, maybe.

Or a wormhole.

Or some other sort of bending of time and space.

Whatever the case—Ginette had moved through space and time in an extraordinary way.

And she was back at the observatory.

And she didn't quite understand how that was possible.

But she didn't care that she didn't quite understand.

Because she realized that now she could go and see Pete and get the explanation she was looking for.

If he was still there.

She looked toward the observatory platform. And, against the bluish glow of the wide-open snowfield, she could make out the silhouette of the bench—and the silhouette of a person sitting on the bench.

It was Pete—she hoped.

He was still there—she hoped.

Ginette started walking toward the bench.

And wondered how long she had been gone.

It felt like forever.

And a moment.

Both at the same time.

As she approached the bench, the northern lights continued to hover above.

And Pete, who was, indeed, still sitting on the bench, saw them.

And watched them dance and shimmer in the sky above.

And then he stood up because they seemed to require him to do so.

And he wished that Ginette had been there with him to see them. And he hoped that—wherever she was—she could see them.

And then he wondered where she was.

And he looked west, toward where Ginette had gone when she had left him.

And Ginette quietly approached the bench.

And watched Pete as he wondered.

And looked up at the glorious celestial phenomenon. And said, "I didn't actually think we'd see 'em."

Ginette hadn't spoken loudly or anything, but the sound of her voice contrasted starkly with the quiet night and made Pete jump a little. He turned toward the sound of the voice, and, even though he knew it was Ginette's, he was still surprised to see her standing on the other side of the bench, looking up at the northern lights.

But he was so happy to see her.

And he wondered, for a moment, if she had tested his theory—successfully. And had walked all the way around the world.

No.

Impossible.

And he almost asked her if she had.

But didn't.

And instead asked, "Where'd you go?"

Ginette had her hands in her pockets and shrugged. And then answered Pete. "I just . . . walked."

"Where?"

Ginette nodded to the west.

And Pete looked toward where Ginette had nodded.

And then looked back at her. And wondered again if she had walked all the way around the world—so she could be close to him again.

And Ginette wondered, too, if she had walked all the way around the world in an instant—because that's what seemed to have happened.

And then she smiled at the mystery of it all.

And just let it be a mystery.

And then she sat on the bench, in the spot Pete had been sitting in when she left him.

And Pete sat next to Ginette, in the spot Ginette had been sitting in when she left him.

And they looked at the northern lights.

They were the same northern lights that appeared in the sky when East started to repair Glory's heart.

And the same northern lights that pulsed in the sky when Randy and Chad fell to the ground—as they fell in love with each other.

And the same northern lights that hovered over Almost when Marvalyn hit Steve with the ironing board the second time and made him say "ow" for the first time.

And the same northern lights that pulsed in the sky when the waitress at the Moose Paddy introduced herself to Jimmy.

And the same northern lights that streaked across the sky when Michelle and Justin danced together and felt like they were dancing on air. And Aunt Belinda saw that they actually were.

And the same northern lights that glimmered and glowed above when Lendall gave Gayle her engagement ring.

And the same northern lights that shimmered and shone above when Marci's other shoe dropped from the sky.

And the same northern lights that visited Almost, Maine, when Hope realized that the strange small man she had been talking to was Daniel.

And the same northern lights that had flickered and fluttered above when Rhonda saw what Dave painted for her.

And the same northern lights that Ginette saw not along after her flashlight died.

Eventually the northern lights disappeared.

And Pete and Ginette were just looking up at the star-filled sky. Which, they had to admit, was a little less interesting now that the northern lights had vanished. But it was still pretty spectacular.

And Pete turned to Ginette and said, "I didn't mean that I wanted you to walk around the world, you know. I wasn't asking that. I was just . . . thinkin'."

"Okay."

"I was just saying I thought it was a cool idea."

"It is."

"'Cause now that I know that I love you and that you love me . . . everything feels bigger."

Ginette felt the lightness fill up her insides again. Because she was happy to hear that Pete loved her. Even though she already knew he did.

"And, now," continued Pete, "you feel farther away from me— and closer to me—than you've ever felt. And you feel known—and unknown. And familiar—and unfamiliar. All at the same time."

And Ginette nodded and said, "Yeah." Because she knew what he meant. And felt the same way.

And it was scary.

But not.

And then Pete slid closer to Ginette.

Until he was right next to her.

And then he scooched down and rested his head on her shoulder.

And was as close to her as he could possibly be.

Which felt right.

Because Ginette and Pete had always been close.

ACKNOWLEDGMENTS

The cover of this book says that I wrote it. And I did. But I couldn't have—without the help of more people than I can list here.

But I would like to thank the following people with my whole heart for making this thing possible:

Ibi Janko, Andrew Polk, Anita Stewart, Gabriel Barre, Wendy Rich Stetson, Justin Hagan, Larry Nathanson, Jan and Dave Cronin, Jack Thomas and Bruce Payne, Finnerty Steeves, Miriam Shor, Todd Cerveris, and Dramatists Play Service for helping *Almost, Maine*, the play, find its way into the world. (Please see the acknowledgments page in *Almost, Maine*: *Third Revised Edition* for a more complete list.)

Will Schwalbe, for finding *Almost, Maine*, the play, and for thinking it would make an interesting book.

Jean Feiwel, for taking a chance on this first-time author. And for being patient and kind and encouraging—and for pushing me to deliver.

Richard Fisher, for encouraging me to give this a shot.

Steve Ross, my agent, for helping me understand the world of book publishing. And for being so supportive. And for talking about books and tennis.

Kat Brzozowski, my editor, for making me cut and cut and cut. And for helping think about forward motion. And for being patient—and always positive.

Linda Minton and Mandy Veloso, for the copyediting expertise. To the proofreaders and the sensitivity readers whose names I never got. You're remarkable.

Barb Lloyd, for giving me good books to read.

Rachel Lloyd, for always making me feel like things are possible.

Kristie and Joe Lloyd, for always asking what I was up to and how it was all going.

Sam Lloyd, for telling me once that you thought I was a good playwright. And for having an imagination that inspires.

Katie and Dennis O'Brien, for always asking how the book was going. And for your new quintessentially Maine digs—which were inspiring.

Bailey O'Brien, for talking to me about storytelling and writing. And for making me feel like I was going to be able to do this.

Julie and Dave Walsh, for caring and always wondering how I was doing—and for the office where I wrote chapters six and ten. And for camp.

The entire Lloyd family, for making me a better Mainer—or, pseudo-Mainer.

Jack Cummings III, Donna Lynne Champlin, Kevin Isola, and Kelly McAndrew, for being excited about the second page I let anyone read—and thinking it was pretty good.

Monica Wood, for the supportive talks and email exchanges. And for writing about Mainers so beautifully.

Cathie Pelletier, for writing such beautiful books about northern Maine. And for your energy and kindness.

Susan Lovell and Michael Borrelli, for being there from the beginning and for reminding me that *Almost, Maine* is a special place.

Kathy McCafferty and Dave Mason, for bringing *Almost, Maine* to life so beautifully so many times. And for believing in me and places like *Almost, Maine*.

Jack Thomas, for the unending support.

Jenn Guare, for always asking how it was going and for talking about books.

Anne Blanchard, for introducing me to Antoine de Saint Exupery.

Liz Fitzpatrick, for all the love.

Mary Bonney, for putting up with our fractured conversations. And for all the good thinking you do.

Louise and Greg Hamlin, for giving me a place to stay when I headed north. (I wrote the prologue at your old house!)

Kim Kiehn, for all the inspiring photos and quotes and texts and pep talks.

Elyse Kiehn, for taking me seriously and for being so thoughtful and fun and kind.

Mindy Wolfe, for picking up when I'd call. And for making me feel better when I was low.

Beth Synnott, for helping me keep my chin up always. And for reminding me that it's almost always all good.

Noelle Umback, for the company and for reminding me to think of the final stretch as an extended finals period.

Kate Reinders, for helping me remember to keep perspective and that there's so much to feel good about.

Emily Skinner, for the meals and the pep talks.

Launa Schweizer, for an extremely valuable pep talk.

Aislinn Frantz, for reading a chapter and making an important cut and for checking in.

Caroline Kinsolving, for saving me when I was drowning in this thing.

Haleh Roshan Stillwell, for the talks.

Annie Brabazon, for checking in on me from time to time.

Betsy Hogg and Kathy Hogg, for letting me know you were there if I needed them.

David Bakis, my new Maine friend, for being so interested in this thing. Rest in peace, my friend.

Tor Hyams and Lisa St. Lou, for helping me make an important cut and for telling me it was all going to be okay.

Alyssa Manning, for sending along all the germane articles. And for checking in often.

Vera Mihailovich, for being there always. And for caring so deeply. And for your great mind and great heart.

Isaac, Henry, and Ruth Cariani, for all the love. You made me want to make this book as good as I could. Because I want you to like it.

Jeff Cariani, for checking in and encouraging me and telling me to stop whining. And for your model work ethic. And for keeping me in a good headspace.

Paul and Sheila Cariani, for moving to northern Maine when I was a kid. And for being honest and true always. And for all the love and support. And for telling me to just get this thing done.

And John Lloyd. This is our story.